Rock blinked, and Jayfeather shivered at the thought that the ancient cat's blind gray eyes could still see him very well. "Your past lies in the mountains," Rock told him. "The place where I was born, the place where cats have returned before. You must go there once more to complete the circle."

"Back to the Tribe of Rushing Water?" Now Jayfeather couldn't get his questions out fast enough. "Are they in trouble?"

Rock didn't reply. The clink of a stone behind him distracted Jayfeather for a heartbeat, and when he turned back, the ancient cat had disappeared.

WARRIORS

Book One: Into the Wild

Book Two: Fire and Ice

Book Three: Forest of Secrets

Book Four: Rising Storm

Book Five: A Dangerous Path

Book Six: The Darkest Hour

THE NEW PROPHECY

Book One: Midnight

Book Two: Moonrise

Book Three: Dawn

Book Four: Starlight

Book Five: Twilight

Book Six: Sunset

POWER OF THREE

Book One: The Sight

Book Two: Dark River

Book Three: Outcast

Book Four: Eclipse

Book Five: Long Shadows

Book Six: Sunrise

OMEN OF THE STARS

Book One: The Fourth Apprentice

Book Two: Fading Echoes

Book Three: Night Whispers

Book Four: Sign of the Moon

Book Five: The Forgotten Warrior

Book Six: The Last Hope

EXPLORE THE
WARRIORS WORLD

Warriors Super Edition: Firestar's Quest

Warriors Super Edition: Bluestar's Prophecy

Warriors Super Edition: SkyClan's Destiny

Warriors Super Edition: Crookedstar's Promise

Warriors Field Guide: Secrets of the Clans

Warriors: Cats of the Clans

Warriors: Code of the Clans

Warriors: Battles of the Clans

MANGA

The Lost Warrior

Warrior's Refuge

Warrior's Return

The Rise of Scourge

Tigerstar and Sasha #1: Into the Woods

Tigerstar and Sasha #2: Escape from the Forest

Tigerstar and Sasha #3: Return to the Clans

Ravenpaw's Path #1: Shattered Peace

Ravenpaw's Path #2: A Clan in Need

Ravenpaw's Path #3: The Heart of a Warrior

SkyClan and the Stranger #1: The Rescue

SkyClan and the Stranger #2: Beyond the Code

SkyClan and the Stranger #3: After the Flood

Also by Erin Hunter

Book One: *The Quest Begins*
Book Two: *Great Bear Lake*
Book Three: *Smoke Mountain*
Book Four: *The Last Wilderness*
Book Five: *Fire in the Sky*
Book Six: *Spirits in the Stars*

RETURN TO THE WILD
Book One: *Island of Shadows*

MANGA
Toklo's Story
Kallik's Adventure

OMEN OF THE STARS

WARRIORS

SIGN OF THE
MOON

**ERIN
HUNTER**

HARPER

An Imprint of HarperCollins*Publishers*

Sign of the Moon

Copyright © 2011 by Working Partners Limited

Warriors Adventure Game © 2009 by Working Partners Limited

"Mission of Mercy" © 2011 by Working Partners Limited

Series created by Working Partners Limited

Library of Congress Cataloging-in-Publication Data

Sign of the moon / Erin Hunter. — 1st ed.

p. cm. — (Warriors, omen of the stars ; #4)

Summary: As Jayfeather, Lionblaze, and Dovepaw continue trying to
understand the mysterious prophecy that binds them, Jayfeather receives a
desperate plea for help from the Tribe of Rushing Water.

ISBN 978-0-06-155521-3

[1. Cats—Fiction. 2. Prophecies—Fiction. 3. Adventure and adventurers—
Fiction. 4. Fantasy.] I. Title.

PZ7.H916625Sj 2011

[Fic]—dc22

Typography by Hilary Zarycky

12 13 14 15 16   CG/BR   10 9 8 7 6 5 4 3 2

❖

First paperback edition, 2012

Special thanks to Cherith Baldry

ALLEGIANCES

THUNDERCLAN

LEADER   **FIRESTAR**—ginger tom with a flame-colored pelt

DEPUTY   **BRAMBLECLAW**—dark brown tabby tom with amber eyes

MEDICINE CAT   **JAYFEATHER**—gray tabby tom with blind blue eyes

WARRIORS   (toms and she-cats without kits)

GRAYSTRIPE—long-haired gray tom

DUSTPELT—dark brown tabby tom

SANDSTORM—pale ginger she-cat with green eyes

BRACKENFUR—golden brown tabby tom

SORRELTAIL—tortoiseshell-and-white she-cat with amber eyes

CLOUDTAIL—long-haired white tom with blue eyes

BRIGHTHEART—white she-cat with ginger patches

MILLIE—striped gray tabby she-cat with blue eyes

THORNCLAW—golden brown tabby tom

SQUIRRELFLIGHT—dark ginger she-cat with green eyes

LEAFPOOL—light brown tabby she-cat with amber eyes, former medicine cat

SPIDERLEG—long-limbed black tom with brown underbelly and amber eyes

BIRCHFALL—light brown tabby tom

WHITEWING—white she-cat with green eyes

BERRYNOSE—cream-colored tom

HAZELTAIL—small gray-and-white she-cat

MOUSEWHISKER—gray-and-white tom

CINDERHEART—gray tabby she-cat
APPRENTICE, IVYPAW

LIONBLAZE—golden tabby tom with amber eyes
APPRENTICE, DOVEPAW

FOXLEAP—reddish tabby tom

ICECLOUD—white she-cat

TOADSTEP—black-and-white tom

ROSEPETAL—dark cream she-cat

BRIARLIGHT—dark brown she-cat

BLOSSOMFALL—tortoiseshell-and-white she-cat

BUMBLESTRIPE—very pale gray tom with black stripes

APPRENTICES (more than six moons old, in training to become warriors)

DOVEPAW—pale gray she-cat with blue eyes

IVYPAW—silver-and-white tabby she-cat with dark blue eyes

QUEENS (she-cats expecting or nursing kits)

FERNCLOUD—pale gray (with darker flecks) she-cat with green eyes

DAISY—cream long-furred cat from the horseplace

POPPYFROST—tortoiseshell she-cat (mother to Cherrykit, a ginger she-cat, and Molekit, a brown-and-cream tom)

ELDERS (former warriors and queens, now retired)

MOUSEFUR—small dusky brown she-cat

PURDY—plump tabby former loner with a gray muzzle

SHADOWCLAN

LEADER **BLACKSTAR**—large white tom with one jet-black forepaw

DEPUTY **ROWANCLAW**—ginger tom

MEDICINE CAT **LITTLECLOUD**—very small tabby tom

WARRIORS **OAKFUR**—small brown tom
APPRENTICE, FERRETPAW (cream-and-gray tom)

SMOKEFOOT—black tom

TOADFOOT—dark brown tom

APPLEFUR—mottled brown she-cat

CROWFROST—black-and-white tom

RATSCAR—brown tom with long scar across his back

APPRENTICE, **PINEPAW** (black she-cat)

SNOWBIRD—pure-white she-cat

TAWNYPELT—tortoiseshell she-cat with green eyes

APPRENTICE, **STARLINGPAW** (ginger tom)

OLIVENOSE—tortoiseshell she-cat

OWLCLAW—light brown tabby tom

SHREWFOOT—gray she-cat with black feet

SCORCHFUR—dark gray tom

REDWILLOW—mottled brown-and-ginger tom

TIGERHEART—dark brown tabby tom

DAWNPELT—cream-furred she-cat

QUEENS

KINKFUR—tabby she-cat, with long fur that sticks out at all angles

IVYTAIL—black, white, and tortoiseshell she-cat

ELDERS

CEDARHEART—dark gray tom

TALLPOPPY—long-legged light brown tabby she-cat

SNAKETAIL—dark brown tom with tabby-striped tail

WHITEWATER—white she-cat with long fur, blind in one eye

WINDCLAN

LEADER
ONESTAR—brown tabby tom

DEPUTY
ASHFOOT—gray she-cat

MEDICINE CAT
KESTRELFLIGHT—mottled gray tom

WARRIORS
CROWFEATHER—dark gray tom

OWLWHISKER—light brown tabby tom
APPRENTICE, WHISKERPAW (light brown tom)

WHITETAIL—small white she-cat

NIGHTCLOUD—black she-cat

GORSETAIL—very pale gray-and-white tom with blue eyes

WEASELFUR—ginger tom with white paws

HARESPRING—brown-and-white tom

LEAFTAIL—dark tabby tom with amber eyes

ANTPELT—brown tom with one black ear

EMBERFOOT—gray tom with two dark paws

HEATHERTAIL—light brown tabby she-cat with blue eyes
APPRENTICE, FURZEPAW (gray-and-white she-cat)

BREEZEPELT—black tom with amber eyes
APPRENTICE, BOULDERPAW (large pale gray tom)

SEDGEWHISKER—light brown tabby she-cat

SWALLOWTAIL—dark gray she-cat

SUNSTRIKE—tortoiseshell she-cat with large white mark on her forehead

ELDERS
WEBFOOT—dark gray tabby tom

TORNEAR—tabby tom

RIVERCLAN

LEADER   **MISTYSTAR**—gray she-cat with blue eyes

DEPUTY   **REEDWHISKER**—black tom
APPRENTICE, HOLLOWPAW (dark brown tabby tom)

MEDICINE CAT   **MOTHWING**—dappled golden she-cat
APPRENTICE, WILLOWSHINE (gray tabby she-cat)

WARRIORS   **GRAYMIST**—pale gray tabby she-cat
APPRENTICE, TROUTPAW (pale gray she-cat)

MINTFUR—light gray tabby tom

ICEWING—white she-cat with blue eyes

MINNOWTAIL—dark gray she-cat
APPRENTICE, MOSSYPAW (brown-and-white she-cat)

PEBBLEFOOT—mottled gray tom
APPRENTICE, RUSHPAW (light brown tabby tom)

MALLOWNOSE—light brown tabby tom

ROBINWING—tortoiseshell-and-white tom

BEETLEWHISKER—brown-and-white tabby tom

PETALFUR—gray-and-white she-cat

GRASSPELT—light brown tom

QUEENS   **DUSKFUR**—brown tabby she-cat

MOSSPELT—tortoiseshell she-cat with blue eyes

ELDERS **DAPPLENOSE**—mottled gray she-cat

POUNCETAIL—ginger-and-white tom

THE TRIBE OF RUSHING WATER

TRIBE-HEALER **TELLER OF THE POINTED STONES (STONETELLER)**—brown tabby tom with amber eyes

PREY-HUNTERS (toms and she-cats responsible for providing food)

GRAY SKY BEFORE DAWN (GRAY)—pale gray tabby tom

WING SHADOW OVER WATER (WING)—gray-and-white she-cat

STORMFUR—dark gray tom with amber eyes, formerly of RiverClan

FLIGHT OF STARTLED HERON (FLIGHT)—brown tabby she-cat

SCREECH OF ANGRY OWL (SCREECH)—black tom

SPLASH WHEN FISH LEAPS (SPLASH)—light brown tabby she-cat

CAVE-GUARDS (toms and she-cats responsible for guarding the cave)

CRAG WHERE EAGLES NEST (CRAG)—dark gray tom (Brook's brother)

SHEER PATH BESIDE WATERFALL (SHEER)—dark brown tabby tom

SWOOP OF CHESTNUT HAWK (SWOOP)— dark ginger she-cat

MOSS THAT GROWS BY RIVER (MOSS)— light brown she-cat

PEBBLE THAT ROLLS DOWN MOUNTAIN (PEBBLE)—gray she-cat

KIT-MOTHERS   (she-cats expecting or nursing kits)

BROOK WHERE SMALL FISH SWIM (BROOK)—brown tabby she-cat (two kits: Lark That Sings at Dawn—Lark—pale tabby she-cat, and Pine That Clings to Rock—Pine—light brown tom)

NIGHT OF NO STARS (NIGHT)—black she-cat (expecting Sheer's kits)

TO·BES   (Tribe apprentices)

DARK SHADOW ON WATER (DARK)—black tom (prey-hunter)

SNOW FALLING ON STONES (SNOW)— white she-cat (cave-guard)

RAIN THAT PASSES QUICKLY (RAIN)— gray speckled she-cat (cave-guard)

ELDERS   (former prey-hunters and cave-guards, now retired)

TALON OF SWOOPING EAGLE (TALON)— dark brown tabby tom

BIRD THAT RIDES THE WIND (BIRD)— gray-brown she-cat

CLOUD WITH STAR IN BELLY (CLOUD)— pale gray she-cat

OTHER CATS IN MOUNTAINS

FLORA—dark brown-and-white she-cat with green eyes

THE ANCIENTS

BROKEN SHADOW—slender orange she-cat with white paws and amber eyes

WHISPERING BREEZE—silver-gray she-cat with blue eyes

STONE SONG—dark gray tabby tom with blue eyes

CHASING CLOUDS—gray-and-white tom with blue eyes

FURLED BRACKEN—dark ginger tabby tom with amber eyes

CLOUDY SUN—pale ginger she-cat with green eyes

RUNNING HORSE—dark brown tom with yellow eyes

RISING MOON—gray-and-white she-cat with blue eyes

JAGGED LIGHTNING—black-and-white tom with amber eyes

SHY FAWN—dusty brown she-cat with amber eyes

DAWN RIVER—tortoiseshell she-cat with amber eyes

FISH LEAP—brown tabby tom with amber eyes

HALF MOON—white she-cat with green eyes

OWL FEATHER—wiry brown she-cat with yellow eyes

JAY'S WING—gray tabby tom with blue eyes

DOVE'S WING—pale gray she-cat with blue eyes

PROLOGUE

Water thundered down from the mountaintop, screening the entrance to the cave with a shimmering cascade. Gray light filtered through it and shadows gathered in the corners of the cavern like soft black wings. Near the sheet of falling water, two kits were scuffling over a bunch of feathers, batting it back and forth and letting out shrill squeals of excitement. The pale tabby fur of the little she-cat and the tom's brown pelt almost blended into the dark stone floor.

At the back of the cave, an old brown tabby tom was crouching in the mouth of a tunnel. His eyes were narrowed, and his amber gaze never left the kits. He was motionless, except for the occasional twitch of his ears.

The tabby kit leaped high into the air, clawing at the feathers; as she landed with the bunch in her paws her brother flung himself on top of her, rolling over and snapping at the feathers with teeth like tiny white thorns.

"That's enough." A gentle voice came from close by as a graceful brown tabby she-cat rose to her paws and padded across to the kits. "Mind you don't get too close to the water. And Pine, why don't you try jumping high like Lark? You need to practice for when you're a prey-hunter."

"I'd rather be a cave-guard," Pine mewed. "I'd fight every cat that tried to trespass on our territory."

"Well, you can't, because I will," Lark retorted. "I'm going to be a cave-guard *and* hunt prey, so there!"

"That's not how we do things," their mother began; a swift glance over her shoulder showed that she was aware of the old cat watching from the shadows. "Every Tribe kit has to—"

She broke off at the sound of paw steps coming from the narrow path that led behind the waterfall and into the cave. A broad-shouldered gray-furred cat appeared, followed by the rest of his patrol. Instantly the kits let out squeals of welcome and hurled themselves at him.

"Careful!" Their mother followed and gathered the kits in with her tail. "Your father has been on border patrol. He must be tired."

"I'm fine, Brook." The gray tom blinked at her affectionately and gave her ear a quick lick. "It was an easy trip today."

"Stormfur, I don't know how you can say that!" a black tom put in, shaking water from his pelt as he left the cliff path. "We waste our time and wear out our paws patrolling that border, and for what?"

"Peace and quiet," Stormfur replied, his voice even. "We aren't going to get rid of those cats, even though we do think they're intruders. The best we can hope for is to protect our own territory."

"The whole of the mountains should be our territory!" the black tom spat.

"Give it a rest, Screech," a dark ginger she-cat meowed, with an irritable twitch of her tail. "Stormfur's right. Things aren't like that anymore."

"But are we safe?" asked Brook. She glanced at the kits, who were now tussling over a morsel of rabbit fur.

"The borders are holding, mostly," Stormfur told Brook, a worried look in his amber eyes. "But we did pick up the scent of other cats in a couple of places. And there were eagle feathers scattered on the rock. They've been stealing prey again."

The ginger she-cat shrugged. "There's nothing we can do about that."

"We can't just let it go, Swoop," Stormfur murmured. "Otherwise they'll think they can do exactly what they like, and there was no point in setting the borders in the first place. I think we should increase the patrols and be ready to fight."

"More patrols?" Screech lashed his tail angrily.

"It makes sense to—"

"No!"

Stormfur jumped as a voice rasped out from the shadows and he saw the old tabby cat standing a tail-length away.

"Stoneteller!" he exclaimed. "I didn't see you there."

"Evidently." The old cat's neck fur was bristling and there was a trace of anger in his eyes. "There will be no more patrols," he went on. "The Tribe has enough to eat, and with the thaw approaching, there will soon be more prey: eggs and young birds stolen from nests."

Stormfur looked as if he wanted to argue, but he picked up a flickering glance from Brook and a tiny shake of her head.

Reluctantly he dipped his head to Stoneteller. "Very well."

The old cat stalked away. Making an effort to flatten the ruffled fur on his neck, Stormfur turned to his kits. "Have you behaved yourselves today?"

"They've been very good," Brook told him, her eyes warm. "Lark is growing so strong and sturdy, and Pine jumps really well."

"We've been hunting," Lark announced, pointing with her tail toward the bedraggled lump of feathers. "I caught three eagles!"

"Didn't," Pine contradicted her. "I killed one, or it would have flown away with you!"

Brook met Stormfur's eyes. "I can't seem to make them understand that they'll have separate duties when they're to-bes."

"They shouldn't have to decide now," Stormfur began, only to break off as Brook flicked her tail toward Stoneteller, who was still in earshot. He let out a sigh. "They'll learn," he murmured, a trace of regret in his tone. "Is there any fresh-kill left? I'm starving!"

As Brook led Stormfur over to the fresh-kill pile, to-bes and their mentors headed back into the cave, and Stormfur's kits shot across the cavern floor to intercept them.

"Tell us about outside!" Lark squeaked. "Did you catch any prey?"

"*I* want to go out," Pine added.

One of the to-bes butted his shoulder gently with his head. "You're too small. An eagle would eat you in one bite."

"No it wouldn't! I'd *fight* it," Pine declared, fluffing up his brown fur.

The to-be let out a *mrrow* of laughter. "I'd like to see that! But you still have to wait until you're eight moons old."

"Mouse dung!"

Stoneteller stood watching the to-bes and kits romping together for a few heartbeats before he headed back toward his tunnel. As he approached it, a gray-brown she-cat rose to her paws and padded up to him.

"Stoneteller, I must talk to you."

The old tabby glared at her. "I've said all I have to say. You know that, Bird."

Bird did not reply, merely stood there waiting, until the old cat let out a long sigh. "Come, then. But don't expect any different answers."

Stoneteller led the way into the second tunnel, and Bird followed. The sounds of the young cats died away behind them, replaced by the steady drip of water.

The tunnel led into a cave much smaller than the one the cats had left. Pointed stones rose up from the floor and hung down from the roof. Some of them had joined in the middle, as if the cats were threading their way through a stone forest. Water trickled down the stones and the cave walls to make pools on the floor; their surface reflected a faint gray light from a jagged crack in the roof. All was silent except for the drip of water and the distant roaring of the falls, now sunk to a whisper.

Stoneteller turned to face Bird. "Well?"

"We've spoken about this before. You know you should have chosen your successor long ago."

The old cat let out a snort of disgust. "There's time yet."

"Don't tell that to me," Bird retorted. "My mother was your littermate. I know exactly how old you are. You were chosen from that litter by the Tribe's previous Healer, the last Teller of the Pointed Stones. You have served the Tribe well, but you can't expect to stay here forever. Sooner or later you will be summoned to the Tribe of Endless Hunting. You *must* choose the next Stoneteller!"

"Why?" Bird flinched at the harshness of the old cat's retort but Stoneteller continued. "So that the Tribe can go on, generation after generation, scrabbling their lives from these uncaring stones?"

Bird's voice quivered with shock when she replied. "This is our *home*! We have earned the right to live here many times over! We fought off the trespassers, remember?" She padded closer to Stoneteller and held out one paw appealingly. "How can you think of betraying our ancestors by not preserving what they began?"

Stoneteller turned his head away; there was a flash of something in his eyes that warned Bird he was not telling her everything.

At that moment a thin claw-scratch of new moon appeared from behind a cloud; its light sliced down through the hole in the cave roof and struck one of the pools of water, turning its surface to silver. Stoneteller gazed at it.

"It is the night of the new moon," he murmured. "The

night when the Tribe of Endless Hunting speaks to me from the sky, through reflections in the water. Very well, Bird That Rides the Wind. I promise you I will look for signs tonight."

"Thank you," Bird whispered. Touching Stoneteller affectionately on the shoulder with her tail-tip, she padded quietly out of the cave. "Good luck," she mewed as she disappeared into the tunnel.

When she had gone, Stoneteller approached the edge of the pool and looked into the water. Then he raised one paw and brought it down with force on the surface, shattering the reflection into shards of light that flickered and died.

"I will never listen to you again!" Each word was forced out through bared teeth. "We trusted the Tribe of Endless Hunting, but you deserted us when we most needed your help."

Turning his back on the pool, he paced among the pointed stones, his claws scraping against the rough cave floor. "I hate what the Tribe has become!" he snarled. "I hate how we have taken on Clan ways. Why could we not survive alone?" Halting beneath the rift in the roof, he raised his head with a burning gaze that challenged the moon. "Why did you bring us here if we were doomed to fail?"

CHAPTER 1

Dovepaw slid out through the thorn tunnel and stood waiting in the forest for her sister, Ivypaw, and their mentors to join her. A hard frost had turned every blade of grass into a sharp spike under her paws, and from the bare branches of the trees, icicles glimmered in the gray dawn light. Dovepaw shivered as claws of cold probed deeply into her fur. Newleaf was still a long way off.

Dovepaw's belly was churning with anxiety, and her tail drooped.

This is your warrior assessment, she told herself. *It's the best thing that can happen to an apprentice. So why don't you feel excited?*

She knew the answer to her question. Too much had happened during the moons of her apprenticeship: important events beside which even the thrill of becoming a warrior paled into insignificance. Taking a deep breath, Dovepaw lifted her tail as she heard the paw steps of cats coming through the tunnel. She couldn't let the cats who were assessing her see how uneasy she was. She needed to do her best to show them that she was ready to be a warrior.

Dovepaw's mentor, Lionblaze, was the first cat to emerge,

fluffing his golden tabby pelt against the early morning chill. Spiderleg followed him closely; Dovepaw gave the skinny black warrior a dubious glance, wondering what it would be like to have him assessing her as well as Lionblaze. Spiderleg looked very stern.

I wish it were just Lionblaze, Dovepaw thought. *Too bad Firestar decided that we should have two judges.*

Cinderheart appeared next, followed closely by her apprentice, Ivypaw, and last of all Millie, who was to be Ivypaw's second assessor. Dovepaw's whiskers quivered as she looked at her sister. Ivypaw looked small and scared, and her dark blue eyes were shadowed with exhaustion.

Padding closer, Dovepaw gave Ivypaw's ear an affectionate lick. "Hey, you'll be fine," she murmured.

Ivypaw turned her head away.

She doesn't even talk to me anymore, Dovepaw thought wretchedly. *She's always busy somewhere else when I try to get close to her. And she cries out in her dreams.* Dovepaw pictured how her sister twitched and batted her paws when they were sleeping side by side in the apprentices' den. She knew that Ivypaw was visiting the Dark Forest, spying on behalf of ThunderClan because Jayfeather and Lionblaze had asked her to, but when she tried to ask her sister what happened there, Ivypaw replied only that there was nothing new to report.

"I suggest we head for the abandoned Twoleg nest," Spiderleg announced. "It's sheltered, so there's a good chance of prey."

Lionblaze blinked as if he was surprised that Spiderleg was trying to take over the assessment, but then nodded and led the way through the trees in the direction of the old Twoleg path. Dovepaw quickened her pace to pad beside him, and the other cats followed.

"Are you ready?" Lionblaze asked.

Dovepaw jumped, startled out of her worries about her sister. "Sorry," she mewed. "I was thinking about Ivypaw. She looks so tired."

Lionblaze glanced back at the silver-and-white she-cat, then at Dovepaw, shock and anxiety mingling in his amber eyes. "I guess the Dark Forest training is taking its toll," he muttered.

"And whose fault is that?" Dovepaw flashed back at him. However urgent it was to find out what the cats of the Dark Forest were plotting, it wasn't fair of Lionblaze and Jayfeather to put the whole burden on her sister's shoulders.

Ivypaw isn't even a warrior yet!

Lionblaze let out a sigh that told Dovepaw he agreed with her privately, but wasn't prepared to say so. "I'm not going to talk about that now," he meowed. "It's time for you to concentrate on your assessment."

Dovepaw gave an irritable shrug.

Lionblaze halted as the old Twoleg nest came into sight. Dovepaw picked up traces of herb scent from Jayfeather's garden, though most of the stems and leaves were blackened by frost. She could hear the faint scutterings of prey in the grass and in the debris under the trees. Spiderleg was right: This would be a good spot to hunt.

"Okay," Lionblaze began. "First we want to assess your

tracking skills. Cinderheart, what do you want Ivypaw to catch?"

"We'll go for mice. Okay, Ivypaw?"

The silver tabby gave a tense nod.

"But not inside the old Twoleg nest," Millie added. "That would be too easy."

"I know." Dovepaw thought her sister sounded too weary to put one paw in front of another, let alone catch mice. But she headed off into the trees without hesitating; Cinderheart and Millie followed at a distance.

Dovepaw watched until the frostbitten bracken hid Ivypaw from her sight, then sent out her extended senses to track her as she padded behind the abandoned nest toward the group of pine trees. Mice were squeaking and scuffling among the fallen needles; Dovepaw hoped that her sister would scent them and make a good catch.

She was concentrating so hard on following Ivypaw that she forgot about her own assessment until Spiderleg flicked his tail-tip over her ear.

"Hey!" she meowed, spinning around to face the black warrior.

"Lionblaze *said* he'd like you to try for a squirrel," Spiderleg meowed. "If you're sure you want to become a warrior, that is."

"I'm sure," Dovepaw growled. "Sorry, Lionblaze."

Lionblaze was standing just behind Spiderleg, looking annoyed. Dovepaw was angry with herself for missing his order, but even more with Spiderleg for being so obnoxious about it.

It's mouse-brained to have two judges, she grumbled to herself. *Mentors have been assessing their own apprentices for more seasons than there are leaves on the trees!*

Raising her head, she tasted the air and brightened when she picked up a nearby scent of squirrel. It was coming from the other side of a clump of bramble; setting her paws down lightly, Dovepaw skirted the thorns until she came out into a small clearing and spotted the squirrel nibbling a nut at the foot of an ivy-covered oak tree.

A wind was rising, rattling the bare branches. Dovepaw slid around the edge of the clearing, using the bracken for cover, until she was downwind of her prey. Its scent flooded strongly over her, making her jaws water.

Dropping into her best hunter's crouch, Dovepaw began to creep up on the squirrel. But she couldn't resist sending out her senses just once more to check on Ivypaw, and she jumped as she picked up the tiny shriek, quickly cut off, of a mouse under her sister's claws.

Her uncontrolled movement rustled a dead leaf, and instantly the squirrel fled up the tree, its bushy tail flowing out behind it. Dovepaw bounded across the grass and hurled herself up the trunk, but the squirrel had vanished into the branches. She clung to an ivy stem, trying to listen for movement beyond the wind and the creaking of the tree, but it was no use.

"Mouse dung!" she spat, letting herself drop to the ground again.

Spiderleg stalked up to her. "For StarClan's sake, what do

you think you're doing?" he demanded. "A kit just out of the nursery could have caught that squirrel! It's a good thing none of the other Clans saw you, or they'd think ThunderClan doesn't know how to train its apprentices."

Dovepaw's neck fur bristled. "Have you never missed a catch?" she muttered under her breath.

"Well?" the black warrior demanded. "Let's hear what you did wrong."

"It wasn't all bad," Lionblaze put in before Dovepaw could answer. "That was good stalking work, when you moved downwind of the squirrel."

Dovepaw flashed him a grateful look. "I guess I got distracted for a heartbeat," she admitted. "I moved a leaf, and the squirrel heard me."

"And you could have been faster chasing it," Spiderleg told her. "You might have caught it if you'd put on a bit more speed."

Dovepaw nodded glumly. *We haven't all got legs as long as yours!* "Does this mean I've failed my assessment?"

Spiderleg flicked his ears but didn't answer. "I'm going to see how Millie is getting on with Ivypaw," he announced, darting off toward the abandoned nest.

Dovepaw gazed at her mentor. "Sorry," she meowed.

"I guess you must be nervous," Lionblaze responded. "You're much better than that on an ordinary hunting patrol."

Now that she was facing failure, Dovepaw realized just how much she wanted to pass her assessment. *Being a warrior is way better than being part of the prophecy with my so-called special powers.*

She tensed as another thought struck her. *What if Ivypaw is made a warrior and I'm not?*

Her sister deserved it, Dovepaw knew. She didn't have any special powers of her own, but every night she put herself in danger to spy for Lionblaze and Jayfeather in the Dark Forest.

Ivypaw's better than me. I can't even catch a stupid squirrel!

"Cheer up," Lionblaze meowed. "Your assessment isn't over yet. But for StarClan's sake, *concentrate*!"

"I'll do my best," Dovepaw promised. "What's next?"

In answer, Lionblaze angled his ears in the direction they had come from. Dovepaw turned to see Icecloud picking her way across the frosty grass.

"Hi," the white she-cat mewed. "Brambleclaw sent me to help you."

"You're just in time." Lionblaze dipped his head. "The next part of the assessment is hunting with a partner," he explained to Dovepaw.

Dovepaw brightened up; she enjoyed hunting as part of a team, and Icecloud would be easy to work with. But she was disconcerted when Icecloud looked at her with her head cocked to one side and asked, "What do you want me to do?"

"I . . . er . . ." Dovepaw wasn't used to giving orders to a warrior. *Come on, mouse-brain! Shape up!*

"Let's try for a blackbird," she suggested. "Icecloud, your white pelt is going to be a problem, though."

"Tell me about it," the white she-cat mewed ruefully.

"So we'll have to find somewhere you can stay in cover until the last moment. When we find a bird, I'll stalk it and try to drive it toward you."

"You'll need to make sure it doesn't fly off, or—"

Lionblaze interrupted Icecloud's warning with a meaningful cough.

"Oops, sorry," Icecloud mewed. "I forgot. Go on, Dovepaw."

"Blackbirds often nest just beyond the old Twoleg den," Dovepaw went on after a moment's thought. "I know it's too early for them to be nesting, but it might be worth scouting there for good places."

Lionblaze nodded encouragingly. "Then what?"

"Well . . . the ground slopes away there. Icecloud could take cover down the slope."

"Okay, let's see you do it," Lionblaze meowed.

Dovepaw had taken only a few paw steps when Spiderleg reappeared, shouldering his way through the bracken. He said nothing; Dovepaw's paws itched with curiosity to find out how her sister was getting on, but there was no time to ask. It felt weird to be padding a pace or two ahead of Icecloud, as if she was leading a patrol, and weirder still to be the one who was making the decisions. Panic pricked at Dovepaw, like ants crawling through her pelt. Her head felt as empty as an echoing cave, as if everything she had ever learned had flown away like birds from a branch.

I've spent more time eavesdropping on other Clans than training to be a warrior!

Dovepaw wanted to finish her assessment without using her special powers. *Ivypaw doesn't have them, so it's only fair.* But it was hard to switch her senses off when she was constantly wondering what her sister was up to. Besides, when she tried to focus on the sounds that were closest to her, she felt trapped and smothered by the trees.

How do the other cats cope? she wondered. *I can hardly catch my breath!*

Dovepaw led the way up the old Thunderpath, then struck off into the trees where the blackbirds nested. Icecloud followed her closely, while Lionblaze and Spiderleg hung back, observing. Sliding into a hazel thicket, Dovepaw raised her tail to warn Icecloud to keep back, where her white pelt wouldn't alert any possible prey. Her paws tingled with satisfaction when she spotted a blackbird, pecking at the ground underneath a hazel bush.

Dovepaw drew back. "Go that way, down the slope," she whispered to Icecloud, signaling with her tail. "I'll scare the bird and send it in your direction."

Icecloud nodded and crept away, silent as a wisp of white mist. Dovepaw watched her until she was out of sight; without meaning to, she extended her senses to track the white she-cat even after she disappeared. Puzzled, she realized that Icecloud's paws sounded different on the ground.

Something isn't right.

Instead of stalking the blackbird, Dovepaw pushed her way through the thick hazel stems, heading after her Clanmate. Spiderleg let out a disapproving snort. Dovepaw barely noticed; Icecloud's paws were thundering inside her head, blotting out everything else.

I shouldn't be able to hear them like that. It's as if they're echoing a long way underground. Suddenly Dovepaw understood. *Oh, no! The ground must be hollow!*

She quickened her pace, thrusting her way out of the thicket and racing down the slope. The blackbird fluttered up into the branches.

"What in the name of StarClan—?" Spiderleg gasped.

Dovepaw heard an awkward mutter from Lionblaze as she streaked away. She burst through a tangle of brambles and spotted Icecloud farther down the slope. At that moment, Icecloud staggered with a screech of alarm, then began to disappear as the ground opened up underneath her paws.

"Icecloud!" Dovepaw yowled. "I'm coming!"

She leaped forward just in time to grab Icecloud's scruff in her teeth before the white she-cat disappeared in a rain of loose earth. Icecloud scrabbled frantically with her forepaws, trying to haul herself out. But it seemed as if the whole slope was giving way, and there was nothing solid to hold on to.

Dovepaw tried to drag her Clanmate out, but the ground was sliding away under her paws as well, and Icecloud's weight dangling down into the hole was too much for her. Icecloud's scruff slipped from between her teeth. Dovepaw stared in horror as she watched the white warrior fall down and down into the darkness. Icecloud's terrified wail was cut off as loose earth poured in to bury her.

CHAPTER 2

Lionblaze pounded around the bramble thicket, wishing he was small enough to head straight through it like Dovepaw. On the other side he halted, panting. Dovepaw was halfway down the slope, crouching at the edge of a hole. Suddenly she lurched backward. Lionblaze heard a shriek and caught a glimpse of a thrashing white paw as Icecloud vanished into the earth.

It's one of the tunnels! Panic throbbed through Lionblaze as he remembered his sister, Hollyleaf. In his mind, he saw her again, darting back into the mouth of the tunnel, ignoring everything he and Jayfeather said to warn her, and then all he could see was the endless fall of soil and rocks that had buried her underground forever.

"What's going on?" Spiderleg's meow jolted Lionblaze back to the present.

The black warrior darted past and joined Dovepaw, who was peering down into the hole. Looking around, Lionblaze spotted a familiar gorse bush and a spot where a tiny spring welled up between two flat stones. He realized that they were a little way up the slope from the exact place where Hollyleaf had disappeared. Icecloud had fallen into the same tunnel!

Lionblaze's belly lurched. *Great StarClan, what might they find down there?*

He rushed down the slope to the edge of the hole, shouldering Spiderleg out of the way. Dovepaw jumped back, clearly startled by the look of horror on his face. There was just enough light in the tunnel to show Lionblaze the walls and floor as he peered down. Several tail-lengths below, Icecloud was scrambling out of a heap of earth and stones, shaking soil from her pelt.

"Get me out of here!" she yowled when she looked up and saw Lionblaze.

"Are you hurt?" he asked.

"Not much. Just my shoulder." Icecloud spat out earth. "Please get me out."

Lionblaze leaned over the edge of the hole as far as he dared, and looked up and down the tunnel. Farther into the hill, it vanished into blackness. Lower down, a fall of earth and stones blocked the former entrance.

Is Hollyleaf under that? Lionblaze wondered, suppressing a shudder. "Spiderleg, go and fetch help," he directed.

As the black warrior dashed off, Lionblaze gazed down again at Icecloud, who was crouching among the soil, her pelt ruffled and her eyes big and scared. "It won't be long now," he promised.

"Thanks, Lionblaze." The young she-cat's voice quivered. "It's really dark down here."

"I'll try to make the hole bigger," Dovepaw mewed. "That'll let in more light."

But as she began scraping at the edge of the hole, more earth started to rain down on Icecloud.

"No! Stop!" she wailed.

"Sorry." Dovepaw stopped scraping and sat at the edge of the hole.

Lionblaze leaned over to hiss close to her ear. "No other cat is to go into the hole except me. Got it?"

The gray apprentice's eyes widened with surprise, but she nodded. Lionblaze let out a tiny sigh of relief. He knew that if there were any dark secrets to be discovered down the hole, he needed to be the first cat to find them. His belly churned as he waited. For the first time in many moons, he wondered if his Clanmates really believed that a passing rogue had killed Ashfur, and that Hollyleaf's disappearance had nothing to do with it.

I don't want the Clan to start thinking about those times again. I have to protect Hollyleaf's memory!

At last he heard the sound of paw steps hurtling through the undergrowth. Spiderleg reappeared at a run, with Cloudtail, Birchfall, and Foxleap just behind. Foxleap dashed up to the edge of the hole, leaning over to see his littermate.

"We're here! We'll get you out soon," he encouraged her.

Icecloud blinked up at him. "Hurry!"

"We need something to pull her out with," Birchfall thought out loud. "Maybe a long, thick tendril. Not bramble, but something like ivy or bindweed."

"There's ivy on that tree." Cloudtail whisked his tail around to point at an ancient oak tree whose trunk was covered in glossy dark green leaves. Foxleap scrambled up the tree and bit off a long tendril; as soon as it was loose Cloudtail tugged it free and bounded back with it trailing behind him.

"Wrap one end around that sapling," Birchfall directed, angling his ears toward a young ash tree that grew near the hole. "Then we can drop the other end down to Icecloud."

When the ivy tendril was secure, Foxleap dangled the free end down to his sister. Icecloud gripped it in her teeth, but as soon as the other cats started to haul it up she let go and dropped back onto the mound of earth.

"I'm too heavy!" she gasped. "I can't hold on."

"Wrap it around yourself, then," Lionblaze suggested.

Icecloud tried, but it was obvious that her injured shoulder was hampering her. "It's no use!" Her voice rose to a wail. "I'll be stuck down here forever!"

"Nonsense," Lionblaze mewed. "We'll think of something."

"What if we drop more earth and stones down the hole?" Spiderleg suggested, peering down. "We could make that heap big enough so she can climb out."

"It might work," Birchfall murmured. "But we'd risk burying her. . . ."

"No, please don't!" Icecloud's panicky mew came up from the bottom of the hole.

The sound of more paw steps approaching distracted Lionblaze. He turned to see Jayfeather and Blossomfall skirting the bramble thicket, and headed back up the slope to meet them.

"I heard Spiderleg telling the Clan what happened,"

Jayfeather meowed as Lionblaze bounded up. He paused; Lionblaze could tell that he knew this was part of the same tunnel where Hollyleaf had disappeared.

Lionblaze waited until Blossomfall had joined the other cats around the hole. "There's nothing there apart from Ice-cloud that I can see," he whispered. "The mudfall is farther down the slope."

"You can't let any other cats go down!" Jayfeather hissed.

"I know that!" Lionblaze retorted. Belly churning again, he led Jayfeather the few paw steps to join the other cats.

"I'm going in," Foxleap announced. "You can lower me into the hole, I'll tie the tendril around Icecloud, and then you can pull her up."

"No," Lionblaze said as he stepped forward. "It's too dangerous. I'll go."

"What?" Birchfall lashed his tail. "Don't be mouse-brained! You're too heavy."

"And why would it be dangerous?" Foxleap argued, stepping forward to confront Lionblaze. "There's nothing down there except Icecloud."

"You don't know that!" Lionblaze snapped.

Cloudtail had been leaning over the hole, peering curiously up and down the tunnel. Finally he drew back. "Are these the tunnels WindClan used to invade us?"

Lionblaze nodded; a familiar pang of guilt clawed him in the belly as he remembered how he and Heathertail had been the first to discover the network of tunnels.

Foxleap drew in a shocked breath. "Great StarClan! There could be WindClan warriors down there now, waiting to attack Icecloud!"

Cloudtail rolled his eyes. "Oh, sure! WindClan must spend all their time down there, waiting for a ThunderClan warrior to fall in."

In spite of the white warrior's scathing words, Lionblaze felt an added urgency among the cats around the hole. A plaintive mew came up from Icecloud in the depths. "Get me out, *please*!"

"I'll go," Dovepaw volunteered, giving Lionblaze a hard stare, as if she remembered how he had told her not to let another cat go down. *Does that include me?* she seemed to be asking.

Jayfeather nodded. "Better her than another cat," he whispered to Lionblaze.

"But she's only an apprentice!" Foxleap protested. Lionblaze could sense that in a couple of heartbeats he would leap into the hole himself, whether he had permission from the senior warriors or not.

"I'm the lightest of all of you," Dovepaw pointed out. "And all I have to do is jump down and wrap the tendril around Icecloud." As if the decision had already been made, she turned to Lionblaze and asked quietly, "Is there anything I should look out for?"

Yes, my dead sister. Lionblaze swallowed hard; instead, he answered, "Just keep your eyes open. Cats don't belong in these tunnels, so we must treat them as hostile territory."

Birchfall wound the tendril around Dovepaw's body; then he and Cloudtail lowered her into the hole. Her eyes widened as she vanished over the edge. Lionblaze looked down to see her unwinding the tendril from herself, and wrapping it securely around Icecloud.

"Ready!" she called.

Birchfall and Cloudtail began hauling on the vine. A yowl of pain came from Icecloud, quickly suppressed. "Sorry," she mewed through gritted teeth. "My shoulder really hurts."

Slowly the white she-cat was drawn up out of the hole. As soon as she appeared over the edge, Foxleap rushed up and supported her with his shoulder. "Come on," he meowed. "We'll get you back to camp and Jayfeather will take a look at you."

"I'll be fine," Icecloud murmured, though she couldn't put one forepaw to the ground, and her breath was coming in rapid gasps of pain. She leaned heavily on Foxleap as they headed toward the camp.

Cloudtail flanked Icecloud on the other side, glancing back with surprise in his blue eyes when Jayfeather didn't move. The ThunderClan medicine cat was still leaning over the hole, his head cocked as if he was listening.

"Come on," Cloudtail urged. "The others can bring Dovepaw up."

Jayfeather hesitated, then followed.

Meanwhile, Birchfall and Spiderleg had passed the vine

back to Dovepaw, and were preparing to haul her up. A moment later she scrabbled her way over the edge of the hole; Lionblaze bent down and tugged her the last tail-length by the scruff.

"Thanks!" Dovepaw panted, shaking earth out of her pelt. "It was horrible down there."

Lionblaze was dying to ask her what she had seen in the tunnel, but he knew he couldn't say anything, not in front of the other cats. *Besides, if Dovepaw had seen a dead cat down there, they would have heard her screeching back in the stone hollow.*

"What are we going to do about this hole?" Birchfall meowed. "We don't want any other cat falling into it."

"It's too big to fill in," Spiderleg commented. "And if we cover it up, the cover might give way if cats walked on it."

"Maybe we can put something around it?" Blossomfall suggested.

"Good idea!" Lionblaze gave the young warrior an approving nod. "Let's pile up sticks to surround it for now. Later on we can figure out how to build something more permanent."

As they collected sticks and constructed the barrier, Lionblaze's paws itched with longing to climb down into the hole and have a look around. But the other cats would have asked too many questions. He had to leave with the others when the barrier was finished, though he cast a reluctant glance over his shoulder as he followed them up the slope.

Dovepaw padded alongside him. Lionblaze could feel her curiosity about the tunnel, but he hadn't decided yet how much he wanted to tell her. To his relief, as they headed for the old Thunderpath, her gaze fell on Spiderleg and she was instantly distracted.

"Oh, no!" she wailed. "I forgot about my assessment. I blew it, didn't I?"

"I'm not sure," Lionblaze admitted. "You weren't at your best when you were hunting, but you did help to save Icecloud. You were very brave, going down into the hole like that."

Looking dejected, Dovepaw glanced at Spiderleg again, but the black warrior was too far ahead to overhear. Lionblaze wanted to reassure her, but there was nothing he could tell her until he had consulted with Spiderleg. As they entered the stone hollow, Ivypaw dashed across the camp and skidded to a halt in front of Dovepaw.

"What happened?" she demanded. "Where have you been? What's the matter with Icecloud?" she added. "I saw her limping into Jayfeather's den."

"She fell down a hole," Dovepaw replied, launching into the story of what they had to do to get Icecloud out again.

Hazeltail came bounding up to listen, followed by Cinderheart and Millie. Brightheart and Bumblestripe pushed their way out of the warriors' den and Molekit and Cherrykit bounced out of the nursery with Poppyfrost chasing after them. Mousewhisker, Berrynose, and Whitewing crowded at the back.

"I heard Icecloud fell into an underground river!" Bumblestripe meowed, interrupting Dovepaw's story. "And you fell in after her."

"No," Whitewing argued. "Birchfall told me it was just a hole."

"Dovepaw didn't fall in." Lionblaze was determined to defend his apprentice. "She *climbed* in to help Icecloud."

"Wow, that was brave!" Bumblestripe gave Dovepaw an admiring glance.

"Maybe Icecloud's back is broken, like Briarlight's!" Berrynose gasped, his eyes wide with horror.

Brightheart flicked his ear with her tail. "Mouse-brain! She was *walking* into Jayfeather's den."

Dovepaw twitched her whiskers. "Do you want to know what really happened, or not?"

"It's tough that you didn't get to finish your assessment," Bumblestripe mewed when Dovepaw had finished.

Dovepaw's tail drooped, and her eyes grew anxious. "I know. Maybe Firestar won't give me my warrior name." Giving herself a shake, she turned to Ivypaw. "How did you do?" she prompted. "Who did the team hunting with you?"

"Hazeltail," Ivypaw replied. Her eyes shone. "It was really great! We caught two mice."

"Fantastic!"

Lionblaze could tell that Dovepaw was making an effort to be glad for her sister, but disappointment still weighed on her like snow on a branch. He was about to step in with a word of encouragement when Ivypaw leaned close to her sister and pressed her muzzle against Dovepaw's shoulder.

"Don't worry," she murmured, so softly that only Dovepaw and Lionblaze could hear. "Firestar knows how important you are to the Clan. You don't have to prove yourself by catching squirrels."

Dovepaw shrugged her off. "I want to be judged like a normal cat for once!" she retorted.

Ivypaw stared at her, puzzled. "But you're not like the rest of us," she pointed out.

"Quiet!" Lionblaze warned them. He had just noticed Firestar emerging from Jayfeather's den, where he must have been visiting Icecloud.

The ThunderClan leader darted across the clearing, leaping across the beech boughs in his way, and ran up the tumbled rocks to stand on the Highledge. His flame-colored pelt glowed, a spot of warmth in the cold leaf-bare light.

"Let all cats old enough to catch their own prey join here beneath the Highledge for a Clan meeting," he announced.

The cats already in the clearing sat down facing the Highledge. Molekit and Cherrykit frisked about at the front of the group until Poppyfrost gathered them with a sweep of her tail and made them sit quietly. Daisy and Ferncloud appeared at the entrance to the nursery and sat with their pelts brushing. Mousefur poked her head out from the beech branches that enclosed the elders' den, then emerged into the open with Purdy hard on her paws. Foxleap padded out from the medicine cat's den, while Jayfeather pushed back the bramble screen so Briarlight could watch from the entrance. Sandstorm, Dustpelt, Cloudtail, and Sorreltail all slid out of the warriors' den and found places at the foot of the cliff; Sorreltail lifted one hind paw and scratched her ear, as if she was chasing a flea.

Firestar raised his tail for silence. "Cats of ThunderClan," he began, "I think you've all heard about Icecloud's accident. She fell into a hole and dislocated her shoulder, but Jayfeather put it back in place." Firestar's tone was firm and reassuring; Lionblaze saw how well he understood his Clan's fears after what happened to Briarlight. "Jayfeather says she will need to rest," Firestar continued, "but she should only be off her paws for a quarter moon."

Murmurs of relief rose from the assembled cats; a couple of them called out, "Jayfeather! Jayfeather!"

"I'll check the hole myself later on," the Clan leader continued. He shot a glance at Lionblaze from glowing green eyes, clearly asking Lionblaze to guide him there; Lionblaze replied with a nod. "Meanwhile, Dustpelt and Brackenfur, you're the best at building. I want a solid barrier around that hole by sunset today. We can't fill it in, and we don't want any other cats falling down there."

"Sure, Firestar," Dustpelt called. "We'll get to it as soon as Brackenfur returns from patrol."

"And don't either of you two dare go anywhere near the hole," Poppyfrost warned her kits, reinforcing her words with a flick of her tail around their ears.

"Like we can!" Molekit complained. "We're not even allowed out of the hollow."

"And that's *totally* unfair," his sister agreed.

"There's another reason that I called the Clan together," Firestar went on. "Two apprentices completed their warrior assessments today."

A ripple of excitement ran through the cats; Ivypaw's eyes were shining, but Dovepaw just studied her paws. A pang of worry shot through Lionblaze and he glanced at Spiderleg, but the black warrior's face was expressionless, giving nothing away.

I hope Spiderleg's not too hard on her, he thought, wishing he had managed to consult the black warrior before the meeting.

"Cinderheart?" Firestar waved his tail, inviting Ivypaw's mentor to speak.

The gray warrior rose to her paws. "Ivypaw works hard," she began. "Her battle training in particular is exceptional. Her hunting could still use some work, though. When she was hunting alone today she caught a vole, but it was a messy catch: She let the vole get downwind of her and it nearly escaped." The gray warrior turned and dipped her head politely to Millie. "What do you think?" she asked.

Millie rose in her turn and took a step forward to stand beside Cinderheart. "Yes, I agree," she meowed. "And when Ivypaw was hunting with Hazeltail, she seemed embarrassed to be telling her what to do. She'll have to shape up if she's ever put in charge of a patrol." She cast a kind glance at Ivypaw, who was listening with wide, troubled eyes. "But Hazeltail and Ivypaw worked well together. They caught two mice, and they were really neat catches. The mice never had a chance!" Her voice grew warm. "In my opinion, Ivypaw deserves to become a warrior of ThunderClan. We're lucky to have her!"

A chorus of approving yowls broke out, while Dovepaw gave her sister's ear a lick. "Congratulations," she purred.

"Millie's right. You do deserve it."

Ivypaw's eyes glowed with relief. "I was so scared when Cinderheart said that about the vole," she confessed. "It was a really awful catch."

"Lionblaze?" The Clan grew quiet again as Firestar spoke. "What about Dovepaw?"

Lionblaze felt a twinge of apprehension as he rose to his paws. He wanted to do the best he could for his apprentice, but he couldn't hide the fact that she hadn't caught anything. "Dovepaw is the best apprentice any cat could hope for," he began. "She works hard, and she learns fast. Today, she started by looking for a squirrel. She found one quickly, and she did some excellent stalking work, getting into position. The squirrel had no idea she was there." He flashed a glance at Dovepaw, who still wasn't looking at him. "But then," he went on, "as she was creeping up on it, she accidentally disturbed a leaf. The squirrel spotted her and fled up a tree."

"She might have caught it if she'd been faster." Spiderleg rose to speak. "But once it got as far as the branches, there was no chance of finding it again."

Lionblaze glared at the black warrior. *There's no need to make it sound as bad as that!*

"What about her team hunting?" Firestar prompted.

"She organized herself and Icecloud well," Lionblaze meowed. "She positioned Icecloud in undergrowth to hide her white pelt, and started driving a blackbird toward her. But then . . ." Lionblaze hesitated. He was aware that this next part wouldn't sound good at all. He couldn't mention Dovepaw's extra powers, to explain why she had suddenly gone chasing after Icecloud. "Then she must have heard something," he went on. "She left the blackbird and ran through a bramble thicket to help Icecloud, who had fallen into the hole. The blackbird got away."

"So Dovepaw didn't catch anything today?" Firestar inquired.

Lionblaze shook his head, feeling hot under his pelt. "No." *Never mind that Dovepaw is one of the best hunters in the Clan,* he thought sadly. *Whether she becomes a warrior or not depends on what she did today.*

"Not a feather, not a whisker," Spiderleg confirmed. "If you ask me, she's far too easily distracted. If she'd kept her mind on what she was doing, she would have caught the squirrel *and* the blackbird."

Lionblaze could see his own disappointment reflected in his Clan leader's eyes. "In that case—" Firestar began.

"Hang on, Firestar, I haven't finished," Spiderleg interrupted. "Dovepaw made a mess of the hunting, true. But she ran to help a Clanmate in trouble when she had no idea what danger she would have to face on the other side of that bramble thicket. And when we couldn't get Icecloud out of the hole, she was quick to volunteer to be lowered down to help her, even though no cat really knew what might have been down there." He gave Dovepaw an approving glance. "These are the qualities ThunderClan needs most," he went on. "Courage, loyalty, and the willingness to face danger for the good of a Clanmate. In my opinion, we'd be mouse-brained not to make her a warrior."

Dovepaw was staring at him incredulously, as her Clan-mates yowled their approval. Her eyes shone as it sunk in that she would become a warrior that day. Ivypaw skipped around her, as excited as a kit.

Firestar waved his tail for silence. "Thank you, Spiderleg," he meowed when he could make himself heard. "Thunder-Clan will be all the stronger for the two new warriors I shall make today." He bounded down the tumbled rocks and stood in front of his Clan, beckoning Ivypaw forward with a flick of his tail. The Clan quieted down to allow their leader to begin the ceremony.

Firestar raised his head and looked around at his Clan-mates. His voice rang out clearly as he spoke the ancient words. "I, Firestar, call upon my warrior ancestors to look down on this apprentice. She has trained hard to understand the ways of your noble code, and I commend her to you as a warrior in her turn." Gazing down at Ivypaw, he continued, "Ivypaw, do you promise to uphold the warrior code and to protect and defend this Clan, even at the cost of your life?"

"I do." Ivypaw's voice shook.

Icy claws raked Lionblaze's pelt as he realized how Ivypaw was already carrying out the oath she had just sworn. Few cats had ever taken the kind of risk she took every night when she walked in her dreams with the cats of the Dark Forest.

"Then by the powers of StarClan," Firestar went on, "I give you your warrior name. Ivypaw, from this moment you will be known as Ivypool. StarClan honors your courage and your loyalty, and we welcome you as a full warrior of Thunder-Clan." Taking a pace forward, Firestar rested his muzzle on the top of Ivypool's head. She licked his shoulder in response.

"Ivypool! Ivypool!" The Clan greeted the new warrior by calling her name. As the yowls died down, Ivypool stepped back between Dustpelt and Cinderheart. The gray warrior laid her tail briefly across her former apprentice's shoulders, and Dustpelt gave her an approving nod.

Firestar raised his tail to beckon Dovepaw, and Lionblaze watched as his apprentice padded forward and halted in front of the flame-colored tom. She held Firestar's gaze without blinking as her leader called upon StarClan to look down upon her. "Dovepaw," he questioned her, "do you promise to uphold the warrior code and to protect and defend this Clan, even at the cost of your life?"

"I do," Dovepaw responded.

Lionblaze realized how much weight the oath carried for his apprentice. Dovepaw had much to offer her Clan, but becoming a warrior meant that even more demands would be laid on the shoulders of the young she-cat. Lionblaze wondered which of Dovepaw's qualities Firestar would choose to single out. *He can't mention her special powers. Not in front of the whole Clan.*

"Then by the powers of StarClan," Firestar continued, "I give you your warrior name. Dovepaw, from this moment you will be known as Dovewing. StarClan honors your intelligence and your enterprise, and we welcome you as a full warrior of ThunderClan."

Once again the Clan leader bent to rest his muzzle on the top of the new warrior's head, and Dovewing licked his shoulder.

"Dovewing! Dovewing!" the Clan yowled their welcome enthusiastically.

Dovewing stepped back a pace, then turned and bounded over to stand beside Lionblaze.

"Well done!" he murmured. "If ever a cat deserved her warrior name, you do."

Dovewing was purring too hard to reply, but her eyes sparkled.

As the noise died down, Firestar raised his tail. "I want to remind the Clan that now we have no apprentices," he meowed. "The younger warriors will have to share the apprentice duties for the time being."

"I knew it!" Bumblestripe sighed. "Back to picking ticks off the elders!"

"*We'll* be apprentices!" Molekit called out. "We'll work as hard as anything."

"I'm sure you will," Poppyfrost purred. "But you have to wait until you're six moons old."

"Why?" Cherrykit demanded.

"Because that's the warrior code," Firestar replied, amusement in his meow. "And you'll be fine apprentices when the time comes. For now, every cat must be patient if the duties are carried out a bit later than usual. Patrols must still go out on time."

"For that matter, we can do our own ticks," Purdy offered,

giving his rumpled tabby pelt a shake. "We may be elders, but we're not helpless."

"Thank you." Firestar dipped his head to the Clan. "The meeting is at an end."

As the cats began to drift apart, Lionblaze padded over to Cinderheart. "Congratulations," he mewed. "Isn't it great that both our apprentices are warriors now?"

Cinderheart dipped her head. "Congratulations to you, too, Lionblaze. I knew Dovewing would make it."

Her tone was friendly, but as distant as if she was a cat from another Clan. Lionblaze's heart ached as her sweet scent flooded over him.

You know what I want, Cinderheart. Why don't you want it too?

But he knew very well why Cinderheart had turned away from him. He had told her about the prophecy. And now she thought that she wasn't special enough to be his mate.

To me, you're the most special cat in the Clan. Lionblaze hated knowing he could never say that aloud to the cat he loved. Cinderheart would be horrified to think she had distracted him from being one of the Three. *I wish I could just be an ordinary Clan cat, and then I could be with you.*

CHAPTER 3

❧

"Can you feel that?" Jayfeather prodded Briarlight's hindquarters with a claw.

"No," Briarlight replied, with an impatient wriggle of her shoulders and forelegs. "I'm not getting any better, am I?"

"Of course you are." Brightheart, who was helping Jayfeather in the medicine cat's den, spoke warmly as she gave the injured cat's ears a brisk lick. "You're getting stronger every day."

"I am, aren't I?" Briarlight's voice brightened. "Icecloud, I'll teach you some of my exercises if you like."

"Not yet," Jayfeather told her. Sensing the young she-cat's disappointment, he added, "Maybe later, if her leg and shoulder stiffen up. But for now she needs to rest."

Crouching down beside Icecloud, who was curled up in a nest on the opposite side of the den, he ran one paw over her injured shoulder. "Feel this, Brightheart. There's no sign of swelling or the heat from a fever. It's coming along well," he said with a nod of satisfaction. "You can have a poppy seed for the pain if you like."

"No, I'm fine," Icecloud insisted. "I just want to get back to

37

my duties. I should be hunting, and instead I'm just an extra mouth to feed."

"That's quite enough of that," Brightheart scolded her affectionately. "Did you mind hunting for Briarlight, or any of the cats who were sick with whitecough?"

"No, but—"

"Brightheart's right," Jayfeather interrupted with a flick of his tail. "If we don't help cats who are sick or injured, we might as well be loners and rogues."

Icecloud let out a sigh. "I know. But I want to do what I can, even here. I'll toss some moss balls for Briarlight."

"Yes!" Briarlight gave a wriggle of excitement. "I bet I can catch anything you throw."

"Okay, but don't overdo it," Brightheart warned the white warrior. "The more you rest, the sooner you'll be back on full warrior duties."

As Icecloud started clawing moss together, Jayfeather withdrew a couple of paw steps to give the young cats space, and sat beside the pool of water that trickled down from the rock wall, stretching out his neck to lap up a few cool drops.

"I'm glad Sandstorm's getting better," he remarked to Brightheart as she settled down beside him. "But she still can't shake off that cough. I hope it'll clear up when newleaf comes."

Brightheart nodded. "Cherrykit's back to her usual energetic self," she mewed. "And the other cats are over the worst of the whitecough."

"Right." Jayfeather rose to his paws and arched his back

to give himself a good stretch, then sat down again with his tail curled around his paws. "I'd far rather be treating injuries than the sickness we've had to deal with in the last few moons."

"So would I." Brightheart's tone was heartfelt. "We don't have to worry that Icecloud's bad shoulder will spread to the rest of the Clan!"

Jayfeather let out a purr of amusement. "I can't wait for newleaf," he went on. "Warmer days and more prey will help the Clan get back to full strength. There'll be more herbs, too, and the plants by the Twoleg nest will have a chance to grow." His humor faded at the memory of how he had been forced to trade herbs with ShadowClan, and his purr gave way to a low growl deep in his throat.

"What's the matter?" Brightheart asked.

"I was just thinking about how I had to give catnip to ShadowClan, to exchange for Ivypaw—Ivypool, I mean," Jayfeather told her. "I was sorry that Littlecloud was ill, but not sorry enough that I wanted to deprive my own Clanmates."

And I'm not happy with how the other medicine cats are behaving at the moment, he added to himself, unwilling to tell Brightheart about the way his counterparts in the other Clans were insisting on keeping themselves apart following warnings from their ancestors. *They're turning aside from the united path that medicine cats have followed for seasons beyond count.* For a heartbeat he asked himself if he was just as guilty, for not wanting to give the herbs to Littlecloud. *That's different,* he told himself firmly. *The health of my Clan has to come first.*

Squeals from nearby told Jayfeather that Icecloud and Bri-arlight were getting overexcited.

"I'll see to them," Brightheart mewed, touching his shoulder with the tip of her tail. "Hey, knock it off, you two! Icecloud, do you want to be stuck in here until greenleaf?"

"But we're having fun!" Icecloud protested.

Jayfeather left Brightheart to deal with them and padded over to the mouth of the den, where he sat beside the bramble screen. Cats passing through the entrance had worn away the twigs that blocked the gap after the beech tree fell, and once again he could feel the breeze on his face.

It's about time the twigs were cleared. I hated not knowing where to put my paws every time I had to go in and out.

He raised his head, whiskers quivering as he checked what was going on in the hollow.

Poppyfrost was rounding up her kits, shooing them back to their nests as the sun went down and the scant warmth of the day began to fade. Sandstorm emerged from the warriors' den and climbed the rocks to join Firestar in his den. Near the mouth of the thorn tunnel, Lionblaze and Cinderheart were instructing their former apprentices about their night vigil.

The camp was peaceful, but Jayfeather's paws itched to be moving. He knew exactly where he wanted to go: to check out the hole that Icecloud had fallen down. He could almost feel the earth beneath him teeming with lost cats, the ones who never made it out of the tunnels to become sharpclaws.

And Rock! Maybe Rock is there, too!

Jayfeather remembered how the ancient cat had come to

him in the lake when he was trying to rescue Flametail, and told him that it wasn't his time to die. Maybe that meant that Rock was prepared to speak to him again.

"Remember, you have to keep silent." Lionblaze's voice drifted across the camp to Jayfeather's ears. "But nothing says you can't help each other. If one of you looks sleepy, the other can prod her awake."

"Off you go, then," Cinderheart meowed.

Jayfeather heard the two new warriors pushing their way out through the thorn tunnel, while Cinderheart headed for the warriors' den. As Lionblaze turned to follow her, Jayfeather rose to his paws and bounded across to intercept him.

"Take me to the hole," he demanded.

"Are you sure?"

"Of course I'm sure." Jayfeather lashed his tail. "Why do you think I asked, mouse-brain?"

"Okay, okay." Lionblaze huffed out his breath. "Keep your fur on. I'll go with you."

"Then let's get moving."

As Jayfeather emerged into the forest behind his brother, he picked up curiosity from both the young she-cats who were on watch by the entrance to the hollow. He guessed that they would be asking questions if they hadn't been on silent vigil.

"We've got . . . er . . . stuff to do," Lionblaze mewed to the new warriors.

Jayfeather sniffed. *Sounding awkward will only make them* more *curious!* "Medicine cat stuff," he snapped. "And I need a warrior with me."

He could feel the she-cats' gazes boring into his back as he padded after Lionblaze toward the old Twoleg nest. It was a relief when the undergrowth closed around them and he knew he was out of their sight. But as Jayfeather followed his brother down the old Thunderpath and veered off to climb the slope, he felt his paws growing heavier. Too many memories were thronging into his mind. He seemed to hear Hollyleaf again as she fled into the tunnel, the underground river roaring behind her.

We couldn't stop her. She wouldn't listen when we tried to warn her.

Jayfeather felt Lionblaze's pelt brushing warmly against his side, jerking him out of the memory. "Stay close to me," his brother murmured. "The ground is rough here, and there are brambles."

Jayfeather doubted that Lionblaze was just trying to guide him across difficult terrain. He must have the same misgivings, the same memories. There was comfort for both of them in the touch of a littermate's pelt. But Jayfeather stopped himself from spying on his brother's memories. He didn't want to relive that terrible moment over and over again.

Once was enough. And I don't think I'll ever be free of it.

"We're passing the old entrance," Lionblaze mewed after a few moments. "At least, I think this is the place. It's covered over with brambles now; no cat will ever get into the tunnels that way again."

For several fox-lengths the two cats went on climbing; Jayfeather felt the ground grow smoother beneath his paws, and he picked up the pace until he was almost running.

"Watch out!" Lionblaze yowled, pushing him aside just as Jayfeather's whiskers touched the outermost sticks of the temporary barrier that had been piled up around the hole.

"Watch it yourself," Jayfeather retorted, ruffling up his fur as he regained his balance. He stretched out one paw and felt the sticks shift. "I thought Dustpelt and Brackenfur were building a proper cover."

"They've started," Lionblaze meowed. "But they haven't had time to get all the way around. We can still get through."

"Good."

"*I'll* go in first," Lionblaze continued. "You wait here until I've checked it out."

Jayfeather opened his jaws for a stinging retort. *I'm not a kit! You don't need to take care of me!* But he bit back the words; Lionblaze sounded tense and angry, and Jayfeather guessed that he was struggling with his memories of Hollyleaf, rather than worrying about a blind littermate. He heard the rattle of sticks as Lionblaze pushed his way through the temporary barrier. He followed, whiskers quivering as he tried to sense the edges of the hole.

"Careful!" Lionblaze warned him.

"I'm *being* careful," Jayfeather insisted as he skirted the hole, getting an idea of how big it was. He stretched out his head and let out a loud meow, listening for the echo as it came up from below. "Deep," he muttered. "I'm not surprised Icecloud couldn't climb out." His ears flicked forward as he listened for the roar of the underground river, but he couldn't hear anything today. *The water must be lower.*

"I have to get down there, into the tunnel," Jayfeather announced.

He heard his brother's sigh of resignation. "I think you're completely mouse-brained." There was anger in Lionblaze's voice, but fear, too: fear of what they might find if they looked too hard.

"Don't you want to know the truth?" Jayfeather asked.

"What truth?" Lionblaze challenged him. "It's been hidden for this long; it can stay hidden forever. Hollyleaf has gone, and we both know that's for the best. What's the point in stirring it all up again?"

Jayfeather stretched out his tail to touch his brother on the shoulder. "The caves below the hills have been giving up secrets ever since the Clans arrived here," he mewed. "Nothing stays hidden down there—nothing."

Down below, in the distance, Jayfeather thought that he could hear the faint voice of Falling Leaves, trapped forever in the tunnels when he failed to become a sharpclaw.

"Help me! Help me find the way out!" the ancient cat's voice echoed.

Lionblaze let out a heavy sigh. "Have it your way. But if you insist on going down there, you're not going alone. I'm coming with you." He stood beside Jayfeather where he could look down into the tunnel. "It's too far to jump," he reported after a moment. "Unless we want a wrenched shoulder like Icecloud."

"What about the ivy tendril they used to pull Icecloud and Dovepaw up?" Jayfeather suggested, his paws itching with a mixture of apprehension and impatience. "Is that still here?"

"Yes," Lionblaze replied. "But it won't bear your weight, let alone mine. We need to think of something else."

Jayfeather heard the sticks shifting as Lionblaze leaped back over the barrier. Frustrated, he clawed the loose earth at the edge of the hole. *I'll jump down on my own if he doesn't get a move on!*

Then he heard his brother returning, dragging something heavy. He hauled it over the remains of the barrier and let it drop with a thump beside Jayfeather.

"I found a fallen branch," Lionblaze panted. "We can slide one end into the hole and then climb down it, like climbing down a tree."

Jayfeather waited, his impatience rising with every heartbeat, while his brother maneuvered the branch into the hole. Finally Lionblaze let out a growl of satisfaction. "Done. I'll go first and make sure it's safe."

A creaking sound told Jayfeather that Lionblaze was climbing down. His claws dug into the soft earth and he felt the hairs on his pelt begin to rise.

"I'm down!" Lionblaze's voice came up from below. "Come on. The end of the branch is about a tail-length in front of where you're standing."

Jayfeather groped his way forward. He hated his helplessness in situations where other cats could at least see where the danger lay.

But you wanted to do this, mouse-brain! Get on with it!

Locating the end of the branch, Jayfeather dug his claws

in and clumsily scrambled onto it. Dead leaves rustled against his fur, and the branch bounced under his weight. Slowly, tail first, he began to edge his way down.

"That's it! You're doing fine!" Lionblaze called.

To Jayfeather's relief, the branch grew wider as he climbed down, with knots in the wood to provide places for his claws to grip. Gaining confidence, he started to move faster, only to halt and nearly lose his hold as a twig poked him in the side. He let out a yowl.

"Are you okay?" Lionblaze asked.

"No! Your branch is clawing my fur off!" Steadying himself, Jayfeather began to creep downward again, until Lionblaze called out, "You're nearly there. You can jump now."

Jayfeather pushed off from the branch and sprang away from it, landing awkwardly on a pile of loose earth. Staggering to his paws, he puffed out a breath. "Made it!"

"I'm not sure this was a good idea," Lionblaze muttered. "It's really dark down here."

I can't say that bothers me, Jayfeather thought. *Blind cats see just as well in the dark.*

Cold, old air washed over him, carrying murmurs and half-memories from the ancient cats who had once lived here. His paws itched to head deeper into the tunnels. "Let's go," he meowed.

"Wait." Jayfeather heard the scraping of rocks and realized that Lionblaze was heaving them away from the pile that blocked the way to the former entrance. "What are you doing?"

"Shifting the stones that fell last time," Lionblaze growled. "Since we're down here, we may as well look."

But do you want to know what you might find? Jayfeather didn't ask the question aloud. He knew very well that arguing with Lionblaze was useless once his brother had made up his mind. Crouching beside Lionblaze, he clawed at the barrier of earth and rocks. The hard edges hurt his paws and as the moments slipped by, his legs began to ache with exhaustion. He could hear Lionblaze panting beside him.

It's like we're trying to move the whole hill!

Jayfeather expected at any moment that his paws would encounter the soft pelt of Hollyleaf's body. Memories of all the rotting crow-food he had ever scented raced through his mind, but the only scents he could pick up were of earth and water and stone. He paused in his scrabbling at the rocks, jaws parted to taste the air more carefully, but there was no trace left of his sister's presence.

Lionblaze pushed a big rock aside and halted. "I can see something," he mewed.

"What? Is it . . . ?"

"No." Lionblaze's voice was tense. "It's just a tuft of fur . . . black fur."

"Hollyleaf's fur . . ." Jayfeather breathed out.

"Then she was hit by the rockfall."

"But she's not here." Jayfeather struggled to keep his voice steady. "If these are the stones that struck her, they didn't trap her." He turned to strain his senses farther down the tunnel. But all he could hear was the whispering, too faint to make out, of the ancient cats. If they knew what had happened to Hollyleaf, they weren't sharing it with him.

"You know what this means, don't you?" Lionblaze spoke close to Jayfeather's ear. "Hollyleaf is alive!"

CHAPTER 4

For a heartbeat, pure joy flooded through Jayfeather. My sister isn't
dead! It was almost like being swept back to the time when
they were kits in the nursery, when they still believed that
Squirrelflight was their mother and they had no idea that one
day Ashfur might be a threat to their safe, peaceful lives.

But reality rushed back all too soon. "We can't know that
for certain," he argued. "Hollyleaf might have been badly
injured; she could have crawled away to die somewhere else in
the tunnels. Or maybe she couldn't find the way out."

"True." Lionblaze's voice was sad. "We both know how hard
that is, especially since WindClan blocked off their entrance."

"And even if she did get out alive, where would she go?"
Jayfeather tried to imagine his sister crawling out of the tunnels, shaking earth out of her pelt, maybe sitting down for a
while to clean her wounds. What would she have done then?
ThunderClan would always be closed to her. Even if no cat
ever discovered the truth about Ashfur's murder, Hollyleaf
had been torn apart by the discovery that Leafpool was her
mother and her father was Crowfeather of WindClan. She
could not bear knowing that the cats she had trusted had

lied to her, and that forced her to give up everything she had trained and hoped for as a loyal ThunderClan warrior.

"She couldn't come back to the Clan," he murmured.

"But she was good at hunting, and fighting to defend herself," Lionblaze pointed out. "She might have settled down somewhere as a loner."

Jayfeather shook his head. "The Clan—the warrior code—was everything to Hollyleaf." *Besides,* he added to himself, *wouldn't I have picked up some sense of her if she was still alive? I should have.*

"Come on," Lionblaze urged him. "We must explore the tunnels. We've got to find out what happened."

But Jayfeather hung back. The whispering of the ancient cats was louder now, and he thought he could hear the pad of paws growing ever more frantic: Fallen Leaves in his eternal search for the way out, and the start of his life as a sharpclaw. Jayfeather recalled how he had padded through the tunnels and found himself living among those ancient cats at the moment they were considering abandoning their home for the stone hills in the distance. Undecided, they had left the lake because of Jayfeather's casting vote.

What would I say to Fallen Leaves now? Does he know that his Clanmates deserted him because of me?

"What are you waiting for?" Lionblaze demanded. He was already standing at the mouth of the tunnel. Reluctantly Jayfeather took a paw step to join him, only to halt as a fat drop of rain splashed onto his head.

"It's raining," he meowed. "We can't go down there now.

It's too dangerous. The river might flood."

"Mouse dung!" Lionblaze growled.

Jayfeather felt slightly ashamed that he couldn't share his brother's annoyance. Instead, he was relieved. As he scrambled back up the branch with Lionblaze behind him, the rain grew heavier. By the time the two cats pulled themselves out of the hole, it was pelting down, plastering their muddy fur to their bodies.

Jayfeather stood shivering while Lionblaze, grunting with effort, pushed the end of the branch down into the hole. "There," he panted. "No other cat will be lost down there. Dustpelt and Brackenfur will finish the barrier in the morning."

Jayfeather followed his brother back to camp, rain driving into their faces as they splashed through mud and lashing wet undergrowth. When they reached the entrance, he located Ivypool and Dovewing still on watch, huddled in the shelter of the thorn barrier. Neither of them paid any attention to the two toms as they brushed through the tunnel and headed for their dens.

"We've got to talk about this again," Lionblaze muttered before they separated.

Jayfeather replied with a curt nod. Between the struggle in the hole, the discovery about Hollyleaf, and being soaked through on his way back to camp, he was exhausted.

Briarlight sat up as Jayfeather brushed past the bramble screen and staggered toward his nest. "Where have you been?" she meowed.

"Out," Jayfeather replied brusquely, then realized that he could scent only one cat inside the den. "Where's Icecloud?"

"She went back to the warriors' den. She said she could rest just as well there."

Jayfeather shrugged. He was too tired to say what he thought about warriors who thought they knew better than their medicine cat. He would check on Icecloud in the morning.

"You're all wet and muddy!" Briarlight exclaimed.

Yeah, and claws are sharp! Anything else obvious you want to point out?

"I'm fine," Jayfeather said aloud.

"No, you're not fine," Briarlight insisted. "You're as wet as a drowned mouse, and asleep on your paws. Come over here and let me clean you up." When Jayfeather didn't reply, she added with a hint of mischief in her voice, "I promise I won't nag you about where you've been."

Too weary to argue, Jayfeather padded over to Briarlight's nest and flopped down beside her. A moment later he felt the rough lap of her tongue, stroking rhythmically over his shoulder. For a moment he felt embarrassed that she was the one looking after him, but the young cat's licks were so soothing that he dozed off, wondering if his mother had ever licked him like this.

But which mother? Leafpool or Squirrelflight?

He could see a face gazing down at him; at first he thought it was Leafpool, but it blurred and became Squirrelflight, then changed to Hollyleaf, her green eyes glowing as they stared at him. Jayfeather jerked awake, half sitting up. His fur felt dry and warm, and his whole body was more relaxed.

"Are you okay?" Briarlight's anxious voice reminded him where he was.

"I'm fine." Jayfeather sighed. Suddenly he wished there was some cat he could talk to: not a cat from StarClan, but a real friend like Lionblaze had in Cinderheart. He didn't think Briarlight could be that cat.

"It must be hard, when you do so much for the Clan, and you have to keep all StarClan's secrets," she murmured.

StarClan's secrets are much easier than our own!

"I'm a medicine cat; it's what I do," he responded. "You'll never have to worry about anything like that."

"Yeah, right," Briarlight muttered in such a low tone that Jayfeather wasn't sure he was meant to hear. "Because I'll never be anything useful, will I?"

Jayfeather rose to his paws. He knew that even though Briarlight had been helping him with medicine cat duties, nothing would make up for not being a warrior. "Thanks for licking my fur dry," he mewed, and padded off to his own nest.

Curled up among the bracken, Jayfeather opened his eyes to find himself back at the bottom of the hole. The rain had stopped. High above, clouds scudded fast across the sky, though Jayfeather couldn't feel any wind. Padding deeper into the tunnel, he saw that the way ahead was dimly lit, as if the stars were shining through the earth and rock above his head. He walked farther in, his ears pricked to catch the slightest sound, but the air around him was empty and silent.

Where are all the ancient cats?

Jayfeather padded on and on into the silver light, until he reached the cave where the river flowed. This time it was thin and black, rushing swiftly between the rocks, not swollen and angry as it had been last time he was here. Hope tingled through his paws as he glanced up at Rock's ledge, but it was bare.

A soft paw step sounded behind Jayfeather. He spun around to see a faint shape slipping out from a different tunnel. "Fallen Leaves?" he meowed.

"No," rasped a familiar voice.

"Rock!"

The ancient cat padded up to Jayfeather, his long, twisted claws clicking on the stone floor. His blind eyes bulged and the pale light glistened on his furless body. His face was solemn as he halted in front of Jayfeather.

"Why did you break my stick?" Rock asked. His tone revealed no anger or sadness, nothing to tell Jayfeather how he was feeling.

"I—I wanted to talk to you, and you weren't there," Jayfeather stumbled. "What was the point of keeping a piece of wood with scratches on it?" Even as he spoke he knew that the stick had been much more than that.

"I am always here," Rock responded, and now Jayfeather could hear sadness in his voice. "I will come to you when I have something to say. It is not for you to summon me."

Jayfeather bowed his head, feeling like a kit being scolded for sneaking out of camp.

"That stick was your history," Rock continued. "You cannot throw that away. The past is all around you, and cats who once were warriors will be warriors again."

Jayfeather tensed and his claws scraped on the rock floor of the cave. "Do you mean Hollyleaf?" he asked urgently. "Have you seen her? Is she still alive?"

Rock blinked, and Jayfeather shivered at the thought that the ancient cat's blind gray eyes could still see him very well. "Your past lies in the mountains," Rock told him. "The place where I was born, the place where cats have returned before. You must go there once more to complete the circle."

"Back to the Tribe of Rushing Water?" Now Jayfeather couldn't get his questions out fast enough. "Are they in trouble?"

Rock didn't reply. The clink of a stone behind him distracted Jayfeather for a heartbeat, and when he turned back, the ancient cat had disappeared.

"Rock!" he called, but the echoes of his voice died away into silence, and there was no answer.

As Jayfeather stood beside the stream, seething with frustration, he heard quiet paw steps approaching and looked around to see a young ginger-and-white tom emerging from a tunnel.

Fallen Leaves padded up to Jayfeather and dipped his head. His eyes were full of sadness. "Greetings, Jay's Wing," he mewed.

Jayfeather tensed as Fallen Leaves called him by the name he had borne in the ancient time. "Greetings."

"The other cats have left, haven't they?"

His tone was quiet, not accusing, but Jayfeather felt even guiltier because of the part he had played in the ancient cats' departure from the lake. *I wonder if Fallen Leaves knows what I did?* "Yes, they've gone," he admitted.

"I feel their absence inside me, like a silence," Fallen Leaves meowed. "But your cats are still here. Come, let me take you to them." Without waiting for Jayfeather to reply, he headed across the cave into the mouth of a different tunnel. Jayfeather hesitated for a heartbeat, then bounded in pursuit.

Fallen Leaves led him along the tunnels, and before Jayfeather thought it could be possible, they were standing in the hole again, in front of the branch. *Of course—he has wandered these tunnels for so long. He knows the quickest way.*

Suddenly, Jayfeather couldn't bear the thought of leaving the young tom alone there again. "Come with me," he urged.

Fallen Leaves shook his head. "We both know that can't happen." He raised his head and looked up at the sky. The clouds had cleared away, and the warriors of StarClan shone in a blaze of icy light. "The stars are still shining," Fallen Leaves whispered with wonder in his eyes. "I never thought I would see them again. It's good to know that they are still there, just as they have always been. The past is all around us."

Jayfeather jumped, startled. *That's what Rock said!*

"Your destiny lies up there, doesn't it?" Fallen Leaves meowed, gesturing with his tail toward the sky. "You don't belong here." He reached out with his tail, and Jayfeather raised his own tail so that they touched for a moment.

"I wish you luck, my friend," Fallen Leaves continued. "If ever you need me, I will be here."

"Thank you," Jayfeather murmured. He picked his way across the loose earth and scrambled up the branch. When he looked down into the hole again, Fallen Leaves had gone. "Hey, Fallen Leaves!" Desperate to see him once more, Jayfeather leaned out over the hole.

Something sharp jabbed into his side. Darkness slammed down over his vision as he opened his eyes and found himself leaning over the edge of his nest, his cheek pressed against the stone floor of his den.

"Jayfeather?" Briarlight's voice was muffled, and Jayfeather realized that she was prodding him with a twig held in her mouth.

"Stop that," he mumbled, sitting up and shaking the moss out of his pelt.

"I thought you were having a bad dream," Briarlight mewed, more clearly now. "You were saying weird things . . . something about leaves falling. What was happening to you?"

Jayfeather ignored her question. Hauling himself to his paws, he stumbled past the bramble screen and out into the camp, almost barging into Mousewhisker as he headed for the fresh-kill pile. "Sorry," he muttered, as the young tom whisked around him.

Over by the nursery, Poppyfrost's kits were squeaking and tumbling about while their mother sat watching. Ivypool and Dovewing brushed through the thorn tunnel and staggered across to the apprentices' den, their paws heavy with weariness after their night's vigil.

Briefly Jayfeather wondered why they were still heading for their old den, until he remembered how little space there was in the warriors' den. *With no other apprentices, they'll get a good sleep there.*

In the middle of the hollow, he could hear Brambleclaw's voice raised as he gave out the instructions for the first patrols of the day. "Graystripe, you can lead the dawn patrol. Take Squirrelflight, Birchfall, and Brightheart."

"We're on our way," Graystripe responded.

"Keep an eye on the ShadowClan border," Brambleclaw warned him. "We don't want any more trouble." As Graystripe's patrol moved off, the deputy continued, "Thornclaw, you can take a hunting patrol along the stream that borders WindClan. There might still be some prey sheltering along the bank."

"Okay, Brambleclaw. Which cats should I take with me?"

The deputy hesitated for a heartbeat, then meowed, "Blossomfall, Berrynose, and Lionblaze. Cinderheart, you lead another patrol down toward the lake. . . ."

As soon as Jayfeather heard his brother's name mentioned, he stopped listening to Brambleclaw and headed across the camp to intercept Lionblaze before he reached the thorns. "Lionblaze, wait! We have to go to the mountains!"

"What?" Lionblaze radiated shock and impatience. "Jayfeather, I'm headed out on patrol. You can't spring something like that on me now."

Jayfeather flicked his tail dismissively. "I had a dream," he insisted. "Our destiny lies there!"

He could tell that he had aroused his brother's interest. "Was it a dream from StarClan?" Lionblaze queried.

"No, from a cat even older than that. I think he knows where the prophecy comes from. Lionblaze, we have to go!"

CHAPTER 5

Ivypool thought her paws might drop off as she stumbled into her den and flopped down on her nest of moss and bracken. "I'm glad that's over! I could sleep for a moon."

"But it was worth it," Dovewing mewed as she curled herself around her sister. "We're warriors!" As Ivypool pressed gratefully into her warm pelt, she added softly, "Don't go to the Dark Forest tonight. You need to rest."

I wish I had the choice, Ivypool thought wearily. Didn't Dovewing understand that she couldn't control her visits to the Place of No Stars? *I'd give anything not to have to wake up there ever again.* But she didn't speak the words aloud. She didn't want to make Dovewing even more worried about her safety.

Warmed by her sister's fur, Ivypool drifted into sleep. When she opened her eyes she hoped for a heartbeat that she would see her familiar den around her, with sunlight filtering in through the grasses that overhung the entrance. Instead, she found herself surrounded by the pale, sickly light of the Dark Forest. She was crouching in the shadow of a clump of bracken, the dead gray fronds arching over her head. A narrow path wound through the undergrowth a tail-length in front of her paws.

Ivypool let out a sigh. *I should have known.*

Before she could move, she heard approaching meows and the sound of several cats brushing through undergrowth. Ivypool waited as the first of them burst into the open.

"Did you see the move Thistleclaw taught me?" Breezepelt boasted. "Wait till I get the chance to try it out on one of those ThunderClan mange-pelts!"

"Thistleclaw's great." His Clanmate Sunstrike followed Breezepelt into the open, along with a gray-and-white apprentice Ivypool didn't recognize. "I can't believe he was ever a ThunderClan cat!"

The WindClan cats raced past Ivypool without noticing her and vanished into the distance. *Of course, it's dawn,* she thought. *They're going home.* She was about to emerge from the clump of bracken when she heard the paw steps of more cats approaching, and picked up ShadowClan scent.

Tigerheart!

Ivypool stayed in the shadows as Tigerheart skirted a nearby bramble thicket and padded toward her. Ratscar and Applefur were with him. As he drew level, Tigerheart hung back, letting his Clanmates go on without him. He waited, nostrils flaring, until they were out of earshot.

"I can smell you," he meowed at last. "So there's no point hiding."

Ivypool sprang out of the gray bracken clump and faced the tabby warrior. "I wasn't hiding!" she retorted. "I only just got here."

"And why are you here now?" Tigerheart asked icily. "Do

you think you can avoid me if you come here at a different time? But it's too late for that," he went on before Ivypool could reply. "I know the truth about you. What would Dovepaw say if she knew that you were prepared to kill an innocent cat?"

For a heartbeat Ivypool froze at the terrible memory of how Brokenstar had tried to make her kill Flametail, wandering in unexpectedly from StarClan, as proof of her loyalty.

Would I have done it, if Tigerheart hadn't interrupted?

"I had no choice—" she began.

Tigerheart lashed his tail. "There is *always* a choice," he hissed.

Anger pulsed through Ivypool like a fire through dry grass. "You mean, like you had a choice about using my sister to find out about ThunderClan's store of herbs? No wonder she doesn't want to see you anymore!"

"I didn't use her." Tigerheart's amber eyes grew shadowed. "But I don't expect you to believe me." He spun around and stalked after his Clanmates.

Ivypool watched him until he disappeared around a bend in the path, then turned and padded in the opposite direction. She had covered only a few fox-lengths when she rounded a clump of thornbushes and almost crashed into Thistleclaw.

"How good to see you," the gray-white warrior purred. "So glad that you decided to join us after all, Ivypaw."

"My name's Ivypool," she retorted with a flash of pride. "I'm a warrior now."

"Not here, you're not," Thistleclaw told her. "Not until I

say so." His voice dripped with sarcasm. "And that won't be for a long time if you can't be bothered to turn up on time for practice."

"I've been keeping my vigil." Ivypool kept her head up, though inwardly her belly fluttered.

"Follow me" was all he replied. Leaving the path, Thistleclaw led her through thick undergrowth until they came to a clearing overhung by gnarled oaks. In the middle of the clearing was a heap of fallen trees, covered by slimy moss. Pale fungus grew on the trunks, seeming to give off its own sickly light.

"Now—" Thistleclaw began.

He was interrupted by the sound of a cat pelting through the bracken; Ivypool picked up WindClan scent a heartbeat before Antpelt burst into view.

"Sorry, Thistleclaw!" he panted. "Onestar sent me on a moonlight patrol. I've only just gone to sleep."

A chill crept through Ivypool's pelt. Just like her, Antpelt had been awake all night. It was daylight in the waking world, with the pale sun of leaf-bare angling through the trees. But darkness still covered the Dark Forest.

Is it always night here? she wondered.

"I've got a new task for you," Thistleclaw meowed, ignoring Antpelt's apology. "See these fallen trees? You're going to attack them, and you"—he swung around to Ivypool, his mottled gray-and-white muzzle a mouse-length from her face—"are going to defend. Antpelt, you've won if you can force Ivypool up to the top of the heap."

Obeying a flick of Thistleclaw's tail, Ivypool bounded onto the lowest tree trunk. A tingle of anticipation ran through her from ears to tail-tip. She was proud of her battle skills. *I'll show this WindClan warrior what ThunderClan cats are made of!*

Antpelt leaped at her, his claws sheathed as if this was a Clan training session. Ivypool reared up, balancing briefly on her hind paws while she batted him over the ears with her forepaws, her own claws sheathed, too. Antpelt took a pace back, then dived at her again, trying to unbalance her by crashing into her side. Ivypool sidestepped neatly and raked a soft paw over his shoulder.

"What? Are you kits?" Thistleclaw snarled. "I said *fight!*"

Antpelt launched himself at Ivypool again. His claws were out this time and his teeth bared as he leaped on her and tried to grab her by the scruff. Pain clawed at Ivypool's flank as she swiped at him; he was too close for her blows to count, and as she struggled to free herself Antpelt shoved her up onto the next log.

Thistleclaw let out a hiss. "Is this the sort of warrior ThunderClan is training now?" he jeered.

Furious, Ivypool hurled herself at Antpelt with an ear-splitting screech. But as she leaped, her paw slipped on one of the pale patches of fungus and she fell clumsily sideways, the breath driven out of her as she landed on the lowest log. Ivypool braced herself for Antpelt to renew his attack, but when she looked up he had stepped to one side, waiting for her to get up and continue the fight.

Giving him a grateful nod, Ivypool struggled to her paws,

but before she could attack again Thistleclaw leaped past her, his teeth bared in a snarl. Antpelt's eyes stretched wide and he backed away from the furious warrior until he balanced precariously on top of the heap of trunks.

"Coward!" Thistleclaw taunted, lashing at him with one immense forepaw. "Show some courage, can't you?"

Snarling, Antpelt leaped on the gray-white tom, sinking his teeth into Thistleclaw's scruff and raking his claws across his shoulder. Thistleclaw threw him off like a dead leaf and pinned him against the logs. Antpelt battered at him with his hind paws, scattering tufts of Thistleclaw's belly fur.

"That's better!" Thistleclaw growled. "*Now* you're fighting like a warrior!"

His powerful claws sank into Antpelt's shoulders and he shook him like a fox. Ivypool watched in dismay as blood sprang into the WindClan warrior's fur; the hot reek of it caught in her throat.

"Thistleclaw, that's enough!" she yowled.

The warrior ignored her. Stretching out his neck he fastened his teeth in Antpelt's scruff and tossed him down the heap, to land hard on the ground in front of Ivypool.

Antpelt was moving feebly, trying to rise to his paws, only to flop down again with a groan. Horrified, Ivypool crouched beside him, reaching out to part his fur and find out where the blood was coming from.

"Leave him!" Thistleclaw ordered from the top of the heap. "He lost the battle, that's all."

"But he's hurt!" Ivypool protested.

"He'll mend," the warrior growled. He began pacing down the trunks toward the two young warriors.

Before he could reach them, Ivypool bent over Antpelt and whispered close to his ear, "Wake up! You're not really here, you're in your nest in WindClan."

Thistleclaw's paw steps were growing closer.

"Quick!" Ivypool hissed.

Antpelt replied with a whimper. Ivypool stroked her paw across his shoulder and to her relief he let out a long sigh and his eyes closed. As he sank into sleep, his shape quivered, then vanished, leaving nothing behind but a few clots of blood on the grass.

At the same moment, Thistleclaw sprang to the ground, his green eyes blazing with fury. "Coward!" he spat, glaring at the spot where Antpelt had vanished. "Is that why WindClan cats run so fast—so they can flee?"

"I always knew he was fox-hearted." Ivypool was well aware that she had to agree with Thistleclaw. "Now I haven't got any cat to practice with."

"Oh, yes, you have." Thistleclaw turned his gaze on her and swiped his tongue around his lips as if he was anticipating a particularly juicy piece of prey. "You can fight me."

Ivypool's heart began pounding so hard that she thought it would leap out of her jaws. "Okay," she mewed, trying to sound eager.

Before she could take a breath, the warrior hurled himself at her, carrying her off her paws so that she landed with a thump on the ground, his weight on top of her. His claws lashed at her shoulders. Instinctively, Ivypool went limp. When she felt Thistleclaw relax she wriggled out from under him and aimed a couple of swift blows to his side before she sprang out of range.

Her head was spinning with weariness and her paws felt heavy as stones, but Thistleclaw's hiss of annoyance gave her strength. As he swung around to attack her again, she crouched down, waiting for him, her tail lashing from side to side. When Thistleclaw leaped, Ivypool slid forward underneath his belly and came up behind him, clawing his hindquarters. His tail lashed across her face and she bit down on it hard, rejoicing to hear his yowl of pain. Yanking his tail free, Thistleclaw spun around on her faster than she would have thought possible. Through blurred, tired vision Ivypool watched him, trying to work out where he would spring. As he launched himself into the air she dodged aside, but he flung out one paw and batted her to the ground. Ivypool let out a screech as they rolled on the grass together, clawing at each other's fur.

Pushing her head against Thistleclaw's neck, Ivypool struggled to sink her teeth into his throat. With a grunt of effort he flung her off, and she slammed against the bottom of the log pile. Fighting for breath, Ivypool clawed her way upward, moss and fungus crumbling in her fur, until she stood on the topmost tree trunk.

"I win!" she yowled.

Thistleclaw scrambled to his paws and glared up at her. "The cat on top of the heap *loses*, mouse-brain," he spat.

"But you didn't force me up here," Ivypool meowed

triumphantly. "I climbed up myself. And I'm ready to leap down on you again—so I win!"

"I set the rules—" Thistleclaw began.

"The young one is right." A growl interrupted him, and the shadowy form of Mapleshade stepped out from behind one of the old oaks. Ivypool wondered how long she had been standing there. "Admit defeat, Thistleclaw. Go lick your wounds."

Thistleclaw let out a snort of disgust and spun around. As he stalked across the clearing and into the trees Ivypool was delighted to see that he was limping.

Mapleshade padded up to the bottom of the log pile and flicked her ears at Ivypool, a signal for her to descend. "I had my doubts about your loyalty," Mapleshade rasped as Ivypool joined her. "But I'm starting to change my mind. When the battle comes, you will fight alongside me."

"When will the battle be?" Ivypool asked, trying to sound eager in the hope that Mapleshade would give her some information she could take back to Jayfeather and Lionblaze.

"Not so fast," Mapleshade murmured with a glint of approval in her eyes. "You may have beaten Thistleclaw, but you still have more to learn before you can take on the Clans' most experienced warriors."

"I just want to be ready," Ivypool assured her.

"You will be," Mapleshade promised. "And it won't be long now. . . ."

To Ivypool's relief, Mapleshade gave her a nod of farewell and faded away into the trees. Weakened by fighting and loss of sleep, Ivypool slumped to the ground, feeling the Dark Forest fade around her as she closed her eyes.

The dusty tang of dry moss and her sister's familiar scent tickled her nose. Letting out a long sigh, Ivypool opened her eyes. Dovewing was still asleep, lying close beside her with one paw flung over her belly. Careful not to wake her, Ivypool wriggled out from her sister's grasp and limped out into the clearing. The sky was gray, but she guessed it must be close to sunhigh. Brackenfur, Sorreltail, and Spiderleg were gossiping beside the fresh-kill pile. Ferncloud was dozing in the entrance to the nursery while just outside the elders' den Purdy was sitting beside Mousefur; Ivypool guessed the former loner was telling her one of his endless stories.

Brambleclaw emerged from the gorse tunnel with a squirrel dangling from his jaws, followed by Birchfall and Whitewing, both carrying mice. Rosepetal brought up the rear with a vole.

It's all so peaceful, Ivypool thought.

But her mind was filled with images of the final battle: cats screeching, claws lashing, blood soaking into the earth floor of the hollow, cats lying dead with their pelts ripped off . . .

Is it up to me to prevent the battle? What if I can't? Will I really be able to save my Clanmates?

CHAPTER 6

Dovewing sat outside the apprentices' den, giving herself a quick grooming while her Clanmates milled around her, waiting to leave for the Gathering. The last of the daylight was fading from the stone hollow, and already the full moon was rising in the sky. Craning to reach the fur on the back of her neck, Dovewing tried to stifle her feelings of apprehension. *I'd be happier to go to this Gathering if Ivypool were with me.*

But Ivypool was still recovering from the injuries she had received in the Dark Forest several days ago, just after they became warriors. Dovewing had been shocked to see the state her sister was in when she woke, with deep scratches on her sides and shoulders and her fur clotted with blood. The wounds had been bad enough for Dovewing to call Jayfeather. He had treated Ivypool with cobwebs and horsetail, and invented a story about her falling into a bramble thicket to explain her injuries to her Clanmates.

Remembering how Icecloud had fallen into the hole, Mousefur had spent some time muttering about clumsy youngsters, but Ivypool had endured it silently. She had refused to tell any cat, even Dovewing, exactly how she came by her injuries.

Worry for her littermate prickled right through Dovewing's pelt. With no sign that the Clan would be leaving soon, she slid back into her den. Ivypool was curled up in her nest; she raised her head as Dovewing entered, her eyes deep pools of weariness.

"Promise me you won't go to the Dark Forest tonight," Dovewing begged.

"I don't have any choice," Ivypool replied with a stubborn shake of her head. "And even if I did, I have to go because we don't know enough about the battle yet."

"But—" Dovewing broke off in frustration, wishing that her sister would confide in her like she used to. *Is she still unhappy with me because I kept my powers a secret from her?* "I'm worried about you, that's all."

"I'll be fine," Ivypool meowed with a hint of pride in her voice. "I can cope."

Dovewing had to fight a twinge of jealousy. *Does she think she's better than me because she's doing this for our Clan?* "Ivypool, I just want—" she began.

"There you are, Dovewing!" Brambleclaw's voice interrupted her; Dovewing turned to see the ThunderClan deputy peering through the grass that masked the entrance to the den. "Come on, we're ready to leave."

"Sorry," Dovewing mewed. "See you later, Ivypool." Scrambling out of the den, she raced across to the thorn barrier, where her Clanmates were waiting to file through the tunnel.

"Hi, Dovewing," Hazeltail greeted her. "Is Ivypool okay?"

"She's fine," Dovewing replied.

She spotted Cinderheart heading her way, a worried expression on her face, and guessed that she wanted to ask about her former apprentice. But there was no time to talk; Cinderheart had to turn and plunge into the tunnel, and Dovewing followed her.

Firestar set a brisk pace through the forest. The moon cast shadows over their path, and frost glittered on every blade of grass and frond of bracken. Dovewing gasped when she broke out of the trees and stood at the top of the slope that led down to the lake. The moon traced a path of molten silver from one side to the other. Ripples washed softly against the pebbled shore.

Following her Clanmates, she raced along the water's edge, splashing through the stream on the WindClan border and heading for the horseplace. She thought back to the shimmering covering of ice, broken by the jagged cracks that had swallowed Flametail. Before that, the lake had been a stretch of drying mud, dotted by dwindling pools where fish flapped and thirsty cats gathered for the last drops of water.

Nothing stays the same, Dovewing realized. *Nothing except the prophecy, and that's no clearer than it ever was.*

"Hey, Dovewing!" Foxleap's voice broke into her thoughts. "Race you to the tree-bridge!"

Thrusting aside her worries, Dovewing sprinted after him, catching up as they crossed the RiverClan scent markings.

Panting, they drew to a halt at the end of the tree-bridge, ahead of all the rest of the Clan.

"You're fast!" Foxleap panted admiringly.

"You're not so bad yourself," Dovewing replied, giving him a flick on the shoulder with her tail.

The rest of the Clan reached them, and Firestar leaped onto the tree-bridge to lead the way over to the island. Sending out her senses, Dovewing realized that the three other Clans were already there. She picked up a strong feeling of uneasiness; her paws prickled with it as she padded along the fallen tree trunk and ran across the shore to push her way through the bushes that encircled the Great Oak.

In the clearing, the cats from the other Clans were milling around restlessly; Dovewing realized they were still in their Clan groups, rather than gossiping with other Clans as they usually did at Gatherings. When ThunderClan appeared, she felt a wave of hostility from the ShadowClan cats. One or two of them stretched out their necks to let out furious hisses, or pointedly turned their backs.

Dovewing couldn't help looking for Tigerheart, and spotted him in the shade of a holly bush. His amber gaze met hers, and at once she looked away, heat washing through her pelt. She could never forgive the tabby tom for using her to get at Jayfeather's supply of herbs. *He turned me into a spy for Shadow-Clan!*

But Dovewing couldn't forget the time she and Tigerheart had spent together, playing in the old Twoleg nest at the edge of ShadowClan's territory. Their moonlight meetings had been more important to her than anything else.

"Dovewing?" She turned at the soft touch of a tail-tip on her shoulder, and turned to see Bumblestripe. "Don't let those ShadowClan cats upset you," the young tom went on. "They're all fox-hearts!"

Dovewing murmured agreement. When Bumblestripe angled his ears toward their own Clanmates, she let him lead her into their midst, though she couldn't resist a last glance back at Tigerheart. He was deep in conversation with a River-Clan cat she hadn't seen before.

Probably another Dark Forest warrior, she guessed with a shudder. *How could I ever have trusted Tigerheart? He is Tigerstar's kin, after all. And every cat knows how evil Tigerstar was!*

Then guilt gusted over her as she remembered that Brambleclaw was Tigerstar's kin, too. *And Brambleclaw isn't evil! He's ThunderClan's loyal deputy!*

By now all four leaders had taken their places in the Great Oak. Firestar was balancing in the fork of a branch, with Mistystar crouched on the branch below. Onestar sat on a higher branch, his tail hanging down. At first Dovewing couldn't see Blackstar at all, until she finally spotted him in a clump of dead oak leaves that clung to the bough, casting dappled shadows on his white pelt; his eyes gleamed, glaring down into the clearing.

Dovewing sat beside Bumblestripe, shivering in the chill, damp air, as Onestar called the Gathering to order.

"Prey is running well in spite of the cold weather," he reported. "And Whiskernose has been made a warrior."

"Whiskernose! Whiskernose!" WindClan welcomed the young tom, who ducked his head, looking pleased and embarrassed.

Dovewing joined in, though she noticed that not many cats from other Clans were doing the same. *Gatherings should be a time for the Clans to be at peace with one another. What is happening to us?*

Onestar sat down again, his gaze raking across the cats as if he was asking himself the same question. Blackstar emerged from his clump of leaves. He surveyed the cats below him in silence before he spoke. "Our medicine cat Littlecloud had a brief attack of whitecough," he announced. "But he is now as strong as ever, and so is ShadowClan." He closed his jaws with a snap and retreated.

"Huh—brief attack of whitecough!" Dovewing muttered. "Littlecloud was dying, and all ThunderClan knows it. Would it have hurt too much for Blackstar to thank us?"

Bumblestripe blinked at her. "That's ShadowClan for you."

Mistystar rose to her paws. "RiverClan is happy to see the ice gone from the lake," she meowed. "It's good to catch fish again. And our Clan has welcomed two new warriors this past moon: Rushtail and Troutstream."

"Rushtail! Troutstream!" More cats from the other Clans joined in this time, as if they were beginning to relax. Or perhaps, Dovewing reflected as she joined her yowls to theirs, Mistystar's confident and friendly manner had begun to win them over. The RiverClan leader had always been willing to work with other Clans.

"Also," Mistystar went on when the noise had died down,

"a badger was seen in our territory, but Reedwhisker tracked it with Robinwing and Petalfur, until it went away."

"Which way?" Ashfoot, the WindClan deputy, called out. "Do we need to watch out for it?"

"I don't think so," Mistystar replied. "It went out past the horseplace, heading for the hills. If I'd thought there was danger," she added politely, "I would have sent a message."

Mistystar finished her report with a nod to Firestar. Dovewing admired his well-muscled body and sleek flame-colored pelt as he stood on the branch. "ThunderClan has good news, too," he meowed. "A few sunrises ago I named two new warriors: Dovewing and Ivypool."

Dovewing felt warm with pride as the Clans called out her name and her sister's. *I wish Ivypool were here to share this.*

"Hey, where's Ivypool?" Sedgewhisker of WindClan asked as the cats fell silent again.

"Yeah, she should be here for her first Gathering as a warrior," Mallownose of RiverClan added.

"Ivypool had an accident," Firestar mewed, before Dovewing could speak. "She had a quarrel with a bramble thicket while she was out hunting. But our medicine cat has treated her scratches, and she'll be back on patrol soon. She'll be here for the next Gathering." There were a few murmurs of sympathy.

Dovewing jumped when Bumblestripe nudged her. "Look at the medicine cats!" he whispered. "They look really uncomfortable. Do you think they've had an argument?"

Dovewing realized that he was right. While the other cats were beginning to mingle, the medicine cats were keeping strictly to their own Clans. Mothwing and Willowshine were talking quietly together, while Littlecloud was staying close to Blackstar, and Kestrelflight crouched under a thornbush, his eyes narrowed as if he was giving the whole Gathering a suspicious glare. Jayfeather sat near the roots of the Great Oak, his tail wrapped around his paws.

"I bet it's Jayfeather's fault," Dovewing whispered to her Clanmate, half joking. "He's so prickly, I wouldn't be surprised if he's upset all the others!"

But a small worm of apprehension nagged in her belly. *Medicine cats don't have the same Clan boundaries that we do. What's gone wrong?*

Looking around, she saw Tornear and Webfoot from WindClan sharing tongues with Tallpoppy from ShadowClan, and wondered if the elders were discussing the Great Journey, which seemed to be their favorite subject when they met at Gatherings. Two or three apprentices had started a mock fight at one side of the clearing. Sedgewhisker and Petalfur were deep in conversation, maybe sharing memories of the battle against the beavers. Dovewing's sense of uneasiness faded.

"Hey, Bumblestripe!" Grasspelt, a young RiverClan tom, bounced up. "What's happened to Briarlight? I haven't seen her at a Gathering for moons!"

Bumblestripe looked startled. Firestar had never announced Briarlight's injuries at a Gathering; Dovewing guessed he thought it would make her, and ThunderClan, seem vulnerable. And this wasn't the right time to pass on the news to other Clans.

"Oh, you know," she jumped in, saving Bumblestripe from having to reply. "She's fine, but she's busy, like the rest of us."

Grasspelt blinked. "Okay," he meowed, sounding disappointed, and headed off toward his own Clan.

Bumblestripe let out a long sigh as he watched the young tom pad away. "Thanks," he murmured to Dovewing.

Dovewing shrugged. "I was only telling the truth."

Bumblestripe's eyes widened. "You know you weren't."

Dovewing could hear the pain in his voice. She reached out with her tail and touched him gently on the shoulder. "It must be hard for you, to see your sister injured like that."

"You don't know what it's like." Bumblestripe bowed his head.

"Oh, yes, I do." Dovewing was thinking of Ivypool. *I worry about my sister, too.*

"I try not to feel sorry for Briarlight," Bumblestripe went on. "I know that's the last thing she'd want. But I *do* feel sorry for her. Even though I'm really proud of her for fighting on when she knows there's no hope that she'll ever walk again."

"I'm sure Briarlight would understand," Dovewing responded awkwardly, wishing there was something more she could say to ease her Clanmate's grief. "She's lucky to have such a great littermate."

Bumblestripe blinked, his eyes shining. "Thanks, Dovewing."

Mintfur and Robinwing from RiverClan padded up, dipping their heads as they approached. "How's the prey running in ThunderClan?" Mintfur inquired.

Dovewing stepped back a pace as Bumblestripe replied, and glanced around the clearing at the groups of cats. *I'm not looking for Tigerheart. Not at all!* Heading for the island's dirtplace, she found herself close to a thornbush where Webfoot and Tornear were sharing tongues with Tallpoppy.

". . . never seen wounds like them, outside a battle," Webfoot was meowing.

"Poor Antpelt," Tallpoppy murmured. "I met him at the last Gathering, and he seemed such a promising young cat. How did he come to be hurt?"

Tornear shook his head. "No cat knows, and Antpelt isn't fit to tell us. It must have been a dog, though. The bites aren't healing, and he's very sick."

Webfoot's voice was hushed as he added, "Kestrelflight doesn't expect him to pull through."

Poor WindClan, Dovewing thought sympathetically. *I'm glad we don't see many dogs in ThunderClan territory.*

Their voices died away behind her as she pushed through the bushes to the dirtplace. As she finished making her dirt and scratched earth over it, she heard Brambleclaw's yowl.

"ThunderClan! It's time to leave."

Heading out through the bushes, Dovewing spotted a shadow across her path; as she drew closer Tigerheart stepped forward to cut her off.

"We need to talk," he meowed.

"We have nothing left to say to each other," Dovewing hissed.

"Please!" Tigerheart's amber eyes were wide and distressed. "I didn't use you, I promise I didn't. Okay, I told Blackstar about Jayfeather's herbs, but that doesn't change how I felt about you." He paused and added in a lower voice, "How I still feel about you."

Dovewing worked her front claws into the ground. Agitation prickled beneath her pelt, a terrible temptation to give in to Tigerheart and believe what he was telling her. "We can't talk about this now," she replied defensively. "Not when any cat could hear us."

"Then meet me in the usual place," Tigerheart urged her.

"No. Tigerheart, I don't have any feelings left for you." Dovewing's heart was heavy as she lied.

Anger glowed in the ShadowClan tom's eyes. "Has your sister been saying things about me?"

Shock crackled through Dovewing. "Like what?"

"Never mind. But maybe you don't know your sister as well as you think you do."

Dovewing stared at him. *He can't mean that Ivypool is training in the Dark Forest. Tigerheart knows I know.*

Suddenly Tigerheart drew closer to her, so that his familiar scent flooded over her. "Ivypool isn't the cat you think she is," he murmured.

And I'm not the cat you think I am. Dovewing wanted to speak the words aloud, but somehow Tigerheart's gentleness frightened her. *It's as if he's sorry for me, and wants to help me!*

To her relief, another yowl from Brambleclaw broke into their conversation, calling the ThunderClan cats together.

"I have to go," Dovewing mewed. "And I don't want to listen to another word from you."

Tigerheart didn't protest, just dipped his head as she stalked away. But even though she had escaped from him, Dovewing felt as though she had left half of herself behind.

Why can't I get him out of my fur?

On the way back from the Gathering Dovewing noticed that Bumblestripe was padding alongside her, a bit closer than usual. But Tigerheart's scent still wreathed around her; she still seemed to see his amber eyes gazing into hers, and hear the warmth of his meow.

She jumped when she realized that Bumblestripe was saying something. "What?" she snapped.

Bumblestripe blinked. "I—I only said I hope Ivypool can be with us next time."

"Sorry." Dovewing tried to push Tigerheart to the back of her mind. "I didn't mean to sound sharp. I guess I'm just tired."

Bumblestripe nodded. "Me too."

He quickened his pace until he caught up to Berrynose and Mousewhisker. Dovewing padded along in silence for a few moments, until she realized that Blossomfall had taken her brother's place at her side.

"You know, you've stolen my brother's heart," the young tortoiseshell warrior murmured. Her tone was teasing, but the gaze she turned on Dovewing was serious.

It sounded as if there was a warning in her words.

"Bumblestripe? You're not serious!" When Blossomfall didn't reply, Dovewing added, "Honestly, I'm sure he doesn't think of me like that."

To her relief, Blossomfall seemed to accept what she said. "It's great that you're a warrior now," she went on. "We can go on patrol together, and all sorts of stuff!" Her eyes widened, reflecting the moonlight. "I don't know how loners and rogues manage on their own, do you, Dovewing?"

"No, being a warrior is great," Dovewing replied, but her heart wasn't in her words. She wished that she could feel the same enthusiasm as Blossomfall.

What was Tigerheart trying to tell me? What could Ivypool be hiding?

Even before Dovewing slid into her den, she could hear her sister whimpering. Ivypool was twitching in her nest of bracken, her tail lashing from side to side. Dovewing crouched into the nest beside her and gave her shoulder a gentle shake.

"Hey, Ivypool, wake up!"

Ivypool started, blinked, then scrambled to her feet, her eyes wide and her claws out. "What? What is it?"

"It's okay," Dovewing murmured, though anxiety prickled every hair on her pelt. "It's only me. Were you in the Dark Forest again?"

Ivypool shook her head. "No, just dreaming." She sat down in her nest and started to groom her fur. "How was the Gathering?"

Dovewing shrugged. "You didn't miss much. None of the leaders had anything unusual to report."

"Firestar must have announced that we're warriors now," Ivypool meowed.

"He did! And lots of cats were sorry you couldn't be there. WindClan and RiverClan have new warriors, too," Dovewing reported. "Oh, and I think WindClan must be having trouble with dogs. Onestar didn't announce it, but I overheard a couple of their elders saying that a dog had savaged Antpelt."

"Antpelt!" Ivypool froze. "What else did they say?"

Dovewing blinked. *Oh, StarClan, don't tell me she's in love with a WindClan warrior!*

"Tell me!" Ivypool insisted.

"I wasn't paying much attention," Dovewing admitted. "They weren't talking to me. They said . . . Antpelt was wounded too badly to tell them what happened, and Kestrelflight didn't think he would pull through."

"Oh, no!" Ivypool let out a horrified wail. "It's all my fault!"

"What do you mean?" But even as she asked the question Dovewing was beginning to understand. "This has something to do with the Dark Forest, doesn't it?"

Ivypool nodded. Her claws worked in the bracken of her nest for a couple of heartbeats before she began to speak. "Thistleclaw was training Antpelt and me," she meowed quietly. "We were fighting like you and I would—practicing the moves, but not trying to hurt each other. When I slipped, Antpelt waited for me to get up." She swallowed. "But that made Thistleclaw call Antpelt a coward, and he went on mocking him and WindClan until Antpelt attacked him. Thistleclaw just *shredded* him. I think he would have killed him, but I told

Antpelt to wake up and he vanished back to WindClan."

"Then it *wasn't* your fault," Dovewing declared. She was trying to suppress the horror she felt, but shivers ran through her as if she had just been dunked in icy water. "Ivypool, you're in real danger," she mewed. "You have to tell Lionblaze and Jayfeather that you can't spy for them anymore."

"I'm not giving up now!" Ivypool protested. "I'm so close to finding out when the battle will be. Mapleshade—she's a really old Dark Forest cat, and all the others seem afraid of her, even Tigerstar—well, Mapleshade is taking a special interest in me. She trusts me now, and I'm so close to the truth!"

Dovewing thought that Mapleshade sounded like the last cat she would want to take an interest in her. Instead, she murmured, "I won't say anything yet, I promise. Why don't you get some more sleep? It won't be dawn for a while."

Ivypool stretched her jaws in an enormous yawn. "I think I will." She curled up in the bracken and closed her eyes; soon her regular breathing told Dovewing that she was asleep.

Lying beside her sister, Dovewing couldn't rest. Her sister's story, and the discovery that yet another warrior was being trained in the Dark Forest, buzzed in her head like a swarm of bees. *Any cat at the Gathering could have allegiance to the Dark Forest. Even some of our Clanmates . . .*

Sighing, Dovewing wondered if she would be certain about anything ever again.

CHAPTER 7
❧

As Jayfeather emerged from the barrier of thorns, he located Firestar heading for his den, side by side with Sandstorm. Though Jayfeather was tired, he knew that he had to talk to his Clan leader right now. He had spent too long wondering what he could say to get Firestar to agree to another journey. He sprinted ahead and caught up to Firestar at the bottom of the tumbled rocks.

"Firestar, I need to speak to you," he called.

He could sense his leader's surprise. "Now? Can't it wait until morning?"

"No."

Firestar hesitated for a heartbeat, then replied, "Okay. Come up to my den."

"I'll go check on Poppyfrost and her kits," Sandstorm mewed tactfully. "They had bellyache last night from eating too much squirrel."

"I gave them watermint," Jayfeather meowed after her as she padded toward the nursery. "Call me if they need more."

Firestar was already climbing the rocks; Jayfeather followed, careful to let his pelt brush the cliff so that he didn't stray too close to the edge of the path.

"What's so urgent that it can't wait?" Firestar's voice came from his nest at the back of his cave.

Jayfeather slipped inside to join him. "I have to go to the mountains," he announced. "I've been summoned."

"By StarClan?"

"No, another cat."

"Oh?" Curiosity radiated from Firestar; Jayfeather could feel it as if he was sitting in a beam of sunlight. "What other cat?"

"That's . . . sort of hard to explain," Jayfeather confessed. Would the ThunderClan leader believe that he had been able to speak with such an ancient cat? "But it's not something I can ignore."

Firestar let out a sigh of exasperation; Jayfeather pictured the tip of his ginger tail twitching. "We can't go on helping the Tribe," he meowed at last. "StarClan knows, I have a lot of sympathy for them, but they have their life and we have ours."

"This isn't about helping the Tribe," Jayfeather told him. "It's about discovering something from the past that's important for the future. Our future, not the Tribe's."

"You couldn't be a bit vaguer, could you?" Firestar's claws scraped on the floor of the den. "Honestly, Jayfeather, you expect me to—"

"I'm sorry, Firestar," Jayfeather interrupted. "I'm telling you everything I can. You have to trust me because of the prophecy."

"No." There was an edge to Firestar's voice. "I trust you

because you're a loyal medicine cat who serves his Clan above all else."

Jayfeather took a breath. "And as a loyal medicine cat, I'm asking you to let me go to the Tribe of Rushing Water, because I believe it's in our best interests."

Firestar was silent, though Jayfeather could almost hear the turmoil of thoughts whirling through his leader's mind. "You need an escort," he mewed at last. "And I'm not happy about leaving ThunderClan without its best warriors or its medicine cat when we're bracing ourselves for an attack."

Though the ThunderClan leader didn't mention the Dark Forest, Jayfeather knew that was where his thoughts lay. *And he's right. But I have to do this!*

"Are you sure this cat isn't trying to lure you away?" Firestar added.

Jayfeather shook his head. "I'm positive." *Rock is the last cat who would be involved in a Dark Forest plot.* "I trust the cat who gave me this message," he went on. "He isn't interested in our battles. He doesn't care who wins. He just knows that this is our destiny, and he has to make it happen."

"Very well," Firestar meowed. "You can go. And I'll choose some warriors to go with you—but you can't have Lionblaze."

"What?" Jayfeather's feeling of triumph was swallowed up in outrage. "But Lionblaze *has* to go. He's one of the Three!"

"You can have Dovewing." Firestar's tone was uncompromising. "But Lionblaze stays here. He's our greatest asset in a battle. And you're not going to the mountains to fight, are you?"

"How do we know that?" Jayfeather muttered mutinously. He was well aware that there was no point in trying to argue when the ThunderClan leader had made up his mind. "Okay," he meowed aloud. "But I don't like it."

"No cat is asking you to," Firestar retorted. "You can have Dovewing, as I said, and . . . let's see . . . Foxleap and Squirrelflight."

"Squirrelflight!" Jayfeather didn't want to travel with the cat who had lied to him and his littermates season after season, the cat he had believed was his mother.

"I don't care what you think about Squirrelflight's actions in the past," Firestar growled as if he could read Jayfeather's mind. "What's done is done. She knows the mountains better than any of us, and she has friends in the Tribe."

Jayfeather dipped his head. "Okay, Firestar." He sighed.

"And while you're away," Firestar went on, "I'll ask Leafpool to step in as medicine cat. Just in case there are any emergencies. If there is a battle, we'll need her trained paws."

Jayfeather felt his neck fur bristle at the mention of the other she-cat who had betrayed him and his littermates. *Yeah, right. . . . Like StarClan will ever speak to Leafpool again, after what she did.*

But he could see the point in making use of Leafpool's vast knowledge of healing, so he just replied with a curt nod. "Brightheart has had some training, too," he pointed out.

"True. Then that's settled." Firestar still didn't sound happy, but Jayfeather knew that he wouldn't go back on what he had agreed. "You can leave tomorrow."

* * *

As Jayfeather reached the bottom of the tumbled rocks, Lionblaze padded across to him; Jayfeather picked up his mingled curiosity and excitement. *You're not going to like this,* he thought. "You're up late," he remarked out loud.

"I spotted a hole in the barrier near the dirtplace tunnel, so I went to fix it," Lionblaze explained. "Nothing to worry about," he added. "Just a few loose branches. There's no sign that any cats had tried to break in."

Jayfeather nodded. A moon or two ago, the idea of any cats trying to break into the ThunderClan camp, deep inside their territory, would have been unthinkable. Now relations between the Clans were so strained that it was all too possible.

"Have you been talking to Firestar?" Lionblaze asked eagerly. "When do we leave for the mountains?"

"You don't," Jayfeather replied, bracing himself for his brother's disappointment.

"What?"

"I'm sorry, but Firestar says he needs you here. If there's a battle with the Dark Forest cats, then you're the strongest warrior we have."

"But I'm one of the Three!" Jayfeather heard his brother's claws raking furiously in the earth, and pictured his golden neck fur bristling with anger. "Surely I have to go to the mountains as well?"

"I wish you could, but . . . well, I think Firestar has a point." Jayfeather reached out with his tail to touch Lionblaze on his shoulder. "If the Dark Forest cats attack, you're the best defense ThunderClan has."

Lionblaze snorted. "Who is going with you, then? Dovewing, I hope."

"Yes, and Foxleap and Squirrelflight."

Lionblaze was silent for a moment. Jayfeather knew his brother would understand how reluctant he was to travel with the cat who had pretended to be their mother. But all Lionblaze said was "I'll give Foxleap some extra training."

"There's no time," Jayfeather told him. "We leave in the morning."

As he spoke he felt a sudden chill; wind swirled around the hollow, making his eyes water and flattening his fur to his sides. He heard the clatter of branches high above as the blast stirred the trees at the top of the cliffs.

"Clouds across the moon . . ." Lionblaze murmured.

Could that be an omen? Jayfeather wondered, suppressing a shiver. "Time is running out for all of us."

Jayfeather padded back to his den. His muscles ached with weariness, but he knew that he couldn't sleep yet. Checking on Briarlight, who was peacefully curled up in her nest, he headed for the cleft in the rock where he kept his supply of herbs. Since he had received Rock's message, he had gathered what he could in preparation for the time when he would be away.

"Plenty of juniper berries," he muttered, identifying each herb by scent and touch. His stores were sparse, but at least he had more than in the previous moon. "Some catmint left . . .

the tansy is a bit low . . . And lots of yarrow." He remembered the bunch of yarrow that had been left outside the camp; he had never identified the cat who had found it. *Whoever it was, they have a good nose for herbs.*

Carefully he selected sorrel, daisy, chamomile, and burnet, the traveling herbs that he and his Clanmates would need for the journey, and made four leaf wraps for the morning. Then he checked on Briarlight once more. She was deeply asleep, worn out by the new exercises he had given her.

Knowing how important it was for him to get some rest before setting out, he stumbled into his nest and curled up, wrapping his tail over his nose. Instantly, as it seemed, he opened his eyes and realized that he was in StarClan. He lay in long grass on the bank of a stream that gurgled over stones. The water reflected red light; Jayfeather looked up to see the sky stained with bars of scarlet as the sun went down in a brilliant blaze. All around him the shadows of evening were gathering, and a chilly wind whispered through the grass and ruffled the surface of the stream. As Jayfeather rose to his paws and looked around, a nearby clump of bracken quivered and a cat emerged into the open. Jayfeather studied the messy, clumped gray fur and snaggly teeth.

"Yellowfang," he greeted her.

"I've been waiting for you," Yellowfang rasped. "What's all this nonsense about going to the mountains?"

Jayfeather flicked up his ears in surprise. "You know about that? Did Rock speak to you too?"

Yellowfang let out a snort of disgust. "That one doesn't

speak much to any cat."

Jayfeather wondered how much the former medicine cat knew about Rock. "You don't think I should go?"

"I think it's a mouse-brained scheme," Yellowfang replied, baring her teeth. "The Dark Forest is rising. You should stay in ThunderClan and protect your Clanmates."

"The Tribe of Rushing Water is linked to the destiny of the Clans," Jayfeather argued.

"That's not your responsibility," Yellowfang snapped.

"But what if it is?" Jayfeather insisted. Yellowfang might change her opinion if she knew that Jayfeather had traveled back to the time of the ancient cats who had once lived beside the lake.

But she doesn't know, and I'm not going to tell her. Not yet. Not here.

Yellowfang let out a sigh. "Come, walk with me," she meowed, abandoning the argument.

Jayfeather padded at her shoulder as she led him along the bank of the stream beside thick clumps of bracken and herbs. Jayfeather breathed in their scents, trying to identify each one, and wishing with all his heart that he could take some of them back with him to ThunderClan.

Comfrey . . . celandine . . . marigold. And I'm trying to cope with a few dried-up leaves!

Other cats brushed through the undergrowth, dipping their heads as they passed. Some of them looked strong, their colors as vivid as if they were still alive. Others were pale, like wisps of vapor, as if the next stiff breeze would blow them into nothingness. Jayfeather spotted Lionheart and Whitestorm from ThunderClan, sharing tongues in the shadow of an elder bush. A beautiful white she-cat, unknown to Jayfeather, was with them, and a tiny kit frolicked around her paws. He would have liked to stop and talk but Yellowfang stalked on with nothing more than a passing nod.

Crookedstar, the former RiverClan leader, was sitting beside the stream, staring down into the water. As Jayfeather watched, he flashed out a paw and hooked a gleaming silver fish. It flapped helplessly on the bank until Crookedstar killed it with a single bite.

"Well caught," Yellowfang remarked.

"Come and share?" Crookedstar invited her.

"Maybe later." Yellowfang didn't look back.

A little farther on, Jayfeather spotted Barkface, the old WindClan medicine cat; his heart gave a leap of sorrow when he saw that the cat with him was Flametail. They stood beside a clump of thyme; Barkface was pointing something out to the younger cat.

"Hey, Jayfeather, come and join us!" Flametail called.

Jayfeather's paws were tugging him toward the medicine cats, but Yellowfang let out an annoyed hiss, and he had to follow her. "Sorry!" he replied. "Another time."

As he turned back to follow Yellowfang, Jayfeather spotted a gray tom running swiftly through the trees. He halted, staring; as if aware of his gaze the other cat stopped and glanced back over his shoulder, returning Jayfeather's stare with burning blue eyes. Then he turned and ran on, vanishing behind a clump of hazel saplings.

"Ashfur!" Jayfeather exclaimed, spinning around to face Yellowfang. He felt cold to the tips of his claws. "He's here?"

"Why not?" The old cat's voice was steady. "His only fault was to love too much."

Jayfeather let out a snort of disbelief. "Hardly. He tried to push us off the cliff!"

"But he didn't," Yellowfang pointed out. "Squirrelflight stopped him—and maybe her only fault is that she loved too much, as well."

"What do you mean?"

Yellowfang shrugged. "Work it out for yourself, mouse-brain. And get a move on. I haven't got all day."

Sighing in exasperation, Jayfeather followed her along a winding track that climbed through the trees until they emerged at the foot of a grassy hill. Yellowfang bounded up the slope and waited for Jayfeather to join her, panting, at the top.

"You need more exercise," she commented, giving him a prod with one paw.

"I've been on my paws all night," Jayfeather retorted. "StarClan cats might not get tired, but I do. What are we doing here, anyway?"

"Just look." Yellowfang waved her tail at the scene below them.

Jayfeather gazed over the tops of the trees. StarClan's forest looked open and inviting, dotted with clearings and lighter-colored trees, and cut through by a sparkling river. Cats were playing in the shallows, throwing up spray and splashing one another with the shining droplets. Jayfeather r... strong bodies and sleek pelts of RiverClan.

"Beautiful, isn't it?" Yellowfang prompted after moments.

"Yes," Jayfeather whispered.

The old medicine cat padded so close to him that their pelts brushed. "All this depends on you, Jayfeather," she mewed. "You're not just protecting ThunderClan now but all the Clans, including this one."

Me? Jayfeather wanted to wail out loud like a lost kit, but he forced himself to stand still, looking across the peaceful landscape. "You don't want me to go to the mountains because you're scared of what will happen to the Clans."

The old cat bowed her head. "Sometimes the right choice can be the hardest one," she rasped.

Scenes flashed through Jayfeather's mind, and he realized that he was seeing her memories: a younger Yellowfang, suckling a dark brown tabby kit; the same kit, big enough now to be an apprentice, fighting savagely with a young black she-cat; then muscular and full-grown, brushing through bracken with a terrified, mewling kit in his jaws; older now, with scarred, blinded eyes, crouched against a thorny barrier with a much younger Dustpelt guarding him. Last of all, Yellowfang herself, casting glances at the dark tom and snagging a scarlet deathberry on one claw.

Jayfeather shivered. *Yellowfang's life was so hard, but she faced it with courage.*

"I'm sorry," he mewed gently. "I understand how you feel, but I have to go to the mountains. It's the right thing to do. I'll come back, I promise."

Yellowfang didn't reply, just gazed at him with scared and sorrowful eyes as she began to fade from Jayfeather's sight. Her gray fur seemed to melt into one enormous shadow, as the last of the light left the sky above StarClan's forest. As darkness swallowed Jayfeather's vision, he blinked open his eyes and found that he was in his den, with a frond of bracken from his nest tickling his nose.

Sneezing, Jayfeather sat up. A sharp dawn breeze ruffled his fur, and he could hear the sound of early-rising cats beginning to move around the clearing. Briarlight was stirring, too; Jayfeather rose to his paws and padded over to her.

"I'm so tired," she complained, her words muffled by an enormous yawn. "Do I have to do my exercises today?"

"Of course you do! You can't miss a single day!"

"Okay." Briarlight sounded surprised that he was so vehement. "Just let me wake up a bit first."

Jayfeather heard her scramble upright in her nest and start to groom her fur. "Briarlight, there's something I have to tell you," he mewed more quietly. "I have to go away for a while."

"No!" Briarlight stopped grooming; her voice was terrified. "You can't!"

"I have to," Jayfeather repeated. "But it won't be for long, I promise. Brightheart and Millie will take good care of you."

"It's not the same," Briarlight whispered. "What if . . . ?"

Her voice trailed off. Jayfeather understood very well what

she was too scared to ask. "I wouldn't go if I thought you were going to die," he meowed bluntly.

He could feel Briarlight relaxing a little. "That's why you've given me all these new exercises," she murmured. "I will do them, I promise."

"Good." Jayfeather touched her ear with his nose. "Look, I've made four leaf wraps of traveling herbs, they're at the entrance to the store. Show the other cats where they are when I send them in."

"Okay."

Leaving her to start her exercises, Jayfeather brushed past the brambles and padded into the clearing. Blossomfall was hurrying past him on her way to join a patrol; Jayfeather checked her with his tail.

"Have you seen Foxleap?"

"Yes, he's still in the warrior's den," the young tortoiseshell replied. "Sleeping like a dead hedgehog. He's not on early patrol."

"Get him for me, would you?"

"But I'm—" Blossomfall began to protest, then sighed. "Okay."

Jayfeather heard her bounding off. A few moments later Foxleap staggered up to him, yawning widely. "What is it, Jayfeather? I thought I'd catch up on my sleep after the Gathering."

Yes, wouldn't that be nice? "You're going on a journey," Jayfeather announced.

"A journey?" Foxleap suddenly sounded wide awake. "Where?"

"To the mountains."

"*Really?* Me?" Excitement made Foxleap's voice quiver and he gave a little bounce of anticipation. "You mean I get to meet the Tribe of Rushing Water, like the cats who made the Great Journey? Wow! I promise I'll protect you, Jayfeather. I'll be the best warrior you can imagine. I'll stay on watch all night—"

"No need to overdo it," Jayfeather murmured, suppressing a small *mrrow* of amusement. "I've made some leaf wraps of traveling herbs in my den," he continued. "Briarlight will show you where they are."

"You mean we're going right now?" Foxleap sounded as if he was about to burst with excitement. At Jayfeather's nod he bounded off toward the medicine cat's den.

Firestar's scent drifted over Jayfeather as the Clan leader padded up. "I see you've told Foxleap," he meowed. "What about Squirrelflight and Dovewing?"

"I haven't seen them yet."

Firestar paused, then called out, "Hey, Squirrelflight! Over here a moment."

"I'm just going to lead the dawn patrol." Squirrelflight's voice came from the direction of the thorn barrier.

"No, you're not," Firestar corrected her.

"What's all this about?" Squirrelflight bounded up.

"Jayfeather had a sign," Firestar began. He explained how he wanted her to go with Jayfeather on a journey to the mountains.

"That's great!" Squirrelflight's enthusiasm bubbled over. "I'll be glad to lead the patrol, Firestar. It'll be a chance to catch up with my friends in the Tribe. I can't wait to see Stormfur and Brook again!"

And who said you were leading *the patrol?* Jayfeather asked himself sourly. But he couldn't say anything aloud: Squirrelflight was the oldest cat to be chosen, and by far the most experienced in the mountains. It made sense for her to take the lead.

"Who else is going?" Squirrelflight asked. "Lionblaze, I suppose, and—"

"No, Lionblaze is staying here," Firestar interrupted. "You don't need him, because you're not going to fight. Jayfeather's omen didn't give him any reason to expect trouble."

"Hmm . . ." Squirrelflight sounded surprised, and not too pleased. "You know best, I suppose. But I hope you don't expect Jayfeather and me to trek all that way by ourselves."

"No," Firestar told her. "Foxleap is going with you, and Dovewing."

"What? Me!"

Jayfeather jumped as an excited squeal sounded behind him. More cats were beginning to gather around to hear what was going on, and he hadn't noticed Dovewing's approach. He turned and explained quickly what had been decided.

"That's so cool!" Dovewing exclaimed. "I've heard so many stories about the mountains, and now I'm really going there! Can Ivypool come, too?"

"No," Jayfeather retorted. *Great StarClan, any cat would think those two were joined at the tail!*

"Why not?" Dovewing hissed close to his ear. "Don't you trust her?"

"That's not the issue at all," Jayfeather answered through gritted teeth. "And we can't discuss it now, not in front of every cat. It's just the four of us and that's all."

"Okay." Dovewing's disappointment made her voice bitter.

"Come on," Jayfeather mewed briskly. "I've prepared traveling herbs for all of us. Let's go and get them."

"You mean, we're going right now?" Squirrelflight asked, astonished.

"There's nothing to wait for," Firestar began.

"Hey, Squirrelflight! Dovewing!" Brambleclaw's voice cut across Firestar's as the deputy came bounding up. "Why haven't you joined your patrols? And why is every cat standing around here?"

It was Squirrelflight who replied. "Firestar is sending us to the mountains. Jayfeather has had a sign."

"I see." Brambleclaw's voice was level. "Firestar, I hope you're not sending too many cats. All of our warriors may be needed here."

"No, just these three and Foxleap," Firestar replied.

"Brambleclaw, do you have any messages for the Tribe?" Squirrelflight asked hesitantly. "I could say hi to Stormfur and Brook for you."

Jayfeather heard something else beneath her words, something she dared not ask for out loud. *She wants Brambleclaw to wish her luck, or tell her to be careful . . . anything to show that he still cares about her.*

But all Brambleclaw said was "Sure. Tell them they're missed in ThunderClan."

Jayfeather could almost taste Squirrelflight's disappointment. *Brambleclaw doesn't seem to feel anything. Has he forgotten that he once thought he was our father?*

Several cats were circling them by now, excitedly asking questions. The dawn patrols hadn't left, and more warriors were pushing their way between the branches of their den.

"What's all the racket about?" Dustpelt asked irritably. "Can't a cat get a wink of sleep around here?"

"Going to the mountains?" That was Cinderheart's voice, filled with longing. "Oh, I *wish* I were going. I can just imagine it . . . bare peaks, the endless blue sky with eagles swooping like specks in the air, and the water so cold and clear . . ."

Jayfeather blinked at the vivid picture her words called up. *Of course, Cinderheart has seen it,* he thought. *She just doesn't know she's remembering.*

"I remember hunting with the Tribe," Cloudtail meowed. "When we passed through there on the Great Journey. I'd like to hunt eagles again."

"So would I," Sandstorm agreed. "Lionblaze, you're so lucky!"

"I'm not going," Lionblaze replied, still sounding disgruntled. "Firestar wants me to stay here and help guard the camp."

"Oh, bad luck," Sandstorm sympathized.

Jayfeather's nostrils twitched at the scent of herbs as Foxleap padded back into the group. He was passing his tongue across his jaws, over and over again. "Why do the traveling herbs have to taste so yucky?" he complained.

Jayfeather jumped as a paw prodded him in the shoulder

and he picked up Purdy's scent. "So you're off on your travels again, young'un," the old loner rasped. "I wish I could go back wi' you and see my old home."

Jayfeather tensed. *Please, StarClan, not that!*

Purdy let out an amused snort. "No need to look so shocked. I don't reckon my old paws would carry me that far. Mind you, I could tell you a thing or two—"

"There isn't time, Purdy," Jayfeather interrupted. "We're leaving now."

"Oh." Purdy hesitated, then added, "Well, mind you stay clear of that farm where your littermates an' that nuisancy WindClan apprentice met the dogs."

"We will, Purdy, don't worry," Jayfeather assured him. Leaning closer to Purdy, he added in an undertone, "Take care of Mousefur while I'm gone."

"Sure I will." Jayfeather heard the pride in Purdy's voice. "You can rely on me."

Jayfeather beckoned with his tail to Dovewing and Squirrelflight, and led them to his den to give them their traveling herbs. Sudden misgivings seized him as he licked up the leaves.

Am I doing the right thing, taking these cats all the way to the mountains, leaving the rest of my Clan vulnerable? Can I really trust Rock?

CHAPTER 8

❧

Lionblaze emerged from the thorns and trotted toward the old Thunderpath at the head of his hunting patrol. Cinderheart, Birchfall, and Leafpool followed him, keeping up easily. After a gray, damp dawn, the clouds were beginning to break up, and ragged scraps of blue sky were appearing through the trees. A breeze blew into Lionblaze's face, bringing with it the scent of prey, but he found it hard to concentrate on hunting. He was still stunned by the speed of Jayfeather's departure, and struggling not to feel angry that he hadn't been allowed to go, too.

"I wonder why Jayfeather has to go to the mountains," Birchfall mewed, bounding up to pad beside Lionblaze. "Did he tell you?"

"He had a sign," Lionblaze grunted. "Don't forget, he's a medicine cat."

"I wish I could have gone," Birchfall continued wistfully. "I was only a kit when we made the Great Journey, but it was so exciting! I'd love to go back there now that I'm a warrior."

"I guess most of the Clan feels like that," Cinderheart

remarked, joining them. "I know I do, even though I wasn't on the Journey."

"There were cliffs that went down forever," Birchfall murmured, his eyes clouded with memory. "And wind that nearly blew your fur off, and the biggest birds I've ever seen. . . ."

You don't have to go on about it, Lionblaze thought. "We're talking too much. It's time we started looking for prey," he reminded them, as the walls of the abandoned Twoleg nest appeared through the leafless trees. "Why don't we split up? Birchfall, you go with Leafpool, and I'll hunt with Cinderheart."

He felt a stab of sadness. If only he could walk beside her for more than just a morning patrol. *For all our life, until we go to hunt with StarClan.*

Birchfall led Leafpool off in the direction of the lake, while Lionblaze veered into the woods behind the Twoleg den.

"You must be worried about Jayfeather," Cinderheart meowed as they paused on the edge of the pine trees. "But remember the prophecy: Nothing will happen to him. He's far too important for the destiny of the Clans."

Lionblaze didn't want to be reminded of the prophecy, especially by Cinderheart, when that was what had come between them. "Jayfeather is an ordinary cat," he argued, desperate for that to be true. "Just like me."

"But you're not ordinary, either of you!" Cinderheart protested. "You're special and different."

Lionblaze dug his claws into the earth, anger tensing every muscle. "Why can't you see past that stupid prophecy to the cat I really am?" he snapped at Cinderheart. "You saw it before, so what has changed?"

"Everything," Cinderheart replied. Her voice was full of pride and excitement. "Because I never knew who you really were. The prophecy is part of you—it was here before you were born!"

She sounds as if she has no regrets at all that we aren't together anymore. "What about you?" he challenged. "Don't you matter, too?"

"Of course I do." Her excitement ebbed and Lionblaze began to sense the sorrow behind her words. "Believe me, I wish that you weren't part of this prophecy. But you are, and we just have to live with it."

"But—" Lionblaze tried to interrupt, but Cinderheart swept on.

"You can't lead your Clanmates into battle worrying about a mate and kits. You're like a medicine cat—your loyalty must be to the whole Clan, equally."

"You could say that about any warrior," Lionblaze retorted.

"No, because you're one of the Three." Cinderheart stretched out her tail as if she was going to touch his shoulder, then drew it back at the last moment. "This is the way things are." Abruptly she turned away. "Let's hunt."

Lionblaze gazed helplessly after her. His heart was full of what he wanted to tell her, but the words wouldn't come. Besides, Cinderheart had already spotted a blackbird, and had dropped into the hunter's crouch, creeping up on it with stealthy paw steps. Suppressing a sigh, Lionblaze began working his way around to the other side of the blackbird, careful not to make a sound. The bird was intent on pecking at the moss beneath a tree, unaware of the cats closing in on it. When Cinderheart was within a couple of tail-lengths, Lionblaze let out a yowl. The blackbird fluttered up in alarm, straight into Cinderheart's claws. She batted it out of the air and gave its neck a swift bite.

Lionblaze padded up to see Cinderheart stroking the bird's limp brown feathers with one paw, her claws sheathed. "It's a female," she mewed softly. "Look, there's moss in her beak. She must have been collecting it for her nest. And now her eggs will never be laid. She'll never go back to her mate."

Lionblaze blinked. He couldn't understand why any warrior would grieve over a piece of fresh-kill. "It was a good catch," he mewed encouragingly.

"That's not the point." Cinderheart was still looking down at the dead bird. "I always wanted a mate and kits," she whispered. "But it wasn't my destiny. Never to feel the warmth of fur . . . never to suckle. . . ."

"You'll find another mate," Lionblaze told her, trying to comfort her even though it wrenched his heart. "You can still have kits."

Cinderheart spun around to face him, blue flame in her eyes. "You don't understand!" she spat. She gouged at the earth with her hind claws, burying the blackbird. "I'll hunt alone!" Without waiting for a response from Lionblaze, she plunged away into the trees.

Lionblaze looked after her, baffled. *What was all that about?* Movement caught his eye and he glanced around to see

Leafpool padding toward him. *How much of that did she hear?*

"Are you okay?" Leafpool asked gently as she drew close to him.

Lionblaze was too dazed to reawaken his old grudge against her. "Not really," he confessed. "Things aren't working out with Cinderheart."

Leafpool nodded, and to his relief she didn't ask him to explain why. He knew that he couldn't tell her about the prophecy.

"Why don't we look for prey beside the lake?" she suggested, turning in that direction with an inviting twitch of her tail.

Surprising himself, Lionblaze fell in beside her and they shouldered through the undergrowth together, the tang of water in the air growing stronger as they drew closer to the waterside.

"Cinderheart seems to think we have different destinies," he meowed after a few moments. "I don't understand her."

"I think I do." Leafpool blinked sympathetically. "And I really believe that she loved you—in fact, I think she still does."

Lionblaze clawed in frustration at a tendril of bramble that snaked across their path. "Then why can't she just be with me? Why does she have to make it all so difficult?"

Leafpool shook her head but didn't reply. For a while they padded along together in silence. As they reached a narrow track that wound its way toward the lake, Leafpool halted, tasting the air. Lionblaze thought she had detected prey, and winced as she darted noisily to the edge of a bramble thicket.

You won't catch anything like that!

But Leafpool was pushing dead leaves aside with one paw, to reveal three bright yellow coltsfoot flowers. "The first this season!" she exclaimed. "I'd better take these back to camp. They'll be good for Mousefur's cough."

"Do you miss being a medicine cat?" Lionblaze asked, as Leafpool carefully nipped off the stems.

"With every breath I take," she murmured.

"Then what was *your* destiny?" Lionblaze mewed, the words tumbling from his jaws. "I mean, if you were meant to be a medicine cat, then you wouldn't . . . StarClan wouldn't have let you and Crowfeather . . ."

Leafpool bowed her head. "Destiny isn't a path that any cat follows blindly," she meowed. "It is always a matter of choice, and sometimes the heart speaks loudest." She paused, then added, "Deep down, I always knew what I had to do, and that's why I came back to the Clan. Lionblaze, whatever else happens, I trust you to know the right thing to do as well. Listen to your heart, because that's where your true destiny lies."

CHAPTER 9

Dovewing's pelt prickled with excitement as she followed Squirrelflight past the horseplace and up the hill. She had never been this way before. New sensations crowded in on her from all sides: the scent of horse, and the way the huge creatures slammed down their hooves as they cantered across their field; strong RiverClan scent borne on the wind that blew from their territory; the scents of reeds and stagnant water from the marshes that bordered the lake.

"This is so cool!" she exclaimed to Jayfeather, who was padding beside her, setting down his paws unerringly in spite of his blindness. Jayfeather just let out a faint grunt and twitched an ear.

Be like that! Dovewing thought crossly. She turned to look at Foxleap, who was gazing around with wide, wondering eyes.

"You can see so much from up here!" he meowed.

Dovewing fell back to walk beside him. "There's a really good view of the island from here," she remarked, flicking her tail to where she could see the Gathering place far below; at this distance the tree-bridge looked like the thinnest twig.

"And there's ShadowClan territory." Foxleap angled his ears toward the dark pines bordering the lake beyond the island.

Dovewing let her senses reach out until she found the ShadowClan camp. Blackstar and his deputy, Rowanclaw, were deep in conversation, while Littlecloud was in his den, muttering under his breath as he counted juniper berries.

I wonder what Foxleap would say if I told him exactly what I can see from here?

"There's RiverClan," she mewed aloud. "You can just see their camp—there, between the two streams."

"Too bad there are so many trees and bushes," Foxleap responded, letting out a mischievous *mrrow.* "We could spy on them!"

I can do that just fine, thanks, trees or no trees. Dovewing located Minnowtail giving her apprentice a fishing lesson. "No, Mossypaw, sit where your shadow is *behind* you, not stretching over the water."

"And the WindClan camp is over there" was all she meowed to Foxleap, waving her tail toward the moorland on their other side. "It's in a hollow, but you can't see it from here."

"I forgot, you've been there." Foxleap's voice held a trace of envy. "Was it scary?"

"Pretty much," Dovewing confessed. "I shouldn't have—"

She broke off, her pelt bristling as a grief-stricken screech sounded in her ears. For a heartbeat she looked around wildly, half fearing that one of the patrol had been grabbed by a fox. But Squirrelflight and Jayfeather were still walking quietly a few tail-lengths ahead. Foxleap was staring at her as if she had gone mad.

The screech came again. "Antpelt! No!"

Dovewing froze. The dreadful cries of grief sounded so close, but they were coming from the WindClan camp.

Then she heard Kestrelflight's voice. "Give me more cobwebs." She was aware of blood pouring from Antpelt's wounds, and sensed the fever raging inside the young tom's body.

"Kestrelflight, do something!" Now Dovewing recognized Swallowtail's voice; she had been the cat who had cried out before. "You can't let him die."

"I'm doing everything I can," the medicine cat hissed. "I've given him horsetail and borage, but I can't stop the infection from spreading."

"Then give him more!"

Dovewing picked up the sound of a cat chewing borage leaves into a pulp and pushing them down Antpelt's throat, but the dying warrior was too weak to swallow.

"Oh, StarClan!" That was Onestar's voice, quiet but full of sorrow. "This is a young cat. Do you have to take him now?"

"I still don't understand how he got wounds like that." Dovewing wasn't sure which cat was speaking now. *Maybe Tornear; I heard him at the Gathering.* "I thought it was a dog bite, but none of the patrols have reported seeing dogs in the territory."

"I know." Dovewing recognized the other elder, Webfoot. "And those wounds don't look like any dog bite *I've* ever seen. You'd almost think he'd been attacked by a cat."

A disbelieving snort came from Tornear. "That's impossible! He would have said something if it had been a rogue."

"Antpelt . . ." Swallowtail whimpered. Dovewing remembered seeing her with Antpelt at a Gathering, and guessed that they had been mates. "Antpelt, please . . ."

"It's no use." Kestrelflight's voice, heavy with defeat. "He hunts with StarClan now."

Swallowtail let out another grief-stricken screech, but it seemed to fade into the background; Dovewing heard another cat much more clearly.

"Sunstrike, Furzepaw, come over here." It was Breezepelt, his voice a low mutter. "Say nothing about the Dark Forest," he warned. "Antpelt may be dead here, but he'll still be in the Place of No Stars. Nothing's changed; he's still on our side."

Oh, Ivypool! Horror shook Dovewing from ears to tail-tip. Cats from the Clans were *dying* because of what was happening in the Dark Forest! *Should I go back to ThunderClan and tell her what happened to Antpelt?*

"Dovewing!"

A yowl from Squirrelflight jerked Dovewing back to her surroundings. The ginger she-cat was standing farther up the hill, looking back at her with annoyance in her green eyes. Jayfeather was beside her, his claws plucking impatiently at the grass.

"You're being left behind!" Squirrelflight scolded. "Get a move on!"

"Sorry! I'm coming!" Dovewing called back, forcing her paws to move. She hated feeling as if she was abandoning the

Clans to the Dark Forest, but there was nothing she could do to help Antpelt. She just had to pray that Ivypool would be careful. Her sister wasn't stupid; she'd know soon enough that Antpelt had died from his injuries. Deliberately Dovewing closed her ears to the sounds of grief coming from the WindClan camp.

Foxleap stayed beside her as she plodded up the hill. "It's okay to be spooked when you're so far away from home," he reassured her. "Don't worry. I'll look after you."

I can look after myself, thanks! Dovewing just stopped herself from snarling the words out loud. *It's not like I can tell him what the real problem is.*

Still quivering from the shock of Antpelt's death, Dovewing drew closer to the top of the hill. A couple of fox-lengths below her, Jayfeather stumbled over a rock. Instantly Squirrelflight was by his side, steadying him.

Jayfeather turned on her with a hiss. "I don't need your help!"

Squirrelflight's tail lashed. "Fine! Sprain your paw and finish your journey before it's started. There's nothing to be ashamed of," she added more quietly. "Even sighted cats trip."

Jayfeather let out a growl of annoyance and stomped away toward the hilltop.

As Dovewing took the final paw steps that brought her up to the ridge, she began to feel strong wind buffeting her fur. Behind her the lake looked small and distant, the different territories blending into one another. Ahead, thick forest covered the downward slope, leading to wide stretches of grass cut through by Thunderpaths. Everywhere she looked, she could see Twoleg dens: some standing alone, some clustered in groups.

All those dens together must be Twoleg camps.

Dovewing stood in a line with her Clanmates, wind flattening their fur and whistling around their ears. Instantly noise blasted through her mind, almost driving her back down the hill. Chaotic visions spiraled in front of her eyes; she froze, paws digging into the ground, as she tried to make sense of what she could see and hear. But the solid hilltop seemed to melt away under her paws, and she was whirled into a storm of noise and color.

A glittering red monster growled out of a flat-roofed Twoleg den; Twoleg kits ran and screeched; a huge black-and-white animal she'd never seen before stared at her from liquid eyes, its jaws moving rhythmically; a male Twoleg pushed a tiny, snarling monster across a stretch of grass, snapping at the stems; more dogs than she'd ever imagined were barking all together; somewhere water was gushing; the scent of crow-food washed over her.

Sick and giddy, Dovewing squeezed her eyes shut, but the whirl of images continued.

"Dovewing! Dovewing!" Foxleap's voice cut faintly across the turmoil.

Dovewing couldn't move. She tried to reply to Foxleap, but she couldn't form the words. Then she became aware of another cat standing close to her.

"Dovewing!" It was Jayfeather's voice, quiet but incisive. "Focus on me. Block out the rest of the noise."

"Can't—" Gasping out a single word was a huge effort.

"Yes, you *can*. Come on—concentrate!"

His voice was sharp, like a splash of icy water. One by one, Dovewing drew her senses back in. She dared to open her eyes and made out the blurred shape of Jayfeather in front of her.

"That's better." She could hear his voice more clearly now. "Focus harder. Don't let go."

There was still a dull, aching roar in Dovewing's head, but she could feel the ground under her paws again, and see her companions; Squirrelflight and Foxleap were staring at her in alarm.

Foxleap drew his tail-tip gently down her side. "It's all right," he whispered.

"Are you okay to go on?" Squirrelflight demanded bluntly. "If you're not, just tell us. It's not too late for you to go back."

Dovewing couldn't stop trembling. She guessed that down by the lake, the hills had shielded her special senses from the outside world. There would be nothing to protect her now. So she'd have to learn to protect herself. The dull roar inside her head threatened to increase, but she pushed it back down. She took a deep breath and faced Squirrelflight, struggling to keep her voice even. "I'll be fine. I want to keep going."

Squirrelflight gave her a hard look, then nodded. "Okay. Let's go." She began to lead the way down the slope into the trees.

Foxleap padded close beside Dovewing, their pelts brushing. "Walk with me," he murmured. "There's nothing to be scared of."

Dovewing was still so shaken that she didn't have the strength to be angry with him for assuming she was frightened of leaving familiar territory.

As they reached the first of the trees, Jayfeather signed to Dovewing to halt, and let Foxleap pad on alone for a few paw steps. "Did you see the mountain cats?" he hissed into Dovewing's ear.

She shook her head. "I don't think so."

Jayfeather let out a frustrated snort. Guilt weighed down Dovewing's paw steps even more. *I should have tried to find out something helpful for the journey.*

As she padded farther into the trees, her feelings of uneasiness faded. She was growing used to blocking out the rush of sensations, and she thought that the surrounding trees were cutting off some of the images that assailed her. This forest was very like ThunderClan territory, too; she began to feel at home, and even to enjoy the journey.

"Bet you can't leap over that!" Foxleap challenged her when they came to a shallow stream.

"Bet I can!" Dovewing retorted, racing up to the bank and pushing off strongly so that her paws landed squarely on the cool moss beyond.

Foxleap jumped after her, but one hind paw slipped as he took off, and he landed with his hindquarters in the stream, droplets splashing up his legs and into his belly fur.

"Clumsy furball!" Dovewing called with a *mrrow* of laughter.

Foxleap hauled himself out, shaking his reddish tabby pelt. "I'll show you who's a furball!" he meowed, launching himself after Dovewing.

With a squeal of excitement, Dovewing pelted away, hiding behind the drooping branches of a willow tree. Foxleap dived after her, chasing her around the trunk and batting at her tail with his forepaws, his claws sheathed.

"Honestly! Are you kits?" Squirrelflight's voice came from outside the screen of willow boughs.

"Oops!" Dovewing exchanged a guilty glance with Foxleap. She poked her head out through the branches to see Squirrelflight standing a couple of tail-lengths away, her tail-tip twitching. "Sorry."

Squirrelflight rolled her eyes. "There's a long way to go," she meowed, not sounding as angry as Dovewing had expected. "You need to save your energy. We're going to hunt now and then rest."

"But I'm not sleepy!" Foxleap protested, popping his head out of the willow screen beside Dovewing. "I could run forever."

Squirrelflight just heaved a long sigh and stalked away. Cautiously Dovewing extended her senses until she found a vole scuffling under the bank of the stream she had just crossed. Setting her paws down as light as leaves falling, she crept up on it. *It has no idea that I'm here,* she thought. *I guess the prey in these woods aren't used to cats hunting.*

Reaching the edge of the stream, she pounced and

straightened up with the vole in her jaws. Glancing around, she spotted Jayfeather sitting on the bank a little farther upstream. "Here," she meowed, padding over and dropping the vole at his paws. "I can easily catch more."

"Thanks. And we need to talk."

Dovewing nodded, then remembered that Jayfeather couldn't see her. "Okay. Just wait for me to find some more prey."

Within a few heartbeats she had located a thrush pecking at the ground near the foot of a beech tree. This was a harder bit of stalking than the vole, she reflected as she slid across the forest floor, alert for any twitching grass or crackling leaf that might betray her presence. She leaped on the thrush from a fox-length away, slamming both her forepaws down on it and snapping its neck.

When she returned to Jayfeather, she spotted Squirrelflight and Foxleap sharing a squirrel nearby. Dovewing padded past them and sat beside Jayfeather, taking a hungry bite of her fresh-kill. "What do you want to say?" she mumbled with her mouth full.

Jayfeather was eating the vole with quick, neat bites. He swallowed before replying. "You need to cast your senses ahead and find the mountain cats as soon as you can."

"I know." Irritation swelled up inside Dovewing, and she had to stop her tail from twitching. "Give me a chance, Jayfeather. I need time to get used to being out here."

Jayfeather grunted. "Don't take too long."

Annoying furball, Dovewing thought as she finished her

thrush and curled up for a nap. Then she reminded herself that all the weight of this expedition lay on Jayfeather's skinny shoulders; it wasn't surprising that he was getting impatient. *I'll do my best,* she promised silently.

Sending out her senses again, she explored the woodland: Small creatures were scuffling in the grass; a couple of foxes were asleep in their den. *Let's hope they stay asleep.* Farther into the woodland the stream grew wider, and by the time it reached the other side there were pools deep enough for fish.

It's good here. I wish Ivypool were with me, she thought drowsily as she sank into sleep.

Heartbeats later, it seemed, Squirrelflight was poking a paw into her side. "Come on. It's time to go."

Dovewing staggered to her paws and blinked sleep out of her eyes. Though the sky was cloudy, she guessed it was just past sunhigh. Foxleap was arching his back in a long stretch while Jayfeather waited, impatiently tearing at the grass with his claws.

Following the stream, Squirrelflight led the way to the other side of the wood. The trees ended in an untidy border of bramble and hazel bushes. Beyond them stretched a dusty slope leading into a valley. Dovewing spotted Twoleg nests in the distance, and made sure that her senses were closed down so she didn't pick up any of the Twoleg racket. On the other side of the valley were more hills covered in trees. Above them, gray peaks rose into the sky. At first Dovewing thought that she was looking at some sort of weird clouds, until Squirrelflight pointed at them with her tail.

"There. The mountains."

"That's where we're going?" Foxleap's tone was a mixture of excitement and apprehension. "They're *huge!*"

And we have to climb them? Dovewing didn't speak—she didn't want Squirrelflight thinking she was scared again—but she suddenly felt very small and insignificant.

"Last time we came, we spent the night here," Squirrelflight meowed with a glance at the sky. "But I think we can go on a bit longer." She led the way down the slope and into the valley. A few horses were cropping the sparse grass; they were smaller than the ones Dovewing had seen at the horseplace, and their pelts were shaggier. They stood under a tree, their tails swinging as they watched the cats with curious eyes. But to Dovewing's relief none of them came closer.

Just beyond the horses was a single Twoleg nest, surrounded by a wall of gray stone. As the patrol padded past, a furious hiss came from the top of the wall above their heads. Dovewing looked up to see a fat ginger kittypet, its back arched and its fur bristling.

"Get out of here!" it snarled. "This is my place!"

"Oh really?" Foxleap spun around to face the kittypet, ready to leap up onto the wall. "You want to prove it, kittypet?"

"No!" Squirrelflight thrust herself in front of Foxleap. "Calm down. We're not looking for trouble."

"But it's a kittypet!" Foxleap protested. "I could beat it with one paw!"

"Come up here and try!" the kittypet yowled. "You've no

business here, flea-pelts!"

"Are you going to let it talk to us like that?" Foxleap asked, outraged.

It was Jayfeather who replied. "Use the sense you were born with, Foxleap. If you get hurt, what am I supposed to do for you out here? Do we know where the nearest cobweb is? Can I find horsetail before you bleed to death?"

"But—" Foxleap was still glaring up at the kittypet.

"Ignore it. We keep moving. *Now*," Squirrelflight meowed.

She turned and padded forward. Jayfeather lashed his tail, gesturing to Foxleap to follow. The young warrior obeyed, though not without a last angry hiss at the kittypet. Dovewing brought up the rear.

"Cowards!" the kittypet screeched after them. "Go away and stay away!"

Dovewing was relieved when they hurried out of earshot, but her relief vanished as Jayfeather turned to her.

"I wish you'd given us some warning," he muttered.

"What?" Dovewing couldn't believe he was blaming her for the encounter with the kittypet. "I don't know this area," she defended herself. "I can't just listen for things up ahead, because I have to watch where I'm putting my paws!"

The medicine cat let out an annoyed growl and lapsed into sulky silence.

"I can scout ahead if you like," Foxleap offered.

"Oh, fine." Squirrelflight's tone was sarcastic. "And then we arrive to find you've got into a fight. No thanks."

"I won't, honestly," Foxleap promised.

"No." Now Squirrelflight sounded calmer. "I trust you to obey orders, Foxleap, but it's better if we stay together."

The patrol walked on. Not much later, the line of a hedge crossed their path, the thorny bushes gray and bare, with grass tangled at their roots.

"We go through here," Squirrelflight explained, "and cross the field beyond. But stay in the shelter of the hedge. It's safer."

Jayfeather murmured agreement. "We're near the farm where Lionblaze and Hollyleaf had trouble with dogs," he meowed. "Let's keep a good lookout." He gave Dovewing a hard gaze as he spoke.

Squirrelflight led the way along the hedge until they came to a gap between two bushes, big enough for a cat to squeeze through.

"Dovewing, you go first," Jayfeather ordered.

"Who's leading this patrol, Jayfeather?" Squirrelflight inquired. Turning to Dovewing, she added, "Okay, but be careful."

Dovewing knew why Jayfeather had chosen her. She was already sending a tendril of her special senses through the hedge and into the field beyond. *No dogs. But some other weird animals . . . oh, I know! Sheep.* She remembered seeing them in the distance on her visit to WindClan. *They won't do us any harm.*

Flattening herself on her belly, she crawled through the gap, feeling thorns rake through the fur on her back. Rising to her paws on the other side, she found herself facing two big white woolly animals, with sharp hooves and placid, incurious faces.

It feels strange seeing them so close, she thought. *They look a bit mouse-brained.*

"Dovewing?" Squirrelflight's voice came anxiously through the hedge. "Are you okay?"

"Fine!" Dovewing replied. "You can come through."

Jayfeather appeared next, shaking his ruffled pelt as he rose to his paws and stepped into the field. Foxleap followed him, and lastly Squirrelflight, panting as she pulled herself through the clustering thorns.

"See?" she mewed triumphantly as she straightened up. "I'm not stuck!" Then she looked disconcerted.

It's like she was talking to a cat who isn't here, Dovewing thought.

Shaking her head as if to clear it, Squirrelflight led the patrol along the line of the hedge. The field was huge; Dovewing couldn't even see the other side. *Everything's so big here,* she thought, suppressing a shiver. *I can't even see the edges of the sky.*

Suddenly loud barking clattered into her ears. She froze, astonished for a heartbeat that the rest of the patrol were quietly plodding on. The scent of dog filled her nostrils. Then she realized that her special senses were giving her advance warning. "Dog!" she yowled. "Take cover!"

Squirrelflight whipped around, gazing across the field. "Where?"

"Over there."

As Dovewing stretched out her tail to point, a dog appeared at the crest of a gentle rise in the middle of the field. Yapping loudly, it raced toward the cats, its tail flying and the wind ruffling its black-and-white pelt.

"Fox dung!" Squirrelflight hissed. "Dovewing, Foxleap, get Jayfeather into the hedge."

Foxleap was already pushing Jayfeather into the bushes. Dovewing spotted a branch where the thorns weren't quite so thick, and slid into the hedge beside Jayfeather. "Put your paws there," she ordered, guiding him with her tail. "Now climb!"

As Jayfeather hauled himself upward, spitting annoyance, Dovewing glanced back to see Squirrelflight standing with her back to the hedge. Her fur was fluffed out so that she looked twice her size; her back was arched and she was snarling as the dog galloped closer.

"Stay back, mange-pelt!" she growled.

Safe for the moment in the tangle of bushes, Dovewing admired Squirrelflight's courage. *She thought of Jayfeather first,* she mused, remembering the stories of how the ginger warrior had raised Jayfeather and his littermates as if they were her own, even though Leafpool was their real mother.

Squirrelflight still feels as if she is their mother, Dovewing realized with a pang of sympathy. *Even now.*

Peering out through the thorny branches, she saw that the dog had halted in front of Squirrelflight, letting out a flurry of excited yelps but not making any move to attack. *StarClan, please make it go away.*

"Oh, no!" Foxleap's voice broke in on her prayer.

Dovewing peered out again and saw another dog crest the rise and bound across the field toward them. *Two of them! They're bound to attack now.*

Squirrelflight stayed on guard, and Dovewing started to struggle out of the thorns again to help her. But before she cleared the hedge, the second dog halted beside the first and started barking at him. Noticing that his muzzle was gray with age, Dovewing realized that the second dog was much older. "He sounds like a mentor telling off an apprentice!" she whispered to Foxleap.

The younger dog crouched low to the ground and let out a whimper. After a few heartbeats, while all the cats waited tensely, both dogs turned and ran off across the field. They started to run after the scattered sheep, herding them into a flock.

"He did!" Foxleap's eyes were sparkling with amusement. "He said, 'Leave those cats alone, you stupid furball, and get on with the job!'"

Sighing with relief, Dovewing clambered out of the hedge, while Foxleap helped Jayfeather down. The medicine cat emerged into the open with a grunt of indignation, craning his neck to pick debris out of his pelt.

"I've got a thorn in my pad," he muttered. "Some cat look for a dock leaf."

Dovewing detected the scent of a clump of dock at the bottom of the hedge and tore off a couple of leaves to give to Jayfeather. While he rubbed the soothing juice on his pad, she sent her senses out after the dogs and the sheep. They had disappeared from view, but she could still track them; the dogs were herding the sheep in a tight cluster to the far end of the field and through a gap into another field. A Twoleg was with them.

"I don't think we'll have any more trouble with them," she mewed.

"I hope you're right." Squirrelflight was smoothing down her pelt. She was the only one of them not to look shaken. "We'll get out of this field and then make camp for the night," the ginger warrior went on. "We could all do with a rest after that."

Dovewing glanced back the way they had come as Squirrelflight set out again along the hedge. Sunlight had broken through a gap in the clouds, bathing the field in scarlet as it went down. Dovewing could still see the range of hills they had crossed, and she tried to picture the lake and the Clans on the far side. Her Clanmates would be returning from the evening patrols and settling down in their dens for the night.

She sent out her senses and felt a shudder deep within her as she discovered that for the first time she couldn't connect with the world she had left behind. There were too many sounds, too many impressions in between.

I'm a long, long way from home.

CHAPTER 10

Ivypool blinked open her eyes to see the pale light of the Dark Forest all around her. She was curled up in the shade of an elder bush, its leaves casting dark patterns on her silver-white fur. Yawning, she scrambled to her paws and slid out. The trees clustered close together here, their branches entwined over Ivypool's head. It was a relief not to be able to see the starless sky, always the most frightening reminder that she wasn't in ThunderClan.

"But it still feels a long, long way from home," she muttered.

Tasting the air, she picked up the scent of many cats, and heard voices coming faintly from among the trees several fox-lengths away. Ivypool padded in that direction and found herself on the edge of a clearing. Halting, she peered out from the shelter of a clump of bracken. Hawkfrost stood in the center with a ragged circle of younger cats around him. Ivypool recognized Tigerheart and Breezepelt, and a white RiverClan she-cat whose name she couldn't remember. Others weren't familiar at all.

Hawkfrost's ice-blue eyes shone in the pallid light. "In a battle, you won't be fighting one-on-one," he meowed. "Cats will come at you from all directions, and you have to be ready. Now, I want all of you to attack me at once."

"All of us?" Breezepelt sounded disbelieving.

"That's what I said." Hawkfrost's voice had an edge. "I'll take you on by myself later, if you want."

"No, that's fine, Hawkfrost," Breezepelt answered hastily.

Mouse-brain! Ivypool thought.

"Okay." Hawkfrost's icy gaze traveled over the group of younger cats. "Attack—now!"

For a moment Ivypool lost sight of the dark tabby warrior as he was buried under a squirming heap of screeching, yowling cats. Then his head reappeared, as if he was trying to swim in a lake of fur. In spite of her dislike of Hawkfrost, Ivypool drew in a breath of admiration as he recovered his paws, lashing out at his attackers. His legs were a blur of motion. His jaws seemed to be everywhere, snapping and tearing. First one, then another of the attacking cats reared back, until Hawkfrost stood alone once again, ruffled and panting but with no injuries that Ivypool could see.

That was awesome, she admitted reluctantly. Almost against her will, her paws were itching to learn how Hawkfrost had managed that.

"Now," the tabby warrior went on when he had caught his breath, "who can tell me what you've learned today?"

"Stay away from your claws," Tigerheart muttered, licking one bleeding paw.

A murmur of amusement rose from the young cats, but Hawkfrost didn't share it. "Anything *useful*?" he prompted.

The white RiverClan warrior raised her tail. "It looked as if you were fighting with all four paws," she mewed.

"Good, Icewing." Hawkfrost gave her an approving nod. "That's exactly what I was doing."

"But how?" another cat demanded.

"Watch, and I'll show you. I'll do it slowly." Hawkfrost balanced on his hind paws and reached out with his forepaws, claws extended. Then with a swift movement he raked them downward. The moment his forepaws touched the ground, he struck out with his hind paws; any cat unlucky enough to be behind him would have received a blow hard enough to knock them to the ground. "Like that," he finished. He repeated the move, faster this time. "Now you try."

Watching the Clan cats practice, Ivypool realized that there were more of them than she had ever seen at one time in the Dark Forest. *So many!* she thought, her belly tight with apprehension. As well as Tigerheart, his Clanmates Redwillow and Ratscar were there, Sunstrike from WindClan, and a RiverClan apprentice with the white warrior Icewing.

"I always thought Ratscar looked a bit shifty," Ivypool muttered under her breath. "I'm not surprised *he's* here. And Breezepelt has always been an annoying lump of fur. But I sort of liked Sunstrike when I met her at Gatherings, and Icewing looks friendly. What are they doing here?"

What am I doing here? she reminded herself. *I'm a spy. So maybe some of these cats are spies for their Clans as well.*

But judging by the eagerness with which they were practicing Hawkfrost's moves, all the young cats wanted to be there for the same reasons as Ivypool first had: to train to be better warriors than their Clans could make them, to be the best they could at fighting and defending their home.

Ivypool knew that if she stayed much longer hiding in the bracken, some cat would scent her. She didn't want to be accused of skulking around. *Even if that's what I'm doing!* Emerging from the bracken clump, she skirted the training cats and padded up to Hawkfrost, giving him a polite nod as she halted in front of him. "Greetings," she mewed.

Hawkfrost's eyes were chips of ice. "You're late," he snapped.

"Sorry. I found it hard to get to sleep."

The dark tabby twitched his ears. "Is your Clan not working you hard enough?" he inquired, his voice a menacing purr. "We can soon take care of that." He raised his voice. "Cats of the Dark Forest!"

At once the cats stopped what they were doing and gathered around him again. Hawkfrost surveyed them approvingly. "Well done," he meowed. "Now you need a chance to practice your new skill in battle. Ivypool is ready to help you. Strike!"

He leaped out of the circle as the Dark Forest cats converged on Ivypool. She hardly had time for a protesting screech before Breezepelt was on her. He tried the balance-and-slash part of Hawkfrost's move, but Ivypool sprang backward and he missed, losing his balance and striking the ground so hard that he staggered.

"Tough, mange-pelt!" Ivypool snarled.

Claws raked down her back; she tried to spin around but another cat landed on top of her and she fell to the ground, the breath driven out of her body as the other cat pressed her down. She saw Tigerheart's amber eyes a mouse-length from her own.

"I'll teach you to attack my brother!" he growled.

Ivypool lashed out with her hind paws, battering at Tigerheart's belly. He rolled away, catching her blow over the ear as he did so. Another cat replaced him, and yet another had teeth fixed in her tail. Ivypool could scarcely move. The vicious yowls and caterwauls were so loud they hurt her ears.

I'm fighting for my life!

Suddenly a shadow fell across the battling cats. The screeching was abruptly cut off. Ivypool felt the weight that was pinning her down vanish. She scrambled to her paws, briefly blinded by blood that trickled down from a scratch above her eye. Swiping at it with a paw, she looked up to see Brokenstar standing at the edge of the clearing. Another cat stood behind him in the shadows.

"Don't let me interrupt," Brokenstar meowed.

Hawkfrost took a pace toward him, dipping his head respectfully. "Welcome, Brokenstar. Can we do anything for you?"

"The question should be, what can I do for you?" the former ShadowClan leader replied. "I have a new apprentice for you to meet." He paced forward into the center of the clearing, and the cat behind him followed. As the brown tabby emerged into the light, Ivypool drew in a horrified breath.

"This is Blossomfall of ThunderClan," Brokenstar went on. "Some of you know her already. Blossomfall, these are your new Clanmates."

Blossomfall glanced around nervously. Recognition flared in her eyes as her gaze fell on Ivypool, but she said nothing, just gave her a curt nod. Ivypool guessed she didn't want to give the Dark Forest cats the idea that she would be more loyal to a ThunderClan cat than any of the others.

Some of the Dark Forest cats murmured greetings to Blossomfall, but none of them said anything more. Ivypool recoiled from how false everything was in the Dark Forest. *Are all the cats here supposed to be a Clan? We don't behave like one! And how can another ThunderClan cat be here? ThunderClan cats are loyal!*

"So," Hawkfrost drawled, "are you going to show us what this new cat is made of, Brokenstar?"

In answer, the ShadowClan cat beckoned to Ratscar with his tail. "Fight," he rasped.

Ratscar had a torn ear from his bout with Hawkfrost, but he didn't hesitate. He hurled himself at Blossomfall, who was so surprised by the sudden attack that she let him carry her off her paws. Ratscar let out a screech of triumph and slammed one paw down on her throat. Ivypool watched, her belly churning with tension, as Blossomfall lashed out with her hind paws and managed to throw Ratscar off. While he still lay on the ground she darted past him and got in a soft blow to his side before she spun around and waited for his next move.

You have to unsheathe your claws! Ivypool thought anxiously. *This isn't a ThunderClan training exercise.*

Ratscar crouched and leaped for Blossomfall; she dived underneath him, but at the last moment he twisted in the air and landed on her haunches, sinking his teeth into the base of her tail. Blossomfall yowled in pain and shock. The ShadowClan warrior had pinned her down again, and this time Blossomfall couldn't free herself. She struck out blindly at Ratscar's head and shoulders, but Ivypool could tell that her blows were growing weaker.

Ivypool couldn't watch her Clanmate being torn to pieces by the bigger, more experienced ShadowClan cat. She darted forward, thrusting her shoulders against Ratscar and rolling him off Blossomfall, raking his ears with her claws as she did so. Ratscar turned on her with a disbelieving snarl as Blossomfall stumbled to her paws.

"Stop!" Brokenstar's voice rang out across the clearing before Ratscar could strike another blow.

All three cats froze as the black cat paced across the open ground to join them. Dismissing Ratscar with a flick of his ears, he loomed over Ivypool and fixed her with a baleful amber gaze. "Just what do you think you were doing?" His voice was low, but the menace in it made Ivypool tremble from ears to paws. "What gives you the right to interfere?"

Striving not to show how frightened she was, Ivypool lifted her head and returned glare for glare. "We're loyal to one another, right?" A gush of genuine anger began to drive out her fear. "Should we stand by like cowards and let one another be defeated in battle?"

Brokenstar narrowed his eyes; every hair on his pelt was proclaiming his distrust of her. "You saved your Clanmate," he pointed out.

"Here, they are all my Clanmates," Ivypool retorted.

StarClan, let him believe me! "I don't see why an apprentice should be lost on her first visit."

Brokenstar stood still for a moment more, his gaze boring into her, then let out a snort and stepped aside. Ivypool was left facing Blossomfall.

"You didn't have to do that," the tortoiseshell warrior hissed, smoothing her ripped fur. "I could have beaten Ratscar in the end."

And hedgehogs can fly, Ivypool thought. Turning away, she spotted a brown tom in the group of Dark Forest cats and recognized him by his one black ear.

"Antpelt!" she exclaimed, bounding over to him. "I didn't see you there. It's great that you're okay."

The WindClan warrior's wounds had healed, leaving long scars that sliced across his back and throat, but he looked strong and free from pain. He gave Ivypool a puzzled look. "This is my home now," he meowed.

For a heartbeat Ivypool didn't understand him; then she felt as though she had fallen into an icy stream. "You—you died?" she gasped.

Antpelt shrugged. "You can see it that way if you want."

"Did you choose to come here?" Ivypool asked, trying to keep the shock out of her voice. *I liked Antpelt! He doesn't belong with these evil cats.*

"These are my Clanmates, more than WindClan ever was," Antpelt told her with a trace of regret in his voice. "Where else would I go?"

Ivypool couldn't answer that question. "I'm sorry you

died," she mewed awkwardly.

"This is where I want to be," Antpelt responded with another shrug.

"Ivypool, come here!"

Almost relieved to hear Hawkfrost calling her, Ivypool dipped her head to the WindClan warrior and ran across the clearing to Hawkfrost. A RiverClan apprentice was standing beside him, looking wide-eyed and anxious.

"This is Hollowpaw," Hawkfrost told her. "He's new. Teach him a move or two, will you?"

"Sure," Ivypool replied. She was pleased that Hawkfrost didn't stay to watch, but padded across the clearing to where Tigerheart and Sunstrike were beginning a practice bout.

"Hi, Hollowpaw," she meowed. "Is this your first visit?"

"Second." Hollowpaw squeaked out the word like a kit, and cleared his throat. "I came here in a dream, and talked to Hawkfrost," he added. "I told him how the other apprentices were bullying me, and he said he'd teach me how to stand up to them."

"Oh, yes, we can do that," Ivypool promised, her heart aching for the nervous apprentice. *He doesn't know what he's getting into, but neither did I. Still,* she thought, *teaching him some good fighting techniques won't do him any harm.*

Hollowpaw brightened up as she spoke. "Great! Troutstream and Mossypaw will get a major surprise! Troutstream is even more of a pain in the butt since he was made a warrior," he added.

"For now, you'd better keep your claws sheathed," Ivypool

advised, hoping that Hawkfrost and Brokenstar wouldn't notice. *I've been in enough trouble for one night.* "Okay," she continued briskly, "I'm a fox coming to attack the RiverClan camp. What are you going to do?"

In response, Hollowpaw flung himself at her, his teeth bared in a snarl and his paws outstretched, leaving himself completely open to attack. Ivypool sidestepped, hooked his paws out from under him, and pinned him to the ground with one paw on his shoulder and another on his belly. Hollowpaw squirmed helplessly underneath her.

Great StarClan! What do they teach them in RiverClan?

Aloud, she mewed, "And now I'm a fox that's going to carry you off to my den and eat you." She released the apprentice, who scrambled to his paws and stood with his head bowed, front claws scraping the ground in his embarrassment.

"Sorry," he mumbled.

"Don't be." Ivypool glanced over her shoulder to make sure that Hawkfrost and Brokenstar were still out of earshot. "You're here to learn, after all. Now you be the fox, and I'll show you what you should have done."

She taught Hollowpaw a fairly basic move, showing him how to dart in, rake the enemy with his claws, and dart out of range again. "Remember that a fox or—StarClan forbid— a badger is much bigger and heavier than you are. Brute strength won't get you anywhere. You have to be fast and clever. Try it."

Hollowpaw sprang at her with an eager look in his eyes, lashed at her side with a sheathed paw, and bounced away again. "Like that?"

"Very good. Again."

While the apprentice practiced, Ivypool shot another glance at Brokenstar and Hawkfrost. They had split up and were padding around the clearing, watching the other practice bouts. *Just don't come over here, okay?*

She had called a halt, and was starting to explain another move to Hollowpaw, when she heard Hawkfrost's voice. "Ivypool!"

Oh, no!

But when Ivypool spun around, the tabby warrior was beckoning all the training cats into the center of the clearing. Ivypool heaved a sigh of relief as she realized that the session was over.

"You've all done well," Hawkfrost meowed when the cats were gathered around him. "Especially you, Blossomfall," he added, giving the new ThunderClan recruit an approving nod. "That leap-and-twist is coming on nicely."

Blossomfall's eyes shone with pride. "Thanks, Hawkfrost," she mewed, ducking her head to the Dark Forest warrior.

"I think you're going to fit in here really well," Hawkfrost told her.

With a sinking heart, Ivypool let her gaze travel around the circle of lean, muscled, battle-hungry warriors. *Oh, StarClan help us,* she thought. *The Dark Forest is trying to recruit an army of loyal warriors from inside all the Clans—and they're succeeding!*

CHAPTER 11

Dovewing halted, her gaze going up and up. She thought that the stretch of snow-covered slopes and jagged rocks would never come to an end, but finally she saw the topmost peaks crisply outlined against a pale blue sky. Clouds drifted around the summit.

"I don't believe it!" she breathed.

"It's just . . . just awesome!" Foxleap's voice was the squeak of a startled kit.

"The mountains are pretty amazing, especially when you first see them," Squirrelflight agreed, coming to stand beside the two younger cats. "I'll never forget my first visit."

"Nor will I." Jayfeather's neck fur was rising and he spat out the words as if he had unexpectedly bitten into crow-food. "It's cold and windy and hard underpaw up there, but we have to go, so we may as well keep moving."

It was the third sunrise since they had left the lake. The sky was clear, but Dovewing fluffed up her fur against the icy wind that blew down from the peaks. "How do cats live up there?" she asked. "Is there any prey?"

"Not that you'd notice," Jayfeather retorted.

138

"Of course there's prey," Squirrelflight meowed, with an exasperated glance at the medicine cat. "But it's different, and there are different ways of hunting. You'll see." Waving her tail, she set off with Jayfeather just behind her. Dovewing exchanged a wide-eyed glance with Foxleap and followed. Their path led them into gently rolling foothills, covered with rough moorland grass and the tough, springy stems of heather. Rocky outcrops poked through the thin soil.

"This feels like WindClan territory," Foxleap grumbled. "I don't like it."

Dovewing murmured agreement. She was uneasy without the cover of trees and she missed the dense, prey-scented undergrowth of the forest. "At least we can see if anything is trying to creep up on us," she pointed out.

Sending out her senses, alert for danger, she encountered nothing but the small sounds of distant, hidden prey and the trickle of streams. A harsh cry rang out from overhead; Dovewing looked up to see a bird hovering high above. She didn't recognize the wide wingspan, but it felt vaguely threatening.

"Eagle," Squirrelflight mewed. "We'll see a lot of those where we're going. We'll need to watch out, because they're big enough to attack a cat."

Dovewing shivered. *What sort of place is this, where the birds are dangerous?*

The cats trekked through the hills for the rest of that day, with only a short stop at sunhigh. Squirrelflight and Foxleap, working together, caught a rabbit, which all four cats shared in quick, uneasy bites. Gradually the slope grew steeper and the grass thinned out, until the cats were toiling over rock with only tufts of grass and scrawny bushes rooted in cracks. The sun was going down, casting stretched-out shadows ahead of them and flooding the snowy mountain slopes with scarlet light.

I hope we find shelter before it gets dark, Dovewing thought.

Squirrelflight led them along a narrow track that twisted among sharp-sided rocks, where snow still drifted in the hollows, then across an open stretch of ground covered with big, smooth boulders. The cats had to scramble over them, Jayfeather spitting with annoyance because he kept slipping, unable to see where he was putting his paws. At the other side of the boulders, snow lay deeply in a dip in the ground. At the bottom was a pool of water, frozen at the edges, with snow-laden grass growing more thickly around the edges.

"Great, a drink!" Foxleap exclaimed, bounding forward. "My tongue feels as dry as these rocks."

"Watch out!" Squirrelflight warned.

Following Foxleap more slowly, Dovewing picked up a powerful scent of cats; her paw steps led her across the strongest part, and she realized it must be a border like the ones that separated the forest territories.

"We're on Tribe territory now," Squirrelflight explained, satisfaction in her voice as she added, "They're still keeping the border markers fresh."

All four cats padded up to the water to drink, but as Dovewing stretched out a paw to break the thin ice at the edge and lap up the first cold drops, a yowl split the air behind her.

"Intruders!"

At the same moment a body slammed into her, carrying her off her paws; she hit the ground at the edge of the pool, throwing up droplets from her flailing paws. Sliding out her claws, she scrambled up, tail lashing, to see a black tom, no bigger than an apprentice, staring at her with undisguised hostility.

"Get off our territory!" he spat.

"Wait—" Squirrelflight yowled.

"Dark! Stop!"

A gray-and-white she-cat emerged from behind a boulder halfway up the slope on the other side of the pool, followed by a dark tabby tom and another young cat, a she-cat with a gray speckled pelt.

"But they're trespassing!" Dark, the black tom, protested.

"No, they're not." The she-cat stalked down the slope to stand beside Dark, and gave him a light cuff over one ear. "They are not intruders, they're guests." She turned to Squirrelflight, surprise in her voice and the set of her ears, and added more warmly, "Squirrelflight, it's good to see you again—and Jaypaw."

"Jay*feather*," the medicine cat corrected her with a twitch of his ears.

"It's Wing Shadow Over Water, isn't it?" Squirrelflight stepped forward to touch noses with the gray she-cat. "And Sheer Path Beside Waterfall," she added with a nod to the dark tabby. "This is Dovewing, and this is Foxleap."

Dovewing dipped her head in greeting, eyeing the Tribe

cats curiously. They were much smaller than the Clan cats, and they all looked as if they could do with a good meal.

"This to-be," Wing went on, pointing with her tail toward the black tom, "the one who has no more sense than to attack four cats all by himself, is Dark Shadow on Water, and this is Rain That Passes Quickly."

The gray speckled cat ducked her head politely.

"To-be?" Dovewing murmured.

"Like our apprentices," Jayfeather hissed into her ear.

"No cat expected to see you here again," Sheer meowed to Squirrelflight. "Are the Clans in trouble? Do you need help?"

"No, everything's fine," Squirrelflight purred. "We just wanted to pay a visit to our old friends."

Wing twitched her whiskers, and Dovewing figured she had guessed that the Clan cats had more reason than that for trekking so far in leaf-bare, but all she said was "We'd better take you to the cave. It will be dark soon."

Following the Tribe cats, the ThunderClan patrol headed deeper into the mountains. The sun had disappeared, and the last streaks of scarlet were fading from the sky. Twilight gathered, making the path even harder to see, but the Tribe cats bounded confidently forward, standing poised on the top of rocks as they waited for the Clan cats to catch up. Wind whined among the peaks; Dovewing blinked as it drove showers of ice into her eyes.

"Why any cat wants to live in such a StarClan-forsaken place as this," Jayfeather panted as he hauled himself over a boulder, "I'll never understand." He hesitated, crouching on the rock; the ground ahead was uneven and Dovewing realized that he could injure himself if he jumped down in the wrong place.

"Wait a moment," she mewed. She let herself drop onto a patch of snow and checked that it was clear of sharp edges. "Jump over here," she instructed Jayfeather. "Follow my voice."

Jayfeather leaped, landing awkwardly; Dovewing steadied him as he staggered. "Thanks," he mumbled.

As they began to toil up a long slope, following Squirrelflight and Foxleap, who had drawn a little way ahead, Dovewing picked up a new sound: a deep, continuous roar that grew louder with every paw step they took.

"What's that noise?" she asked Jayfeather.

"Oh, you can hear it already?" Jayfeather spoke in a low voice, and Dovewing guessed that without knowing it she had been using her special senses. "It's the waterfall. That's where the Tribe of Rushing Water lives."

Soon all the cats could hear the rumble of the falls. They scrambled up one last steep slope and came out onto a flat stretch of rock where a river flowed past between boulders. Wind scoured across it, buffeting Dovewing's fur and threatening to sweep her off her paws, but the sound of it was drowned by the deafening thunder of the cascade.

Dovewing padded to the edge of the cliff, where water slid over the lip of the rocks in a smooth curve. "Wow!" she exclaimed to Sheer, who stood beside her, one paw stretched out as if warning her to be careful. "You really live here?"

"Our cave is behind the waterfall," he explained with pride in his voice.

"Awesome!" *We actually have to walk behind that wall of foaming water?* she thought privately. *That's no place for cats to live!*

Sheer guided the Clan cats down the rocks beside the falls. The surface was wet and slippery; Dovewing tried to dig her claws into the hard surface and waved her tail wildly for balance. Her heart beat fast as she fought not to show these strange cats how scared she was. Jayfeather struggled down between Wing and Squirrelflight, grunting with every paw step.

Finally, every cat stood on a narrow path that led behind the waterfall. Dovewing walked along it carefully, keeping to Sheer's paw steps, with the rock face on one side and the endlessly falling water on the other. She shivered as spray soaked her fur.

By now it was almost completely dark. The waterfall was a screen of rippling gray, shot through with silver where it reflected the moon and the slowly emerging stars. As Dovewing padded forward, a dark space opened up on the opposite side from the water; Sheer vanished into it and his voice came back to Dovewing, echoing strangely.

"Welcome to the Tribe of Rushing Water!"

Blinking, Dovewing entered the cave, followed by Squirrelflight, Jayfeather, and Foxleap, with the other Tribe cats bringing up the rear. Shaking her pelt dry, she gazed at the soaring cave walls, the roof lost in shadows high above her head. At the far end, two tunnels led away into darkness. Cats were crouching on ledges, staring down at the new arrivals. Others stalked around one another on the floor of the cave; it looked to Dovewing as if they were in the middle of some kind of training exercise. All of them froze as the visitors halted, bunched together, near the entrance. Dovewing's pelt prickled.

Almost at once a voice yowled from the other side of the cavern. "I don't believe it! Squirrelflight! Jaypaw!"

"Jay*feather*," he muttered.

A dark gray tom, longer legged than the other cats, bounded out of the shadows and skidded to a halt in front of Squirrelflight. "It's great to see you again," he meowed.

"Crag." Squirrelflight's voice was a warm purr. "It's great to be here."

More cats started to crowd around, offering greetings and asking questions about the Clans. Dovewing's head began to spin; Squirrelflight tried to introduce every cat, but it was hard to remember, or to tell them all apart when they looked so much like one another: small and skinny, and mostly with gray-brown pelts.

And they have such long names! No wonder they cut them short.

"Remember when we ambushed you the first time you came here?" An old cat named Talon was speaking to Squirrelflight. "I nearly ripped your pelt off, but you managed to convince us you were on our side."

"You might have been surprised at who did the pelt-ripping." To Dovewing's astonishment Squirrelflight butted the old tabby affectionately in the shoulder. "And we all fought on the same side against Sharptooth."

Talon nodded, blinking sadly, then shook his head as if he was banishing painful memories. "Where's Brook?" he asked, looking around. Pushing his way to the edge of the cats clustered around the visitors, he called out, "Brook, come see who's here!"

A graceful tabby she-cat emerged from a corner near the back of the cave, herding two tiny kits in front of her.

Squirrelflight's eyes widened, her green gaze sparkling. "Brook! You have kits!"

Brook padded up to Squirrelflight and touched noses with her, purring as if she would never stop. She parted her jaws to drink in Squirrelflight's scent. "Welcome back," she mewed, then added proudly, "This is Lark That Sings at Dawn, and Pine That Clings to Rock. Lark looks like her father, don't you think?"

"I'm so happy for you and Stormfur!" Squirrelflight gasped. She bent her head to give each of the kits a sniff.

The two little creatures looked up at her with wide, curious eyes. "Have you come to join the Tribe?" Lark mewed.

Squirrelflight shook her head. "No, we're just visiting."

"You should stay," Pine told her, his stumpy tail quivering eagerly. "Tribe cats are the best!"

"I'll need some advice from you about raising kits," Brook went on to Squirrelflight. "Your three turned out so well!"

Dovewing stiffened, waiting for Squirrelflight's response. For a moment it looked as if Squirrelflight didn't know what to say. Then she dipped her head. "You seem to be managing fine, without any help from me," she mewed. "They're lovely kits—so strong and healthy. Where's Stormfur?" she added, clearly glad to change the subject.

"On border patrol," Brook explained. "He should be back anytime now."

"Yes, how are the patrols working out?" Squirrelflight asked. "Are you managing to defend the border against those rival cats?"

"It's hard work," a black tom replied; Dovewing remembered that his name was Screech of Angry Owl. "It doesn't leave much time for catching prey when cats are tired from patrolling the border."

"But you don't have to go out all the time," Foxleap protested, glancing around at the cave thronged with cats. "There are loads of you. Why don't some of you patrol the border while others go hunting? That's what we do."

"The Tribe doesn't work like that," Squirrelflight explained. "They have two different kinds of cats, prey-hunters who catch prey and cave-guards who protect the prey-hunters. So more cats are needed to catch prey."

"Yes, but they still could—"

Dovewing never found out what Foxleap was going to suggest. Her acute hearing picked up a soft paw step coming from the back of the cave. A voice rasped, "What are they doing here this time?"

Spinning around, Dovewing saw the crowd of cats part to reveal a skinny old tabby tom. He was no taller than a new apprentice, and his bony haunches strained at his patchy fur.

As he paced forward, Dovewing was shocked to hear the uneven beating of his heart and his labored breathing. A whiff of scent like rotting crow-food came from his open jaws as he halted in front of Squirrelflight.

This cat is dying! Dovewing realized in alarm.

"Stoneteller . . ." Brook stammered. "Look who came to visit."

"I can see who it is," Stoneteller snapped. "I want to know what they're doing here."

Squirrelflight flashed a glance at Brook as she stepped forward and dipped her head courteously to the old tom. "Greetings, Stoneteller," she meowed. "My Clanmates and I just came to visit. We wanted to see how you're all getting on."

"Do you think we can't survive without you?" Stoneteller growled.

Dovewing could see that Squirrelflight was getting flustered, her claws scraping the hard floor of the cave. "It's not like that—" she began.

Stoneteller cut her off with a snarl deep in his throat and a single lash of his tail. Foxleap's eyes widened; he leaned over to Dovewing and hissed in her ear, "Who made dirt in his fresh-kill?"

Jayfeather stepped forward. Dovewing tensed; the short-tempered medicine cat was bound to make things worse with some cutting remark. Instead, she was surprised by Jayfeather's even tones as he began to speak.

"Nothing is wrong, Stoneteller, believe me. We come in peace, as friends." Waving his tail toward Foxleap and

Dovewing, he added, "We thought it would be a good experience for these two young cats to see how the Tribe lives. We have as much to learn from you as you have learned from us in the past."

Stoneteller let out a snort but didn't challenge the visitors any further.

"Well done, Jayfeather," Squirrelflight whispered.

Wing weaved her way through the cats and dipped her head to Stoneteller. "Healer, may these cats share today's meal?"

"Today's meal?" Foxleap sounded dismayed. "You mean you only eat once a day? Don't you get hungry?"

"Don't you get fat?" a young she-cat countered, looking Foxleap up and down.

Stoneteller gave his permission, though Dovewing could tell he wasn't thrilled. He stood back as Wing and Brook led the visiting cats across the cave and halted in front of a fresh-kill pile.

"Help yourselves," Wing invited.

Following Squirrelflight, Dovewing pulled a bird out of the pile and bit into it hungrily. A heartbeat later she was struggling to swallow. *Great StarClan, that tastes bitter!* She studied the prey carefully; the bird wasn't any kind she had seen before: bigger than the forest birds, with brown feathers and a hooked beak.

"I don't see how any cat could catch a bird like this alone," she murmured, half to herself.

"That's ridiculous!" Dark exclaimed, overhearing her. He blinked at her scornfully. "As if any cat would be expected to hunt alone. Prey-hunters work together; even kits know that. Watch; we'll show you. Here—Rain, Snow!" He called to the other to-be who had met them in the mountains, and another young she-cat with a white pelt. "Snow, you be an eagle."

"Okay." Snow leaped up onto a ledge in the cave wall.

"Rain, be a prey-hunter with me," Dark went on.

"But I'm a cave-guard," Rain objected.

Dark sighed. "So? You can pretend, right? You know what prey-hunters do."

Rain shrugged and crouched at the bottom of a boulder. Dark also dropped into a crouch a couple of tail-lengths away. The two young cats stayed where they were, quite motionless, while Dovewing watched, puzzled.

"They aren't doing anything," Foxleap whispered, looking up from his own prey.

At that moment, Snow dived off her ledge onto the cave floor below. Instantly Dark and Rain pounced in unison, bundling on top of her and slapping her to the ground with their paws when she tried to get up.

"Hey, not so hard!" she yowled.

"What are you doing?" A black she-cat, her belly heavy with kits, glanced over her shoulder with an irritated expression. "You to-bes! This is the time for eating, not for playing."

"Sorry, Night," Rain mumbled.

"We were only showing these strange cats—" Dark protested.

"I know, I know," Night interrupted. "Always excuses. . . . Show them at sunrise, okay?"

Dark ducked his head and yanked a rabbit out of the pile, dragging it away to share with the other to-bes.

"Weird," Dovewing murmured to Foxleap. She felt a pang of homesickness for her Clan, where any cat who was hungry could eat when they felt like it, provided there was enough prey, and no cat told apprentices off for playing, if they'd finished their duties. "The Tribe cats are really strict!"

Foxleap moved closer to her. "Strict *and* weird," he agreed.

When the Clan cats had finished eating, Brook led them across the cavern. "You can sleep here," she announced. Peering around Squirrelflight, Dovewing saw several shallow scoops in the cave floor, lined with feathers. *Those are nests?* she wondered, longing for the soft moss and crackly bracken in her own den in the stone hollow.

Brook's kit Pine leaned over the edge of the biggest scoop and sniffed at the feathers. "That looks really cozy!" he mewed.

"I want to sleep there!" Lark announced, taking a flying leap into the middle of the nest. Feathers swirled up around her and she sneezed as one settled on her nose.

"Certainly not!" Brook exclaimed, her fur fluffing up. "Come out of there *at once*. We have a perfectly good nest of our own."

Lashing her tiny tail, Lark scrambled out with feathers clinging to her pelt. Brook brushed them off with her tail and patted her daughter's fur down again. "Sorry," she murmured to Squirrelflight. "But you know what they're like at this age. Sleep well," she added, as she gathered her kits together with her tail and prodded them away.

"Good night!" Squirrelflight called after her.

Curled up in one of the scoops, Dovewing found it impossible to sleep. The thunder of the waterfall was so loud that it hurt her ears, and there was no way to shut it out. She felt trapped by it; the noise drowned out any other sounds that she might have picked up from beyond it. Never before had she been so closed in by stone and water.

This isn't right, she thought.

Raising her head, she saw that her three Clanmates were already asleep; Jayfeather was twitching uneasily, as if he walked in some ominous dream with the cats of StarClan . . . or in the Dark Forest. Farther away in the cave, she could hear the Tribe cats as they settled down for the night.

"Close your eyes, Lark." Brook's voice. "Or you'll be too tired to play tomorrow."

"Good night, Bird." That was the old tom, Talon.

"Good night," an unfamiliar she-cat's voice replied. "Dream well."

"Snow, if you don't take your paw out of my ear, I'll scratch you!" Dovewing stifled a *mrrow* of amusement at Dark's indignant mutter.

Gradually the voices died away to silence. Dovewing cautiously pulled herself out of her nest and padded across to the cave toward the waterfall. Her paws tingled and she kept casting glances over her shoulder, aware that if any of the Tribe cats spotted her they might think she was spying. But no cat called out to her as she reached the path that led behind the waterfall and slipped along it. The falling water glittered in the moonlight, and as Dovewing emerged onto the rocks beside the pool the spray filled the air with a mist of silver.

It's beautiful, she realized, catching for the first time a glimpse of what kept the Tribe in their inhospitable home.

Climbing with extra care in the darkness, Dovewing hauled herself up the rocks beside the waterfall until she reached the cliff top. She gave herself a good shake to dry her pelt before sitting down and looking around. Her breath snagged in her throat. She was surrounded by mountain peaks streaked with snow, rolling away into the distance as far as she could see. The waterfall was below her now, its roar still louder than thunder, but not making her feel trapped in the way it had when she was inside the cave.

Dovewing cast her senses out over the snowy landscape, her sight and hearing sharpened in the clear air. She could hear the stir of huge birds—*eagles?*—in their twiggy nests on the bare precipices; ice thawing on small streams hidden among the rocks; white-furred hares scuffling among snow and pebbles to find blades of grass. The mountains that seemed so barren were full of tiny lives.

Then Dovewing realized she could hear cats, too. They were too heavy-footed to be Tribe cats; they sprang arrogantly over the rocks, padding up to a Tribe scent marker, and giving it a sniff.

"Ooh, this is the Tribe's border." A mocking mew reached Dovewing's ears. "Should we cross it? I'm shaking in my fur!"

"These cats have bees in their brain," another voice responded. "They think they can keep us out with a barrier of air!"

Dovewing listened, anger growing in her belly as first one cat, then the second, jumped across the border, then back again, and for a third time, ending up inside the Tribe's territory.

"Where are you?" the first cat yowled. "Where's your patrol to drive us out?"

"Hiding like scared rabbits," the second cat meowed. "Let's hunt."

Dovewing heard them padding off in search of prey—prey that belonged to the Tribe. She slid out her claws, scraping them against the rock. Jayfeather and Lionblaze had told her about their previous visit, how they had established the border and made the intruding cats promise to respect it.

What's the point? she wondered angrily. *The other cats don't have any kind of code, so how can we expect them to stay on their side of the boundary?*

A soft paw step sounded behind her; expecting to see a Tribe cat, she rose to her paws and turned. To her surprise, it was Jayfeather.

"How did you get up the rocks?" she asked, her belly twisting as she realized how easily a blind cat could slip and fall into the pool.

"With difficulty," Jayfeather growled, giving himself a shake and sending a mist of spray into the air. With a long sigh he sat down beside Dovewing and waved his tail at the peaks that encircled them. "Amazing, isn't it?" he puffed.

"How do you know?" Dovewing meowed, startled. The

words were hardly out before she answered her own question, guessing that he had walked here in his dreams. "Why are we here?" she added.

"The Tribe has ancestors, too," Jayfeather replied as he wrapped his tail around his paws. "The Tribe of Endless Hunting. I think they have something to tell me—something to do with the prophecy."

"If we truly have the power of the stars in our paws," Dovewing mused aloud, "then maybe we have power over the Tribe, too."

Jayfeather twitched his ears. "I don't think it's as straight-forward as that. Remember that Stoneteller has a lot of power—more than a Clan leader or a medicine cat alone. But I'm convinced that our destiny has something to do with the Tribe."

"We've helped them so much before," Dovewing meowed. "Maybe now it's their turn to help us."

"Maybe," Jayfeather agreed.

As he spoke, Dovewing picked up the sound of another cat scrambling up the rocks, and a broad-shouldered gray tom hauled himself onto the plateau. He padded over to Jayfeather and dipped his head. "Greetings. It's good to see Clan cats again."

"Stormfur." Jayfeather dipped his head in response. "This is Dovewing, Whitewing's kit."

Dovewing blinked, impressed that she was face-to-face with a cat who was almost a legend among the Clans. Born of a ThunderClan father and RiverClan mother, Stormfur had made the journey to the sun-drown-place to meet Midnight, and later had taken part in the Great Journey when the Clans discovered their new home by the lake. But he had loved Brook so much that he had abandoned his Clan to live with her and make his home with the Tribe.

"How are things beside the lake?" Stormfur asked. There was a hunger in his voice, and Dovewing understood that even though he had decided to stay here in the mountains, part of his heart would always be with the Clans.

"Pretty good," Jayfeather replied. "We had a drought last greenleaf, and the lake almost dried up, but Dovewing went with a patrol to bring the water back."

Stormfur's amber eyes shone as he looked at Dovewing. "Well done! That must have been hard."

Dovewing ducked her head. "I was scared most of the time. We had a tree fall into the stone hollow, too," she added, eager to change the subject. "All the dens look very different now."

Stormfur nodded. "And RiverClan?" he asked.

"I think they're okay," Dovewing told him. "But Leopard-star died."

Stormfur bowed his head. "I'm sorry to hear that. She was a great leader." He paused, then continued. "So is Mistystar Clan leader now?"

Dovewing nodded. "She's a great leader, too."

"I can imagine. StarClan made the right choice."

"So who will Stoneteller's successor be?" Jayfeather asked, with an edge to his voice that hinted there was more to the question than Dovewing understood.

Stormfur shook his head. "Stoneteller has refused to name any cat as his successor," he meowed. "You can imagine how the Tribe feels about that."

Dovewing felt puzzled. "Why is that such a problem?"

Stormfur turned to her. "Each Tribe Healer has the same name," he explained. "Teller of the Pointed Stones, or Stoneteller. Usually each future Stoneteller is chosen as a kit, to be mentored by the current Stoneteller for as long as possible. Now the Tribe is afraid that a new Stoneteller won't have time to learn everything before the present Stoneteller dies."

"That means you might not have a leader!" Dovewing exclaimed. She knew that Stoneteller was both leader and medicine cat of his Tribe. How would the Tribe cope without either?

"So what is the Tribe of Endless Hunting doing about this?" Jayfeather asked. "If they—"

Stormfur interrupted him, signaling for silence with a sharp flick of his tail. He crept to the edge of the rock and looked over. Dovewing slid up beside him. Less than a tail-length away, the waterfall thundered down into the pool below.

"Careful," Stormfur warned her softly.

Far below, where the path led behind the water to the cave, a cat had emerged. Dovewing recognized the scrawny shape of Stoneteller. "What's the matter?" she whispered to Stormfur. "Maybe he just wants some peace and fresh air."

Stormfur shook his head. "The Healer *never* leaves the cave," he explained, "except to perform ceremonies here on the cliff top. And there aren't very many of those . . . usually just when a cat dies. He's supposed to stay in the cave the whole time, to receive messages from the Tribe of Endless Hunting."

"He *never* leaves the cave?" Dovewing echoed, suddenly sorry for the fragile old cat imprisoned in those walls of stone and water.

"Never. Especially at night, when the reflections of stars are most vivid. So by coming out now, Stoneteller is defying his ancestors and the ancient laws of his Tribe."

Dovewing looked down at Stoneteller, who was sitting at the edge of the pool, gazing at the mountains. She wondered what he was thinking, and why he was so angry that the Clan cats had come. Would he feel differently if he knew that Jayfeather and Dovewing had been promised the power of the stars?

What if the prophecy means that we have to protect the future of the Tribe as well as the Clans?

CHAPTER 12

Lionblaze jumped onto a fallen tree trunk and arched his back in a long stretch, enjoying the feeling of sunlight on his golden fur. Buds were appearing on the trees, and in the clumps of dead brown bracken, vivid green fronds were beginning to unfurl. The branches seemed full of birdsong, and he could hear the scuffling of small creatures in the undergrowth.

Newleaf is almost here, he thought.

Behind him, his patrol emerged into the open: Cinderheart, ears and whiskers alert for the signs of prey; Toadstep, making more noise than a whole pack of badgers; and Rosepetal bringing up the rear.

"Right." Lionblaze sprang down from the tree into the clearing on the other side. "This is a good place. Firestar asked Cinderheart and me to help you brush up your hunting techniques," he added to the two younger cats.

"Oh, great!" Toadstep gazed at Lionblaze with shining eyes. "Will you teach us some fighting moves, too?"

"Please?" Rosepetal added eagerly.

"Another time, maybe." Cinderheart gave her tail a flick. "Today we're concentrating on hunting. Let's see how much prey we can bring back for the Clan."

Toadstep looked disappointed. "You're the best at fighting," he told Lionblaze. "ThunderClan's so lucky to have you. I don't think you'll ever get hurt!" Brightening, he added, "I'm going to be like that one day. I'll defend my Clan, and none of my enemies will be able to touch me!"

Lionblaze suppressed a sigh. *If he tries to fight the way I do, he'll get seriously injured.* "Toadstep," he began awkwardly, "you need to fight like yourself, not like me or any other cat."

"But you're so good, why wouldn't I want to fight like you?"

Lionblaze's pelt prickled with embarrassment. He cast a glance at Cinderheart, who was watching him with a sympathetic look in her blue eyes.

"Every cat is vulnerable," he persisted. "Every cat has weaknesses. Part of being a good fighter is being aware of that and—"

"Watch this!"

Lionblaze broke off as Toadstep hurled himself at the fallen tree, battering it with his paws, scoring his claws down the bark and grabbing a protruding branch between his teeth.

"Stop!" Lionblaze yowled, bounding over to the younger cat and hauling him away by the scruff. "Throwing yourself into battle like that is the quickest way to get yourself killed."

He stood over the younger warrior, who gazed up at him in shock. Lionblaze felt his anger spilling over, fueled by his resentment of the prophecy that had taken his life and twisted it without giving him any choice. *I'd give up my fighting skills if I could just be an ordinary Clan cat . . . if I could have Cinderheart.*

"Hey, Lionblaze, take it easy." Cinderheart padded over and rested her tail-tip on Toadstep's shoulder. "Toadstep is enthusiastic, that's all." Glancing at the young cat with a glimmer of amusement in her eyes, she added, "But you won't get anywhere by trying to kill a tree."

"Sorry, Lionblaze," Toadstep stammered. "I only wanted to show you . . ."

"I know." Lionblaze twitched his whiskers. "Just remember that every cat has limits, and you need to know what yours are."

Toadstep nodded, withdrawing a pace or two into the clearing, his gaze still on Lionblaze as if he felt that the golden tabby was likely to spring at him without warning.

"Mouse-brained young idiot," Lionblaze murmured to Cinderheart, his voice a soft, frustrated growl. "How do you think I would feel if he got his pelt ripped off trying to be like me?"

Cinderheart nodded understandingly. "You'll sort him out," she mewed.

Warmed by her response, Lionblaze turned back to the two younger warriors. "Right, let's see if we've frightened off all the prey in the forest," he began. "Can you scent anything?"

Toadstep raised his head at once, jaws parted to taste the air, while Rosepetal sniffed around the tangled roots of the fallen tree.

"Squirrel!" Toadstep exclaimed.

"Okay, but don't tell the whole forest," Lionblaze murmured. "The idea is that the prey doesn't know we're here."

Toadstep ducked his head, forepaws scrabbling among the dead leaves. "Sorry. I forgot."

"So where's this squirrel?" Cinderheart asked.

Toadstep pointed with his tail toward a bramble thicket. The squirrel was almost completely hidden by a tangle of tendrils, only the tip of its tail visible. Toadstep had tracked it by its scent alone.

"Well done." Lionblaze gave him an approving nod. "Now let's see your hunter's crouch. Both of you."

Toadstep crouched down, and after a heartbeat's pause Rosepetal padded to his side and joined him. Lionblaze and Cinderheart eyed their stance critically.

"Not bad," Lionblaze told Toadstep, flicking his hindquarters with his tail. "Pull your hind legs in a bit farther. You'll get more power in your pounce that way."

"Rosepetal, that's very good," Cinderheart added. "Your weight's nicely balanced."

"Okay, we'll practice hunting in pairs. Toadstep, it's your squirrel," Lionblaze went on, checking that the animal was still there. "You'll creep up on it. Rosepetal, move over toward that tree"—he angled his ears toward an ivy-covered oak—"so if the squirrel tries to flee that way, you'll be in the right place to catch it."

Rosepetal nodded and began padding toward the oak, while Toadstep slid through the grass. He was almost within striking distance of the squirrel when one of his hind paws brushed against a bracken frond. The squirrel sat up, alert, at the faint rustling sound, then broke away from the thicket and fled across the clearing, straight toward Rosepetal's oak.

Rosepetal reached out, but the squirrel shot past her a mouse-length from her paws and hurled itself up the tree. Rosepetal jumped and spun around, but by then only the shaking tendrils of ivy showed where the prey had gone.

"Fox dung!" Toadstep exclaimed, bounding over in a fury. "Rosepetal, you should have caught that!"

"Rosepetal, you have to focus," Cinderheart admonished.

"Yes, anything could happen at any time." Lionblaze looked sternly at the young warrior. "We have to be ready."

"What could happen here?" Rosepetal flicked her ears dismissively as she looked around at the peaceful forest, the trees covered by the green mist of approaching newleaf. "Even the bees are sleepy!"

Her last few words were drowned by the screech of a cat from somewhere close by. "Help! Dog!"

Lionblaze froze. "That's Bumblestripe!"

"Go!" Cinderheart urged him. When he cast a worried glance at the two younger cats she added, "I'll keep them safe. Just go!"

Lionblaze leaped over the fallen tree and plunged through the undergrowth, back in the direction of the camp. His heart began to pound as he heard the deep-throated barking of a dog, a defiant cat-shriek cutting across it. Bursting out of a clump of bracken, Lionblaze halted at the edge of a clearing where Bumblestripe, his back arched and his pale fur bristling, stood nose-to-nose with a huge black dog.

"Stay back!" Bumblestripe yowled, stretching out one paw

with claws extended. "Stay back or I'll shred your ears!"

The dog's mouth gaped, its tongue lolling out between sharp white fangs. It sprang at Bumblestripe; before Lionblaze could do anything, the young tom darted forward, away from the cover of the brambles behind him, and fled across the clearing with the dog snapping at his paws. Bumblestripe clawed his way up the nearest tree and balanced on the lowest branch, looking down. The dog jumped up at him, yelping; Bumblestripe's dangling tail was no more than a mouselength away from the deadly paws.

Lionblaze charged forward, letting out an earsplitting yowl. The dog stopped jumping and whipped around, fixing its yellow-eyed glare on him.

"Over here, mange-pelt!" Lionblaze jumped as a voice rang out beside him and he turned his head to see Toadstep scrambling to his side. "Come and get us!"

"You were supposed to stay with Cinderheart!" Lionblaze snapped.

Toadstep's eyes were blazing. "I want to help you!"

"Get back!" Lionblaze shouldered the black-and-white tom back into the bracken. "Bumblestripe, you'll be okay," he called to his other Clanmate. "Try to climb a bit higher."

He didn't look to see if Bumblestripe obeyed. All his attention was on the dog. For a moment it had paused, looking baffled, its head swinging from Lionblaze to Bumblestripe and back again. Now it hurtled across the clearing, its jaws wide; Lionblaze could hear its panting breath.

"Stay there!" he hissed at Toadstep, who had lost his balance after Lionblaze shoved him, and was struggling to his paws in the middle of the bracken clump. Leaping out in front of the dog, Lionblaze swerved toward the other side of the clearing, hoping that he could draw it away from his Clanmates.

"No!" Bumblestripe screeched, bouncing on his low branch. "Don't go that way—Briarlight is there!"

"What?" *How could a crippled cat be out in the forest?* He couldn't see Briarlight, but the dog's breath was hot on his tail, and there was no time to ask questions. Lionblaze knew that he could attack the dog and not be hurt, but that would give away too much with Toadstep and Bumblestripe watching. Especially Toadstep: *He has to learn to be more defensive, not just blindly copy me.*

As he doubled back, he spotted Cinderheart and Rosepetal at the edge of the clearing, with wide eyes and identical expressions of horror.

"Briarlight is over there!" Lionblaze yowled, gesturing with his tail.

Cinderheart gasped, then began to work her way around the edge of the clearing. The dog immediately veered away and raced after her with a flurry of excited yelps. Lionblaze hurled himself forward to intercept it, keeping his claws sheathed but brushing past its muzzle so that it picked up his scent and swerved away from the she-cats once again. Plunging into the trees, he led it away from the clearing, racing through the ferns in the direction of the lake, with the dog so close that he could hear the rasp of its breath and the pounding of its paws on the ground. He could have saved himself by climbing a tree, but he was afraid that if he did, the dog would turn back into the clearing where Briarlight was lying defenseless.

He could see the glitter of the lake through the trees ahead. *And what then?* he asked himself. *Do I start swimming?* His heart thumped and his breath became short; a sharp pain pierced his paw as he trod on a thorn, but he still raced on.

A bramble thicket appeared in front of him; Lionblaze leaped over the outlying tendrils. But he had misjudged the leap; one tendril wrapped around his paw and brought him crashing to the ground. With a startled yowl Lionblaze rolled over and over, halting only when he thumped into a tree. He tried to struggle to his paws, but the tendril was still gripping him tightly. The dog pounded into view, its eyes gleaming when it saw he was trapped.

StarClan help me! Lionblaze prayed.

A screech from overhead made him look up. To his astonishment he spotted Toadstep balancing on the branch of a beech tree. *He must have followed us through the forest, like a squirrel!*

The black-and-white tom leaped down in front of the dog, his tail lashing. "Come and get me, flea-pelt!" he challenged.

The dog turned on its haunches, its paws spraying turf and soil as it bore down on Toadstep. Horror at the thought of seeing his Clanmate torn apart gave Lionblaze extra strength. He wrenched himself away from the brambles, leaving tufts of golden fur on the thorns. Racing toward the dog, he caught its tail in his jaws and bit down hard, before turning and fleeing toward the lake.

The dog let out a howl of pain and pounded after him.

Lionblaze glanced over his shoulder and saw it was no more than a tail-length behind, with Toadstep bounding along in the rear.

"Stay back!" Lionblaze yowled, but the young tom ignored his order.

With the dog snapping at his paws, Lionblaze exploded out of the bushes and onto the lakeshore. He thought of flinging himself into the water, but he knew that dogs could swim.

I'll never get away from it!

Then he spotted a male Twoleg a few fox-lengths farther along the shore. He was calling into the trees, and waving a long tendril gripped in one of his forepaws. When he saw the dog, he let out an angry yowl. The dog skidded to a halt, then turned and trotted off in the direction of the Twoleg with its ears down. The Twoleg fastened the tendril to its collar and dragged it away.

Lionblaze watched it go, then circled back and joined Toadstep in the undergrowth at the edge of the shore. "Thanks," he panted, flopping down in a clump of ferns. "It would have got me for sure if you hadn't been there."

Toadstep sank down beside him. "I couldn't leave you to face it alone."

"Exactly." Lionblaze realized that he had a chance to drive home the point he had been trying to make earlier. "It's a good lesson in not trying to tackle enemies by yourself. It's always better to fight in pairs."

The younger warrior nodded, his eyes wide with wonder. "Yeah, but you fell in that patch of brambles, and you still don't have a scratch on you!"

"It's a good thing I have a thick pelt," Lionblaze mewed, glad of the excuse. Glancing at his flanks, he added, "And I think I left most of it on the thorns!"

When Lionblaze and Toadstep returned to the clearing, they found Cinderheart, Bumblestripe, and Rosepetal clustered around Briarlight. The she-cat was lying crookedly beneath a holly bush; Lionblaze guessed that Bumblestripe had shoved her under there when the dog first appeared.

"Has it gone?" Cinderheart asked, swinging around as Lionblaze and Toadstep approached.

Lionblaze nodded. "A Twoleg took it away." Peering under the bush, he called, "Are you okay, Briarlight?"

"I would be, if you'd just get me out of here," Briarlight retorted, sounding fed up and embarrassed.

"We don't want to hurt you," Cinderheart meowed. "We'll get you out now that Lionblaze is here to help."

"Oh, just drag me out like an old stick!" Briarlight snapped. "It's not like you can hurt me any more, can you?"

"Take it easy." Cinderheart reached under the bush to rest a comforting paw on the young she-cat's shoulder.

Briarlight shrugged her off. "I'm going to get into so much trouble!" she wailed. "But I can't stand to be stuck in that den any longer."

"It's my fault," Bumblestripe admitted. "I'm the one who brought you out here."

Lionblaze looked at the young warrior, impressed by his

dedication to his littermate. It must have been a struggle to drag her all the way from the camp.

"I won't let any cat blame you, Bumblestripe," Briarlight insisted, her voice strained and high-pitched. "I talked you into it!"

This isn't getting us anywhere, Lionblaze thought. Feeling uncomfortable in the face of so much emotion, he added, "We need to get both of you back to camp."

Working together, Lionblaze and Cinderheart gently drew Briarlight out of the holly bush. Lionblaze crouched down so that the other cats could drape her over his back. He rose to his paws, unsteady under her weight, and set out for the hollow, with Bumblestripe and Toadstep steadying her on either side.

"There's some thyme." Cinderheart pointed with her tail to where a few green leaves were growing in the shelter of a rock. "It'll calm you down, Briarlight, and help if you have any muscle pain after this." She bounded across to the herb and brought back some leaves.

"Thanks, Cinderheart," Briarlight mumbled as she chewed them up. "You know a lot about herbs."

When the entrance to the camp was in sight, Cinderheart halted. "Lionblaze, let's stop for a moment." She angled her ears to where a trickle of water sprang up among some rocks, falling to make a tiny pool. "We'll all feel better if we have a drink."

Lionblaze padded over to the water's edge and slid Briarlight off his back so that she could drink. "Toadstep, Rosepetal," he meowed when every cat had lapped up a few mouthfuls, "you go back to the camp first. It'll create more of a fuss if we all arrive together."

"And there's no need to mention the dog," Cinderheart added. "I don't think it will come back, so there's no point in scaring every cat."

"Toadstep," Lionblaze mewed as the young cats began to move off, "you were very brave today."

"Thanks, Lionblaze." The young warrior glowed.

"You learned a good lesson about fighting as a team," Lionblaze went on. "Remember that no warrior needs to be a hero. The most heroic actions take more than one cat."

Toadstep nodded earnestly before bounding after Rosepetal and slipping through the thorns.

"Thank StarClan," Lionblaze muttered to Cinderheart. It was a relief to talk to a cat who understood his fears about others trying to copy his actions. "I think he's got the point."

Cinderheart murmured agreement and turned to Briarlight, who was lapping at the little pool again. "What were you doing so far from the camp?" she asked gently.

"I wanted to look for herbs, to help Leafpool and Brightheart while Jayfeather is away." Briarlight's fighting spirit flashed in her eyes, and her voice rose to a wail. "I just want to be useful!"

Lionblaze felt a stab of pity in his heart.

"I know I'm not going to get better," Briarlight went on more quietly, her claws digging into the moss at the edge of the pool. "But I—"

"You don't know that," Cinderheart interrupted. "It's early days yet."

Briarlight shook her head. "I know. And I have to find a way to live like this, as half a cat."

"You're not half a cat!" Bumblestripe protested, drawing his tail-tip down his littermate's flank. "You're just . . . different."

"Yeah, but not in a good way." Briarlight's tone was matter-of-fact. "And I can't see why the Clan should care for me when I don't contribute anything. I'm not an elder; I haven't had a lifetime of hunting and fighting that needs to be rewarded. I'd only just become a warrior!"

"We'll find a way for you to be useful, I promise," Cinderheart meowed solemnly. "You are different," she added with a glance at Lionblaze. "Because you're more determined and braver than any other cat I know."

Briarlight's eyes widened with excitement.

"I can't promise things will change overnight," Cinderheart warned, "but I'll speak to Firestar, and to Jayfeather when he gets back, and they'll figure out everything that you can do."

"But no more leaving the camp without any cat knowing," Lionblaze added.

The young she-cat nodded. "I promise."

"For now," Cinderheart mewed, "we'll just say that you went out a little way. And we won't mention any scary meetings with dogs! If Millie hears about that, she'll never let you out of your nest again."

"Okay," Briarlight agreed.

"I'll remind Rosepetal and Toadstep not to say too much," Lionblaze put in.

"I'm really sorry for taking her out in the first place," Bumblestripe meowed, giving his sister an affectionate lick on her ear.

"No, you did a good thing," Lionblaze told him. "You listened to what your sister wanted, when the rest of the Clan tried to decide for her."

Bumblestripe crouched down beside his littermate and she wrapped her forepaws around his neck. "We'll get you home now," he murmured, beginning to drag her in the direction of the hollow.

Lionblaze's heart ached for the injured she-cat as he watched their slow progress. "That was exactly the right thing to say," he meowed to Cinderheart. "You've given her hope."

"So did you," Cinderheart responded. "And I'm glad I didn't have to see you fight that dog!"

"Thank StarClan it didn't come to that!" For a heartbeat Lionblaze imagined he could hear the dog barking again, and feel its breath hot on his pelt. "I don't fight for the fun of it, you know."

"I'm so glad you don't," Cinderheart murmured.

"Well," Lionblaze meowed awkwardly, "I'd better see if Brambleclaw wants me on patrol."

"Me too," Cinderheart agreed.

The gray she-cat stayed near him as they pushed their way through the thorns. Lionblaze stumbled, anxious that their pelts shouldn't brush against each other. Cinderheart seemed to be squeezing herself into the thorns, as if she was embarrassed, too. Inside the camp, Lionblaze spotted Bumblestripe setting Briarlight down gently just outside the medicine cat's den, while Millie burst from the warriors' den and bounded across to her.

"Where have you been?" she demanded, crouching beside Briarlight and covering her with anxious licks.

"I just wanted to go out for a bit," Briarlight replied. "Honestly, I'm fine."

Lionblaze exchanged a glance with Cinderheart.

"She'll be okay," the gray she-cat mewed.

"Are you sure?"

"I'll make sure." Cinderheart's voice was determined. "She's my Clanmate. Oh, and Lionblaze," she added as he headed for the warriors' den in search of Brambleclaw. "You got something wrong, what you said to Toadstep. To many cats, you are a hero."

CHAPTER 13
❧

Dark shapes flitted around Jayfeather, and from far away he could hear the wailing of unseen cats. *Who are you? What do you want from me?*

But there was no answer, and the mournful sound went on and on. Gradually the roar of the waterfall replaced the distant cries, and Jayfeather became aware of soft whispering, much closer to him. The shadowy shapes faded into blackness as he woke from troubled sleep.

"Don't worry, Lark." Jayfeather recognized the voice of Brook's kit Pine. "He's blind! He won't know we're creeping up on him."

Oh, won't he?

Jayfeather tensed his muscles as he detected the pad of tiny paws on the stone floor of the cave, and heard a stifled *mrrow* of laughter. He waited as their scent grew stronger, and he sensed soft breath riffling the tips of his whiskers.

"Looking for something?" As he spoke, Jayfeather leaped to his paws.

Two high-pitched squeals bounced around the cave. He

listened with satisfaction to the sound of paw steps skittering away.

"Mother, that weird cat scared us!"

"He's going to eat us!"

Jayfeather's satisfaction faded and his pelt grew hot with embarrassment. *They're only small. They didn't mean any harm.*

"Sorry!" he called out. "I wouldn't hurt you, kits!"

He could still sense the young cats' fear, and heard Brook's gentle voice from the other side of the cave as she soothed them.

"Mouse dung!" he muttered.

"I wouldn't worry." Another voice spoke closer to him, and after a heartbeat's thought Jayfeather recognized the voice of the prey-hunter Screech. "I saw them stalking you. They could do with a few lessons in respect." Turning away, he added, "It's hard for them. They're strong and active, but they're not allowed outside the cave at all until they become to-bes."

Jayfeather nodded, reminding himself to apologize to Brook later. He climbed out of the dip in the cave floor where he had slept, and began to groom himself, hissing with annoyance at the downy feathers that clung to his pelt.

Give me moss any day!

"Hey, Jayfeather!" Dovewing's excited voice broke in on his thoughts. "Crag has invited Foxleap and me to go on a border patrol."

Jayfeather could feel how eager she was to get out of the cave and start exploring. "That's good," he mewed. "But be careful, and don't forget to keep your ears open."

Dovewing sighed. "I always do."

Squirrelflight padded up with Brook. The two kits were behind them. Jayfeather could picture them peering at him, round-eyed, from the safety of their mother's hindquarters.

"Brook and I are going hunting," Squirrelflight announced.

"Stormfur is coming, too," Brook added. "Talon and Bird will look after the kits, Jayfeather, so they shouldn't bother you again."

"We don't want to stay in the cave," Lark squeaked.

"Yeah, that blind cat might scare us again," Pine added.

"Nonsense!" Stormfur meowed as he joined them. "You startled Jayfeather, that's all. You should say sorry."

"Sorry," Pine muttered.

"We won't do it again," Lark mewed, then added to her brother in a whisper, "It was fun, though!"

"While we're out," Stormfur went on to the kits, "you can ask Talon to tell you the story of Sharptooth, and how I first came to the mountains with the cats from the Clans."

"Yes!" Lark jumped up and down.

"That's the *best* story!" Pine squealed, as both kits scurried off to where the elders made their nests.

Jayfeather was aware of an orderly bustle in the cave as the patrols gathered together and went out. No cat was giving them orders; they all seemed to know what to do and what their duties were without being told by a senior member of the Tribe.

Where's Stoneteller? Shouldn't he be supervising this?

But there was no sign of the Tribe's old Healer. Jayfeather couldn't even pick up his scent.

"Will you be okay, left behind?" Squirrelflight asked Jayfeather as her patrol was moving off.

"Yes, of course," Jayfeather replied, wondering why she bothered to ask. *No harm is going to come to me in here.* He could sense Squirrelflight's awkwardness, and wondered why she was delaying when Brook and Stormfur were already waiting beside the waterfall for their turn to take the path that led out onto the mountain.

"Jayfeather . . ." she began quietly after a couple of heartbeats, "have you worked out why we're here?"

Jayfeather shook his head. "No," he admitted. "I have no idea."

Squirrelflight suppressed a sigh. He knew that she wanted to ask more, but just then Brook called to her from across the cavern.

"Coming!" Squirrelflight called back. "We'll talk later," she added to Jayfeather before she bounded away.

Once the patrols had gone, the cave fell quiet, except for the roar of the water; Jayfeather was growing so used to the sound that he hardly noticed it anymore. *It's so different from our camp,* he thought. *There's always something going on there, even when the patrols are out.* He went on with his grooming; before he had finished he heard the kits come bouncing back into the middle of the cavern, followed by the slower paw steps of Talon and Bird.

"Okay, we're going to play a game," Talon instructed, raising his voice over the excited squeaks of the kits. "This bunch of feathers is a bird."

"What sort of bird?" Lark mewed. "A lark like me?"

"An eagle!" Pine suggested.

"It doesn't matter what sort of bird," Talon told them. "Let's make it a crow, okay? And you're going to catch it."

"Yes!" A scuffling sound told Jayfeather that Pine had tried to pounce on the feathers already.

"Wait a moment." Bird's quieter voice broke in. "It's not as easy as that. You have to creep up on the crow across this patch of stones." Jayfeather heard the sound of pebbles sliding across the cave floor. "If you disturb one and make a noise, the crow will fly away."

"Oh, cool!" Lark exclaimed. "I bet I can do it."

"So can I," Pine declared. "*I'm* going to be the prey-hunter."

Leaving the kits to their game, Jayfeather crossed the cavern to the tunnel that led into the Cave of Pointed Stones. The stone closed around him as he padded forward; after no more than a few paw steps he blundered into the wall, his paws almost skidding out from under him on the damp floor.

He let out a hiss. He hated having to squeeze through the narrow passage, and found it hard to check his position by the echoing drip of water when all other sounds were muffled by the rumble of the falls. Recovering his balance, he edged forward more slowly, frustrated by the way that every paw step felt the same; he missed the forest, where the covering of moss, twigs, ferns, and grass could tell him everything he wanted to know about where he was.

At last Jayfeather sensed that the tunnel walls had opened into a larger cave. The noise of the falls was fainter here, the drips of water echoing more loudly in contrast. There was movement in the cool air against his whiskers; he knew it came from the hole in the roof where moon and starlight could enter, bringing signs from the Tribe of Endless Hunting. Tasting the air, he located Stoneteller at the far side of the cave.

"Who's there?" the old cat growled. Before Jayfeather could reply, he added, "Oh, it's you."

Jayfeather padded forward, skirting the stones and pools of water until he stood in front of Stoneteller.

"Why are you here?" the Healer growled. "And don't give me that nonsense about wanting your young cats to gain experience. You can be honest with me."

Jayfeather chose his words carefully. "I was told to come."

To his surprise, Stoneteller didn't ask who had summoned him. "We don't need your help," he insisted. "There's nothing you can do."

"You haven't chosen a successor," Jayfeather challenged him. "Is that because you don't believe your Tribe will survive without you?"

Stoneteller let out a contemptuous snort. "Their survival doesn't depend on me. Even while I'm alive, I can do nothing to help them. Nor can our ancestors," he added bitterly.

Jayfeather knew that the old cat felt he had been betrayed by the Tribe of Endless Hunting, who had refused to guide him when the intruders came to the mountains. "The Tribe has to be given a chance to survive!" he protested. "It would be too easy to give up the first time something goes wrong."

"It's not the first time!" Stoneteller snapped. "Have you forgotten how so many of us were hunted like prey by Sharptooth? Our endless struggle against the cold and snow? The danger from eagles that means half the Tribe must stand guard while the other half hunts? We could catch twice as much prey if there were no eagles. Queens can't even nurse their kits in peace; they have to go straight out on patrol again." He lashed his tail. "Cats do not belong here!"

While Stoneteller was speaking, Jayfeather became aware of a faint light coming from above, illuminating one wall of the cave, slick with water, and one tapering column of stone that rose from the cave floor to meet another spike jutting from the roof, with no more than a mouse-length between their two points. If he could see, and he wasn't asleep, that meant only one thing. . . .

A shiver tingled through Jayfeather from ears to paws as he made out the shape of Rock in a beam of moonlight. The ancient, hairless cat stood with his head bowed. Then he looked up and turned his sightless eyes on Jayfeather.

"We do belong here," he rasped. "This was my home once, before the cats lived by the lake, before they came back here to start again."

Stoneteller didn't react; he had no idea of the ancient visitor to his cave. Jayfeather opened his jaws to ask a question, but before he could speak Rock went on.

"I was the very first Stoneteller, though my legacy was long forgotten by the time my kin left here to find the lake. If the Tribe of Rushing Water leaves, it will not be forever. Cats must live here *always*."

"*You* were the first Stoneteller?" Jayfeather whispered, but the vision was already fading and darkness covered his eyes once more.

"Of course not." Stoneteller sounded puzzled. "I was chosen by my mentor."

"Then you have to choose another one!"

"Why?" Stoneteller shot back.

Jayfeather scraped his claws against the wet rock in frustration. "Because cats must always live in the mountains."

"Cats *do* live in the mountains," Stoneteller responded dryly. "And more successfully than us, it seems. That's why we have to waste time patrolling every day, to keep the invaders away from what we can catch."

"But those aren't the right cats!" Jayfeather protested. "The Tribe of Endless Hunting didn't bring them here."

Stoneteller snorted dismissively. "I just want to be left in peace," the old cat muttered. He sounded old and very tired. "All that I was proud of has gone. The time of the Tribe is over. When I die, my Tribemates will leave the mountains and find other homes where they will be safe."

As the old cat's words faded into silence, Jayfeather's ears were filled with the sound of roaring water and his vision became washed with gray, splashed with white foam. He was inside the waterfall! For a heartbeat he froze, waiting to feel himself crashing down with it, tossed in the torrent like a fallen leaf. But he could still feel his paws standing on the solid floor of the cave.

Then he choked back a yowl of horror. All around him, the cascade of dark water was full of cats, their paws and tails flailing helplessly, their jaws stretching wide in a soundless screech. They fell down, down, down, into a whirlpool of darkness and foam, and vanished.

But . . . I know these cats! Jayfeather started to shake. *There's Yellowfang . . . and Crookedstar . . . and Lionheart. . . . Is StarClan being destroyed?*

Mistystar . . . and Kestrelwing . . . and the Tribe cats, too. Brook . . . Crag . . .

"No!" Jayfeather choked as he spotted Firestar, the ThunderClan leader reduced to a scrap of orange fur tossed in the crashing torrent.

Dustpelt . . . Mousewhisker . . . Brambleclaw . . .

All his Clanmates, all the cats of the Tribe, falling, falling, to be consumed in water and blackness.

Jayfeather let out a screech and sprang forward as he saw Lionblaze carried past him, his claws outstretched to snag his brother's pelt and drag him to safety. Instead, darkness slammed down over his vision once more and he found himself back in the Cave of Pointed Stones. Dazed with terror, he stumbled forward and crashed into one of the spikes of stone. His feet shot out from under him and he fell on his side in a pool of water.

Stoneteller began to speak, but Jayfeather wasn't listening. Scrambling to his paws, he fled, and this time managed to get himself into the tunnel. He bounced off the narrow walls until he emerged in the cavern, gasping. The cave was cool and gray around him, silver light filtering in through the screen of water. A throng of cats were milling around restlessly, or slumped near the cave wall, and for a moment Jayfeather thought that the patrols had come back.

Then, as he tried to steady his breathing and quiet his pounding heart, he realized that he was *looking* at the cats in the cave.

Is this another vision?

As he hesitated at the mouth of the tunnel, a young white she-cat raced across the floor of the cave and skidded to a halt beside him. Her jaws gaped with astonishment.

"Jay's Wing!"

Jayfeather stared at her. "Half Moon!"

The cats in the cave started to look vaguely familiar as his gaze flickered from one half-remembered face to the next. His thoughts flew back to when he had emerged from the tunnels below ThunderClan in the time of the ancient cats, who had lived by the lake seasons upon seasons ago, whose paw prints dimpled the path that led down to the Moonpool.

While I was with them, they decided to leave because it was too dangerous to live by the lake. I told them they could find a home in the mountains . . . and now they're here!

Half Moon was still gazing at him, her green eyes stretched wide as two small moons. "You disappeared when we set out on our journey from the lake. I thought you didn't want to be with me—with us, anymore."

Jayfeather fought back panic, while inside his head thoughts skittered like a mouse trying to escape from a hunting patrol. "I stayed behind. I was scared," he blurted out. "But when you'd all gone, I was lonely. I decided to follow you."

Half Moon blinked, and her eyes were clouded. "You . . . you didn't even say good-bye. I thought I'd never see you again."

Before he could answer, Jayfeather spotted Stone Song, the powerful gray tabby tom who had led the ancient cats away from the lake. He was standing in the middle of the cavern with Jagged Lightning by his side, close enough for Jayfeather to hear what they were talking about.

"I'm still convinced that coming here was the right thing to do," Stone Song meowed. "Back where we came from, we were losing too many cats. Badgers, Twolegs—"

"That's all very well," Jagged Lightning interrupted with a flick of his black-and-white tail. "But are we any better off here? We're all hungry and exhausted, and I've never been so cold in my entire life. It was all Owl Feather and I could do to get our kits here. And Dark Whiskers didn't even make it," he added with a note of challenge in his voice. "If we'd stayed by the lake, he wouldn't have been blown off a ledge in the middle of an ice storm!"

Stone Song bowed his head. "Perhaps we should be grateful that we lost only one cat," he murmured.

"Try telling that to Shy Fawn!" Jagged Lightning snapped. "She's carrying Dark Whiskers's kits! How is she supposed to bring them up in this icy excuse for a den?"

Stone Song looked blank, as if he didn't know what to say. He was saved from the rest of the conversation when Rising Moon hurried up to him and began speaking urgently, waving her tail toward the cats who were lying beside the cave walls.

"Chasing Clouds just came in with some prey," she meowed. "But Shy Fawn is refusing to eat. Cloudy Sun's pads are bleeding, and Running Horse says that he's going back to the lake once the storm lifts."

"You see?" Jagged Lightning flattened his ears. "Stone Song, you have to admit that this is a disaster."

Stone Song let out a harassed sigh. "I won't," he retorted. "Rising Moon, as soon as the storm is over, can you go out and look for some dock leaves for Cloudy Sun's pads? I'll talk to Running Horse; there's no question of an elder wandering about these mountains on his own, and deep down he knows it. As for Shy Fawn, we have to give her time to grieve."

Jagged Lightning began to reply, but just then an excited yowl sounded from the other side of the cavern. "Jay's Wing!"

Jayfeather spotted Fish Leap, the young tabby tom who had befriended him by the lake; he bounded across the cave and butted Jayfeather in the shoulder with his head. "Where have you been?" he demanded. "We thought we'd lost you."

"I . . . er . . . I sort of changed my mind."

Jayfeather realized that Stone Song had spotted him and was heading in his direction, with Jagged Lightning and Rising Moon at his heels. Whispering Breeze came running up to see what was going on, her silver tabby pelt glimmering in the light from the cave entrance. The other cats fell silent and stared at Jayfeather until his pelt felt as if it were going to crawl off his skin.

"Isn't it wonderful?" Half Moon burst out. "Jay's Wing came back!"

Stone Song's gaze traveled over Jayfeather, his eyes narrowed in suspicion. "How did you get here? The journey was hard enough for all of us together. One cat alone would find it far harder."

"Does it matter?" Fish Leap mewed. "He's here now."

Jayfeather shrugged. "I followed your trail for most of the way, and guessed the rest."

"And how did you get into the cave?" Jagged Lightning growled. "Some cat should have seen you. I don't like all this sneaking around."

"I wasn't sneaking!" Jayfeather retorted, feeling his neck fur beginning to bristle. "If you were all too tired to notice me, that's not my fault. I thought I'd explore these smaller caves," he added, eager to change the subject. "They might be useful for something."

Jayfeather noticed that Half Moon had moved to stand closer to his side, as if she was ready to defend him; her sweet scent tickled his nose, and he remembered how empty he had felt when he had returned to his own time through the tunnels, and left her behind.

"Well?" Whispering Breeze gave him a nudge with her shoulder. "What did you find in the caves?"

"Er . . . pointed stones in the one behind me. Lots of them," Jayfeather replied. "And pools of water. It's not a good place to sleep, because there's a hole in the roof."

Stone Song grunted. "What about the other cave? Could we use that for shelter?"

Jayfeather shot a swift glance at the passage that led to Stoneteller's den. "Oh . . . er . . . that one's fine," he reported. *If Stoneteller sleeps there, it must at least be watertight.*

Whispering Breeze turned her blue gaze on Stone Song. "You're surely not thinking of *staying* here?" she asked, shocked. "Not for any longer than we have to?"

Stone Song angled his ears across the cave to where Chasing Clouds was grooming ice out of his gray-and-white pelt. "You can see that the storm isn't over yet," he meowed. "We may as well be comfortable while we wait."

"Comfortable?" Whispering Breeze's neck fur started to bristle. "You're crazy if you think any cat could be comfortable here."

"We should never have left the lake." A soft voice, ragged with grief and exhaustion, came from the darkness at the edge of the cave, and Broken Shadows limped into view. Jayfeather felt a rush of pity. The mother of Fallen Leaves was even more gaunt than when he last saw her, her orange pelt thin and her amber eyes dull.

"We should never have left," she repeated. "What if Fallen Leaves finds his way out of the tunnels, and we're not there?"

Half Moon padded over to her and drew her tail gently down Broken Shadows's side. "That won't happen," she murmured.

"You don't know that!" Broken Shadows hissed. "He'll

think I abandoned him. He'll be all alone!" She wrenched herself away from Half Moon and rounded on Jayfeather. "This is all your fault! You cast the final stone! You made me leave my son behind!"

CHAPTER 14

❧

"Why did I ever want to leave the lake behind?" Dovewing panted as she scrambled up a narrow gully, her paws slipping on hard-packed snow. "I can't believe cats actually live here!"

Foxleap, slogging up the gully a tail-length ahead of her, simply grunted in reply. The two ThunderClan cats were almost at the rear of the patrol; only Swoop, one of the cave-guards, followed them, glancing around as she moved confidently over the ice. Stormfur and the other two prey-hunters, Gray and Splash, were strung out ahead, while Crag took the lead. They were no more than blurred shapes to Dovewing, glimpsed through the flurries of snow.

It's almost newleaf in the forest! she thought, shivering.

A shape loomed up beside her. "Are you okay? Do you want to lean on my shoulder for a bit?"

Dovewing recognized Stormfur. "No, I'm fine," she gasped. "I can keep going."

Stormfur dipped his head, his eyes warm and friendly, amber like the glow of tiny suns in this wasteland of white. "Just say if you need help."

"They haven't got their snow-paws yet," Splash remarked,

halting to let Stormfur, Foxleap, and Dovewing catch up. "Don't worry," she added with a gentle *mrrow* of laughter. "You'll be snow cats before you know it."

"I'm a snow cat now!" Foxleap meowed with a shiver, shaking lumps of snow from his pelt.

I wish Jayfeather would work out what we're supposed to be doing here, Dovewing thought as she clambered out of yet another drift. *Then we could all go home.*

To her relief the snow died to a few drifting flakes, then stopped, and the clouds began to clear, torn into tatters by the wind. A little farther on, the walls of the gully tapered off, leaving the cats at the top of an exposed peak. Dovewing gasped as she emerged from the shelter of the gully; the wind felt like thorns in her throat, and the blast almost carried her off her paws. Digging her claws into the ice and grit, she raised her head and looked around. They were surrounded by an endless roll of mountain peaks, covered with snow. There was beauty in the jagged shapes and stark colors, but it was nothing like home.

"Look!"

A sharp meow from Crag startled Dovewing; following the cave-guard's gaze, she spotted two tiny dots circling far above them in the pale sky.

"What's that?" Foxleap asked.

"Eagle attack!" Swoop's voice was terse.

The two dots grew larger; Dovewing realized that they were circling lower, homing in on the group of cats.

"What should we do?" she mewed, fighting panic as she

gazed around for cover, while Foxleap crouched and slid his claws out as if he was ready to do battle.

"This way!" Crag and Swoop shoved the two Clan cats back into the mouth of the gully and under the shelter of an overhanging rock. Stormfur, Gray, and Splash crouched down beside them, while Crag and Swoop backed under the outer edge of the overhang, their claws out and their teeth bared.

A heartbeat later the eagles swooped down, their wide brown wings brushing the rocky opening. Dovewing caught a glimpse of glaring yellow eyes and cruel hooked beaks before the birds pulled away again with angry screeches that echoed among the rocks.

"They're our prey—but they're attacking us!" she yelped.

"We don't often hunt eagles," Splash explained calmly. "But we hunt the things that eagles do, like hares and mice and smaller birds."

"So we're in competition," Gray added.

And birds don't respect borders, Dovewing realized with a shudder.

Crag was peering out from under the overhang. "They've gone," he reported. "Let's be on our way."

Dovewing felt very exposed as she ventured out from under the rock. She imagined those cruel talons sinking into her shoulders, whisking her up into the sky. As she padded across the peak and down into a gully on the far side, she kept glancing up, trying to send out her senses to track the position of the eagles.

The next thing she knew, the ground gave way under her

paws. She let out a yowl of alarm, cut off as she landed on soft snow. Blinking in confusion, Dovewing realized that she had fallen down a narrow cleft in the path. Foxleap was gazing down at her, his head and ears outlined against the sky.

"Are you okay?" he asked anxiously.

Dovewing floundered to her paws, the snow too loose to give her a proper footing. "I think so," she mewed. Glancing up at the sheer stone walls that stretched up around her, she added, "I don't think I can get out."

"Okay, don't panic." Foxleap was replaced by Crag, his voice brisk and confident. "We'll get you out."

How? Dovewing wondered helplessly. She remembered what happened when Icecloud fell into the hole, back in the forest. They had used a branch and an ivy tendril to get her out. *But there are no branches or ivy here!*

"Here, I'll do it. I'm the smallest," Splash meowed. She backed over the edge of the gap, clinging to the top with her forepaws while she dangled her tail down to Dovewing. "Can you grab my tail?"

"But I'll hurt you!" Dovewing exclaimed.

"No, I'll be fine," Splash assured her. "Just do it."

Dovewing stretched up as far as she could and sank her teeth into Splash's tail. Thankfully the wall of the cleft wasn't as sheer as she had first thought; there were paw holds that she could use to balance herself and take at least part of the weight off Splash's tail.

Crag and Stormfur were holding on to the she-cat, bracing her, as Dovewing scrambled over the edge of the cleft and collapsed on one side. "Thank you!" she gasped. "I'm really sorry!"

Splash gave her tail a couple of experimental flicks. "You're welcome," she replied. "No harm done."

"Next time I'll watch where I'm putting my paws," Dovewing promised. Shivering, she hauled herself up. Her pelt was covered with snow and grit; she felt she would never be clean or warm again.

"Do you want to go back to the cave?" Stormfur asked. "Swoop will go with you."

Dovewing shook her head. She didn't want to be a nuisance and leave the patrol with only one cave-guard, especially with eagles about. "No, I can keep going," she insisted.

Foxleap padded up and gave her ear a quick lick. "Just tell me if you need any help," he whispered.

Dovewing's muscles ached and her pads were sore from scrambling out of the cleft, but she kept pace with the others as Crag led the patrol down the gully and across a ridge before halting in front of a tall spike of stone where a narrow stream bubbled up from between two rocks and wound away into the distance. The surface was frozen, but Dovewing could hear water trickling underneath.

"This is a border marker," Crag told the Clan cats, angling his ears at the rocky spike. "Gray, would you renew the scent markers?"

While they waited, Dovewing gazed across the rolling hills, the wind buffeting her fur. "Where's the next marker?" she asked Crag.

The cave-guard pointed with his tail. "You see that dead tree, next to the stream? That's it."

On the far side of the valley, almost as far as the distance between ThunderClan's camp and the ShadowClan border, was a tiny stunted tree clinging to the edge of a narrow gully. Dovewing stared at Crag; she hadn't realized that the Tribe's territory was so big. "But it's so far away! How do you check the borders? It must take the whole day to do one patrol."

"We patrol only certain sections," Swoop explained, padding up to stand beside Crag. "Other groups will protect the rest of the border."

Dovewing nodded, privately thinking that it wouldn't take a lot of effort for enemies to figure out there were gaps between each patrol. She cast out her senses and almost at once picked up the sound of cats far away, beyond the border.

They must be the intruders the Tribe is always talking about. But they don't sound threatening now. They're hunting, but they're not trespassing on Tribe territory.

She tensed as she heard the raucous screech of an eagle and instinctively looked up, but the bird was no more than a speck in the sky, well away from where her patrol was standing. Farther away still, she could hear the answering call of eagle chicks and caught a glimpse of them, bald and scrawny, in a mountaintop nest.

Then Dovewing heard a scratching sound much closer by. She identified a vole, pushing its way through the moss at the edge of the frozen stream, hidden by the ice that overhung the bank. She could smell it, too, just a faint trace beneath the clean, sharp scent of snow.

"Vole!" she yowled, leaping for the stream.

To her amazement, Stormfur knocked her aside; Dovewing sprawled on the ice at the water's edge.

"What—?" she began, scrambling up.

"If you fall through the snow into the stream, you'll get dangerously cold," Stormfur explained. "Sorry if I hurt you."

Dovewing shook her head. "I'm fine." *Is he saying that I could die, just from getting wet?* "But there's prey under there," she added, guessing that none of the others had heard the vole. Listening again, she realized that the vole had stopped moving. *Mouse dung! It heard us. That will make it far more difficult to catch.*

Gray and Splash padded up, their ears pricked and their jaws parted to pick up the least trace of prey. "Well done for spotting it," Splash murmured to Dovewing. "Can you hear it now?"

Dovewing stretched all her senses, and finally heard a faint, cautious scuffling that told her the vole was on the move again. Without speaking, she nodded toward the spot on the bank where she thought the vole was hiding.

"Just under the bank," Gray whispered, and Splash nodded.

Taking up positions on either side of the vole, the two Tribe prey-hunters dug down into the snow with strong, thin legs. Crag and Swoop stood guard over each of their Tribemates.

"The cave-guards stay with the prey-hunters," Stormfur explained to Dovewing and Foxleap. "See how they're watching the sky? They'll warn Gray and Splash if any eagles appear."

Dovewing noticed that both prey-hunters were pushing through the snow at an angle, so that they left the top layer undisturbed. "They're getting as close as they can to the vole without alerting it," she murmured. "We might try that back home if we get snow next leaf-bare."

"Right," Stormfur meowed. "And when the vole *does* realize, there's a cat waiting wherever it decides to run."

Just as he spoke, there was a splash as both cats reached the stream. They sprang back, and the vole appeared scurrying downstream along the bank next to Splash. The she-cat pounced, but the vole darted to one side and her paws hit the icy surface of the stream.

"Mouse dung!" Splash snarled.

"Bad luck!" Foxleap called to her.

Meanwhile the vole fled back upstream, where Gray was waiting for it. He pounced from the bank right on top of it and killed it with a swift bite to the back of its neck. "Thanks to the Tribe of Endless Hunting!" he mewed.

"Great teamwork!" Foxleap exclaimed.

Dovewing murmured agreement, but privately she was a bit shocked that it had taken four cats to catch one miserable little vole.

"Are you going to bury it while we do the rest of the patrol?" Foxleap went on. "That's what we do in the forest."

Gray shook his head. "If we did that out here, it would freeze," he pointed out. "I'll take it back to the cave. In the Tribe, we like to eat our prey warm."

He picked up the vole and bounded away, back in the

direction they had come. Crag watched until he had gone, his lithe gray shape hidden by the rocks, then turned and headed toward the next border marker. Dovewing followed, and Splash came to pad alongside her.

"It must be really strange for you up here," the tabby she-cat began in a friendly tone. "What's it like, living in a Clan?"

For a few heartbeats Dovewing was silent, hardly knowing where to start. "There are more of us, to start with," she replied at last. "Four Clans, not just one. We share our borders, but we live by the warrior code, and don't often have to worry about other Clans invading us. And our territories aren't as big as yours, so it doesn't take as long to patrol the border."

"We *need* a big territory," Splash responded defensively. "Prey's scarce up here, and we have to survive."

"Oh, I understand that," Dovewing assured her. "And we don't have cave-guards or prey-hunters," she went on. "In a Clan, every cat learns how to do all the duties."

Splash nodded. "Stormfur told us about that. But surely it makes sense for each cat to specialize in what they do best?"

Dovewing was beginning to feel embarrassed. She wasn't trying to say that Clan life was so much better than Tribe life, even though Splash seemed determined to defend her Tribe.

"Cats have survived here for many, many seasons," Splash meowed quietly, as if she had guessed Dovewing's thoughts. "I couldn't live anywhere else. This is where I belong, between the snow and the sky."

"I feel the same way about the forest," Dovewing admitted.

"I need grass and earth beneath my paws, and the rustle of branches over my head."

Splash gave her a long, considering look. "I think you'd do just fine if you lived up here," she meowed. "Look at the way you heard that vole under the snow!"

"I couldn't leave my home," Dovewing replied. "Not forever."

Splash sighed, pausing for a moment to gaze out over the snow-covered peaks. "I might have to leave mine," she mewed sadly.

"You mean if Stoneteller dies without choosing a successor?" Dovewing asked. "Can't you just choose one yourselves?"

Splash stared at her, eyes stretched wide with shock. "Never! That's for the Tribe of Endless Hunting to decide. Do they watch over you as well?"

Dovewing shook her head. Quickening her pace so they wouldn't get left behind by the rest of the patrol, she explained, "No, we have StarClan to watch over us. They're the spirits of our warrior ancestors. They send signs to our medicine cats, and when a cat dies they go to join them."

Splash blinked. "That sounds just like the Tribe of Endless Hunting. Are they the same cats?"

"I don't think so," Dovewing meowed. "And among the Clans, StarClan doesn't exactly choose the new leader. They give nine lives to the leader the Clan chooses."

"Well, it doesn't work like that for us," Splash argued, sounding defensive again. "Stoneteller will look after us. He always has." Glancing around, she spotted a bunch of feathers lying on the snow. "Oh, look! The kits will love those," she mewed, darting away.

She doesn't want to talk about Stoneteller, Dovewing thought as she watched her go. *But it's clear that she's terrified of what will happen to the Tribe if he doesn't choose a successor.*

CHAPTER 15

"That's enough." Stone Song stepped between Jayfeather and Broken Shadows. His voice was firm but his eyes were sympathetic as he gazed at the grieving she-cat. "You were one of the cats who chose to come, Broken Shadows. And we all abide by the casting of the stones." Laying his tail over her shoulder, he drew her away to the edge of the cave. "Let's find you some fresh-kill," he meowed. "And then you should rest. We'll all feel better after a good sleep."

Rising Moon followed them and stayed with Broken Shadows, while Stone Song returned to Jayfeather. "Are you okay?" he asked, sounding friendlier. "You must have had a hard time, following us on your own. Whatever made you stay behind by yourself?"

"I got scared." Jayfeather offered the same lie that he had given to Half Moon.

"You?" Stone Song sounded incredulous. "But you were the one who wanted to leave! You convinced me that there was a place for us among these stone hills."

"I know." Jayfeather scraped his forepaws across the hard rock of the cave floor, hoping that his confusion would be put down to guilt and embarrassment. "That's what scared me. I'd sort of taken responsibility, and I couldn't face it. I'm sorry."

"But you're here now," Half Moon murmured. "You didn't want to leave us after all." There was hope in her voice.

"That's right. And even though I was scared, I never doubted what we were doing. This is the place where we're supposed to be." Suddenly a wave of exhaustion swept over Jayfeather. The light in the cave was gray; it could have been dawn or twilight for all he knew. He had no idea how he had come to be here among the ancient cats, or what he was supposed to do now.

While he stood trying to collect his chaotic thoughts, Chasing Clouds came plodding up, his fur still damp and clumped from the storm outside. "We need more fresh-kill," he announced. "That means going outside to hunt."

Jayfeather thought that the gray-and-white tom looked tired enough for a mouse to knock him over, but there was a look of determination in his blue eyes.

"And what about nests?" Whispering Breeze demanded. "Where's all the moss? Or grass, or feathers? Are we supposed to sleep on bare rock?"

"We'll take a look when the storm is over," Stone Song promised. "But I don't know what we'll find up here to make nests."

Whispering Breeze gave her whiskers an angry twitch, but said nothing more. Looking at her, and at all the other cats milling about in despair, Jayfeather felt a flash of panic. *How will they survive here? Because they're meant to stay, aren't they? They're Rock's descendants; they have to settle here and form the Tribe of Rushing Water.*

As if the thought of Rock had summoned him, Jayfeather was suddenly aware of the ancient cat's presence at his shoulder, though he could see nothing. Soft breathing stirred the fur around his ear. "You helped them leave the lake," Rock murmured. "This is their home now. You must make them stay."

How? Jayfeather wanted to yowl the words aloud, but he knew better than to expect a straight answer from Rock. Besides, the presence of the ancient cat faded as soon as he had spoken. Jayfeather looked around once more. He couldn't imagine how this pitiful collection of exhausted, dispirited cats could be transformed into the Tribe who made these mountains their home. *Where do I begin?*

"What about this hunting patrol?" Chasing Clouds's voice broke in on his musing.

"I'll come with you," Stone Song meowed. "Half Moon?"

The white she-cat nodded. "I'm up for it."

"I'll come, too," Jayfeather added, surprised at himself. *You can't hunt, mouse-brain,* he reminded himself. *But I can see here,* he argued. *And how hard can it be?*

Half Moon gave him a glowing look and padded beside him as they headed out of the cave. In front of the screen of falling water, Jayfeather turned and looked back. The two elders, Cloudy Sun and Running Horse, were both stretched out, asleep or unconscious. Shy Fawn lay panting on one side, her belly swollen; Jayfeather could see that her kits weren't far from being born. *There's no way she can travel any farther.*

As Jayfeather watched, a small gray she-cat padded up and mewed something to Shy Fawn; Jayfeather recognized Dove's Wing, who was his sister in this time. Something about her anxious sense of responsibility seemed familiar to Jayfeather, but he was distracted by Half Moon prodding him in the shoulder with one paw.

"Are you feeling up to hunting?" she mewed. "You look as if a badger fell on you."

"I'm fine," Jayfeather responded, and followed her along the path that led behind the falls.

Outside, the storm was still raging. Shiny gray ice held the mountains prisoner and the wind whined around the peaks, flinging ice crystals against the cats' faces. Shards of it flew into their eyes and clung to their fur. Keeping his head down against the stinging blast, Jayfeather followed Chasing Clouds as he scrambled up a steep slope of loose pebbles opposite the waterfall. There was a terrifying moment as they crossed the ridge when Jayfeather was sure that the wind would carry him off his paws; he scrambled thankfully into the shelter of a rock, and the rest of the patrol huddled around him to catch their breath.

Jayfeather tried to remember what he could about the way the Tribe hunted. "What do they catch?" he muttered to himself. "Do they use regular hunting skills?"

"What?" Half Moon turned toward him, backing up a pace so that she could look into his eyes.

"Oh, I . . . I was just wondering what to do," Jayfeather stammered.

Half Moon opened her jaws to reply, but a gust of wind caught her and sent her sliding across the icy rock. She let out a wail of alarm as she slipped over the edge and clung by her forepaws, trying vainly to dig her claws into the hard surface.

"Hold on!" Jayfeather meowed, darting forward to help her. He fastened his teeth into her shoulder and heaved, closing his eyes so that he didn't have to see the sheer drop below Half Moon's hindquarters. Terror on her behalf gave strength to his paws as he backed away from the edge, aware of Chasing Clouds pressing up beside him and grabbing Half Moon's other shoulder.

Half Moon scrabbled frantically with her hind legs; with the others' help she managed to drag herself back onto the rock, where she lay for a moment, trembling.

"Are you okay?" Chasing Clouds asked anxiously, leaning toward her so that she could use his shoulder to haul herself to her paws again. His blue eyes were sharp with fear; Jayfeather remembered that he was Half Moon's father.

"Thanks, both of you," Half Moon panted, blinking gratefully. "I'm fine. But let's get off this ridge, before we're all blown off."

Chasing Clouds nodded and took the lead again, down into a steep valley where jagged rocks poked through the snow. Jayfeather followed, and realized that Stone Song was padding at his side.

"Maybe we've made a mistake," the dark tabby tom confided, gazing at Jayfeather with worry in his blue eyes. "How can cats live somewhere when even the wind is our enemy?"

"We didn't make a mistake!" Jayfeather insisted. "We are supposed to be here."

But Stone Song didn't look convinced.

Jayfeather's belly felt hollow with anxiety as he struggled down into the valley through the snow and icy wind. *Somehow I have to make them stay! I have to show them how the Tribe hunts.* Inside his head he seemed to hear a derisive little voice. *You're going to teach these cats how to hunt? Are you completely mouse-brained?* Jayfeather let out a growl deep in his throat. *Who will do it if I don't?*

Peering through the swirling ice, he spotted a narrow gully leading away from the main valley. Steep rocky sides sheltered it from the worst of the wind, and farther down he could just make out a dark, bushy mass of thorns.

"Hey!" he called out to the patrol who had drawn a few tail-lengths ahead of him. "This looks like a good place to start."

The other three cats slogged back to his side and followed his lead as he trudged down into the gully. Jayfeather felt a vast relief to be out of the wind, though the ground was covered with deep, powdery drifts of snow that clung to their fur as they thrust their way through.

"There might be small creatures sheltering under there," he meowed, waving his tail toward the thorn thicket. "It's worth a try, at least."

"True," Stone Song grunted. "Well spotted."

Cautiously approaching the bushes, Jayfeather pricked his ears to listen for prey, and opened his jaws to taste the air. Though the wind still blustered among the rocks above his head, he thought he could pick up the tiny scratching sounds that meant mice or shrews might be moving around inside the thicket.

"Let's hunt as a team," he suggested, trying to remember what Lionblaze and Hollyleaf had told him about hunting with the Tribe on their last visit. "Two of us could go into the bushes and chase the prey out, and two of us stay here to catch it."

"Good idea!" Half Moon mewed, flexing her claws with excitement. "I'm the smallest, so I get to go in!" Crouching down until her belly fur brushed the snow, she crept underneath the outermost branches. But as she tried to pull herself farther in, thorns snagged in the fur on her back, and however much she tugged, she couldn't free herself.

"I'm stuck!" she wailed.

"Be quiet or you'll scare the prey," Stone Song told her.

"I thought that was the idea," Half Moon muttered.

Chasing Clouds clawed at the branch with a raised forepaw. "Keep still," he mewed, "and I'll soon have you out of there."

The whole bush started to shake as Chasing Clouds dug his claws harder into the branch, trying to tear it away from his daughter's pelt. As Jayfeather watched, he glimpsed movement at the corner of his eye, and spotted a shrew darting out from the shelter of the bush.

"Yes!"

The shrew was heading straight for Jayfeather, but as he swiped at it, his paws felt slow and clumsy. He grabbed at it with claws outstretched, missing it by a whisker. The shrew veered away and dived into a gap between two rocks before

Jayfeather could pounce again.

"Fox dung!" he exclaimed.

"Bad luck." To Jayfeather's surprise, Stone Song didn't sound angry, or even particularly disappointed. "At least it shows that there *is* prey here," he went on. "More than the puny little mouse Chasing Clouds caught this morning."

Chasing Clouds had managed to free Half Moon from the thorns, and she backed out from under the bushes, shivering and craning her neck to see whether she had lost any fur.

"I don't think there's anything else under there," Chasing Clouds meowed. "And the storm is getting worse. We'll all freeze to death if we get lost out here."

Stone Song nodded. "Let's go back to the cave, and we'll see if we can pick up some prey on the way."

Taking the lead, he headed back to the top of the gully and then, instead of climbing to the ridge where Half Moon had nearly fallen, he made for a gap between the rocks. Jayfeather thought his paws might freeze to the ground as he followed, stumbling from rock to rock in an effort to find shelter from the wind. Suddenly the air grew darker above him and he let out a groan, wondering what more vile weather the mountains could throw at them. A heartbeat later a rank scent flooded over him and a screech sounded in his ears. The air was full of a storm of wings; horrified, Jayfeather looked up to see a huge brown bird swooping down on them, its talons extended toward Half Moon.

"Look out!" he yowled.

Chasing Clouds and Stone Song flung themselves sideways,

out of the path of the bird. Half Moon leaped for the shelter of a rock, but her paws slipped on the ice and she fell with her feet flailing helplessly in the snow. With a triumphant screech the bird hurtled down and fastened its claws into Half Moon's back. Desperately Jayfeather scrabbled toward her, his paws skidding over the icy rocks. The bird's outstretched wings seemed to cover the whole sky as Jayfeather flung himself on Half Moon to hold her down, meeting her terrified gaze.

"I won't let you go!" he gasped, feeling himself lifted into the air as the bird tried to take off again.

A long caterwaul ripped through the air as Chasing Clouds hurled himself at the bird, fastening claws and teeth into one of its wings, dragging it away from his daughter. The bird let go; Jayfeather and Half Moon hit the ground in a tangle of legs and tails. Looking up, the breath driven out of his body, Jayfeather saw the bird twist in the air, throwing Chasing Clouds off its wing. While the big cat lay half stunned, the bird swooped down again and gripped him by the shoulders in its cruel talons.

"No!" Half Moon shrieked.

Together Jayfeather and Stone Song sprang to Chasing Clouds's side, and hung on to his legs as the bird tried to climb into the sky. For a moment Jayfeather thought it would carry all three of them away. Then they fell to the ground with Chasing Clouds landing heavily on top of them; scarlet blood began to flow over Chasing Clouds's pale pelt where thorn-sharp claws had ripped his fur away.

The bird's furious cry was lost in a louder rumble. Jayfeather looked up, dizzy from shock, and saw snow breaking away from the rocks above his head, pouring down toward them in a rolling cloud of white.

"Run!" he croaked feebly.

But the cats barely had time to struggle to their paws before the snow was upon them. Jayfeather lost his balance, tumbling over and over. The mass of snow thundered around him as it swept him down the mountain. The bird had vanished; he lost sight of the other cats. Nothing was left but a storm of white, roaring louder and louder until it blotted out everything.

What's happening? Jayfeather yowled silently. *Is this the end?*

CHAPTER 16

"Come on, move your tail, Mousewhisker! We haven't got all day!"

Ivypool's ears flicked up at the sound of Brambleclaw's cheerful yowl. She was crouching among the ferns at the entrance to the apprentices' den, watching as a soft milky light strengthened in the sky above the hollow, and the warriors began to emerge for the dawn patrols.

The ThunderClan deputy shoved Mousewhisker in front of him as they slid out of their den between the beech branches; the younger cat spun around and playfully swiped at him, his paw missing Brambleclaw's nose by a mouse-length. Ivypool sighed as she listened to the happy buzz of waking cats. The day was cool and gray and damp, but the air was full of the scent of leaves and growing things. In the last few days the sun had shone, buds on the trees had begun to unfold, and new shoots had poked through the earth. The fresh-kill pile was well stocked for the first time in moons.

But Ivypool couldn't share her Clanmates' excitement about the arrival of the new season. Since Dovewing left for the mountains, her sleep had been broken; she couldn't get used to being alone in the den, and uneasiness prickled in her pelt like a whole nest of ants.

Heaving a sigh, Ivypool padded out into the clearing, where Brambleclaw was assigning the cats to patrols. Cloudtail was emerging from the warriors' den, his jaws stretched wide in an enormous yawn, while Dustpelt slid out more quickly and arched his back in a long stretch. Whitewing and Bracken-fur were stalking around each other, looking as if they were maneuvering for a mock fight. Sorreltail watched them, licking one paw and drawing it over her ears.

Ivypool's gaze flicked around the clearing, but she couldn't spot Blossomfall. *Where is she? Did she go to the Dark Forest last night?* Ivypool dug her claws into the earth floor of the clearing. With so little sleep, she hadn't visited the Dark Forest for the last couple of nights, but she was sure that the bitter and bloody training sessions were still continuing. So far, she hadn't had the chance to talk to Blossomfall about what she was doing there.

Perhaps today I should.

"Hey, Ivypool!" Lionblaze called. "Cinderheart and I are doing a border patrol. Do you want to come with us?"

"Great. Thanks."

"We're going along the ShadowClan border—" Lionblaze began, but Ivypool's attention was distracted as she spotted Blossomfall stumbling out of the warriors' den with Bum-blestripe at her side. The young she-cat looked ruffled and exhausted, and she was trying not to limp.

I know all the signs, Ivypool thought, wincing.

Hazeltail stepped forward to intercept Blossomfall as she

headed toward Brambleclaw. "Blossomfall, are you okay?" she asked, concern in her eyes.

Blossomfall halted. "Yes, I'm fine."

"I don't think you're fine at all," Hazeltail responded sharply. "Hey, Millie!" She waved her tail at Blossomfall's mother, who was crossing the clearing toward the medicine cat's den. "I think Blossomfall is sick."

"What?" Millie glanced at Blossomfall. "Oh, she's fine. I have to go check on Briarlight."

Ivypool spotted a flash of anger in Blossomfall's eyes as her mother spoke, but Millie was clearly unaware of it as she bounded away and disappeared behind the bramble screen.

"Blossomfall, I was going to send you to patrol the Wind-Clan border with Bumblestripe, Sandstorm, and Thornclaw," Brambleclaw announced, padding up to the tortoiseshell-and-white she-cat. "But you don't look as if you could scare off a dead leaf this morning. Your patrol had better go hunting instead."

Blossomfall nodded, but Bumblestripe's tail drooped in disappointment. "I went hunting twice yesterday," he told Brambleclaw. "I was looking forward to a border patrol."

Brambleclaw gave the young tom a hard stare. "Last time I looked, it was the deputy's job to organize patrols."

Bumblestripe muttered something under his breath, scuffling loose earth with his forepaws. Seizing her chance, Ivypool bounded up to his side. "I'm in a border patrol with Lionblaze and Cinderheart," she mewed. "I don't mind swapping—if that's okay with you, Brambleclaw."

"Feel free," the deputy responded dryly. "Maybe I should just go back to my nest and let you sort yourselves out?"

"Thanks, Ivypool!" Bumblestripe brightened up and ran off to join Lionblaze and Cinderheart, who were getting ready to leave. Ivypool watched as the two warriors padded side by side toward the thorn tunnel, envying the easy friendliness between them. Bumblestripe caught up to them, and all three cats vanished into the forest.

"Right." Sandstorm swished her tail. "Let's get moving. I thought we'd try around the Twoleg nest. I don't think a patrol has been there for the last day or two."

As they emerged into the forest, Sandstorm and Thornclaw took the lead, while Ivypool found herself padding along the old Thunderpath beside Blossomfall. The young tortoiseshell was breathing hard, and still trying not to limp; Ivypool spotted a torn claw on one of her forepaws.

"Was it tough in the Dark Forest last night?" she asked, feeling a little awkward to be questioning a more experienced warrior. "Were you—?"

"Hush!" Blossomfall exclaimed, angling her ears toward the two cats ahead of them. "We can't talk here." With an obvious effort she quickened her pace to draw ahead, and Ivypool followed, wondering if there was any way to get Blossomfall alone.

Outside the old Twoleg nest, Sandstorm picked her way through the clumps of herbs Jayfeather had planted, sniffing delicately at the new growth. "The catmint is starting to sprout," she meowed, "but there'd be a lot more of it if

ShadowClan hadn't forced us to give them some."

"Sorry," Ivypool muttered. She still felt guilty that Shadow-Clan had kept her imprisoned until they could exchange her for herbs.

At least Dovewing isn't seeing Tigerheart anymore. We can't trust him, because he's in the Dark Forest. But then, so am I, she added, feeling an icy trickle down her spine. *And Blossomfall . . .*

"Ivypool, wake up!" Ivypool jumped as Thornclaw gave her a flick around the ear with his tail. "Stop daydreaming. Did you hear what Sandstorm said to you?"

Embarrassed, Ivypool shook her head.

"She wants you to head up the slope on the other side of the Thunderpath," the tabby warrior explained, pointing with his tail. "There should be plenty of squirrels up there, hunting for their stores of nuts underneath the oak trees."

"And we'll scour the Twoleg nest," Sandstorm added, her green eyes gleaming. "There should be mice in there, or I'm a badger."

She padded toward the entrance to the den, almost immediately disturbing a mouse that scuttled frantically for a gap in the wall. Thornclaw leaped after it, cutting it off from its refuge. It turned back, and ran straight into Sandstorm's waiting claws.

"What did I tell you?" she mewed, her voice full of satisfaction as she scratched earth over her prey.

"What are you two waiting for?" Thornclaw flicked Blossomfall and Ivypool away with his tail. "Or is this an apprentice training session?"

"He's so bossy!" Ivypool muttered as she headed up the steep slope. Blossomfall let out a puff of agreement, already laboring as she hauled herself through the thick undergrowth. Once they were out of sight of the Twoleg nest, Ivypool stopped. "Do you want to rest for a bit? I know what hunting at night can be like," she added warily.

Blossomfall met her gaze. "I don't think we're supposed to talk about it."

Who swore you to secrecy? Ivypool wondered. *Tigerstar? Hawkfrost?* She twitched her tail in frustration. If Blossomfall refused to talk about the Dark Forest, there was no chance of discouraging her from going there.

Blossomfall was already struggling on through the undergrowth, and Ivypool had to follow her, brushing past a clump of nettles and ducking under the low-growing boughs of a hazel bush. Ivypool padded up to her, brushing aside a bramble tendril so that she could stand facing her. "How did you know it was there?"

There was a glimmer of anger in Blossomfall's eyes, and an edge in her voice as she replied. "I was invited, okay? By Hawkfrost. He said it was a chance to be a better warrior than I could be just training with my Clanmates, and he was right. I bet he told you exactly the same thing." She turned away and headed up the slope again, glancing over her shoulder to add, "Now, can we just get on with hunting?"

Ivypool's mind whirled as she hurried after her. *Does Blossomfall really not know the purpose of the Dark Forest? To wage war against all living Clans?* She wanted to tell Blossomfall the truth, to warn her to stay away from the Dark Forest for her own sake. But if she did that, she would have to admit that she was a traitor to the Dark Forest, spying on behalf of ThunderClan.

If I'm going to save the Clans, will I have to let Blossomfall continue, and maybe die there?

"Hold on!"

Ivypool was dragged out of her dark thoughts by Blossomfall's voice up ahead. The tortoiseshell warrior had paused at a spot where the trees thinned out; bounding forward, Ivypool found herself at the edge of the clearing where Icecloud had fallen into the tunnel. She could see the pile of sticks that Dustpelt and Brackenfur had placed there, weaving them together to cover the hole.

Her pads prickled with curiosity. She had passed this place before on patrol, but this was her first chance to have a closer look at it. She exchanged a glance with Blossomfall, seeing her own excitement reflected in the other cat's eyes.

"Shall we?" she prompted.

Blossomfall nodded, and the two she-cats padded down the slope side by side. Reaching the hole, Ivypool stretched out her neck to sniff at the covering. Blossomfall gave the woven sticks a nudge with her head, and let out a trill of surprise as the whole covering shifted to one side.

"Hey, look," she meowed, pushing it farther. "We can see right down into the tunnel! Let's explore!"

A weird feeling crept over Ivypool as she gazed down into the hole. She felt strangely reluctant to go near it. "What about hunting?"

"We can hunt later," Blossomfall replied, her eyes sparkling. Fueled by excitement, she seemed to have thrown off her earlier exhaustion. "Let's explore!"

While Ivypool remained standing beside the hole, fighting against the apprehension that had seized her, Blossomfall searched through the long grass and came back dragging a branch. "Help me lower it," she puffed, pushing one end into the hole. "Then we can use it to climb." She scrambled down as soon as she and Ivypool had maneuvered the branch into position, with the narrow end resting on the lip of the hole.

"Come on!" she called to Ivypool. "The tunnel goes on forever, all the way under the hill!"

Still reluctant, Ivypool edged her way into the hole, feeling the branch bounce beneath her paws. She dug in her claws, but the bark was dry and crumbly. She was no more than halfway to the bottom when it gave way and she felt her paws slipping from under her. Letting out a startled screech, Ivypool crashed down into the hole with the branch falling on top of her. Scrabbling her way through dry leaves and twigs, she gazed up at the ragged scrap of blue sky above her head. There was no way to climb out now.

"We're stuck!" she whispered.

Shadows wreathed around her, and every hair on her pelt rose. She couldn't explain it, but she was certain that there was something terribly wrong down here. Chilly darkness loomed from the mouth of the tunnel and somehow she knew that they weren't alone.

Blossomfall's eyes were gleaming in the half-light. "Now we *have* to keep going," she mewed delightedly.

"But it's dangerous!" Ivypool protested.

Blossomfall snorted. "What's the worst that can happen? We might lose the use of our legs?"

They padded farther into the tunnel, with the light from the hole fading behind them. Blossomfall glanced back to where they could just make out the remains of the branch lying on the tunnel floor. "There's no point in going back. We might wait for ages for some cat to pass by the hole," she pointed out. "And when they do, we'll get into major trouble. There must be another way out, right?"

As she followed her Clanmate into the darkness, Ivypool hoped that they weren't making a huge mistake. But in spite of her misgivings, she couldn't help beginning to share Blossomfall's excitement. When Icecloud fell into the hole, she was hauled out right away. She had never been this far underground.

We're the first cats to set paw down here, ever!

By now the two she-cats were padding along in complete darkness, their pelts brushing the side of the tunnel. Their path twisted and turned until Ivypool lost all sense of which way they were facing. Now and again she was aware of other tunnels leading off the main one, and she shivered at the thought of plunging even deeper into the hill.

"I can feel a tiny draft of air," Blossomfall, in the lead, reported after a while. "That should lead us to a way out."

They plodded on; Ivypool's pads were aching from walking

on the cold, hard rock by the time she realized that she could see her Clanmate's head and pricked ears outlined against a pale light up ahead. "We're getting somewhere!" she mewed.

Blossomfall picked up the pace and Ivypool bounded after her, almost bumping into her when she stopped dead. Peering around her Clanmate, Ivypool saw that the tunnel ended in a huge cave, its walls soaring far above their heads. A dark river ran through it, and on the opposite side a wide ledge was cut into the rock.

"This is the strangest place I've ever seen," Blossomfall whispered, venturing a little farther in.

Light was angling down through a tiny hole in the cave roof, too high above their heads for the cats to think of climbing out that way. Padding forward cautiously, Ivypool bent her head and lapped up a mouthful of water from the river.

"That's cold!" she exclaimed, stepping back and twitching her whiskers to shake off the drops.

Glancing around while Blossomfall drank, Ivypool felt a strong sensation of being watched, as if a cat's gaze was boring into her back from the ledge in the cave wall. She whipped around; the ledge was empty, but the feeling wouldn't leave her. Her pelt crawled.

"We shouldn't be here," she mewed, her voice sounding unnaturally loud in the echoing cave.

"Why not?" Blossomfall looked up, swiping her tongue around her jaws. "There's no cat here to tell us to go away."

"Then who left those?" Ivypool's voice rasped in her throat as her gaze fell on fresh paw prints dimpling the damp sand at the edge of the river, a couple of tail-lengths from where she and Blossomfall were standing. Every hair on her pelt bristled and she slid out her claws, scraping them on the rock.

"There are cats living down here!"

CHAPTER 17

❧

A thick, heavy silence surrounded Jayfeather. Everything was dark and for a moment he thought that he was blind again. Then he realized that ice crystals were sealing his eyes shut; in spite of the pain he forced them open, only to see nothing but glimmering white all around him. When he tried to gasp in air, beads of snow stung the back of his throat.

I'm buried!

The light seemed to be coming from somewhere above his head. Jayfeather scrabbled toward it; a few heartbeats later his head broke out into the air and he looked around. The storm was over. Stillness covered the valley; the peaks were dark shapes cutting into an indigo sky where the last scarlet streaks of sunset were beginning to fade. He was completely alone.

Terror that the other cats had died in the snowfall rooted Jayfeather to the ground, but he forced himself to start moving. Kicking out with his hind legs, he climbed out of the snow and stood for a moment shaking clots of it from his pelt.

"Jay's Wing!"

The shout came from behind him; Jayfeather spun around to see Stone Song fighting his way out of a drift a little farther up the valley. Jayfeather floundered through the loose snow and dragged him out. At first the gray tabby tom was silent with shock, gazing at the mountains as if he didn't remember where they were.

"Are you okay?" Jayfeather prompted. "We have to look for the others."

Stone Song shook his head to clear it. "I'm okay," he panted. "Have you seen them?"

Jayfeather shook his head.

"They have to be here somewhere," Stone Song muttered. "We have to find them."

By digging up all this snow? Jayfeather thought, appalled. Then he spotted a dark patch of color on top of the snow a few fox-lengths away. Plodding over to it, he saw that it was blood. "Over here!" he called to Stone Song. "Chasing Clouds was hurt; this must be his blood."

Working together, the two cats scraped away the snow until Chasing Clouds's body appeared. Jayfeather's heart beat faster when he saw how still the cat lay, a limp scrap of fur tossed aside by the power of the snow.

Then Chasing Clouds coughed and opened his eyes. "What happened?"

"The snow fell on us," Stone Song explained. "I think we must have dislodged it, fighting that giant bird. Come on, let's get you out of there."

Jayfeather and Stone Song hauled Chasing Clouds out of the hole; he crouched on the surface of the snow, still looking dazed, and occasionally licking at the raw flesh on his shoulder where the bird had torn out his fur.

"Half Moon?" Jayfeather called. "Half Moon!"

There was no reply, but a slight movement on the surface a couple of tail-lengths away caught his eye. He thrust his way through the snow toward it; relief crashed over him when he saw Half Moon's ears and nose emerge from the white covering, followed a heartbeat later by the rest of her head.

Jayfeather scraped energetically at the snow around her until she was able to scramble out. "Thanks," she gasped. "Have you found—?"

She broke off with a wordless wail of anguish as she saw her father. Struggling to his side, she crouched beside him and began to lick his injuries. Jayfeather could see scratches from the bird's claws on her back, too, but if she was in pain, she wasn't showing it, too caught up in concern for Chasing Clouds.

In the dim light, Jayfeather noticed something growing in the hole where Half Moon had been lying. Bending down, he sniffed and recognized the scent of ragwort. *That's good for strength,* he thought, remembering what he had learned about mountain herbs on his previous visit to the Tribe. It should help with shock. Craning his neck down into the hole, he managed to nip off a few stems and carried them back to the others.

"Here, eat these," he ordered, setting the herbs down in front of them. "They'll make you feel better."

All three cats looked up at him, then bent their heads to lick up the herbs.

They've been through too much to wonder how I know about plants that grow here, Jayfeather guessed, wondering if there were any cobwebs around to stop bleeding. The cave would be the best place to look.

"We should go back," he meowed. When none of the cats moved, he gave Stone Song a prod. "Come on. Do you want to die out here? Give up when we already came this far? We need to have faith."

Stone Song looked at him with dull eyes. "Faith? Faith in what?"

Jayfeather flinched, wishing he could call upon StarClan, or the Tribe of Endless Hunting. But those names would mean nothing to these cats. *Are there any ancestors watching us right now?*

"We should have faith in ourselves," he told them, trying to put conviction into his voice. "We came this far. We will survive. We must give ourselves time."

Stone Song blinked. "We might not have time. The mountains might kill us first."

Jayfeather thought of all the generations of cats to come, all the seasons when the Tribe would live in the mountains until they were discovered by a patrol of cats who had journeyed to visit the sun-drown-place.

"You do have time," he mewed. "I promise."

Yowls of horror broke out from the cats in the cave as Jayfeather and Stone Song struggled back through the entrance, practically carrying Chasing Clouds between them while Half Moon limped behind.

"What happened?" Jagged Lightning demanded. "Were you attacked by a fox?"

"No, a bird," Stone Song replied.

"A bird?" Whispering Leaves pressed up behind Jagged Lightning, gazing at Chasing Clouds's injuries with horrified blue eyes. "A bird did that to you?"

"It was a really big bird," Chasing Clouds muttered.

More of the cats were gathering around, jostling one another to get a good look, letting out exclamations of fear and despair. Owl Feather's kits came bouncing up, sniffing curiously at Chasing Clouds, then shrank back close to their mother as they caught the tang of blood.

"I told you so!" Running Horse muttered. "We should never have come here."

Rising Moon turned her head away as if she couldn't bear to look. Jayfeather remembered that back in the forest he had learned that she and Chasing Clouds were mates. "This place will kill us all," she whispered.

Annoyance prickled Jayfeather's pelt and set his tail-tip twitching. *Are they all going to stand around and moan and do nothing?* Back among the Clans, he would have taken an injured cat straight to the medicine cat's den, but here there was no medicine cat. *It looks as if it's up to me.*

Stone Song let Chasing Clouds sink gently to the ground, and pushed his way into the midst of the panicking cats.

"That's enough!" he called out. "Calm down. Chasing Clouds is going to be fine. Let's all concentrate on what we can do to help."

But in spite of their leader's words, there was barely a pause in the horrified exclamations. Jayfeather spotted Half Moon in the middle of the crush. Angling his ears, he gestured to her to meet him at the edge of the crowd. "We need cobwebs to stop the bleeding," he meowed, when they had both fought their way out of the press of cats. "There might be some in the little caves back there."

Half Moon nodded and pattered behind Jayfeather as he headed for the caves. She slipped into the one that would become Stoneteller's den, while Jayfeather padded down the tunnel that led to the Cave of Pointed Stones. The cavern looked just the same to Jayfeather as when he had seen it in visions in his own time: the sharp spikes of rock rising from the floor to meet other spikes hanging from the roof; the puddles of water dotted here and there, reflecting a pale light from the moon that shone down through the hole in the roof. His pelt stood on end and he shivered.

How long has this place been here? How many seasons, lying as thick as leaves on the forest floor?

Then he gave himself a shake. Padding forward, he searched around the edges of the cave and in cracks in the rock. There weren't any cobwebs, but beside one of the pools he found some stubbly moss. Clawing up a pawful, he dipped it in the water; it would be the next best thing to cobwebs for dressing Chasing Clouds's wounds. Carrying a mouthful of dripping moss, Jayfeather returned to the main cave.

Half Moon was emerging from the other tunnel. "I couldn't find anything in there," she meowed. "It's so dark!"

The crowd of cats by the entrance had begun to disperse, and Chasing Clouds was staggering into the center of the cavern, supported by Stone Song. Jayfeather looked around. There was nowhere to make a proper medicine cat's den, but he spotted a sandy stretch of ground in the shelter of a boulder; that would have to do. "Bring him over here," he mumbled around the moss, beckoning to Stone Song with his tail.

Some of the other cats were still following, but Half Moon stepped forward to intercept them. "He needs quiet now," she mewed. "You can see him later."

Rising Moon looked as if she was about to object, but Whispering Breeze laid her tail over her shoulders and led her away. Jayfeather and Stone Song settled Chasing Clouds on the sandy floor and Jayfeather dabbed the soaking moss on his shoulder where the bird had torn away his fur.

"That feels good!" Chasing Clouds grunted.

When the wound was clean, Jayfeather pressed more moss over it, patting it down at the edges to make sure it would stick. "Keep still so you don't dislodge it," he told Chasing Clouds. "Sleep if you can."

He thought he detected a flicker of surprise in Stone Song's eyes at his tone of authority, but he shrugged it off. *I don't know how much Jay's Wing knew about healing, but this is me. I'm doing what I have to.*

"You next," he meowed to Half Moon.

As he cleaned up the white she-cat's scratches, Jayfeather spotted Furled Bracken in the center of the cavern, with most of the other cats clustered around him.

Trouble? Jayfeather wondered, though he said nothing, and didn't pause in his careful cleaning of Half Moon's wounds.

Furled Bracken had been the leader of the ancient cats when Jayfeather first met them beside the lake. He had cast his stone in favor of staying, and when the decision went against him, he had yielded the leadership to Stone Song.

"I think most of us agree that coming here was a mistake," Furled Bracken was meowing. "We should never have left the lake. As soon as the ice storm is over, I will lead those cats who want to return."

"About time!" Jagged Lightning exclaimed. "I'll go with you."

"So will I," Fish Leap meowed. "I never wanted to come in the first place."

Shy Fawn raised her tail to speak. "Furled Bracken, we haven't all agreed." Her voice grew more determined as she went on. "Did the father of my kits die for nothing?" She whisked her tail-tip along her swollen belly and added, "I can't travel, not until my kits are born and strong enough to make the journey."

"I want to stay, too," Dove's Wing put in. "We had problems by the lake, and they won't have gone away."

"But maybe Fallen Leaves will be there," Broken Shadows suggested, a brighter gleam in her eyes than Jayfeather had ever seen. "Take us home, Furled Bracken."

Whispering Breeze let out a sigh. "I cast my stone to leave," she mewed. "And now I regret that bitterly. This was a mistake. We should go home."

"I wanted to leave, too, but now I want to go back." Owl Feather drew her kits toward her with a sweep of her tail. "I'm afraid my kits will die if we stay here." The kits set up a frightened mewling; their mother curved her body around them, soothing them with gentle licks.

"Then we're agreed that—" Furled Bracken began.

"No!" Jayfeather interrupted. The eyes of every cat in the cave turned toward him, shining in the dim gray light. "You can't go back—I mean, we can't go back!"

Owl Feather drew her kits closer and glared at Jayfeather. "That's easy for you to say," she hissed. "You don't have kits."

Suddenly Jayfeather was conscious of Half Moon standing beside him. Flicking her a quick glance, he pressed on. "We can't give up so soon. We should at least wait until the storm is over to see if we can find a way to catch prey."

Rising Moon took a pace toward him, lashing her tail. "But we are prey!" she snarled. "How can we hunt if we're being hunted ourselves?"

Jayfeather's mind whirled. "We have to find a different way of hunting." He suddenly recalled how the Tribe divided up the cats into cave-guards and prey-hunters, with their own special duties. "Some of us will hunt, while others will protect them—and our prey—against big birds."

The cats looked at one another, muttering. Jayfeather could

tell that they didn't have any faith in his idea. *But it will work! I've seen it working!*

"We could try," Half Moon meowed, standing closer to Jayfeather so that their pelts brushed.

A trickle of warmth crept through Jayfeather at her touch. It was good to have one cat who supported him. "Thanks," he whispered, touching her ear with his nose.

"Oh, yes, try and have more cats with their fur ripped off!" Jagged Lightning's neck fur bristled as he stared at Jayfeather.

Yowls of agreement followed his words. Jayfeather almost staggered backward at the wave of hostility he sensed coming from the crowd of cats around Furled Bracken. Half Moon's support hadn't been enough.

"Then that's settled." Furled Bracken's gaze swept over the rest of the cats. "We'll wait until the storm is over, then go back to the lake."

Jayfeather stood blinking in disbelief as the cats began to shuffle toward the edges of the cave and find places to sleep. *This can't be happening!*

"I'm sorry," Stone Song murmured; he had stood in silence while the argument was going on. "We tried; it's not our fault we failed. Maybe we're not supposed to live in the stone hills after all."

Jayfeather looked into his blue eyes and saw genuine regret there. He was the cat who was most committed to this . . . and now he was giving up, too! With nothing to say to him, Jayfeather stumbled away. *Stone Song doesn't understand. We've failed. . . . I've failed!*

"If these cats leave so soon," he muttered, "how will the Tribe of Rushing Water end up in the mountains?"

Hardly aware of what he was doing, he found his paw steps leading him into the Cave of Pointed Stones. Soft paw steps sounded behind him; glancing back, he saw that Half Moon had followed him. She halted at the mouth of the tunnel, her eyes stretching wide as she took in the cave.

"Wow!" she breathed.

Jayfeather shared some of her wonder as he gazed around at the tapering columns and pinnacles of white stone. Being in the cave with Half Moon somehow made him realize how beautiful it really was.

"Let's explore!" Half Moon mewed, giving a little bounce like an excited kit.

Jayfeather followed her as she darted around the puddles and stretched her forepaws as far as she could reach up the side of one of the stony spikes. "Look!" she exclaimed. "This stone is growing from the floor, and it almost meets the icicle of stone that's hanging from the ceiling."

"Those two have met." Jayfeather pointed with his tail to one of the completed columns.

"It's so strange!" Half Moon bounded farther in among the forest of stone, dodging around the base of one and poking her head out playfully on the other side. Jayfeather launched himself at her with a mock growl, but before he reached her his paws slipped on the slick rock at the edge of one of the pools. Water splashed up as he planted one paw in the water; he saved himself from going deeper only with an awkward sideways scramble.

"Oops, you got a wet paw!" Half Moon teased.

"I'll show you wet paws!" Jayfeather growled.

Scooping up some water, he flicked it at her; Half Moon shrieked and ran away. Jayfeather raced after her, losing sight of her for a moment among the clustering columns. Suddenly she darted out at him and they collided. Jayfeather found himself looking into her eyes; they were the lustrous green of forest pools. Her warm fur brushed his.

"The moon's up," he meowed, breaking away from her to stand on the edge of a pool. "It must be night outside."

As his breathing steadied, he became aware of cats moving restlessly in the main cave. Owl Feather's kits were wailing with hunger. A pang of sadness pierced Jayfeather, sharp as a claw. *I can understand why they don't want to stay here.*

"Look!" Half Moon padded up to stand beside him. "You can see the moon in the water."

Looking into the puddle in front of him, Jayfeather saw a reflection of the tiny new moon, shining down through the hole in the roof. Half Moon couldn't take her eyes off it.

"It's so beautiful!" she whispered. "So tiny—just like a claw scratch."

She dabbed at the surface of the water with one paw, and the moon fluttered like silver wings before settling again as the water stilled. Letting out a faint *mrrow* of wonder, Half Moon dabbed again and again. However often she disturbed the surface, the moon was still there.

"It doesn't give up, does it?" Half Moon blinked at

Jayfeather. "It's always there, constant like the stones in this cave. Maybe we should be like the moon's reflection, holding fast whatever happens?" Padding farther into the cave, she gazed around at the stones again, a new sense of understanding beginning to creep into her eyes. Jayfeather felt his pelt prickle.

"They have been here for so many seasons," Half Moon murmured. "If we stay, will our descendants survive for as long as these columns of stone?"

Jayfeather jumped to her side. "Yes, they will! I promise."

Half Moon shot him a look of alarm. "How do you know?"

"I just do," Jayfeather replied. "Trust me."

Her green gaze grew warm as she looked into his eyes. "I do trust you. Always." Jayfeather felt his tail entwining with hers. "I wish the others would trust you too," Half Moon mewed.

Over her shoulder, Jayfeather spotted movement; he shivered as Rock stepped out from behind a distant column, the moonlight shining on his hairless body. He fixed his bulging eyes on Jayfeather and nodded once.

"Half Moon!"

The sharp voice came from the entrance to the cave. The vision of Rock winked out. Jayfeather and Half Moon broke apart to see Rising Moon standing at the mouth of the tunnel.

"Half Moon, what are you doing here?" Rising Moon gave her daughter a disapproving glare, and her voice was like ice. "Jay's Wing, Chasing Clouds wants to speak to you. I've hunted all over for you."

Jayfeather dipped his head politely and brushed past her to

go out again into the main cavern. Chasing Clouds was lying where Jayfeather had left him, in the shallow scoop of sand. He raised his head as Jayfeather padded up. "You saved my life," he rasped. "Thank you."

Jayfeather scuffled the cave floor with his forepaws. "We all played a part," he mumbled.

"I can't believe we fought off that bird!" Chasing Clouds's voice grew stronger, and a gleam of pride appeared in his eyes.

"Well, you did," Jayfeather told him. "And you could do it again. Any of us could, if we tried hard enough."

"Not that again!" Rising Moon was close enough to overhear. "It's too dangerous."

"She's right." Jagged Lightning padded up to the gray-and-white she-cat's side. "Why should we risk our lives to catch our prey?"

"Because it's the only way to survive here." Half Moon faced the older cats. "And if we train properly, we won't be risking our lives every time."

Anger flashed in Rising Moon's eyes. She opened her jaws to retort, but Stone Song interrupted. "Look, we're all exhausted. This isn't the right time to be making decisions. Let's get some sleep and talk about it again tomorrow."

For a heartbeat Rising Moon and Jagged Lightning looked as if they wanted to argue, but then they turned away and stalked off to the other side of the cave. Stone Song and Half Moon found scoops in the floor, and curled up there, ready to sleep.

Jayfeather hesitated for a heartbeat, then took the few paw steps that brought him to Half Moon's side. She looked up at him, letting out a warm purr. Lying down beside her felt natural and right. Usually, Jayfeather slept close to a cat only if they were sick enough to be in the medicine cat's den. Even then, they would be in separate nests.

This is better, Jayfeather thought, yawning as he closed his eyes. *Comforting, even without the moss and feathers I'd have in the stone hollow* . . . He could still hear Half Moon's gentle breathing as he drifted into sleep.

A plaintive wail woke Jayfeather, cutting through the endless thunder of the falls. The gray light that filtered through the screen of falling water was strengthening, and he guessed that outside the sky was growing pale with the approach of dawn. Raising his head, he spotted Owl Feather's kits at the other side of the cave, pummeling their mother's belly with tiny paws as they tried to make the milk come.

"I'm sorry, kits," Owl Feather mewed sadly. "I've no more milk for you, because I haven't had enough to eat."

The miserable wailing went on. Other cats were stirring too; Dawn River was grooming herself, but most of the others just sat slumped on the cave floor. Jayfeather could feel their despair like a cold, smothering fog.

"We won't get a chance to go back to the lake," Whispering Breeze muttered. "This place will kill us first."

Jagged Lightning heaved himself out of the scoop in the cave floor and padded over to Owl Feather, resting his muzzle briefly on her head. "We have to hunt," he announced. "I won't let my kits starve."

Fish Leap turned toward Jayfeather, beckoning to him with his tail. "Jay's Wing, what was it you were saying yesterday about hunting in pairs?"

"More than pairs." Jayfeather scrambled out of his nest and padded across the cavern to join the others. Disturbed by his movement, Half Moon rose to her paws, gave herself a quick stretch, and followed. "We need a whole patrol to protect the hunters," he went on. "Two or three of the best hunters to catch the prey, and a few of the strongest cats and the best fighters to watch out for attacking birds."

"You mean fight off birds that can carry a cat into the sky?" Jagged Lightning sounded disbelieving. "I'd like to see that!"

"Oh, no!" Owl Feather looked up, distraught. "They'll steal my kits!"

"Then the kits mustn't leave the cave." Stone Song padded up to join them. "There's plenty of room here for them to play."

"And there's no need to worry," Dawn River added. "We're not going to be here that long."

"But what about the rest of us?" Rising Moon demanded. "Trying to fight birds like that is a mouse-brained idea."

"I wouldn't be too sure," Stone Song responded. "We fought off that bird yesterday. Okay, Chasing Clouds was hurt, but that doesn't need to happen if we can figure out the best way to defend ourselves."

Rising Moon let out a disbelieving snort.

"I think we ought to give Jay's Wing's idea a try," Dove's Wing meowed. "Even if we do decide to go back to the lake, we won't get far without food in our bellies."

"But how can we fight birds that big?" Fish Leap asked. "We can't fly up and attack them in the air."

"No, we'll have to lure one down to us." Stone Song sounded reluctant, as if he knew how his suggestion would be received. "Then we can work out the skills we need."

"You're not using my kits!" Owl Feather glared at him, protecting the three tiny cats with her paws and tail.

"Of course not," Stone Song reassured her.

"I'll do it," Half Moon offered. "I'll pretend to be injured."

Jayfeather felt his heart lurch. "No way," he mewed. "I'll do it. This was my idea."

Stone Song blinked at him. "You're taking quite a risk."

"Some cat has to," Jayfeather replied, forcing his voice to be steady, though inside he was shaking. It was too easy to imagine being whisked into the sky, gripped in cruel talons. "Are we going to do this or not? We need food right away."

Though some of the cats still seemed uncertain, enough of them gathered around Jayfeather to make up a patrol. Jayfeather looked at them: Stone Song, Jagged Lightning, and—to his surprise—Furled Bracken, along with Half Moon, Fish Leap, and Dove's Wing. All of them looked tense but determined.

"Let's go," Jayfeather meowed, leading the way out of the cave. Emerging from behind the waterfall, he realized that the storm was over. The howling wind had sunk to a stiff breeze, with a few flakes of snow tossed in the air, and gaps showed in the rolling gray clouds above their heads. The patrol crunched through the snow and clambered up the rocks beside the waterfall until they stood on top of the cliff.

Jayfeather took a deep breath. He had never trained another cat, especially not in fighting skills. The safety of these cats was his responsibility—not just now, when they were luring the bird down deliberately, but for all the generations to come. *Is this what it means, to have the power of the stars in my paws?*

"I'll stay out here while the rest of you hide," he directed. "Remember, you mustn't be seen from above because that's where the bird will come from. Stone Song, Jagged Lightning, and Furled Bracken, you get ready to leap out and attack. Fish Leap, Dove's Wing, Half Moon: You stay hidden and watch what happens. Then we can discuss tactics later."

"I'm not watching behind a rock while you get torn apart," Half Moon objected.

Her concern warmed Jayfeather. "You can join in if there's trouble," he told her.

Half Moon's tail lashed once. "Try stopping me!"

"What do we do when it comes?" Fish Leap asked. "We can't pounce on it as if it was a blackbird!"

"I think we should go for the wings," Stone Song suggested. "It can't carry one of us off if it can't fly."

Furled Bracken nodded. "Leaping for its neck would be good, too. That's a weak point on any bird, I don't care how big it is."

"Good idea," Jayfeather agreed. "Now, get out of sight before it spots you all."

The rest of the patrol slunk away to take up positions among the rocks.

"This is going to work," Half Moon encouraged Jayfeather before she left. "I just know it!"

I hope so, Jayfeather thought, aware of fear like a chunk of ice in his belly. *I have to do this, for the sake of the Tribe of Rushing Water.*

Standing at the edge of the river, Jayfeather felt very alone. The other cats had disappeared; all he could see was the tip of Fish Leap's tail, brown against the snow. He looked up into the sky; it was gray and endless, and there were no signs of any birds. His belly felt hollow and sore.

"Look!" Half Moon's low voice came from behind a nearby rock.

Blinking, Jayfeather gazed up into the sky again. A tiny speck had appeared, circling lazily far above. His paws felt frozen to the rock as he watched it; the bird came close enough for him to see that it was an eagle, like the ones he had heard about from the Tribe of Rushing Water. It was even bigger than the bird that had attacked them yesterday. He braced himself for it to swoop down on him, but then it circled away, losing interest.

No! Jayfeather wanted to yowl. *I'm a juicy bit of prey! Come and get me!*

He began to limp forward, holding up one paw as if he was injured, and let out a wail. The eagle swept through the sky, gliding down in a wide circle, until Jayfeather could make out its hooked talons and yellow, staring eyes.

Great StarClan—it's huge!

He crouched down in the snow, mewling piteously. The wing shadow covered him and spread around him; he squeezed his eyes shut tight as the bird's strong scent washed over him.

I hope the others are ready to pounce. . . .

The beating of the eagle's wings was like thunder. Then fearsome claws dug down into Jayfeather's shoulders and he let out a shriek. In the same heartbeat, caterwauling pierced the air around him. As his paws left the ground, the rocks sprang to life.

"Go for the wings!" Stone Song yowled. "Don't let it fly away!"

His words were swallowed up in the chaos of screeching cats and wildly flapping wings. Jayfeather spotted Furled Bracken leaping for the eagle's throat, missing it by a mouse-length as his claws slashed at air. Half Moon bit down on the edge of the eagle's wing and was flung off; she hit the rock with a thump, clutching a mouthful of feathers. Fish Leap grabbed at Jayfeather's tail and tried to hold him down.

"No! Let go!" Jayfeather shrieked, feeling his pelt begin to rip away with the added weight.

Fish Leap dropped back, and for a heartbeat Jayfeather thought that the eagle had won as it began to lift away from the cliff top. He could do nothing but flail his paws helplessly. Then Stone Song and Jagged Lightning raced in, one from either side, and made a leap for the eagle's wings. Both sank their claws in at the same moment; the eagle let out a furious cry, but it couldn't take to the air with the weight of a cat on each wing. While they held it down, Dove's Wing ducked underneath, close to Jayfeather, and gave a swift nip to each of the bird's legs, one after the other.

With another raucous screech, the eagle let Jayfeather go; he crashed down onto the rock, half-stunned, and watched as Stone Song and Jagged Lightning slashed at the bird's shoulders, scoring their claws through its feathers, then leaped aside to safety. The eagle mounted into the sky, shedding feathers as it went, blood dripping from its naked legs. Jayfeather watched, panting, as it dwindled to a speck in the sky and was gone.

"Are you okay?" Half Moon crouched panting on the cliff edge, but her green eyes glowed as she gazed at Jayfeather.

"I'm fine," Jayfeather gasped, though his shoulders where the eagle had gripped him felt as if they were on fire.

Half Moon rose to her paws and padded over to him, giving his wounds a sniff. "We ought to put moss on those, like you did for Chasing Clouds last night," she mewed. "I wonder if there's any dock growing around here. That's good to stop bleeding."

The rest of the patrol began to stagger to their paws, checking their own scratches.

"We did it!" Fish Leap croaked.

"Yes, we did." Stone Song's gaze rested on Jayfeather. "Jay's Wing, your plan to protect our hunters just might work. At least to find enough food until we leave." Waving his tail at the rest of the patrol, he added, "Come on. Let's go and tell the others."

He led the way down the rocks beside the waterfall, leaving Jayfeather and Half Moon alone on the cliff top.

"I was so scared for you," Half Moon murmured, brushing

her muzzle along his flank. "And I'm so proud of you! If we had kits, just think how brave they would be!"

Kits! "Half Moon . . ." he began awkwardly.

Before he could say more, he saw another cat emerge from behind one of the boulders at the water's edge. *Rock! Not now, please!*

The sightless cat stood waiting; though she was looking in that direction, Half Moon had no idea that he was there.

"Why don't you go down with the others?" Jayfeather suggested. "I'll follow you in a moment."

"Okay." There was a trace of disappointment in Half Moon's green eyes, but she headed down the cliff without protesting.

"What do you want now?" Jayfeather demanded.

Rock did not reply. For a moment they stood side by side at the edge of the cliff. Far away, a red glow on the snow showed where the sun would rise.

"So much is the same. . . ." Rock breathed. Then he turned to Jayfeather. "You can't stay here. You know that, don't you?"

"Why not?" Jayfeather demanded, with a sudden tug of anguish.

"You are too powerful to be lost in the past."

"I can be powerful here!" Jayfeather protested. "I could raise kits, teach them everything I know, and then go back to the Clans." He stared at Rock. "I . . . I don't want to leave."

CHAPTER 18

☘

"We have to get out of here!" Ivypool whispered, expecting hostile cats to leap out at them at any moment.

"We're only exploring," Blossomfall pointed out, padding up to the paw prints and giving them a curious sniff. "We're not doing any harm."

"Well, it doesn't feel like that," Ivypool retorted, annoyed by Blossomfall's nonchalance. "It feels like we're trespassing, and I want to leave."

Blossomfall shrugged. "Okay, let's find a way out."

On the opposite side of the river, more tunnels opened up, leading away into darkness. Ivypool leaped across the stream and headed into the nearest one. But she hadn't taken many paw steps when she was confronted by a solid wall of mud.

"No good," she told Blossomfall, who was following her. "This one's blocked."

Retracing their paw steps into the cave, they chose another opening. This one seemed more promising at first, leading upward with the occasional chink in the roof to let in light. Then Blossomfall, who was in the lead again, halted abruptly when the tunnel took a sharp turn to one side.

"Mouse dung!" she spat.

Ivypool craned her neck to see past her Clanmate; in the dim light she could make out a tumbled heap of stones and rock stretching right up to the tunnel roof. Ivypool's heart began to beat faster as they returned to the cave again. "We'll have to go back the way we came," she meowed, "and just hope that some cat comes along to help us out of the hole."

Blossomfall heaved a sigh. "I suppose you're right."

But as they leaped back across the river, Ivypool noticed for the first time that several tunnels led away from the cave on this side. "Do you remember which way we came in?" she asked her Clanmate.

Blossomfall shook her head. "We'll have to follow our scent trail."

But no scent lingered on the damp rock, and away from the edge of the water there was no trace of their paw prints on the hard floor.

"We're lost!" Ivypool yelped.

"We'll be fine," Blossomfall reassured her, though Ivypool could detect a hint of panic in her voice. "We'll just pick a tunnel. Come on!" Racing across the cave floor, she dived into a wide black opening. Ivypool was almost sure it was the wrong one, but she bounded after her Clanmate, terrified that they would be separated.

"Wait!" she yowled. "We can't—" She broke off at the clatter of falling rocks from up ahead. "Blossomfall!" she called. "What was that?"

There was no reply. Ivypool went limp with terror and she

had to force her legs to carry her along the tunnel. A few paw steps farther, she made out Blossomfall in the dim light; the tortoiseshell warrior was lying motionless on the floor with rocks scattered around her. Looking up, Ivypool saw a fresh scar on the roof, and guessed that the rocks must have fallen from there.

"Blossomfall?" she whispered, crouching beside her Clanmate. *StarClan, please don't let her be dead!*

A shudder of relief ran through her as Blossomfall's whiskers twitched and her eyes opened. "Ivypool?" she murmured. "What happened? My head hurts."

"I think a rock fell from the roof and hit you," Ivypool replied. "Can you get up?"

Blossomfall scrabbled with her paws, raising her shoulders off the floor, then collapsed with a whimper of pain. "Everything's whirling," she complained, her eyes wide and scared. "Oh, Ivypool, do you think we're going to die down here?"

"Of course we're not," Ivypool told her.

"But what if we do? Do you think Millie will miss me?"

Pity rushed through Ivypool from ears to tail-tip. "Of course!" she assured Blossomfall. "Millie loves you just as much as Briarlight."

As she reassured her Clanmate, Ivypool guessed that this was how Hawkfrost had won Blossomfall over: by giving her the chance to get as much attention as her sister, Briarlight.

Just as he did with Dovewing and me.

She felt sad that Blossomfall was so jealous of her sister for the amount of time her mother and her Clanmates spent with her. Briarlight had lost the use of her legs!

But then, Ivypool thought, *I don't suppose Dovewing's gift is always so much fun, either. Maybe we should both be grateful for what we have. . . .*

Blossomfall hesitated, then shrugged. "Maybe Millie loves me, when she remembers that she has more than one kit." Stretching out one forepaw, she scraped it against the hard stone of the tunnel floor, so violently that Ivypool was surprised she didn't wrench her claws out. "I hate myself for feeling jealous of Briarlight," Blossomfall confessed, not looking at Ivypool. "I can't bear seeing her suffer and I know Briarlight would give anything to be better and whole again. It's all so unfair!" Scoring her claws across the rock again, she added, "But I can't help what I feel, and that proves I'm not a good cat."

"Of course you are!" Ivypool exclaimed, shocked.

"No. A good cat wouldn't be jealous of an injured littermate. So that's why I've ended up in the Dark Forest." She gave Ivypool a sidelong glance. "I'm not stupid. I know it's where cats go if they're not allowed into StarClan. But I guess I won't get into StarClan either, because I hate my sister for being injured. So the Dark Forest is where I fit in, and I'm getting good training, better than anything we get here." She took in a long, shaking breath and looked around. "Will Hawkfrost come to get us, do you think?"

"I told you, we're not going to die!" Ivypool put every scrap of conviction she could muster into the words. *But what if we do?* She couldn't bear the thought of being trapped in the Dark Forest forever. "Blossomfall, do you think you could try again to get up?"

"Maybe." Blossomfall gathered her legs under her and managed to stand, though she still looked shaky.

As Ivypool was wondering how far her Clanmate would be able to go, she heard the soft pad of paw steps approaching from behind. Every hair on her pelt rose; she felt as though icy water was creeping over her entire body. It took all the courage she had to turn around.

A strange cat padded out of the shadows, a scrawny tom with ginger fur and wide, haunted eyes. "Oh!" he gasped. "I was expecting the other one."

"What other one?" Ivypool demanded, her voice cracking.

The stranger ignored her question; he was examining her and Blossomfall with puzzled eyes. "Two of you?" he meowed. "Are you all right?"

"No." Ivypool was too scared to waste time wondering who this strange cat was, or what he was doing here. "We need to get out. My Clanmate is hurt!"

"But if I show you the way out," the strange cat told her, "I'll be on my own again. You always promise to come back, but you never do."

Ivypool stared at him. "We've never been here before!" she meowed. "Please, you have to get us out of here."

The ginger tom flicked his ears crossly. "There's no need to shout. You shouldn't have come down here if you didn't want to stay. It's not safe, not unless you know what you're doing."

"Well, we don't," Ivypool replied, wondering what she could do to make him listen to her pleading. "We just want to go home."

The stranger came nearer, his eyes narrowed in suspicion; Ivypool tensed as he sniffed her, then Blossomfall. His scent spooked her: He smelled of earth and water and cold ancient stone.

"You're right, you don't belong down here," he murmured, and added more briskly, "All right. Go down this tunnel and take the turn after the rock shaped like a mushroom. Follow that passage for ten fox-lengths, and you'll see that the tunnel splits into three. Take the middle one. That should start leading upward, and you'll come to a heap of stones. There's enough space at the top for you to squeeze through, and from there you can see the way out."

Ivypool's mind buzzed like a hollow tree full of bees as she tried to remember the directions. "Can you show us?"

"No." The ginger tom was already backing away. "You must go on your own."

Before Ivypool could protest, he had vanished into the shadows. "Mange-pelt!" she muttered, lashing her tail. For a couple of heartbeats she stared down the tunnel where he had disappeared, then turned back to Blossomfall. "Come on. Let's get moving."

Sending Blossomfall in front, in case the tortoiseshell warrior collapsed again, Ivypool headed along the tunnel. They found the mushroom-shaped rock the ginger tom had mentioned, but the tunnel they had to turn into was completely dark, and there was no way to tell where they were.

"I'm sure we've come more than ten fox-lengths," Ivypool meowed as they padded cautiously forward, "but we haven't found the place where the tunnel divides.'"

"Maybe we've passed it without realizing," Blossomfall suggested. "I think we should go back."

"Okay." Ivypool turned and padded into the darkness, straining her eyes for the first signs of light. But the shadows were never-ending.

"We should have reached the first turn by now," Blossomfall mewed, her voice quavering.

"I know." As she spoke, Ivypool realized that a faint breeze was ruffling her fur on one side. "I think it's here," she mewed, relieved. "This way."

Almost as soon as they turned into the new passage, Ivypool realized that they had gone wrong again. There was no sign of the mushroom-shaped rock. The passage led steeply downward and her paws slipped on slick, damp rock as she padded along it.

I hope we don't have to go back. I'm not sure Blossomfall could climb up this way again.

Then Ivypool began to make out a faint gray light filtering from farther down the passage. "We're getting somewhere!" she called out encouragingly, picking up the pace.

With Blossomfall struggling along behind her, Ivypool stepped out of the mouth of the tunnel and halted, letting out a yowl of disappointment. They were back in the cave with the underground river.

"I don't believe this!" Blossomfall hissed, flopping down on the ground. "We'll never get out."

"I wish I'd asked that cat his name," Ivypool meowed. "We

could call for him." Twitching her whiskers angrily, she added, "I don't suppose he would have come, anyway."

Blossomfall lay on her side, panting. "I'm sorry," she whispered. "This is all my fault. I was the one who wanted to come down here."

"I could have stopped you," Ivypool argued.

"How?" Incredibly, there was a gleam of humor in Blossomfall's eyes. "By hanging on to my tail?"

Ivypool let out a snort of amusement. She couldn't help picturing herself with her teeth sunk into Blossomfall's tail while the tortoiseshell warrior dangled over the hole.

"Come on! What are you waiting for?"

The voice came from behind them; Ivypool stiffened, her pelt bristling and her paws tingling with fear. A heartbeat later she forced herself to turn around, but she could see nothing, unless perhaps there was a gleam of eyes in the darkest recesses of the cave. She was sure, though, that it wasn't the ginger tom they had met before.

"You do want to get out, don't you?" the voice went on impatiently. "You know you shouldn't be here."

"Oh, yes—please help us!" Blossomfall begged.

"Very well. Follow me."

Ivypool spotted a dark cat shape whisking into one of the tunnels a few tail-lengths away, but however hard she peered she couldn't make out anything that would help her identify the cat. She hauled Blossomfall to her paws and followed. The tunnel was narrow and dark; Ivypool couldn't see anything of the cat they were following, knowing its presence only by the pad of paw steps and the scent of earth and water and green forest growth.

The trek went on for a long time, through twisting tunnels and down cross-passages, until Blossomfall began to falter. The tunnel had grown a little wider, so that Ivypool could pad by her side and let her lean on her shoulder.

"Is it much farther?" Ivypool called to the cat in front of them.

There was no reply, but the next turn in the tunnel showed bright daylight ahead. The path leading up to the burst of light was steep, covered in bare earth with a few paw prints here and there. But the cat who had rescued them had vanished.

"Where did it go?" Ivypool asked, puzzled.

Blossomfall was too exhausted to reply. She dragged herself into the open and collapsed into a patch of sunlight beside an oak stump. Looking around, Ivypool thought she caught a glimpse of movement among the ferns a few tail-lengths away.

"Thank you!" she called.

There was no response, and in the same heartbeat the movement ceased. The mouth of the tunnel gaped open among rocks where water had trickled down to form a small pool. Ivypool clawed up a pawful of moss and soaked it in the water for Blossomfall to drink.

"Thanks!" the she-cat gasped, sitting up. "Wow, that place was weird! It's good to be out in the sun again."

"We'd better get back to camp," Ivypool meowed. "Are you fit to travel?"

"I'd better be," Blossomfall replied grimly.

Examining her Clanmate, Ivypool wasn't so sure. Both cats were filthy and exhausted, their pads cracked from walking on hard stone. But as well as her injuries from the Dark Forest training, Blossomfall had a bump on her head from the rock fall that almost closed one of her eyes.

"We'll take it slowly," Ivypool murmured. She wasn't even sure where they were. *There are too many trees for this to be WindClan,* she thought, gazing around at the ancient oaks and beeches, and the tangled undergrowth between them. *But suppose we've come up in the middle of ShadowClan? What if we meet a patrol?*

She said nothing of her worries to Blossomfall, but she thought that her Clanmate had worked out the dangers for herself. She was nervous, jumping at the slightest rustle in the undergrowth, and Ivypool's paws prickled with apprehension with every step she took. She felt vast relief as she detected an overwhelming scent of ThunderClan just ahead, and a few heartbeats later they crossed the border into their own territory.

"Thank StarClan for that!" Blossomfall exclaimed. "Ivypool, what do you think we ought to say when we get back to camp?"

"Not the truth," Ivypool responded instantly.

Blossomfall halted, bristling, and Ivypool added, "We're already lying to our Clanmates, in a way, by not telling them about the Dark Forest."

"That's different," Blossomfall muttered.

Though Ivypool didn't argue, she felt privately that one lie more or less wasn't going to make much difference.

"We'll have to say that we got lost," Blossomfall went on, limping forward once more.

Well, that's not being entirely honest, is it? Ivypool thought. "Right, *really* lost," she mewed out loud.

As they drew closer to the stone hollow, they managed to pick up the pace, but it was well after sunhigh by the time they stumbled through the thorn tunnel and into the camp. Several of their Clanmates were crouched around the fresh-kill pile; Ivypool spotted Sandstorm and Thornclaw, back from the hunting patrol. Firestar and Graystripe were both there, along with her mother, Whitewing, and more of the senior warriors. She braced herself for trouble. When Ivypool and Blossomfall padded forward, their Clanmates looked up, staring at them mid-mouthful; Brackenfur had a mousetail dangling from his jaws, while Sorreltail had a blackbird feather stuck to her nose.

"What happened to you?" Sandstorm demanded, rising to her paws and coming to meet the two she-cats. "Thornclaw and I thought you must have followed a prey trail. Didn't you catch anything?"

Blossomfall shook her head. "We got lost."

Ivypool realized how lame the explanation sounded. She couldn't blame some of the cats for looking at them with suspicion, and her heart pounded harder as Firestar summoned them over to him with a flick of his tail. The ThunderClan leader studied them, his brilliant green eyes narrowed. "You got *lost?*" he echoed. "In ThunderClan territory?"

"And why do you look as if some cat pulled you through a bramble thicket backward?" Thornclaw asked. "Did you meet rogues? Or WindClan?"

"No," Ivypool meowed. "We just—"

"Ivypool!" To Ivypool's relief, her mother, Whitewing, padded up, pushing past Thornclaw and shooting a glare at Firestar. "What does it matter where they've been?" she demanded, in between covering Ivypool's face and neck with licks. "They're obviously hurt. I thought you'd just been distracted by newleaf prey," she added to Ivypool. "I can't bear to think that you were in real trouble."

"We're fine, honestly," Ivypool insisted.

Whitewing's green gaze was loving. "It's hard enough having one daughter out of sight," she mewed. "I can't lose track of another one."

Ivypool noticed that Millie had appeared from the medicine cat's den, helping Briarlight over to the fresh-kill pile. She seemed not to notice Blossomfall until Whitewing called out to her.

"Millie, Blossomfall and Ivypool got lost. It looks as if they've had a tough time."

Millie looked up, then left Briarlight to carry on dragging herself across the camp, while she stalked up to Blossomfall. Her tail-tip was twitching in annoyance.

Wow, Ivypool thought, feeling a pang of guilt that Whitewing had been so kind and sympathetic to her. *Millie really does think she's got only one kit now.*

"Where have you been?" Millie snapped. "You've wasted a whole morning when you could have been hunting!" Glancing back at Briarlight, who was struggling to join the group at the fresh-kill pile, she added, "Your sister would give anything to be able to help feed the Clan! It's time you grew up, Blossomfall, and started to behave like a proper warrior."

Several of the cats stretched their eyes wide.

"There's no harm done," Brackenfur meowed, blinking at Blossomfall in concern. "Both cats are home safe, and that's the main thing, isn't it?"

"Is it?" Millie drew her lips back in a snarl. Her eyes were full of bitterness as she went back to Briarlight.

Feeling awkward, Ivypool padded over to Blossomfall. "Your mother doesn't mean it. . . ." she began.

Blossomfall dismissed her words with a swish of her tail. "Whatever," she muttered, her gaze following Millie as she helped Briarlight pick out a plump vole from the fresh-kill pile. "This is just the way it is now. I'd better get used to it. At least I get noticed in the Dark Forest."

Her words sent a chill running through Ivypool. *I wonder how many other cats would be ready to listen to Hawkfrost's clever words,* she asked herself as she looked at her Clanmates, peacefully settled around the fresh-kill pile. *It could be any of them training to fight their own Clanmates when the final battle comes!*

CHAPTER 19

"Please," Jayfeather begged. *"Let me stay* here with Half Moon. This is my only chance to live like my Clanmates, to raise kits and grow old with a mate."

"That is not why you have returned to these cats," Rock meowed somberly. "And this is not where Half Moon's future lies. She must become the first Teller of the Pointed Stones."

"Why?" Anger and frustration gripped Jayfeather with all the force of the eagle's talons. "Why not some other cat?"

"Because Half Moon can read the reflections," Rock replied. "She saw the sign of the moon."

"Any cat could have seen that!"

Rock shook his head. "It is not her destiny to have kits and live the same life as her companions. You must help her see that."

"Couldn't you have done that on your own?" Jayfeather's anger was rising now, spinning out of his control. "Why did you need me? Did you know what would happen, how I would feel about Half Moon?"

Rock dipped his head, an admission that he had known it

all. "You have the power of the stars, Jayfeather. There are some things you must do, however hard they may seem."

"It's not fair." Jayfeather flexed his claws. "And you can't make me."

He turned away, meaning to go back to the cave and seek out Half Moon, but suddenly Rock was in front of him, barring his way with ominous strength, in spite of his blindness and scrawny, hairless body.

"I can make you if I have to," he warned Jayfeather quietly. "Where do you think the prophecy came from? This is your destiny. Yours and Half Moon's."

Trembling with fury, Jayfeather brushed past him and scrambled down beside the waterfall. Between his anger and his soreness from fighting the eagle, he lost his footing a few tail-lengths from the ground and fell, the breath driven from his body as he landed beside the pool. Struggling to his paws, he spotted Rising Moon at the end of the path that led behind the waterfall. He braced himself for more cold words as she padded toward him, but as she drew closer he saw that her eyes were full of gentle concern.

"Thank you for your courage, Jay's Wing," she mewed. "If we can survive here until we are strong enough to go back to the lake, you have done us a great favor."

Following her back into the cave, Jayfeather saw that most of the cats were clustered around Stone Song and the rest of the patrol.

"So we leaped up onto the eagle's wings. . . ." Stone Song

gave a huge jump into the air as he spoke.

Owl Feather's three kits were watching with open mouths, their hunger forgotten.

"Come on, Strong Pounce," one of them mewed to his littermate. "I'm going to be an eagle, and you and Running Fox can attack me."

"You're so bossy, Lapping Wave," another kit replied. "I want to be the eagle!" He flung himself at his littermate and all three kits wrestled together on the floor.

Jayfeather suppressed a *mrrow* of laughter to see the tiny cats behaving like kits again. For the first time he sensed optimism and humor among these cats.

"So the eagle let Jayfeather go, and flew off," Stone Song finished. "We won!"

Yowls of approval rose up from the cats who surrounded him. Stone Song let them continue for a moment, then raised his tail for silence. "We need a hunting patrol," he went on. "Jagged Lightning, you come with me, and Dove's Wing and Fish Leap. You were best at fighting the eagle, so we'll protect the hunters."

"Rising Moon and Dawn River should do the hunting," Jagged Lightning meowed with a nod of agreement. "They were the best at catching prey by the lake."

"Right." Stone Song gathered his patrol together with a wave of his tail. "We'll take Whispering Breeze, too. That should be enough for now."

The patrol headed toward the entrance to the cave, the rest of the cats clustering together to watch them go. "Good luck!"

Half Moon called.

"Bring us back something tasty!" Running Horse added.

Jayfeather knew that he should feel hopeful. Although the cats were still thinking about returning to the lake, they were at least making an effort to adapt to life in the mountains. But he had no room for hope; all he could think about was how he had to teach Half Moon to become Stoneteller, and then return to the time of the Clans.

Stone Song nodded to Jayfeather as the patrol padded past him on their way to the path behind the waterfall. "We owe you a lot," he meowed. "You should stay here and get some rest after your struggle."

Jayfeather dipped his head, though inwardly he was wincing. *They treat me like one of them.*

But all the time he belonged somewhere else, far, far away.

Half Moon bounded up to him. "Are you fit to go out again? I was thinking about those herbs that you found yesterday, when we were buried in the snow. We ought to go see if there are any more."

Jayfeather's heart weighed heavier than the mountains as he gazed into her eager eyes. "Can we go to the cave with the pointed stones first?"

Half Moon looked puzzled, then nodded. "If you want to."

As they crossed the cavern, Jayfeather spotted Shy Fawn lying near Owl Feather, with her swollen belly propped awkwardly. *Her kits will be born soon,* he thought.

Half Moon paused and touched Shy Fawn's shoulder with her tail-tip. "You'll be fine now," she murmured. "The patrol will bring you some prey."

Shy Fawn blinked gratefully.

Jayfeather led the way down the tunnel into the Cave of Pointed Stones. Dawn light spilled through the hole in the roof, turning the pools to sheets of glimmering silver. Jayfeather let his gaze travel over the spikes of stone. Everything looked just the same as it did in the time of the Tribe of Rushing Water. If the stones had grown by then, he couldn't tell. The cave seemed alive with the sound of dripping water, the light rippling over the columns and pinnacles.

"I wonder whether any other cats have visited here," Half Moon meowed, her voice echoing. "Do you think the moon shines in the pool every night?"

Jayfeather swallowed uncomfortably. "I've got something to tell you."

Half Moon padded close to him, her beautiful green eyes expectant. "Yes, Jay's Wing?"

Taking a deep breath, Jayfeather stared down at the pool as he spoke. "I followed you here for a reason. I . . . I know some things you don't." When he dared to glance at Half Moon again, he saw that she was bristling playfully. Clearly she thought she knew what he was going to say.

"No . . . not like that." Every word was being wrenched out of Jayfeather. "Half Moon, this is the place where you are meant to be. You and all the cats from the lake. Other cats have lived here before and survived, however hard it seems. You can't go back. Your future lies here."

Half Moon stared at him as if he had grown a second head.

Continuing to talk to her was the hardest thing Jayfeather had ever done. *I'd face all the eagles in the mountains rather than tell her this.*

"You will become their leader," he went on. "This cave will be your den, and your ancestors will guide you with signs in the pool, like the reflection of the new moon you saw last night. You will be known as the Teller of the Pointed Stones. This is your destiny."

For a few heartbeats there was silence. "Well, that's a mouthful of a name!" Half Moon meowed at last. Her voice was shaking—with outrage or amusement, Jayfeather couldn't tell. "Is this some kind of joke?"

"No. I promise you it isn't." Jayfeather's heart sank when he saw anger gathering in the green eyes that had looked at him so warmly.

"You came all this way to tell me this?" she burst out. "Where did you get all these mouse-brained ideas? Jay's Wing, I've shown you how I feel! Is it so awful that I might have wanted to have your kits? If you're not interested, then why can't you just turn me down, like any normal tom?"

Her fury, her sense of betrayal, crashed over Jayfeather like a wave. Overwhelmed, drowning in it, he murmured, "This has nothing to do with me. It's your destiny! I'm sorry!"

For a heartbeat, Half Moon faced him, glaring; then she whipped around and stormed out of the cave.

"Wait—"

Jayfeather bounded after her; when he emerged from the tunnel he saw her racing across the cavern to the entrance. *She mustn't go out there alone! It's dangerous!*

"Stop!" he yowled.

Half Moon ignored him. But then a feeble wail rose from the side of the cave where Shy Fawn was lying. "Half Moon, help me! My kits are coming!"

Half Moon halted, then spun around, looking for Jayfeather. "Jay's Wing! Over here!" she called.

Jayfeather hurried across the cave and met her in front of Shy Fawn. Owl Feather was heading in her direction, too, but she was held up by her kits tumbling around her paws.

"Stay back there," the she-cat scolded her litter. "This isn't for kits."

"But we want to see!" Strong Pounce protested.

"No! Go over there and play, and don't make too much noise. This is a hard time for Shy Fawn."

Looking down at the pregnant she-cat, Jayfeather had to agree. Shy Fawn's distended belly was huge for such a small cat, and he wondered how many kits she was carrying. Her eyes were wide and scared.

"Please help me," she whispered. "I don't know what to do."

Anger clawed at Jayfeather as he realized how frightened she was. She should have given birth among the soft moss and bracken of a proper nursery, not here on this rocky floor without even the right herbs.

At least she's got a medicine cat, he thought.

"Half Moon," he began briskly, "you remember where we got the moss for Chasing Clouds? Can you get some more, and soak it with water so that Shy Fawn can have a drink?"

Half Moon nodded and sped off.

"Owl Feather, I need a stick. Something good and stout that Shy Fawn can bite down on when the pains come. You should find one by the bushes around the pool."

Owl Feather blinked in surprise at being ordered around, but she didn't protest, just called over her shoulder as she padded toward the entrance, "Make sure my kits don't follow me out."

Jayfeather turned his attention back to Shy Fawn. Powerful ripples were passing across her belly, and she gasped with pain.

"Relax as much as you can," Jayfeather advised her. "It won't be long now."

Half Moon reappeared with a bundle of wet moss in her jaws and sat down beside Shy Fawn's head, helping her to drink, then licking her ears gently to keep her calm.

Another ripple coursed over Shy Fawn's belly, and she let out a sharp cry of pain as she began straining.

"That's good," Jayfeather reassured her. "You're coming along nicely."

Owl Feather bounded up with the stick Jayfeather had asked for, and dropped it on the ground so that Shy Fawn could grip it in her jaws. "How many kits, do you think?" she asked Jayfeather.

Jayfeather felt Shy Fawn's belly with his forepaw. "Three, at least," he replied, realizing how weird it was to be able to see as he delivered kits. "Hang on, I think the first one's coming."

Shy Fawn's belly convulsed. Jayfeather heard the stick crack in her teeth, and a small bundle of wet fur slid out onto the cave floor. Half Moon cushioned it with her paws and nudged it over to Shy Fawn.

"It's a little tom," she mewed. "Isn't he beautiful?"

Shy Fawn gazed down at her kit, all the fear gone from her eyes, swallowed up in overwhelming love. "He's black, just like Dark Whiskers," she murmured, bending her head to lick his fur.

Jayfeather gave her shoulder a prod with one paw. "Concentrate. There's more to come."

"Yes, I—oh!" Shy Fawn's words ended in a yowl as the pain gripped her again.

Jayfeather massaged her belly, while Half Moon stroked her head. "Breathe deeply," she encouraged her. "It'll be over soon."

As she spoke, a second kit slid out; Jayfeather trapped it gently between his forepaws and placed it beside its littermate. "Another tom," he meowed. "And the next one's right behind it."

As Shy Fawn strained to bring her next kit into the world, Jayfeather heard jubilant yowls from outside the cave and turned his head to see the hunting patrol jostling through the entrance. Stone Song was carrying a vole, while Jagged Lightning was dragging an enormous snow-white hare.

"It worked!" Fish Leap bounded into the middle of the cavern. "A hawk swooped down on us, but it took one look at our claws and flew away again."

"We should be able to work out a way to catch birds," Dove's

Wing meowed. "An eagle would feed all of us for days!"

Then the hunting patrol fell silent as they realized what was going on. Stone Song dropped his vole and raced across the cavern to Shy Fawn. "Her kits are here!" he exclaimed. "Is she going to be okay?"

"She'll be fine," Jayfeather replied. Shy Fawn's third kit—a little she-cat—had made her appearance. Looking down at the exhausted mother cat, he had his doubts about what he had just said, but he wasn't going to voice them. Shy Fawn had been hungry and worn out by the journey before she ever got here, grieving for her mate, and life in the cavern still looked pretty bleak. But at least the hunting had been successful.

"Bring her something to eat," he directed. "And when it's ready, that hare's pelt would be good to keep the kits warm."

By now Shy Fawn's three kits were beginning to squeak and wriggle. She guided them toward her teats, but Jayfeather fended them off with one forepaw while he ran the other over her belly.

"You're not finished yet," he told her. "There's another kit in there."

Shy Fawn made one last effort, letting out a high-pitched screech. The final kit slithered out and lay motionless on the cave floor.

"There!" Half Moon exclaimed. "Well done!"

Shy Fawn collapsed, exhausted, and Half Moon guided the kits into the curve of her belly. Each of them latched on to a teat, and their high-pitched complaints died away into silence as they began to suckle.

Jayfeather felt the fourth kit gently with one paw; it was another tom, this time with a golden tabby pelt, and though he was so small, he looked compact and strong. But he still didn't move.

"Is he dead?" Half Moon whispered.

Jayfeather thought he could detect the feeble flutter of a heartbeat, but the kit didn't seem to be breathing. "He's not dead," he replied. "And I'm not going to let him give up that easily!"

He pawed a little mucus out of the kit's mouth, then began licking him vigorously, thrusting the fur the wrong way to warm the kit up and start his body working. Shy Fawn raised her head and watched anxiously. Suddenly the tiny kit convulsed between Jayfeather's paws. He took a gulp of air and let out a loud yowl straight at Jayfeather, who stared at the familiar golden pelt and the set of the shoulders, and marveled at the strength in the tiny body.

"He has a roar like a lion," some cat commented from behind Jayfeather.

"Then I'll call him Lion's Roar," Shy Fawn murmured proudly.

No, Jayfeather thought. *This is Lionblaze. Welcome, brother.*

He gave the kit a lick between the ears and nudged him into the curve of Shy Fawn's belly, where he began to suckle strongly next to his littermates. Jayfeather glanced over his shoulder to see Dove's Wing among the cats who were crowding around. The gray she-cat's eyes were wide with wonder as she watched Shy Fawn caring for her litter.

And there you are, as well, Jayfeather thought. *How weird: She's called Dovewing in our time, too.* Glancing from Dove's Wing to Lion's Roar, he added to himself, *The three of us are here now, even if the other two don't realize it. The Power of Three has begun.*

Suddenly he sensed a familiar presence at his shoulder.

"It is nearly time," Rock whispered.

Jayfeather tensed, and for a heartbeat he considered ignoring the ancient cat's warning. Then he sighed. He knew there was no use fighting destiny. Glancing around, he spotted Half Moon and made his way to her side. "Come on. Let's go out for some air," he murmured.

Half Moon nodded and followed him along the path and up the rocks beside the waterfall. To Jayfeather's astonishment, he saw that the short leaf-bare day had ended and the moon was shining, a little brighter and plumper than the night before.

Standing at the edge of the cliff, her fur ruffled by the breeze, Half Moon looked up at the thin crescent. "It's still there," she whispered.

"Yes, and it will always be there," Jayfeather responded. "Just as your descendants will be here. It's up to you to make them stay, Half Moon, to persuade them that they can survive with their new ways of hunting. You must use all your skills with herbs to look after them."

Half Moon's green eyes were worried. "I don't want to be a leader," she protested.

"Then call yourself their Healer."

The she-cat looked away as if she didn't want Jayfeather to

see the pain in her eyes. "You truly believe this, don't you?"

Jayfeather stepped closer to her and touched the tip of her ear with his muzzle. "Yes, I do. This is all meant to be. However much I wish things could be different."

Half Moon let out a long sigh. Closing her eyes, she leaned against Jayfeather. "You're going to leave me again, aren't you?"

Jayfeather nodded. "I'm so sorry. I wish I could stay." He gave her ear a lick, but there was little comfort in it. "You will be a great Healer," he went on. "Let the moon and the stars guide you. I promise everything will be okay."

Half Moon looked up at him. "I believe you, because I trust you," she whispered.

Jayfeather stepped back, the light of the slender moon spilling around them, turning Half Moon's white fur to silver. As if there was a voice prompting him from inside his head, he knew what he had to say. "From this moment on, you will be known as the Teller of the Pointed Stones. Others will come after you, moon upon moon upon moon. Choose them well, train them well, and trust the future of your Tribe to them."

"Tribe?" Half Moon echoed.

"Yes," Jayfeather replied. "You are a Tribe now, united in loyalty to everything you represent. It won't be easy, but the other cats will understand what needs to be done to keep you safe here forever."

"I'll miss you." Half Moon's voice was desolate.

"And I you. I won't ever forget you, I promise."

Jayfeather leaned toward her, and their noses touched. *If*

only . . . Jayfeather thought.

Half Moon was the first to break away. Jayfeather watched as she jumped neatly down beside the waterfall, paused at the end of the path for one brief glance at him over her shoulder, then vanished into the cave.

"Good-bye, Stoneteller," Jayfeather murmured. "May the Tribe of Endless Hunting light your path, always."

CHAPTER 20

"Mouse dung! Which cat thought night training would be a good idea?" Thornclaw muttered, pulling away from a trailing bramble tendril and leaving a tuft of tabby fur behind. "I can't see my own paws!"

Lionblaze suppressed a *mrrow* of amusement. "That would be Firestar," he meowed. "You know he wants us to keep all our skills sharp."

Thornclaw let out a snort of disgust as he headed after the rest of the patrol. Lionblaze brought up the rear with his ears pricked, but all he could hear was the faint pad of his Clanmates' paw steps and the rustle of branches in the breeze. The forest was cool and quiet, with only a thin sliver of moon to light the cats' path.

Brackenfur, who was leading the patrol, halted in the next clearing. "Right, this is the exercise," he began. "We split into two patrols. I'll lead one, with Thornclaw, Bumblestripe, and Birchfall. Sorreltail, you can lead the other, with Ivypool, Lionblaze, and Berrynose."

"So what are we supposed to be doing?" Berrynose asked, scuffling his paws through the dead leaves.

"Each patrol has to approach and seize control of the old Twoleg nest," Brackenfur explained. "And stop the other patrol from taking it, of course. Even better if we can track down and capture some of the opposing patrol."

"Sounds like fun!" Bumblestripe exclaimed.

Sorreltail raised her tail. "Brackenfur, we don't want to get into serious fights, do we? If one of us jumps on your patrol, then we've won, right?"

"In your dreams!" Brackenfur blinked at his mate with warm amber eyes. "But yes, good point. If you're jumped on, you surrender. This is an exercise in night tracking, not fighting."

When there were no more questions, Brackenfur waved his tail as a signal to his own patrol to move off. Sorreltail watched them go, her eyes narrowed; Lionblaze guessed she was trying to work out which route they would take. Then she summoned her own patrol with a flick of her ears and led the way into the trees.

The undergrowth was thicker here; it was hard to move quietly and harder still to see the other cats. The thin claw-scratch of moon and the weak starlight were hardly any use at all. Trying to creep down a slope covered with bracken, Lionblaze crashed into Sorreltail's rump and realized that she had halted.

"Sorry!"

Sorreltail gave him a brief nod, then twitched her tail to summon the others. "Any suggestions?" she whispered. "Ivypool?"

Ivypool's eyes were shining in the dim light. "We need

to stick to the shadows," she meowed, "and try not to brush against the undergrowth. We should think how we find prey while we're hunting."

Sorreltail gave an approving nod. "Very good."

Lionblaze had felt a chill of unease as Ivypool spoke. Training in the Dark Forest had given her an edge on stalking by night.

"Why are we sitting here?" Berrynose demanded. "The others could be at the Twoleg nest by now."

"I don't think so," Sorreltail murmured. "I know how Brackenfur thinks. They'll make a wide circle and try to come at the nest from the other side, so that we can't track them down." Her eyes gleamed. "At least, that's what he *hopes* will happen. Let's go!"

The patrol headed down the slope and through a hazel thicket. Lionblaze watched how sure-footed Ivypool was, winding her way through the undergrowth like a passing shadow, seeming to know instinctively when to duck low beneath overhanging branches and when to slip almost unseen from one patch of darkness to the next. Admiration battled inside him with apprehension. Were the tactics of the Dark Forest becoming part of ThunderClan's skills? Was that what Tigerstar thought would happen?

Or will Ivypool be in trouble on her next visit to the Dark Forest, for giving away their secrets? Lionblaze sighed. *At least she's here now, and not training with our enemies in her dreams.*

"Hey! Mouse-brain! Are you asleep?"

Lionblaze jumped at Berrynose's irritated hiss, and spotted

the cream-colored tom a few paces ahead, glaring back over his shoulder.

"Okay, I'm coming," he whispered back, hurrying to catch up.

Sorreltail halted again on the edge of the old Thunderpath; the Twoleg nest was on the other side, several fox-lengths farther down but still out of sight. "We're going to win this, no question." Her voice was a soft murmur, barely audible. "Berrynose, you'll come with me, and we'll take the nest." The young tom puffed his chest out. "Lionblaze, you and Ivypool are going to capture one of Brackenfur's patrol. If I'm right, they'll be somewhere over there." Sorreltail pointed across the Thunderpath with her tail.

Lionblaze nodded to show that he understood; Ivypool was quivering with impatience to be off. Sorreltail flicked her ears to send them on their way, then jerked her head for Berrynose to follow her. They headed down the Thunderpath, keeping close to the edge where they were hidden by overhanging ferns; after a few moments Lionblaze couldn't see them anymore. He tasted the air, but he couldn't pick up any trace of the other patrol. *Good. That means they can't scent us, either.* Signaling with his ears to Ivypool, he slunk across the exposed stone of the Thunderpath, crouching low with his belly fur brushing the ground.

He crawled into the dense undergrowth on the other side, heading toward the back of the old Twoleg den. Pushing his way through thick stems, he became conscious of his own bulk, and once more admired Ivypool's slinky, deft movements, confident and swift in spite of the darkness.

Lionblaze tasted the air again, and this time picked up a definite trace of cat. *Sorreltail was right about where Brackenfur would approach the nest!* Angling his ears toward Ivypool, he veered in a slightly different direction to home in on the scent. Moving faster than he could manage in the shadows, Ivypool drew ahead, then raised her tail, warning him to stop. The cat scent was stronger now. Lionblaze strained his ears for signs of movement. At first there was nothing. Then he heard a faint crunching, as if some cat had stepped on a dry leaf.

Ivypool had heard it, too. She gestured with her tail, directing Lionblaze to circle around so that they could attack the other patrol from both sides. Lionblaze slid into the new position and waited under a holly bush at the edge of a bramble thicket. Though he couldn't see Brackenfur's patrol, he had a pretty good idea of where they were, and he couldn't understand why Ivypool was still signaling to him to wait.

He twitched his tail in frustration. *What is she playing at?*

There was a faint rustling and the first of the patrol—Thornclaw—emerged from a clump of ferns. He was heading for the bramble thicket, and Lionblaze noticed for the first time a narrow path leading through the thorns, in the direction of the Twoleg nest. Thornclaw slid along the path, followed by Birchfall and Bumblestripe. Brackenfur brought up the rear, glancing over his shoulder from time to time as if he was checking that Sorreltail's patrol wasn't following them.

No, we're not, mouse-brain! Lionblaze thought gleefully. *We're already here!*

Now he understood Ivypool's strategy. Glancing at where she crouched in the shelter of a rock, he saw her poised to pounce, and gathered his own muscles, ready for a leap.

The first three cats had entered the thicket, strung out along the narrow path that would only let them pass in single file. Brackenfur paused at the edge for a last glance around. He opened his jaws to taste the air, his eyes suddenly narrowing in suspicion.

Now!

Leaping in the same heartbeat, Lionblaze and Ivypool crashed into Brackenfur and brought him down in a tangle of flailing legs and tails. The ginger tom let out a screech of surprise.

"Got you!" Lionblaze declared. "You're our prisoner now, right?"

"Right," Brackenfur admitted ruefully, with Ivypool's paws planted on his chest.

Yowls came from the bramble thicket. Lionblaze heard Thornclaw's voice raised in exasperation. "Turn around, for StarClan's sake. Go back!"

"I can't!" That was Bumblestripe. "There isn't room!"

"Fox dung! I'm stuck!" Birchfall snarled. "We'll have to go forward."

Amusement bubbling inside him, Lionblaze waved his tail for Ivypool to let Brackenfur stand up. "We don't need to worry about *them* for a bit," he meowed. "Let's head for the den."

Now they could race through the forest without worrying

about being seen or heard. Lionblaze took the lead as they burst out of the undergrowth, across the stand of pine trees at the back of the Twoleg den, and through a gap in the stone wall.

"Get out—oh, it's you." Berrynose stopped himself just in time from leaping on Lionblaze as he slid through the gap, followed by Brackenfur and Ivypool. Sorreltail, who was circling the walls trying to keep an eye on all the possible ways in at once, halted. Her tail shot up in surprise and approval.

"Great! You got one!" She padded up to Brackenfur and touched noses with him. "Welcome to *our* den."

Brackenfur purred and brushed his muzzle against her shoulder. "Well done!"

A few heartbeats later, the rest of Brackenfur's patrol came panting up and pushed their way through the gap. All of them were missing tufts of fur, and Birchfall had a scratch across his nose. The bramble thicket had done the hard work for the winning patrol!

"Okay, you beat us." Thornclaw flopped down on his side. "That was a clever move."

"We ought to discuss what we've learned," Brackenfur meowed, sitting down beside his mate. "What would we do differently if we did this exercise again?"

"Stay out of brambles," Birchfall replied in a heartfelt tone, licking one paw and dabbing it on his nose.

"It was a good idea to split up," Bumblestripe commented. "Why didn't we think of that?"

"Yes, it was an excellent idea," Brackenfur agreed, giving

Lionblaze an approving nod. "You and Ivypool distracted us while Sorreltail and Berrynose captured the nest."

"I had nothing to do with it," Lionblaze corrected him. "Sorreltail thought of splitting up, and it was Ivypool's idea to wait for you beside those brambles."

The rest of the cats looked impressed, while Sorreltail and Ivypool both purred with satisfaction.

"We can learn from what we did wrong, too," Brackenfur went on, brushing at a scrap of fern that was caught up in his pelt. "I should have kept two cats on watch at the end of that narrow path through the brambles."

"Or found a different route," Thornclaw added. "We were far too vulnerable on a narrow path like that. When Lionblaze and Ivypool attacked, we couldn't get back in time to help you."

"We didn't get it all right, either," Sorreltail meowed. "I'd forgotten just how many ways there are to get into this nest. When Berrynose and I got here, we practically ran our paws off trying to keep an eye on all the entrances at once. We'd have been in trouble if your patrol had arrived first," she added to Brackenfur.

Brackenfur flicked her ear with this tail. "Then we've all learned something. Firestar will be pleased when I report to him in the morning." Waving his tail for the rest to follow him, the warrior rose to his paws and headed out of the nest, with Sorreltail beside him.

Lionblaze found himself padding at the back of the patrol, matching his paw steps with Ivypool's. "Good work!" he mewed, briefly touching her shoulder with his tail.

Ivypool gave her chest fur a couple of embarrassed licks. "Thanks."

"You . . . you learned most of those skills in the Dark Forest, didn't you?" Lionblaze ventured.

Ivypool's head lifted sharply; there was a defensive look in her eyes. "Yes, but I would never use them against my own Clanmates."

"Of course not," Lionblaze reassured her. "I just meant that you're getting good, that's all."

"I . . . I do feel bad about using my Dark Forest skills as a ThunderClan warrior," Ivypool admitted, leaping over a fallen tree branch. "It's as if I'm betraying the training I've received from the Clan."

Lionblaze blinked, remembering his own nights of training with Tigerstar, and how he still used moves and tactics that he had learned from the murderous Dark Forest warrior. "Any source of training is a good one," he mewed aloud. "A battle is a battle, and winning is everything."

Ivypool nodded, though she still seemed uncertain. Thinking over what he had just said, Lionblaze began to wonder if any other cats were being trained by hidden sources. "Have you ever seen any other ThunderClan cats in the Dark Forest?" he asked, trying to sound casual.

He was aware of Ivypool tensing beside him, and a few heartbeats passed before she answered. "We're kept separate," she replied. "I've seen a WindClan cat—the one who was injured, Antpelt—but mostly I train with other Dark Forest cats. I think they keep us apart deliberately."

It was obvious to Lionblaze that she didn't feel comfortable talking about the Dark Forest. Seeing the hollow not far away among the trees, he gave Ivypool a nod and a wave of his tail, releasing her to run ahead of him. Padding more slowly after her, he thought over what she had said. Suddenly he halted, a chill running through his pelt.

She didn't answer my question! She never said she hadn't *seen any other ThunderClan cats in the Place of No Stars.*

Lionblaze's chill grew stronger.

Who else among my Clanmates is being trained by the cats who want to destroy all the Clans?

CHAPTER 21

Dovewing's ears ached from the snow that blocked them; snow filled her eyes and froze her paws until she felt as if they were burning. "I hate snow," she grumbled. "I'd give anything to be back in the forest."

"So would I," Foxleap agreed.

Dovewing had noticed that the Tribe cats moved far more easily through the landscape. They seemed to know instinctively where there were rocks to jump onto, even when they were covered by a thin layer of white. Admiring Splash's easy grace, Dovewing forgot to watch where she was putting her paws. The snow gave way underneath her and she felt herself sinking into a drift.

"No! Help!" she yowled, flailing her paws as if she was trying to swim through the powdery white flakes.

Crag bounded back toward her and bent over, fastening his teeth into her scruff. *Just as if I was a kit!* Dovewing thought crossly, scrabbling for a paw hold as the cave-guard hauled her out and set her down again on solid rock.

"Thanks!" she gasped.

Crag's eyes gleamed with humor. "Anytime," he purred. "Just ask."

"How much farther do we have to go?" Foxleap asked, flicking his ears to shake snow off them.

"You see the pine tree over there?" Swoop pointed with her tail. "The one blasted by lightning? That's the next border marker."

"When we get there, we'll have covered half the border," Crag added. "Then we can head back. We'll keep looking out for prey, though."

Dovewing sighed as she looked at the withered pine tree. It was halfway up the opposite side of the valley; it looked a long, long way away.

"Prey!" Foxleap muttered into her ear. "Only the skeleton of a squirrel could live in that blackened tree."

In spite of her discomfort, Dovewing let out an amused *mrrow*. "At least we could chew on the bones!"

Following Crag, the patrol slogged down into the valley, across a frozen stream, and up the far slope. They had almost reached the tree when Dovewing heard a yowl of alarm, followed by the screeches of a cat in pain. Wings beat furiously, and paws thudded on hard stone. For a heartbeat she froze. Obviously her companions hadn't heard anything, but the sounds went on, growing louder and more agonized. Spinning around, Dovewing stared across the valley.

Are Tribe cats in trouble?

Much farther up the slope on the other side, she spotted a

knot of cats thrashing in the snow. A huge gold-brown bird hovered over them, striking out with hooked talons.

"Look!" Dovewing called.

Splash glanced around, narrowing her eyes. "It looks like the intruders have got into trouble with an eagle." Her voice was grim. "Serves them right. They're inside our territory!"

"Shouldn't we go help?" Dovewing asked.

Swoop shrugged. "They'll have to learn to defend themselves, like our ancestors did."

"But we can't just watch them be killed!" Foxleap protested.

"The eagle won't kill all of them," Crag meowed calmly. "It might take one, that's all."

The light of battle gleamed in Foxleap's eyes. "When Clans have a common enemy," he meowed, "we unite to defend ourselves. We have to help those cats!"

Swoop still looked doubtful, but Splash nodded reluctantly. "He's right, you know. We can't just stand here and watch. And if we help, they might owe us any prey they've caught!"

Crag hesitated, then nodded and set off, waving his tail for the others to follow him. As she drew closer, Dovewing was almost deafened by the shrieks of horror and pain. *That eagle isn't giving up!*

Racing over a low crest, they scrambled up the opposite slope toward the battle. Four cats were fighting with an enormous eagle. The eagle's talons were fixed in the pelt of a brown-and-white she-cat; her paws waved feebly while the other three cats leaped and clawed at the bird's wings.

"That's Flora!" Splash exclaimed.

"Splash, you take the farthest wing with Swoop," Crag ordered. "I'll take the nearest. Wait for my signal."

"What can we do?" Dovewing called.

"Stay out of the way," Crag replied, as Swoop and Splash raced around the eagle. "You're not trained in this sort of fighting."

Dovewing and Foxleap stood close together in the shelter of a boulder, watching the eagle as it flung the intruding cats away. One of them, a young tortoiseshell no bigger than an apprentice, was hurled against a rock, where she lay stunned and bleeding from one ear.

"Now!" Crag yowled.

As he leaped at one of the eagle's wings, Swoop and Splash sprang at the other, trying to hold the bird down between them. It let out a raucous screech of fury, and Dovewing imagined that its talons were gripping Flora even more tightly. She shivered with terror as she stared at the eagle's glaring yellow eyes. *Is this how prey feels?*

The other two intruders, a black tom and a skinny brown tom with big ears, threw themselves back into the battle, clawing at the eagle's legs, but they were already hurt and exhausted from the struggle, and their blows were feeble. The eagle was big and determined, almost managing to take off with the little she-cat, in spite of the Tribe cats weighing down its wings.

There are only three of them, Dovewing thought, fear flooding through her. *They can't do this on their own.*

"I've had enough of this," Foxleap muttered. "I'm not standing here like a useless lump of fur!"

He sprang forward and latched his claws into the eagle's wing, just as it shook off Crag with a screech. Crag twisted in midair and attacked the eagle's naked, gnarly legs, clawing first at one and then the other. With a shriek of rage the eagle let go of Flora; she hit the ground and lay still. Swoop and Splash leaped gracefully to the ground.

"Okay, Foxleap!" Crag meowed. "You can let go!"

But Foxleap didn't release his grip. Dovewing's heart began to thud as she realized that her Clanmate was stuck. He dangled from the eagle's wing by his claws, twisting and wrenching to free himself as the bird battled into the air.

Before any other cat could move, Swoop let out a furious screech. "No!" She leaped up again, grabbing at the eagle's wing with one forepaw, while with the other she batted at Foxleap. His claws dislodged, Foxleap crashed to the ground, where he lay winded.

But just as Swoop began to drop to the ground again, the eagle whirled around in a storm of wings. Blood-splashed talons shot out and sank into her back.

"Swoop!" Splash shrieked. She tried to jump into the air, but the eagle was already climbing higher.

"No!" Swoop screamed, battering the air with her paws. "Help! Crag! Splash . . ."

Dovewing could still hear her as the eagle's wings beat more strongly and carried him off, vanishing over a distant peak. The sound of Swoop's terror filled her head until she thought she would never hear anything else again.

Trembling, Dovewing blocked her ears with her paws. "I'm

sorry, Swoop," she whispered. "There's nothing I can do. . . ."

Silence fell. The snow-covered slope was stained with blood and strewn with feathers. The Tribe cats stood silent, watching Dovewing as she writhed in agony. The intruders had picked themselves up; even Flora was standing shakily on her paws. They exchanged swift, guilty glances, but said nothing.

Dovewing lifted her head, feeling cold horror course through her veins. She couldn't hear Swoop screaming now—and that was the most terrible sound of all. "She's dead," she whispered.

Foxleap staggered to his paws and faced the Tribe cats. "I'm sorry," he mewed, his voice full of anguish. "It was my fault."

"Yes!" Splash hissed, her eyes narrowed with grief and hostility. "You were told to stay out of it. If you'd done as Crag told you, Swoop would be alive now."

"I know. I'm sorry," Foxleap repeated.

Dovewing padded over to him and pressed her muzzle against his shoulder. "It wasn't your fault," she murmured. "You were only trying to help. Without you, the eagle might have taken Flora."

"Better an intruder than one of the Tribe!" Splash snapped.

Foxleap said nothing, just stared at his paws with numb grief in his eyes.

Crag let out a long sigh. "Blaming Foxleap won't help. We'd better get back to the cave."

As they set off, the black tom took a pace forward. "Wait!" Splash spun around, flexing her claws. "What?"

"Nothing." The black tom looked embarrassed and guilty. "Just . . . er . . . thanks."

The Tribe she-cat let out a snort of disgust and bounded away with a last glance over her shoulder. "Don't even think about crossing the border again," she snarled.

Dovewing stumbled blindly back through the snow. She felt so much pain inside that she scarcely noticed her frozen paws or aching ears. All she could hear was the echo of Swoop's terrified shrieks as the eagle carried her away.

We should never have come here. This has nothing to do with the prophecy, nothing to do with keeping the Clans safe from the Dark Forest.

The sun was sinking into a troubled mass of cloud by the time the waterfall came in sight. When the patrol finally staggered into the cave, Squirrelflight sprang up from where she had been talking to Talon and Bird. "What happened?" she demanded, fear in her eyes as she bounded over to Dovewing.

"We went to help—" Crag began, but Splash cut him off with a lash of her tail.

"Swoop is dead," she rasped. "An eagle took her while she was trying to save *this* cat." She glared at Foxleap. "He forced his way into the fight when he'd been told to stay out of it."

Squirrelflight let out a gasp of horror. More cats gathered around them, Stormfur and Brook in the lead.

"That's terrible!" Stormfur exclaimed.

Brook nodded, stroking her tail over Splash's shoulder. "No cat has been taken by an eagle for many moons."

"They have now!" Splash spat.

"I'd better report to Stoneteller," Crag muttered, bounding to the back of the cave.

Brook's kits, Lark and Pine, were staring up at her with wide, frightened eyes. "Will the big bird come and take us, too?" Lark whimpered.

"No." Brook bent down and touched each of their noses in turn. "You're safe inside the cave."

Dovewing stood close to Foxleap so that their pelts brushed. "We should never have made this journey," she murmured. "Jayfeather won't tell us why we had to come, and now a cat is dead."

Foxleap nodded. "I want to go home."

Movement in the shadows of the cave caught Dovewing's eye, and she spotted Stoneteller stalking toward them, with Crag at his shoulder. The old cat halted in front of the group, his amber eyes glaring with anger and hatred.

"No cat wanted you here," he snarled. "And now one of the Tribe is dead because of you."

"You can't blame Foxleap!" Dovewing stepped forward, her neck fur bristling with anger. "He was very brave."

"I don't blame Foxleap," Stoneteller rasped. "I blame *all* of you. If you had never come to the mountains, Swoop would still be alive."

Squirrelflight stretched out her tail to touch Dovewing's shoulder. "He's right," she murmured. "We'll leave as soon as we can. Stoneteller, we are all sorrier than we can say."

As the old cat opened his jaws to reply, a muffled noise

sounded behind them; Dovewing turned to see Jayfeather padding from the Cave of Pointed Stones. His blind blue eyes stared at her. "It's my fault," he rasped. "I was the one who said we had to come. I will do what I have to, and then we will leave."

CHAPTER 22
❧

Jayfeather felt as if all the weight of the mountains was resting on his shoulders, but he braced himself and turned to Stoneteller. "Your Tribe will always be loyal to the Teller of the Pointed Stones," he meowed. "You need to return their loyalty by having faith that you are destined to be here. Your descendants will survive if you give them hope now."

"But—" Stoneteller began.

Jayfeather didn't let him speak. "The time has come to choose your successor."

His words fell into silence. Jayfeather was conscious of the Tribe of Rushing Water around him, waiting for their Healer's reply.

The old cat hauled himself to his paws. "It's too late," he growled. "Our ancestors no longer watch over us. We are alone." Turning, he limped down the tunnel into his den-cave. Jayfeather pictured his Tribemates staring after him, as murmurs of protest began to rise from them.

"What does he mean?"

"Has the Tribe of Endless Hunting abandoned us?"

"What's going to happen?"

"Calm down." Bird's voice rose above the rest. "Stoneteller is very troubled, but he is still our Healer. He will protect us. Let him sleep."

The murmuring died away, but Jayfeather could tell that the cats were still uneasy.

"I want to go *now*." Jayfeather heard the slap of Dovewing's paw on the stone floor.

"So do I," Foxleap added.

"I know. I want to leave, too," Squirrelflight meowed. "But we can't set off when night is falling. We'll go home tomorrow. Is that all right with you, Jayfeather? Will you have finished whatever you need to do here?"

Jayfeather nodded, ignoring Dovewing's hiss of impatience. "Yes, we can leave tomorrow."

"Let's find you a nest." Squirrelflight drew Dovewing away, and Foxleap padded after them. "You'll both need a good night's sleep if we're to travel tomorrow."

"I don't want to sleep," Dovewing retorted. "I'll keep on seeing Swoop, I know I will."

Jayfeather waited until their voices had died away, then padded back into the Cave of Pointed Stones. Blind once again, he could still remember the pinnacles of stone and the thin shaft of moonlight cast into the shallow pools. He remembered how Half Moon had patted the water and set the reflection flickering. Taking a deep breath, he searched for her scent, but all he could smell was stone and water.

He found a dry spot at the foot of one of the columns and lay down, curling up and wrapping his tail over his nose. He felt very much alone, grief and regret for Swoop biting deep into him.

I know what I have to do to help the Tribe, but was Swoop's life too great a price to pay for our visit?

Jayfeather's eyes flickered open and he saw a sheet of dark water stretching in front of him. Starlight shimmered on its surface. Springing to his paws, he realized that he had returned to the stone hollow in the mountains that he had visited once before, led there by an elder of the Tribe of Endless Hunting. Sheer cliffs rose all around him, lined by cats whose pelts glowed with starshine. In silence they gazed down at Jayfeather.

He lifted his head and boldly returned their gaze, scanning the ranks of starry cats. He recognized Fall and Slant, who had spoken to him before, and Rain, who had been an elder when Jayfeather first visited the Tribe. Farther up the cliff, he made out the fainter outlines of Owl Feather, Stone Song, and Rising Moon. They dipped their heads to him, but did not speak.

Jayfeather's heart lurched. *Is Half Moon here?* It seemed like only a heartbeat since he had been with her on the cliff top, yet he knew that she had been dead for seasons upon seasons. He searched the cliff face, but there was no sign of her graceful white pelt.

Has she faded away completely? Am I too late to keep her here with my memories?

He couldn't see Jay's Wing, Dove's Wing, or Lion's Roar,

either, then scolded himself for being mouse-brained enough to look for them. *Of course they're not with the Tribe of Endless Hunting! We live on in ThunderClan!*

A pale gray she-cat rose to her paws and jumped down from a boulder at the bottom of the cliff. Padding around the edge of the pool, she halted in front of Jayfeather. "I am Cloud with Storm in Belly," she introduced herself.

"I know you, don't I?" Jayfeather recalled. "You were a Tribe elder when I first came to the mountains."

"I was. And I am the mother of the present Stoneteller. Now it is time for my son to join the Tribe of Endless Hunting."

A shiver ran through Jayfeather. "But he hasn't chosen a successor!"

"I know." Cloud's eyes, like tiny moons, were fixed on Jayfeather. "Tomorrow it will be your duty to name the next Stoneteller." As Jayfeather gaped at her in dismay, she went on. "Not all of us have abandoned the Tribe. Some of us still have faith that it will survive."

"But—but how can I appoint a new Healer?" Jayfeather stammered.

Cloud leaned forward and whispered into his ear. "Because you appointed the first, remember?" She turned to look up the cliff, angling her ears toward a shape at the very top of the ranks of cats, glowing and barely visible.

"Half Moon . . ." Jayfeather breathed. He strained to see more clearly, but he was too far away to make out her features.

"We have been grateful to you for all these years," Cloud

went on. "We always knew that you would come back. What you do now will affect all cats, past and future, from the lake and the mountains and the old forest where your Clans lived for so long."

Jayfeather wrenched his gaze from Half Moon and stared at Cloud. "I don't understand. . . ." he faltered.

"The end of the stars draws near," Cloud continued. "Three must become four, to challenge the darkness that lasts forever."

Jayfeather stepped back, realizing that the ranks of starry cats around them had begun to fade. There was darkness on all sides of the hollow, penetrated by only the tiniest faint gleams of light.

"But we have always been three!" he cried. "Who is the fourth?"

The icy glow of starlight from Cloud's pelt grew dimmer. Her voice grew fainter, too, as she replied, "The fourth is with you already. You will not have to search far."

Jayfeather jerked awake to darkness and the endless dripping of water in the Cave of Pointed Stones. Scrambling to his paws, he ran into the main cavern and down the tunnel that led into Stoneteller's den. The old cat's scent wreathed around him as he halted, panting. Jayfeather could hear Stoneteller's breath bubbling as he tried to speak.

"I see them now!" Every word was a struggle. "My ancestors! They have not abandoned us! I am so sorry. . . ."

His voice faded. Jayfeather waited for the hoarse breathing

to start up again, but there was only silence. He stood with his head bowed. "Rest well, Stoneteller," he murmured. "The Tribe of Endless Hunting is waiting for you."

He padded out into the cavern and picked up Wing's scent as the she-cat approached. "Is everything okay?" she mewed.

"No," Jayfeather replied. "Stoneteller has died."

Wing let out a wail of grief and terror; disturbed by the noise, the rest of the Tribe began to stir. Their dismay churned around Jayfeather like waves: grief and loss and the fear of being without a leader.

"Did Stoneteller name his successor before he died?" Wing asked.

A tense silence slammed down in the cave. Jayfeather realized that the whole Tribe was waiting to hear his answer. He took a deep breath.

"Yes," he meowed. "Yes, he did."

With the tumble of the waterfall beside him, Jayfeather led the way out of the cavern and up to the top of the cliff. The Tribe followed him. Some of the cats carried Stoneteller's body from his den, and laid him on the stones next to the river.

Bird padded up and stood beside Stoneteller's body. "Farewell, Teller of the Pointed Stones. May you hunt endlessly among the stars with those who watch over us."

She stepped back, and an expectant silence fell. Jayfeather could feel that the gaze of every cat in the Tribe was fixed on him. He knew what he had to do, but his mind was whirling.

He had lied to every one of these cats. Stoneteller had died too soon.

How can I choose the new Healer?

Then he gathered himself. The Tribe of Endless Hunting had known that this would happen. They had faith in him to make the right choice—for the second time. The Healer mustn't be too young, he thought; the Tribe needed a cat with experience and courage, who had seen these cats through their darkest times and had faith that they could survive. A cat who would put his Tribe before himself, and work tirelessly to keep them safe.

"Crag Where Eagles Nest, stand forward," he meowed.

"Me?" The shocked exclamation was followed by Crag's paw steps as he approached Jayfeather; astonishment and doubt flooded from him.

"From this moment on," Jayfeather declared, "you will be known as the Teller of the Pointed Stones." His heart twisted with pain as he remembered the last time he had spoken these words. "Others will come after you, moon upon moon upon moon. Choose them well, train them well, and trust the future of your Tribe to them."

"I am honored to have been chosen." Crag's voice was solemn. "I will serve my Tribe until the end of my days."

Bird padded forward. "Greetings, Stoneteller," she mewed. "May the Tribe of Endless Hunting watch over you and send you their wisdom."

She headed down the cliff, her paw steps growing fainter

as she jumped from rock to rock, and Talon took her place, acknowledging the new Stoneteller with the same words. Jayfeather waited until all the Tribe had spoken and filed away, back to the cave.

At last, Stoneteller and Jayfeather stood alone on the cliff top.

"I wasn't expecting this," the Teller of the Pointed Stones admitted. "Stoneteller—the last one—said nothing to prepare me. But I cannot doubt his choice. I will do my best to honor him, and the rest of the Tribe of Endless Hunting." He took a deep breath. "It's so beautiful up here," he murmured. Jayfeather realized that he must be looking out at the vista of mountain peaks. "But I guess I won't be seeing it for a while—not until those to-bes finish their training, anyway."

He sighed faintly and Jayfeather heard his paw steps recede as he headed toward the cave. Suddenly, Jayfeather felt a slight stirring in the air beside him. An achingly familiar sweet scent wreathed around him.

"Half Moon?" he whispered.

He couldn't see the white she-cat, but he knew that she was there beside him. Her muzzle lightly touched his ear; it felt as if lightning crackled through him.

"You chose well," she murmured.

Jayfeather swallowed. "I won't forget you," he promised.

"And I never forgot you," Half Moon replied. "Not through all the moons since we last met. Go well, return to your Clan now. Find the fourth."

As her scent faded away, Jayfeather realized that Squirrelflight, Foxleap, and Dovewing had joined him on the cliff top.

"Can we go home now?" Squirrelflight asked.

"Yes," Jayfeather told her. "We have done what we had to."

He waited for the two she-cats to climb back down the rocks and prepared to follow them. But as he cautiously lowered himself over the edge, he heard Half Moon's voice calling after him.

"I will wait for you forever, Jay's Wing!"

WARRIORS
ADVENTURE GAME

Visit www.warriorcats.com
*to download game rules, character sheets,
a practice mission, and more!*

Written by Stan! • Art by James L. Barry

Mission of Mercy

Whatever the previous adventure you played, consider that one moon has passed since then. Determine what age that makes all of the cat characters (including the one belonging to the person who will take the first turn as Narrator) and use the information found in the "Improving Your Cat" section of Chapter Four in the game rules to make the necessary improvements.

Unless you are the first person who will act as Narrator in this adventure, you should stop reading here. The information beginning in the next paragraph is for the Narrator only.

The Adventure Begins

Hello, Narrator! It's time to begin playing "Mission of Mercy." Make sure all the players have their character sheets, the correct number of chips, a piece of paper, and a pencil. Remember that the point of the game is to have fun, so don't be afraid to go slow, keep the players involved, and refer to the rules if you aren't sure exactly what should happen next.

When you're ready, begin with **1** below.

1. Twoleg Trouble

Special Note: "Mission of Mercy" involves the players' cats interacting with a little girl (who they will refer to as a "Twoleg kit"). This presents a kind of storytelling challenge that is different than any of the previous adventures: Players will need to set aside their human knowledge and embrace the perspective of their cat characters.

The players will certainly have a better understanding of

what the girl knows, feels, and wants than their cats would. The challenge for everyone will be to keep the focus on the cats' point of view—for the players to pretend not to know things they clearly do (like how humans react in different situations) and for the Narrator to avoid explaining things from a person's perspective (for example, saying that she "howls" rather than "cries").

This kind of roleplaying is at the heart of what makes the *Warriors Adventure Game*, and other games like it, so much fun. Help the players to let their imaginations flow and you will all begin to see your characters, as well as the characters in the novels, in a new light.

Read Aloud: "Greenleaf is nearing its end. The days are still warm and lazy, but they're growing shorter and there's a chill in the air at moonhigh. The coming of leaf-fall usually marks a time of peace and quiet among the Clans, so it seems particularly odd that warriors from all four Clans have suddenly been gathered together."

Narrator Tips: When all the warriors are together, the leaders of all the Clans tell them about a dire emergency. A Twoleg kit is lost in the woods above the lake. The kit has wandered too far from where she entered the woods—and the cats have seen older Twolegs looking for her in the wrong places.

The cats have an idea where the kit is by luck—a ThunderClan patrol saw her and reported that she was wandering farther and farther away from where the older Twolegs were searching. In fact, she's moving so unpredictably that the same patrol failed to locate the kit again even at sunhigh. Later, a ShadowClan hunting party saw her from a long way off, and then a WindClan patrol heard her as moonhigh approached.

Several groups of warriors have tried to lead the older Twolegs to the right areas, but they are so distraught over their missing kit that they have completely failed to notice what the cats have been trying to tell them.

3

The players' cats' assignment is to find the missing Twoleg kit and bring her back to someplace where she can be found by her own kind.

Let the players ask questions of the leaders. The leaders will answer as best they can, but very little is known. Twolegs are unpredictable, and their kits even more so. What's more, they often wander into dangerous situations without even noticing that they're doing so. Many warriors are being sent out to different locations with the same assignment: Find the kit and bring her back to where other Twolegs can find her. A few other warriors are being sent to keep track of the older Twolegs so that they can try to lead them to the kit, once she is found.

After the players' questions have been answered, tell them that their cats have been assigned a stretch of woods far up the hill above ShadowClan territory.

Once the cats reach their assigned area, let them search around. There are signs that the Twoleg kit has been this way recently—tracks in the dirt and mud, broken twigs on the underbrush, and the strong scent of a Twoleg kit in the air. Allow all cats the opportunity to make Smell Checks to see if they can pick up the trail (the Track or Alertness Knacks can be used here, if the cats have access to either). To figure out how successful the search is, add the cats' results together to get a group total.

What Happens Next: If the group total is 20 or higher, continue with **9**.

If the group total is under 20, continue with **4**.

2. The First Leg

Read Aloud: "The kit seems happy to follow you. She must have been terribly lonely, because now that she's found you she keeps calling out in her tiny little Twoleg voice."

Narrator Tips: The cats have passed the first major obstacle—getting the kit to follow them. Of course, as the Narrator you know that it is extremely difficult to get a five-year-old child to focus on anything for long periods of time.

This scene is about the difficulty the cats have in getting the Twoleg kit to stay focused on the simple task of walking back toward her home.

Think about the kids you've known and the things that would grab their attention; then improvise a scene where the kit has a similar distraction. Perhaps she sees a butterfly and begins to chase it. Perhaps she gets tired and wants a nap. Perhaps she wants to pick some wildflowers. Choose whatever seems the most interesting to you.

The players will then have to come up with a plan to get the kit back on task. This plan can involve the "Improvised Actions" rules or just be played out through roleplaying, whichever you prefer.

Eventually, the cats should be able to get the Twoleg kit moving again. Then the question will be where to take her. The two most likely places to find Twoleg adults are the area where the adults were searching yesterday or near the edge of the lake, where many Twolegs gather during greenleaf.

What Happens Next: If the players' cats decide to take the kit to where the Twoleg adults were searching yesterday, continue with **5**.

If the players' cats decide to take the kit to the lake, continue with **16**.

3. Frustration

Read Aloud: "Despite your best efforts, the kit is becoming upset again. Between the fear and her inability to understand the things you're trying to tell her, it's more than one small Twoleg can take. With a howl of frustration, she dashes away."

Narrator Tips: Twolegs often do irrational things when they're under a great deal of stress, and it's understandable that this kit is upset that, having found a familiar area, no one is there to help her.

As the Narrator, you should help the players understand why the Twoleg kit is acting this way, even if their cats might not be able to. (Although, any cat that has the Twoleg Lore Knack can make a Ponder Check to try to understand. The total for the check must be 10 or higher for the cat to get a true insight into the kit's motivations.)

The cats must come up with a plan to get the kit to calm down and start following them again. Use the rules for "Improvised Actions" to determine if the action succeeds. If so, the Twoleg kit follows the cats to the only other place it makes sense to go—the lake. If the action fails, but the plan was good or excellent, the kit keeps running and the cats must try a different plan. If the plan was bad, or this is the second time that the cats have failed with a good or excellent plan, the kit will no longer pay attention to the cats and will run blindly off into the woods.

What Happens Next: If the Twoleg kit follows the cats toward the lake, continue with **16**.

If the kit ignores the cats and runs blindly into the woods, continue with **7**.

4. Wrong Tracks

Read Aloud: "After following the tracks for a while, you find yourself back where you started."

Narrator Tips: The cats were following the wrong tracks and they must start their search over. Fortunately, they now have their own scents to mark a trail they know is incorrect. Oddly, that makes it easier to find and follow the right tracks.

Have each cat make a new Smell Check (this time allowing both Track and Twoleg Lore Knacks to be used, if the cats can use them and wish to do so). Again, add all the results together to get a group total.

What Happens Next: If the group total is 15 or higher, continue with **9**.

If the group total is less than 15, continue with **7**.

5. Familiar Territory

Read Aloud: "As you lead the Twoleg kit toward the area where the adult Twolegs were searching yesterday, the forest grows quiet—too quiet, you think, but you're not sure why. Before you can ponder it much, though, the Twoleg kit starts to make happy chirping noises. She must recognize this area."

Narrator Tips: If the players are curious as to the significance of the quiet in the forest, ask them to tell you what they think is so important about it. The answer is that, with so many groups of Clan cats searching the woods, and with all the noise that the Twoleg kit is making, it is strange that no other cats have come out to greet you as you bring the kit through the woods. If any of the players guess the correct reason, tell them so. If none of them do, have the cats all make Ponder Checks. Those whose total is 8 or higher figure out the reason.

As the Narrator, you should know that the reason the other cats are not here is that they are off chasing the older Twolegs. The adults were here earlier today but they packed up and moved on. The Clan leaders told the cats who were searching in this part of the forest to chase after the adult Twolegs and bring them back, knowing that it was very likely that one of the other groups would actually bring the kit here. However, there is no way for the players' cats to know this. They will just have to guess at the reason.

One thing that seems sure is that there are no longer any adult Twolegs in this area, and if there are no adults here then this is the wrong place to bring the kit. Have each cat make

7

a Smell Check to confirm that there are no more Twolegs in the area. Any cat with a total of 4 or higher is certain of that fact, and anyone that gets a 6 or higher can tell that there were adult Twolegs here earlier in the day, but they've been gone for a while. Any cat that gets a total of 10 or higher, though, will smell a different scent on the wind. A dangerous scent that's growing closer. The scent of a bear!

The players' cats will have to come up with a plan to get the Twoleg kit to follow them out of the area. Use the "Improvised Actions" rules to determine how well the plan works. If the plan succeeds, then the Twoleg kit will follow the cats toward the lake. If it fails but it was a good or excellent plan, the kit refuses to leave the area and continues to look for other Twolegs. If the plan was a bad one and it fails, the kit becomes so upset at having found this spot but not finding the other Twolegs that she runs blindly into the woods.

What Happens Next: If the kit follows the cats toward the lake, continue with **16.**

If the kit refuses to leave the area, continue with **11.**

If the kit runs blindly into the woods, continue with **3.**

6. Follow Us!

Read Aloud: "Twolegs can be very unpredictable. This one is lost and obviously frightened. Maybe it's best to call out to her from a distance."

Narrator Tips: The players' cats have a plan that in some way calls for them to avoid approaching the Twoleg kit and instead trying to get her to come to them. Perhaps they call out to her the way a Clan queen would to a missing kit. Perhaps they try to act the way they think kittypets act, knowing the Twolegs find those pampered, spoiled kinds of cats appealing.

You may also want to remind the players about the differences between what they know and what their cats know. Clan cats have no idea what a Twoleg kit likes, dislikes, or fears—everything should be thought of from a cat's perspective.

Use the method described in the "Improvise Actions" sidebar to determine the success of the players' plan. In this case, there are three likely results. If the action works, the Twoleg kit will follow the cats. If the action fails but it was a good or excellent plan, the Twoleg kit will stay where she is but will remain curious about the cats—and they will have to approach her in order to get her to follow them. If the action fails and the plan was bad, the Twoleg kit will become frightened and run away.

What Happens Next: If the Twoleg kit follows the cats, this is the end of the chapter. Hand the adventure to the next Narrator and tell him or her to continue with **2**.

If the cats decide to approach the Twoleg kit, continue with **12**.

If the Twoleg kit runs away, continue with **8**.

7. Some Kits Stay Lost

Read Aloud: "The trail is nearly impossible to follow—twisting, turning, and going in circles that make no sense. If prey could leave trails this confusing, the Clans would go hungry!"

Narrator Tips: There are several reasons the adventure may end up at this juncture. Improvise a short closing scene based on the appropriate section below.

The most likely reason the story wound up here is that the players' cats have followed the wrong trail completely. If this is the case, they have no hope of finding the right trail, but you may have fun describing some of the strange ways the trail leads them.

Another likely reason for reaching this scene is that the Twoleg kit simply runs into the woods and away from the players' cats. They may chase her for a while, but the kit will not stop.

As the Narrator, you get to decide the ultimate fate of the

Twoleg kit. Does the group of Clan cats manage to lead her home? Do the adult Twolegs figure out the right place to look and find her on their own? Does she simply run into the woods, never to be heard from again—leaving her ultimate fate a mystery?

What Happens Next: No matter what the details are, this scene means that the adventure has ended badly. The players' cats do *not* get any Experience rewards for this adventure. The group can, however, play the adventure again, hopefully making smarter decisions along the way and guiding the Twoleg kit more carefully.

8. Frightened Kit

Read Aloud: "The Twoleg kit's eyes go wide with terror and she lets out an ear-piercing yowl. Then she turns and runs deeper into the woods."

Narrator Tips: The Twoleg kit is so scared by everything that's happened to her that the only thing she can think to do is run away, even though the players' cats want nothing other than to help her. Unfortunately for the kit, running away is only going to make things worse for her.

The cats must think of some way to stop the kit and get her

IMPROVISED ACTIONS

In most scenes, the text will tell you exactly what the players' cats must do—what Skills or Attributes to use and what the results are based on the totals of the Checks. Beginning in this adventure, some scenes will call for the Narrator to let the players come up with their own solutions.

When this happens, the Narrator will let the players decide what their cats want to do and, where appropriate, ask them for details about how they plan to make it happen. This is a storytelling game, so be sure to encourage them to put in all the important details.

Once the course of action is chosen, it is up to you, the Narrator, to decide how that plan will work in the game—meaning what Skill or Ability Check should be used to represent it. The Narrator also has to decide what chance the plan has to succeed. This may sound difficult, but it's really not.

First, select the Check that will represent the action. If you're having difficulty remembering them all, the *Quick Start* document (found on www.warriorcats.com) has all the Abilities and Skills listed (as does Chapter Two of the game rules). There may not be a perfect answer, so just choose the one that makes sense to you. You'll also have to decide if any Knacks can be used as part of this action. You will probably find that the players will ask if they can use a particular Knack and you will just have to make a yes or no judgment, rather than having to decide for all the Knacks ahead of time. (But if there is a Knack that you think would be especially helpful, it is usually a good idea to tell the players that.)

The results of the Check will be determined based on how good you think the players' plan is (based on how likely it is to get the result the players intend) — excellent, good, or bad. This will tell you what number the Check must beat. Once you've made that decision, use the chart below to pick the target number for the Check. (Remember that you can always make actions slightly more or less difficult by raising or lowering the target number by one or two points. As the Narrator, you have the power to make any adjustment you think will make the game more fun.)

Quality of the Plan	Individual Target Number	Group Target Number
Excellent	6	10
Good	8	15
Bad	10	20

Using these guidelines will make it easier for you to improvise scenes in all of the published *Warriors Adventure Game* adventures, and to make up adventures of your own.

headed in the right direction. Perhaps they run with her for a while and try to slowly turn her course so that while she thinks she's still running away, she actually is going where the cats want her to. Perhaps they will run ahead and pretend to be hurt, hoping that the kit will stop to help them. Perhaps they will run back and forth in front of her hoping that if she slows down a bit it will clear her mind and help her understand that blindly running away is the worst thing she can do.

Use the method described in the "Improvise Actions" sidebar to determine the success of the players' plan. In this case, there are only two likely outcomes. Either they get the kit calmed down enough that she will be reasonable, or the kit is so frightened that running is the only thing she is willing to do. **What Happens Next:** If the cats get the Twoleg kit calmed down enough to be reasonable, continue with **12**.

If the Twoleg kit is so frightened that nothing can stop her from running, continue with **7**.

9. The Missing Kit

Read Aloud: "The scent trail grows stronger and fresher. You must be on the right track!"

Narrator Tips: Describe the winding, unfocused trail the players' cats are following—going one way then another, doubling back along its own route and then circling around back in the original direction again. Clearly the Twoleg kit is lost and doesn't know where to go. But the cats are certain that she must be around somewhere.

Have the cats each make a Listen Check (to which the Track or Alertness Knacks may be applied, if the players like). Any cat whose total is 10 or higher hears the Twoleg kit nearby, though it's not clear what she is doing. The noises are not like those that Twolegs usually make.

In fact, the kit is crying. She's grown tired from all her

wandering around and she is terrified. She has been on her own in the wild for an entire day, and she has no idea if she'll ever see her family again. Of course, the cats don't know these particular facts but you, as the Narrator, should use them to figure out how the Twoleg kit is acting and describe just those actions and sounds to the players. Let them figure out for themselves what she's doing (even if they guess wrong).

At this point, the players need to figure out what they're going to do. Their mission is to get the kit to follow them to a place where the adult Twolegs are more likely to find her. The question is: How are they going to do that? The possibilities are as limitless as the players' imaginations, but they are likely to come down to two broad categories—either the cats will stay away from the Twoleg kit and try to tempt her to come their way on her own, or they will go up to the kit and then try to lead her in some direction.

What Happens Next: If the cats decide to go up to the Twoleg kit, continue with **12**.

If the cats decide to call to the kit from some distance away, continue with **6**.

If the players come up with a plan that does not fall into one of those broad categories, it will be up to you to improvise a scene that suits the situation, then use the choices at the end of scene **12** to progress the story further.

10. Distraught Kit

Read Aloud: "The Twoleg kit has been frightened beyond belief for almost a whole day. Now, with the cats having befriended her, she relaxes just enough for all the emotions she's held inside to finally come pouring out."

Narrator Tips: The players' cats might not understand why the kit is so upset, particularly now that she has the cats as friends, but any cat with the Twoleg Lore Knack will know that crying

is often a Twoleg's natural reaction to moments of relief—it's their way of letting go of all the bad feelings and fears they've been holding inside.

The cats may want to do something to help, but really there isn't much to do. If they try to comfort the Twoleg kit by rubbing against her and purring or sitting in her lap, she will calm down more quickly. But even if they do nothing, she will get back to normal soon enough.

It's only if the players' cats pester the Twoleg kit, yowling with annoyance, poking her with their claws, or nipping at her fingers and toes, that they have to worry. If they make the kit feel more anxious, she will run away. Otherwise, she will soon be ready to follow the cats wherever they want to lead her.

What Happens Next: If the cats pester the Twoleg kit and she runs away, continue with **8**.

If the cats let her finish crying so she can calm down, this is the end of the chapter. Hand the adventure to the next Narrator and tell him or her to continue with **2**.

11. A Different Kind of Kit

Read Aloud: "The Twoleg kit looks up when she hears a rustling sound in the nearby woods. At first, you think she must have realized the same thing you did—that there's a bear nearby—but clearly her senses aren't as sharp as yours. Instead of running away from the sound, she runs straight toward it. Perhaps all creatures walking through the woods sound the same to her."

Narrator Tips: The Twoleg kit has no idea that there's a bear ahead—she thinks that the sounds are being made by people looking for her. Luckily for her, the bear is just a cub, too.

If the cats stay with the Twoleg kit as she runs toward the sound, describe the scene as she sees the bear cub and understands what the situation really is. As the Narrator, you get to decide what her reaction to the bear is. Does she get scared and run away? Is she overwhelmed by how cute and furry it is? Does she try to play with it? Is she stunned and unable to move, giving the players' cats the chance to try to guide her away? Decide for yourself what the Twoleg kit will *want* to do and tell the players how she *begins* to act. Then let the players have their cats react accordingly.

In real life, it is always a bad idea to approach a bear cub. It is, after all, a wild animal. This game, though, is a piece of fiction, and can afford to be slightly more generous in letting fun things happen rather than sticking to pure realism. If the Twoleg kit approaches the bear cub, it is okay for them to play together safely (at least for a little while). If this is what happens in the adventure, let the players' cats come up with a plan for what to do next. Will they play, too? Will they stand off, frightened of the bear cub? Will they call to the Twoleg kit, or use some other method to try to coax her away?

Use the "Improvised Actions" rules to determine the results.

What Happens Next: If the Twoleg kit gets scared and runs into the woods, continue with **8**.

If the Twoleg kit stays and plays with the bear cub for a while longer,

continue with **13**.

If the Twoleg kit follows the cats away from the bear cub, continue with **16**.

12. The Friendly Approach

Read Aloud: "The Twoleg kit seems happy to see you approach. She calls to you and reaches out her hand to feel your fur."

Narrator Tips: After being alone and scared for so long, the Twoleg kit is very happy to see cats (although she thinks of them as kittypets).

The players' cats will need a plan to get the Twoleg kit to befriend them and then follow as they lead her out of the woods. Perhaps they will start by rubbing against her legs and purring. Perhaps they will bring her freshkill to eat. Perhaps they will tug on the coverings of her feet.

Whatever their plan, use the method described in the "Improvised Actions" sidebar to determine its success. In this case, there are three most likely results. If the action works, the Twoleg kit will follow the cats. If the action fails but the plan was good or excellent, the Twoleg kit forgets about the cats, focuses on her problems, and becomes upset. If the action fails and the plan was bad, the Twoleg kit will become so upset that she runs away.

What Happens Next: If the Twoleg kit follows the cats, this is the end of the chapter. Hand the adventure to the next Narrator and tell him or her to continue with **2**.

If the Twoleg kit ignores the cats and becomes upset, continue with **10**.

If the Twoleg kit runs away, continue with **8**.

13. Mama's Home

Read Aloud: "The happy laughter of the two very different kits playing together fills the woods—until the mother of one of the kits arrives. With a bellowing roar, the adult bear bursts through the bushes, stands on her hind legs, and roars even louder."

Narrator Tips: This may be a tricky scene for you, as the Narrator. Clearly, no person or cat should ever stand up to a mother bear that is protecting her cub. But it's possible that the players may want their cats to fight against the beast in order to protect the Twoleg kit. In addition, in real life, running away from a bear often just encourages it to chase you. But running may seem like the best thing for the cats and Twoleg kit to do, and is a good way to get them out of immediate danger.

You should know your friends well enough to know what type of adventure the group enjoys most—realistic, heroically fictional, or somewhere in the middle. Use that knowledge when determining the outcome of this scene, and remember that the most important thing is always that everyone has fun playing the game.

First, determine how the Twoleg kit reacts to the mother bear's arrival. Does she panic and run into the woods? Does she become frozen with fear? Once you've figured that out, tell the players what she *begins* to do, and allow them a chance to react with their own plans and actions. Some effective strategies would be to distract the bear, cause the bear cub to run away, or even attack or scare the Twoleg kit so that she runs away.

The mother bear has no real interest in fighting the Twoleg kit or the cats but, if pressed, she certainly will fight. The bear has 50 points of Strength, 5 points of Intelligence, and 10 points of Spirit. Her Swat Skill is at level 5, her Bite Skill is at level 4, and her Jump, Pounce, and Wrestle Skills are all at level 3. The mother bear has 65 chips to represent the damage she can take, but she cannot spend any of those chips on actions.

If the Twoleg kit gets hit by the bear even once, she will

become badly hurt. There is no need to use the Abilities, Skills, and Knacks to determine the outcome if the bear attacks the Twoleg kit—it is purely a part of the story. So, as the Narrator, you get to decide when it makes sense for the bear to miss the kit, and when it makes sense that she strike her. (But know that if the scene gets to the point where the bear is attacking the Twoleg kit, things have already gone terribly wrong.)

If any of the players' cats are Knocked Out by the mother bear, or if two or more members of the group have had their chip pools reduced to half or lower, then it counts as the cats having been badly hurt.

There are many, very different ways this scene could play out, so use your best judgment and make us of the "Improvised Actions" rules, if they can be of help.

What Happens Next: If the Twoleg kit gets scared and runs into the woods, continue with **8**.

If the Twoleg kit or any of the cats are badly hurt by the mother bear, continue with **17**.

If the Twoleg kit follows the cats away from the bear cub, continue with **16**.

14. Horses!

Read Aloud: "All Clan cats know how dangerous the horseplace is. Those gigantic beasts could crush a cat with just one stomp of their powerful hooves. But

Twolegs seem to like being around the beasts. The question is, are they there now?"

Narrator Tips: There are two main parts of the horseplace—the area where the horses stay and the area where the Twolegs stay.

Cats get nervous around horses, so make the scene feel very tense. Chances are that the players' cats have never been in horseplace before, and the only things they know about horses come from rumors and tall tales.

The great unknown in this scene is how the Twoleg kit will react when she sees the horses. Can the cats get her to go right to the place where the Twolegs usually gather, or will she want to go see a horse up close?

Let the players' cats make a plan for how they are going to lead the Twoleg kit here. At the same time, decide for yourself how the kit will react to seeing real, live horses. Will she be excited, disinterested, or even a little scared? Will she want to go pet a horse or will she instead focus on the house (where she can be pretty sure she'll find some help)? Then improvise a scene that plays through all that information.

Be sure to give the cats a chance to affect what the Twoleg kit does, using the "Improvised Actions" rules if there isn't an obvious outcome to their action.

What Happens Next: If the Twoleg kit decides to approach a horse, continue with **21**.

If the Twoleg kit decides to look for other Twolegs, continue with **18**.

15. Bare Your Claws!

Read Aloud: "A Clan warrior must always be ready to fight for survival, and it's time for you to do just that. But you've never even dreamed about dangers as big and vicious as the dog whose teeth now are snapping near your face."

Narrator Tips: Fighting the dog is very difficult and even more dangerous.

The dog has Strength 20, Intelligence 8, and Spirit 12, plus the appropriate number of Ability Chips for each (which it can spend to improve its actions). It does not Swat, but it can Bite three times every Round with a Bite Skill of level 4. The dog also has the Chomp, Dash, and Pin Knacks. It will stand and fight until the cats have done 20 chips worth of damage to it, at which point it will run away.

In almost every case, the dog will attack the cats before it attacks the Twoleg kit. If there is more than one cat for the dog to choose from, it will pick targets randomly. (Select the dog's targets by a rock-paper-scissors contest, rolling dice, or any other method that seems fair to the group.) The only thing that will make the dog focus on the kit is if she tries to approach the Twoleg den—that is what the dog guards most jealously.

If the cats run away from the dog, they and the Twoleg kit can get to the far side of the fence in one Round. Once there, they can reconsider their course of action.

What Happens Next: If the cats want to make a new plan, continue with **18**.

If any of the cats or the Twoleg kit are Knocked Out, continue with **17**.

If the Twoleg kit is able to knock on the door, continue with **20**.

16. To The Lake!

Refresh Chips: Before playing through this scene, tell the players that it is time for them to refresh their chips (as described in Chapter Five of the game rules).

Read Aloud: "During greenleaf, many Twolegs come to the lake. Sometimes the Twolegs swim, sometimes they go to the horseplace, sometimes they simply walk through the woods. They always eat and make a great deal of noise. But leaf-fall is nearly here, and there's no way to tell where the Twolegs will be, if they are at the lake at all."

Narrator Tips: After the players' cats have gotten the Twoleg kit to follow them toward the lake, they have to decide where they want to take her. The two most likely areas are the water's edge near the greenleaf Twolegplace and the horseplace. (Look at a map of the Lake Territories to see exactly where these things are.)

Alternatively, if the players' cats want to lead the kit to the area where Twolegs like to spend the night (a small campground, though the cats would not call it that), you can improvise a scene that lets them do so. At this time of year, there are no Twolegs staying there. Still, you can create an interesting scene as the cats explore the various things that have been left behind—long-cooled remnants of campfires, scraps of food, trash, etc. Perhaps they could encounter some other animals—rabbits, skunks, or raccoons, for example.

What Happens Next: If the cats take the Twoleg kit to the water's edge, this is the end of the chapter. Hand the adventure to the next Narrator and tell him or her to continue with **19**.

If the cats take the Twoleg kit to the horseplace, this is the end of the chapter. Hand the adventure to the next Narrator and tell him or her to continue with **14**.

17. It's All Fun Until Someone Gets Hurt

Narrator Tips: If the players arrive at this scene, it is because one of their cats, or perhaps the Twoleg kit, was badly hurt. Although it may be possible to rescue the kit, the players' cats cannot claim to have been fully successful in their mission and this is a bad end for the adventure.

Using the details of the scenes that led to this point, improvise an ending for the story, remembering that other cats could still bring the Twoleg kit to her family (or the other way around). If the cats were wounded while taking heroic actions, they should be praised by the other members of their Clans—a sort of "consolation prize" for doing the right thing, but not having it turn out well. If the Twoleg kit was hurt while under their protection, though, the players' cats will probably receive a lecture about the strength and dedication that is expected from a Clan warrior.

What Happens Next: No matter what the details are, this scene means that the adventure has ended badly. The players' cats do *not* get any Experience rewards for this adventure. The group *can*, however, play the adventure again, hopefully making smarter decisions along the way and guiding the Twoleg kit more carefully.

18. The Guard Dog

Read Aloud: "As the group nears the place where Twolegs often stay, you can smell something nearby—something other than the horses. Then you hear it: heavy paws on the grass."

Narrator Tips: There is a fence around the farmhouse, so the dog cannot get to the cats or the Twoleg kit directly. But it does stand between them and the place where Twolegs may be staying. (The people inside are so used to the dog barking at everything, they do not even come to see why it's making so much noise now.) The question is, can the cats help the kit get past the dog?

The two most likely plans are to get the dog to chase after one or more of the cats as they run away from the fence gate, or for the cats to fight the dog and do enough damage to it to scare it away. If the players have a different idea on how to get the Twoleg kit past the dog and it seems reasonable, let them try it. Use the "Improvised Actions" rules to determine whether or not their plan is successful.

What Happens Next: If the cats try to get the dog to chase them, continue with **22**.

If the cats try to fight the dog, continue with **15**.

19. A Quick Drink

Read Aloud: "Thinking about it, you're sure that the Twoleg kit cannot have had anything to eat or drink since dawn. It's no wonder she's running to the lake edge so quickly. But she'd better be careful—those rocks get very slippery!"

Narrator Tips: The Twoleg kit is heading straight to the water's edge, which the players' cats know is not the best place to get a drink. Twolegs enter and leave the lake at this point so often, the water near here doesn't taste as good (brought on by the pollution and algae, though the cats would not understand those terms). Also, the rocks where the kit is heading are covered with moss and are very slippery—she

is likely to fall into the water.

Let the players decide if their cats want to do anything about this. They can use any of the tricks that have gotten the Twoleg kit to follow them so far, or try something new. Whatever action they attempt must beat a total of 12 to succeed. If it does succeed, the cats lead the Twoleg kit to a place where she can drink safely. If it fails, the kit falls into the water and must be rescued. She can't swim and will immediately panic if she falls into the lake, in spite of the fact that it is less than one foot deep at that spot and she is in no real danger.

Rescuing the Twoleg kit requires the cats to get into the lake and swim with her. All the cats who are doing so may attempt Swim Checks, adding their results together for a group total. If the group total is 15 or higher, they successfully guide the Twoleg kit to the shore. If not, she continues to splash around in the water and the cats may try again. If they fail a second time, the kit makes it to shore but is so tired by the process that she falls down and is Knocked Out by the exhaustion.

As long as the Twoleg kit is on land and awake, the cats can lead her toward the horseplace and the adventure can continue.

What Happens Next: If the Twoleg kit is Knocked Out, continue with **17**.

If the group leads the Twoleg kit toward the horseplace, this is the end of the chapter. Hand the adventure to the next Narrator and tell him or her to continue with **14**.

20. Grown-Ups!

Read Aloud: "The kit goes up to the Twoleg den and bats it loudly with her paw. A few moments later, two grown-up Twolegs come out and look down at the kit. Suddenly, the kit begins to cry."

Narrator Tips: Although the players' cats won't understand these actions completely, it is important that you, as the

Narrator, do so that you can properly describe this scene. The little girl is crying because she is so relieved to finally find someone who can help her. The couple at the door are the owners of the riding stables, and though they don't know the girl, they have heard that someone was lost in the woods and they're happy to help. They invite the girl inside and call the police. After a while, the police will arrive and will take the little girl back to her family.

From the players' cats' perspective, all they know is that the adult Twolegs are now taking care of the kit, so they have successfully completed their mission. They can go back to the Clan leaders and tell them so. All the cats from all the Clans will be proud of the players' cats.

What Happens Next: The players' cats should be proud of what they've done. You can improvise a short scene where the Clan leaders tell the cats how well they've done. A few of the cats' Clanmates, though, are skeptical and wonder how the players' cats can be sure that the other Twolegs will really take care of the kit. It's a question no one can answer, but the players will know that their cats did the right thing.

21. Skittish Mare

Read Aloud: "The Twoleg kit is mesmerized by the horse, her eyes wide as she walks up and tries to stroke its nose. She seems to have no idea how nervous the beast is. It snorts, thumps the ground with its front hoof, and looks as though it wants absolutely nothing to do with the kit."

Narrator Tips: The players' cats are certain that the horse will not let the Twoleg kit get close to it. They have to either find a way to calm the horse down or convince the kit to stay away. Neither one is an easy task.

Let the players talk about ways in which their cats could calm the horse. Then have the cats make a group Ponder Check (to which the Animal Lore Knack may be applied) to see if they can figure out the best way to put that plan into action. (If the players' plan is excellent you, as Narrator, may decide to give the group a +2 bonus to their group Ponder Check.) If the group total for this Check is 16 or higher, the cats have performed their plan perfectly and the horse is calm enough that it lets the Twoleg kit approach and pet it. If the group total is 15 or lower, the horse remains skittish and will rear up if the kit comes near it.

The cats can also try to convince the Twoleg kit to stay away from the horse. They can do this by trying to draw the kit's attention to the place where Twolegs usually stay, or by scaring the kit, or any other plan that seems reasonable to the players. Use the "Improvised Actions" rules to determine the success of their plan (in this case it should almost certainly be a group action, rather than something an individual cat can do). If the action succeeds, the Twoleg kit leaves the horse and goes toward the Twoleg den.

If the horse rears up, the Twoleg kit will be too scared to move.

At that point, the horse is going to stomp its hoof on something, the question is what. Let each cat attempt something to help. They each can try to scare the horse using the Hiss or Arch Skill, they can attack the horse, or they can perform some other action that they think will help. Any action they choose will need a total of 10 or higher to succeed. If more than half of the cats succeed at their actions, the horse will go away without stomping its hoof. If the horse does stomp its hoof, the Twoleg kit will be Knocked Out (she will just have fainted from fear, but the cats won't be able to tell the difference between that and real damage—the results are the same).

Alternatively, if the horse is about to stomp, one of the cats can jump in to block the blow. In this case the Twoleg kit realizes the danger and runs away toward the place where Twolegs usually stay, but the cat will be injured by the hoof stomp. Any cat that blocks the horse's hoof must take 10 chips worth of damage. Depending on how many chips the cat has spent on various actions, this may be enough to Knock Out the cat.

What Happens Next: If the Twoleg kit or any of the cats are Knocked Out, continue with **17**.

If the kit leaves the horse and goes to where the Twolegs stay, continue with **18**.

22. Follow Me!

Read Aloud: "It's hard to tell whether the dog is more interested in you or in the Twoleg kit. All your warrior experience tells you that if you run, the dog will chase you."

Narrator Tips: The first thing the players have to decide is which side of the fence they will run on while trying to get the dog to chase them.

Getting the dog's interest is difficult if the cats stay on the far side of the fence. Doing so requires a contest of wills. One cat must make a Spirit Check. If the total is higher than the dog's Spirit score, the dog will chase the cat. The dog has Strength 20, Intelligence 8, and Spirit 12, plus the appropriate number of Ability Chips for each, which it can spend to improve its actions (see Chapter Five of the game rules). The dog has a Bite Skill of level 4. It also has the Chomp, Dash, and Pin Knacks.

If the cat wins the contest of wills, the dog will chase it. But the dog will switch its attention to the Twoleg kit if she comes inside the fence. At that point, the cat must make another contest of wills, exactly as described earlier. If the cat loses that contest, the dog will ignore the cat and instead run back toward the kit. Then the kit must retreat back outside the fence (and she or the cats must close the gate) or the dog will attack her and any cats around her. If the cat wins that contest, the Twoleg kit can walk up and knock on the door of the Twoleg den.

It is easier to get the dog to chase cats that are inside the fence, but much more dangerous. (The cats can easily jump over the fence or squeeze through its slats.) The dog will chase any cat that comes into its yard and try to bite it. If the cat stands still, it must fight the dog. If the cat runs away, the dog will chase after it and try to Bite it one time every Round. The cat must make a Jump Check to determine the target number for the dog's bite. If the Bite Check total is higher than the cat's Jump Check total, the dog successfully bites the cat and does damage. If the dog is chasing a cat inside the fence, it will ignore the Twoleg kit even if she enters the yard, too (which allows her to go up and knock on the door).

Even if the first attempt to get the dog to chase them fails, the cats can try again as many times as they like (so long as neither they nor the Twoleg kit is forced to fight the dog).

What Happens Next: If either the cats or the Twoleg kit must fight the dog, continue with **15.**

If a cat is Knocked Out by the dog's bite, continue with **17.**

If the Twoleg kit is able to knock on the door, continue with **20.**

AFTER THE ADVENTURE

Åfter the last scene of the adventure has been played, the game itself is not necessarily over. There still are a few things you can do if the players want to keep at it.

Play It Again

Maybe you just want to try the whole thing a second time, starting back at the beginning or perhaps picking up somewhere in the middle where it feels like things went wrong. In either case, your cat would be right back where he or she was and have another chance to try to find a more favorable outcome.

One of the great things about storytelling games is that you can always tell the story again. And, since there are so many ways that the Twoleg kit can react to any of the situations in this adventure, the story could unwind in a different way every time you play (particularly as different Narrators get to guide the storyline).

Experience

If the cats completed the adventure successfully, then they all get Experience rewards. It is important to note, though, that each cat can only get experience from this adventure *once*! If you play through and successfully finish the adventure several times, your cat only gains the rewards listed below after *first* time he or she completes the adventure.

If you use different cats each time, though, each one can get the Experience rewards. The rule is not that a player can only get experience once, it's that a cat can.

Age: Although the action in this adventure clearly all happens over the course of a day or two, the presumption is that this is the most interesting and exciting thing that happens to your cat during the whole of that moon. Increase your cat's age by 1 moon and make any appropriate improvements described in Chapter Four of the game rules.

Skill: On top of the improvements your cat gets from aging, he or she also can gains 1 level in the Ponder Skill.

Knack: If the adventure had a perfect ending (that is, if the last scene you played through was 20), your cat also gains one level of the Twoleg Lore Knack.

More adventures can be found at the back of each novel in the Omen of the Stars series, and you can find extra information at www.warriorcats.com.

Jayfeather's dream dissolved into darkness as he woke and stretched his jaws in a massive yawn. His whole body seemed heavy, and when he sat up in his nest he felt as though ivy tendrils were wrapped around him, dragging him back to the ground. The air was hotter than usual for late newleaf, filled with the scents of prey and lush green growth. Noise filtered through the brambles that screened the medicine cat's den from the rest of the stone hollow: pawsteps and the excited murmuring of many cats as they gathered for the first patrols of the day.

But Jayfeather couldn't share his Clanmates' excitement. Although a moon had passed since he and his companions had returned from their visit to the Tribe, he felt cold and bleak inside. His head was full of images of mountains, endless snow-covered peaks stretching into the distance, outlined crisply against an ice-blue sky. His belly cramped with pain as he recalled one particular image: a white cat with green eyes who gave him a long, sorrowful look before she turned away and padded along a cliff top above a thundering waterfall.

Jayfeather shook his head. *What's the matter with me? That was all a long, long time ago. My life has always been here with the Clans. So why do I feel as if something has been lost?*

"Hi, Jayfeather." Briarlight's voice had a muffled, echoing sound, and Jayfeather realized she must have her head inside the cleft where he stored his herbs. "You're awake at last."

Jayfeather replied with a grunt. Briarlight was another of his problems. He couldn't forget what Lionblaze had told him when he returned to the mountains: how Briarlight was so frustrated by being confined to the hollow, trapped by her damaged hindlegs, that she'd persuaded her brother Bumblestripe to carry her into the forest to look for herbs.

"There was a dog running loose," Lionblaze had told him. "A cat with four functioning legs would have been hard-pressed to outrun it. If it hadn't been for me and Toadstep luring it away, Briarlight would have been torn to pieces."

"Mouse-brain!" Jayfeather snapped. "Why would she put herself in danger like that?"

"Because she's convinced that she's useless," Lionblaze explained. "Can't you give her more to do? Cinderheart and I promised her we'd help her find a proper part to play in the life of the Clan."

"You had no right to promise her anything without speaking to me first," Jayfeather retorted. "Are you suggesting I take her as my apprentice? Because I don't want an apprentice!"

"That's not what I meant," Lionblaze meowed, his tail-tip twitching in annoyance. "But you could find more interesting duties for her, couldn't you?"

Still reluctant, Jayfeather had done as his brother asked. He had to admit that Briarlight was easy to teach. She had been stuck in the medicine cat's den for so long that she had already picked up a lot.

She's actually useful, he mused. *Her paws are neat and quick when she sorts the herbs, and she's good at soaking wilted leaves in the pool without letting them fall to pieces.*

"Jayfeather?" Briarlight's voice roused Jayfeather from his thoughts. He heard her wriggling around, and then her voice came more clearly as if she was poking her head out of the cleft. "Are you okay? You were tossing and turning all night."

"I'm fine," Jayfeather muttered, unwilling to dwell any longer on the dreams that had plagued him.

"We're running low on marigold," Briarlight went on. "We used up a lot on Dovewing's scratches when you got back from the mountains. Should I ask Brightheart to collect some more?"

"No, I'll go," Jayfeather muttered.

"Fine." Briarlight's voice was determinedly cheerful. "I'll get on with sorting the herbs. Oh, one more thing . . ."

Jayfeather heard the young she-cat dragging herself across the floor of the den until she reached his nest and pushed something toward him. "Could you throw this out on your way past the dirtplace?" she asked. "It was stuck at the back of the herb store."

Jayfeather stretched out his neck until his nose touched a tuft of fur with a few dried scraps of leaf dusted on it. He stiffened as he recognized the faint scent that clung to it.

"Who would have put an old bit of fur among the herbs?" Briarlight continued. "It must have been in there for ages. I don't recognize the scent or color."

For a moment Jayfeather didn't reply. He breathed in his lost sister's scent, overwhelmed by longing for the time when he and Hollyleaf and Lionblaze had played and trained together, before they knew anything about the prophecy, before they learned how Squirrelflight and Leafpool had lied to them.

I don't know how Hollyleaf's fur got into the store, he thought, *but I should have thrown it out when I first found it there, not left it for another cat to find.*

"I wonder where it came from," Briarlight meowed. "Maybe a cat from another Clan got in here to steal herbs." She stifled a *mrrow* of laughter. "Maybe the kits got in and hid it."

"How would I know?" Jayfeather snapped, irritated at being jerked out of his memories. "You should stop letting your imagination run away with you."

Turning so that Briarlight couldn't see what he was doing, he tucked the scrap of fur deep inside the moss of his nest, and rose to his paws. "I'm going to fetch that marigold," he mewed, and headed out of the den.

Lusa

Excitement tingled through Lusa's paws as she padded down the snow-covered beach. Ice stretched ahead of her, flat, sparkly white, unchanging as far as the horizon. She didn't belong here—no black bears did—yet here she was, walking confidently onto the frozen ocean beside a brown bear and two white bears. Ujurak had gone, but Yakone, a white bear from Star Island, had joined Lusa, Kallik, and Toklo. They were still four. And a new journey lay ahead: a journey that would take them back home.

Glancing over her shoulder, Lusa saw the low hills of Star Island looming dark beneath the mauve clouds. The outlines of the white bears who lived there were growing smaller with each pawstep. *Good-bye,* she thought, with a twinge of regret that she would never see them again. Her home lay among trees, green leaves, and sun-warmed grass, a long, long way from this place of ice and wind as sharp as claws.

Lusa wondered if Yakone was feeling regret, too. The bears

of Star Island were his family, yet he had chosen to leave them so that he could be with Kallik. But he was striding along resolutely beside Kallik, his unusual red-shaded pelt glowing in the sunrise, and he didn't look back.

Toklo plodded along at the front of the little group, his head down. He looked exhausted, but Lusa knew that exhaustion was not what made his steps drag and kept his eyes on his paws and his shoulders hunched.

He's grieving for Ujurak.

Their friend had died saving them from an avalanche. Lusa grieved for him, too, but she clung to the certainty that it hadn't been the end of Ujurak's life, not really. The achingly familiar shape of the bear who had led them all the way to Star Island had returned with stars in his fur, skimming over the snow and soaring up into the sky with his mother, Silaluk. Two starry bears making patterns in the sky forever, following the endless circle of Arcturus, the constant star. Lusa knew that Ujurak would be with them always. But she wasn't sure if Toklo felt the same. A cold claw of pain seemed to close around her heart, and she wished that she could do something to help him.

Maybe if I distracted him....

"Hey, Toklo!" Lusa called, bounding forward past Kallik and Yakone until she reached the grizzly's side. "Do you think we should hunt now?"

Toklo started, as if Lusa's voice had dragged him back from somewhere far away. "What?"

"I said, should we hunt now?" This close to shore, they

might pick up a seal above the ice, or even a young walrus.

Toklo gave her a brief glance before trudging on. "No. It'll be dark soon. We need to travel while we can."

Then it'll be too dark to hunt. Lusa bit the words back. It wasn't the time to start arguing. But she wanted to help Toklo wrench his thoughts away from the friend he was convinced he had lost.

"Do you think geese ever come down to rest on the ice?" she asked.

This time Toklo didn't even look at her. "Don't be bee-brained," he said scathingly. "Why would they do that? Geese find their food on *land*." He quickened his pace to leave her behind.

Lusa gazed sadly after him. Most times when Toklo was in a grouchy mood, she would give as good as she got, or tease him out of his bad temper. But this time his pain was too deep to deal with lightly.

Best to leave him alone, she decided. *For now, anyway.*

As Star Island dwindled behind the bears, the short snow-sky day faded into shadows that seemed to grow up from the ice and reach down from the sky until the whole white world was swallowed in shades of gray and black. When Lusa looked back, the last traces of the hills that had become so familiar had vanished into the twilight. Star spirits began to appear overhead, and the silver moon hung close to the horizon like a shining claw. The bears trekked between snowbanks that glimmered in the pale light, reaching above their backs in strange shapes formed by the scouring wind.

"It's time we stopped for the night," Kallik announced, halting at the foot of a deep drift. "This looks like a good place to make a den."

"I'll help you dig," Yakone offered. He began to scrape at the bottom of the snowbank.

Lusa watched the two white bears as they burrowed vigorously into the snow. This would be Yakone's first night away from his family, away from the permanent den where he had been raised. Yet he seemed unfazed—enthusiastic, even, as he helped Kallik carve a shallow niche that would keep off the worst of the wind. The white bears' heads were close together now as they scraped at the harder, gritty snow underneath the fluffy top layer. Yakone said something that made Kallik huff with amusement, and she flicked a pawful of snow at him in response.

Lusa turned away, not wanting to eavesdrop. A pang of sorrow clawed once more at her heart when she spotted Toklo standing a little way off, watching the white bears without saying anything. After a moment he turned his back on Kallik and Yakone and raised his head to fix his gaze on the stars.

Looking up, Lusa made out the shining shape of Silaluk, the Great Bear, and close to her side the Little Bear, Ujurak. Seeing him there made her feel safe, because she knew that their friend was watching over them. It helped to comfort her grief.

But there was no comfort for Toklo. All he knew was that

his friend, the other brown bear on this strange and endless journey, had left them. His bleak gaze announced his loneliness to Lusa as clearly as if he had put it into words.

"We're here, Toklo," she murmured, too faintly for the brown bear to hear. "You're *not* alone."

She knew that Toklo had been closer to Ujurak than any of them; he had taken on the responsibility of protecting the smaller brown bear. *Toklo felt like he failed when Ujurak died,* Lusa thought. *He's wrong, but how can any bear make him understand that?*

Kallik's cheerful voice sounded behind her. "The den's nearly ready."

Lusa turned to see the white she-bear backing out of the cave that she and Yakone had dug into the snow. Kallik shook herself, scattering clots of snow from her fur. "Are you okay, Lusa?" she asked. "You look worried."

Lusa glanced toward Toklo, still staring up at the stars. "He's missing Ujurak. I wish I knew what to say to him."

Kallik gazed at Toklo for a moment, then shook her head with a trace of exasperation in her eyes. "We're all missing Ujurak," she responded. "But we know that he's not really dead."

"Toklo doesn't see it like that," Lusa pointed out.

"I know." Kallik's voice softened for a moment. "It's hard out here without Ujurak. But think what we've achieved together! We destroyed the oil rig and brought the spirits back so the wild will be safe. Toklo should remember that."

"Toklo just remembers that Ujurak gave his life for us."

While Lusa was speaking, Yakone emerged from the den, thrusting heaps of newly dug snow aside with strong paws.

Kallik padded toward him, then glanced back over her shoulder at Lusa.

"Ujurak has gone home," she said. "He's happy now, with his star mother. There's nothing for Toklo or any other bear to worry about."

Lusa shook her head. *It's not as simple as Kallik thinks,* she told herself. *And not as simple as Toklo thinks, either. He might not be here on the ground with us, but I think we've still got a lot to learn about Ujurak.*

ERIN HUNTER

is inspired by a love of cats and a fascination with the ferocity of the natural world. As well as having great respect for nature in all its forms, Erin enjoys creating rich, mythical explanations for animal behavior. She is also the author of the bestselling Seekers series.

Download the free Warriors app
and play Warriors games at
www.warriorcats.com.

For exclusive information on your
favorite authors and artists, visit
www.authortracker.com.

Warriors: Power of Three

Firestar's grandchildren begin their training as warrior cats.
Prophecy foretells that they will hold more power than any cats before them.

Warriors: Omen of the Stars

Which ThunderClan apprentice will complete the prophecy that
foretells that three Clanmates hold the future of the Clans in their paws?

Includes Warriors ADVENTURE GAME

Also available unabridged from HarperChildren's *Audio*

HARPER
An imprint of HarperCollinsPublishers

Delve Deeper into the Clans

Warrior Cats Come to Life in Manga!